DEAD LAWYERS DON'T LIE

MARK NOLAN

COPYRIGHT

In Memory of Josh

CHAPTER 1

Some men are alive simply because
it is against the law to kill them.
—E. W. Howe

San Francisco Superior Court Building
Criminal Courtroom Number 8

On the morning before attorney Richard Caxton was shot, he spent an hour in court doing what he did best—lying to the jury.

This time around, Caxton's client was the son of a wealthy mortgage banker. Brice Riabraun had "allegedly" been driving under the influence of alcohol when he'd crashed his luxury SUV into the Tate family's economy car. In court, Caxton claimed that the police had mishandled the case.

In Caxton's successful cases, he often found a loophole in the law, or a small procedural error by the police, or a semi-believable alibi that would hold up just long enough to bamboozle a jury. He exploited these opportunities with the smooth-talking technique of a used car salesman. Other attorneys in the city marveled at—and envied—the creatively dishonest con man.

After arguing relentlessly for his version of the truth, Caxton listened to the court clerk read the jury's verdict aloud and pronounce Riabraun not guilty.

Judge Emerson frowned.

Caxton had to make an effort not to laugh.

Brian Tate bolted from his chair and railed at the jury. "How could you find him innocent when he was driving with a 0.15 blood alcohol level? Witnesses said he drank seven beers before he crashed into our car and almost killed my wife and kids!"

Tate's wife, Judy, sat next to him with her arm in a plaster cast. The twelve jurors seated in the jury box averted their eyes and didn't reply to him. Tate turned and stared at Caxton and his client with the righteous fury of someone who had been cheated out of justice.

Judge Emerson slammed his gavel down. "Order! Sit down, Mr. Tate."

Caxton and his client just sat there gloating, and trying not to laugh at Tate, the working man in his department store suit and tie.

Tate curled his lip and ignored Judge Emerson's warning and jabbed his finger at Caxton. "Anyone else would be going to prison now, but your client had the cash to hire the best lying lawyer that money can buy. Somebody ought to teach you two a lesson—the hard way."

"Mr. Tate, that is enough!" Judge Emerson said as he banged his gavel again. "Do not test my patience, or you will find yourself held in contempt of court."

Tate took a deep breath and let it out, struggling for control. "Yes, Your Honor." He sat down, but continued to glare at Caxton.

Caxton shrugged and maintained his cool and professional appearance. He had perfect teeth, a year-round tan, manicured fingernails, and the latest hairstyle. His suits, shirts, and ties were all custom-made by the finest tailors in the Financial District.

Caxton was used to having that level of helpless anger leveled at him. He couldn't have cared less about it. He'd earned a reputation as *the lawyer you loved to hate*. But as he often said, being hated sure did pay well.

Caxton's favorite story was about a client who had asked him if he could seek justice. He'd answered, "Yes, and how much justice can you afford to buy today?"

"You are now free to go, Mr. Riabraun," Judge Emerson announced.

Riabraun grinned and shook hands with Caxton, then exited through a side door. He was already sliding into a waiting limousine when Emerson dismissed the jury.

Caxton headed toward the front entrance of the court building with his head held high. He went outside and faced the news reporters and gave a brief but well-rehearsed speech. "Today, justice was served. My client was found not guilty by a jury in a court of law. Thank goodness we live in a country where lawyers can protect honest, hardworking people such as my client from false accusations."

Reporters yelled questions at Caxton about his celebrity client, but he walked away, looking pious. His publicist would issue a statement to the press any minute now. As he strolled toward the parking lot and his brand-new BMW, he didn't notice someone sitting in a car watching him.

CHAPTER 2

Photojournalist Jake Wolfe sat in his Jeep Grand Cherokee and watched Caxton walk toward the parking area. The television news station where Jake worked had assigned him to get photos or video of Caxton doing something scandalous. He'd been following the lawyer for days.

Jake glared at the slick attorney as his thoughts turned once again to the previous weekend. It was all he could think about lately. His boss had told him to follow Caxton to a strip club and record him with a hidden camera. The pounding music at the club had been so loud that Jake had missed a call from Stuart, one of his best friends from when he'd served in the Marines. Later that night, Stuart had been found dead from a heroin overdose and Jake blamed himself for not answering Stuart's call in his time of need. And he resented his employer—and Caxton—for causing him to go on the assignment.

He took a deep breath and let it out. His hangover today wasn't as bad as the one he'd had yesterday, or the day before. He took a drink from a bottle of water and promised himself he'd stop using whiskey to numb the pain. Last night his fiancée, Gwen, had told him he needed to get over Stuart and move on. She may have been right, but when she talked that way, Jake felt he should get over her and move on.

For a moment, he considered quitting his job, cancelling the wedding, and borrowing a friend's motor yacht. A few weeks alone at sea might do him good. He shoved that reckless idea aside and reminded himself to take life one day at a time. He was going to Stuart's funeral tomorrow; maybe that would bring some closure and peace. Maybe then he could forgive himself and stop thinking about hunting down the drug dealers who deserved to die.

Jake was observant, a people watcher, and as he waited for Caxton to drive out of the lot, he noticed an attractive, well-dressed woman who wore her gray hair in an updo. She reminded him of his own grandmother, so full of life and love and wisdom. As she was getting into her car, a man in a dark hoodie and filthy jeans stood up from where he'd been crouched between two parked cars. He grabbed her purse, shoved her to the ground, and took off running toward Jake's vehicle. Jake opened his car door, shoving it fast and hard and straight-arming it like a football player.

The door and the purse snatcher collided—and the door won. The thief's face smacked into the window, his knees banging against the metal. He bounced off and landed flat on his back on the pavement, dropping the purse as he fell. Jake got out of his vehicle, closed the door, and stood looking down at the thief. A bruise began forming on the man's forehead. He struggled to his knees and glanced at the purse on the ground near Jake's feet.

Jake shook his head. "Leave it."

The thief had the sunken eyes and sallow complexion of a meth addict. He looked Jake up and down and grimaced as if seeing his worst-case scenario, a vigilante who still believed in chivalry.

Jake took a step forward and raised his eyebrows. "I'm going to give you to the count of three. One … two …"

The man reacted in a fight-or-flight response that came from deep within the recesses of his chemically cooked lizard brain. He got up and ran across the street with surprising speed, vanishing around the corner into a crowd of pedestrians.

Jake picked up the purse and walked past several parked cars to where the woman was standing, and handed it to her. "Are you all right, ma'am?"

"Yes, I'm fine. Thank you for stopping that thief."

"You're welcome."

"Are you an undercover police officer or simply a man who believes in doing the right thing?"

"Actually, I just lost my temper there for a minute."

Her eyes opened wide. Jake held the car door as she got into her vehicle. He stood there and waited until her door was closed and locked and the engine running. She waved as she drove off. Jake nodded and walked back to his Jeep.

Two young women stared at him as he walked, discussing him and observing the controlled, deliberate, and dangerous way his animal-like body moved. He stood out from the people in business suits. Tall, with wavy dark hair and dark eyes, he wore jeans and boots, with a black t-shirt and a black leather jacket. His face was devoid of expression, and his muscular body and confident walk gave the impression that he could handle himself in just about any situation.

After Richard Caxton got into his brand new BMW 7-Series, he sat on the buttery leather seats and sighed in contentment. His phone buzzed with a call from his son, whom he rarely saw or talked to since the divorce. He ignored the call and let it go to voicemail.

Caxton pulled out into the street, giving just a little goose to the gas pedal. The wheels squealed as the twelve-cylinder engine purred like a big cat. He didn't notice the black Jeep following behind him at a discreet distance.

He pushed a button to open the power sunroof and then tuned the radio to a local news station. The current top news story was about his court victory. Hearing his name mentioned on the news made him smile. After the report, he turned on some music and drove to his favorite place for a beautiful day by the San Francisco Bay—the exclusive and expensive Paradise Golf Club.

Caxton was in the mood to enjoy a celebratory round of golf with some attorney friends, drink a few craft beers, and smoke a fine cigar. Later tonight he and his buddies would enjoy a lavish dinner at a fancy restaurant and then go drinking at their favorite dance club. The young ladies there always gravitated toward his table, and they weren't doing it simply because he bought top-shelf liquor they could drink for free. They were genuinely attracted to him because he was so handsome, witty, and charming.

Caxton's lips curled into a satisfied smile, anticipating his typical Friday afternoon and evening indulging with his friends. However, there was someone else racing ahead of Caxton to the golf course—someone armed with a deadly weapon. He had a vastly different and far less pleasant plan for *the lawyer you loved to hate.*

CHAPTER 3

Jake Wolfe pulled into the private country club a minute or so after Caxton. He sat in his Jeep and shot some video of Caxton and the rest of his golf foursome near the first tee. He switched from the dash-cam to a professional high-definition camcorder and pointed the zoom lens and long-range shotgun microphone out of his open window.

The four lawyers never even glanced in Jake's direction. If one of them happened to look, he wouldn't have seen much. Jake was parked among many other cars and the camcorder and window tray blended in with the Jeep's black paint and leather interior.

Once Jake had everything zeroed in, he set the video camera on a window tray designed for such a purpose and began shooting photographs with a DSLR camera and a telephoto lens.

The lawyers sat at one of the picnic tables underneath the shade of a large wooden pavilion, drinking beers and smoking cigars. Caxton's friends congratulated him for getting yet another guilty client off the hook in exchange for a huge fee from Riabraun's wealthy father.

Jake knew there were a number of honest, hardworking lawyers in the city, but these four were not among them. During the time he'd been working on this investigative news story about Caxton and his friends, he'd seen them engage in all kinds of unethical behavior.

~

A further distance away, another man was also watching Caxton, stalking him through binoculars. The watcher smiled, set down the binoculars and picked up a high-powered rifle with a scope.

~

The golf group prepared to tee off. Caxton stood and puffed on his Cuban Montecristo cigar while he waited his turn.

Two of the men were divorce lawyers who used the private meeting to compare notes on a divorcing couple.

"The Hattons' divorce case is going well. I've got the wife mad at her husband. She wants to make him suffer."

"Same here. The husband is so angry he can't see straight. He won't be settling anytime soon."

"Great, the longer we keep the hostilities going, more hours we can bill. They'll be at it for at least another month or two."

Caxton's phone buzzed and he read a text message from his long-suffering legal secretary. He sent a text in reply and then grinned at his friends. "My telemarketer client is in hot water again with the attorney general. I told my secretary to send out the standard boilerplate letter. That text only took me one minute to respond to, but my client doesn't need to know that. Especially when I'm billing him at five hundred dollars an hour."

His attorney friends all laughed. One of them raised his beer bottle and said, "Here's to people who get involved in lawsuits."

As Jake observed the lawyers, he felt a weird sense of impending danger. There was a tingling at the back of his neck. It was something he'd felt a few times when he'd been deployed. He checked his mirrors and looked around at the greens and the woods but didn't see anything unusual. He turned his attention back to Caxton but stayed alert for any surprises.

The lawyers were just starting on their second round of beers when there was a strange sound, like somebody had been punched hard in the chest by a fist.

Caxton staggered back several steps and fell flat on his back. The other lawyers gathered around him and gasped in shock as their friend groaned in agony, bleeding from a sucking chest wound. In a split second, the seemingly invincible lawyer was dying on the lush green lawn with a look of total surprise on his face.

"Help me," he groaned as foamy blood bubbled from his lips and from the hole in his chest.

One of the lawyers looked toward the woods and took off running for the clubhouse. The others quickly followed suit. None of them tried to help Caxton. It was every lawyer for himself.

As Caxton lay dying, he wondered who among his law firm's many victims had finally followed through on their promise of revenge. His last thought was about who'd fight over his money and assets. At 12:18 p.m. Pacific Time, Caxton let out a final gasp of breath, his dishonest heart stopped beating, and his days of lying for a living came to an end.

CHAPTER 4

Jake stared at Caxton in surprise. As the other lawyers ran in a panic, he made an effort to remain professional and detached. He'd seen people get hit by gunfire during his days in combat. Many of them by his own weapon. He heard one of the fleeing lawyers yelling into his phone. "Send the police. Send an ambulance."

Jake took a deep breath and assessed the situation. In his opinion, Caxton was dead; it was too late for an ambulance. Judging by the sound of the suppressed shot, and the direction and angle it appeared to have come from, Jake figured the shooter was probably in a tree. Using his camera to scan the woods, Jake saw a brief flash of light as the sun reflected off the glass lens of a rifle scope. Then he saw the killer up in a tree, aiming the rifle right at him.

Not good, not good at all.

Jake's reflexes had been trained to pull a rifle trigger in this situation. His trigger finger pressed the camera's shutter button instead and snapped a photo as he ducked down to his right on the front seat, below the dash. He waited for rounds to hit his car, seeking his body, but none came. Maybe the killer had decided to make a quick getaway. Or maybe he was just waiting for Jake to sit up in the driver's seat so he could shoot him in the head.

The front seats weren't meant to be a bed for a six foot tall guy built like a running back, but he adjusted himself as well as he could before using his tablet to connect with the TV camera on the tray outside his car window. He made the camera tilt and turn as he pointed it at the woods and zoomed in for a closer look. The shooter was no longer visible in the tree. Was he hiding behind camouflage and pointing his rifle at the Jeep, or moving rapidly in Jake's direction?

Jake cursed at himself. "You just had to get a picture, didn't you?" He grabbed his phone and called his good friend Terrell Hayes, a plainclothes police inspector with the SFPD Homicide Division.

Terrell answered. "Hayes."

"It's Jake, I need some help."

"What kind of help? Financial help? Mental help?"

"Police help. I just witnessed a murder at the Paradise Golf Club."

"I'm on my way. Give me a report."

"A lawyer named Richard Caxton was shot by a sniper near the first tee."

"And you saw it happen?"

"Yes, I was taking photos and video for a news assignment."

"Please tell me you took cover and you're out of the line of fire."

"I'm behind cover right now, but when I did recon with my telephoto lens, I saw the shooter up in a tree at the two o'clock position from the first tee. I shot a photo of him as a reflex."

"That was crazy, you're lucky he didn't see you."

"Actually, he did see me and had me in his sights. Right now I'm lying low on the front seat of my Jeep."

"Keep your head down, I'll be there soon." Terrell ended the call.

Jake checked the tablet again. He made the camera scan along the edge of the woods and across the greens. Soon he grew impatient with hiding like a sitting duck. He studied the area for a vantage point from which he could see but not be seen. If he could find a good observation post, he could provide recon intel for Terrell.

The pavilion near the first tee looked like his best bet. It was a large open-sided wooden structure with an octagonal roof. He stuffed his camera gear into a small backpack and double-checked to make sure his pistol was in there too. He removed the tray, raised the car window, and locked the door. As he ran to the pavilion, his heart was beating fast. Hopefully, the sniper wasn't taking aim at him right now. All he had to do was find a way to get up on top of the roof quickly and hide on one of the eight sides without being shot. What could go wrong?

CHAPTER 5

The assassin whispered, "As Shakespeare said ... *Kill all the lawyers.*"

He scanned the scene with his rifle scope and watched the other lawyers panic and run to the clubhouse. It would've been amusing to pick them off one by one, but that was not part of his plan.

He frowned when he saw a man sitting in a parked vehicle, pointing a telephoto camera lens directly at him. The man must have seen the rifle aimed at his head, because he ducked out of sight.

The shooter was tempted to remain in the tree for a while longer and try to get a head shot on this inconvenient witness, or to fire round after round into his vehicle and kill him that way. However, to avoid being arrested, he had to stick to his plan and schedule, even more so now that he'd been spotted. He climbed down from the tree and retrieved his golf bag and pushcart from where they were hidden in some bushes, covered with a small camo-patterned tarp.

Working quickly, he removed the suppressor from the end of the barrel and dropped it into the golf bag. Next he folded over the skeleton stock of the rifle and placed it into his bag with the butt end down and the barrel pointing up.

From a zippered pocket in the golf bag, he took out a knitted sock cover that matched the same ones on the rest of his clubs. There was a golf club head inside, with a custom-made hollow shaft that fit over the end of the rifle barrel.

Lastly, he rolled up the camouflaged tarp and stuffed it into the bag between the club shafts and on top of the suppressor. The golf bag was on a three-wheeled cart and he pushed it along as he walked up a path leading out of the woods to a nearby neighborhood. Once he reached the street, he strolled toward his parked car. Dressed in golf shoes, khaki pants, and a designer polo shirt, he looked just like any other golfer coming from the course. He adjusted his nondescript white baseball cap and slid on a pair of stylish sunglasses to hide his light brown hair and blue-gray eyes.

He didn't see any residents of the neighborhood looking at him as he tucked his bag into his vehicle and drove away. He made sure to keep his speed at or below the posted limit, and while he drove along, he whistled softly to himself, a strange and melancholy tune seldom heard in America.

A few minutes later, he was miles from the scene of the crime and he'd made a clean getaway. It was almost the perfect crime, except for that unfortunate man with the camera. Had he taken a photo, or not? The killer decided he'd have to find out who the man was, put a bullet in his brain, and confiscate his camera. The only good witness was a dead witness.

CHAPTER 6

Terrell Hayes arrived at the crime scene before his fellow officers. He stood near the first tee, looking down at the body on the perfectly manicured grass. Caxton's mouth was open. His dead eyes stared at the sky. Flies buzzed around the wound in his chest.

When several beat cops drove up and saw the plainclothes police lieutenant already there, one of them said, "How is he always one step ahead of everyone?"

The CSI Unit arrived, along with a police photographer from the Forensics Photographic Unit. Uniformed officers began setting up fence posts and police tape.

Terrell's previous experience as a Marine Corps infantry rifleman "grunt" came in handy now that he worked on the SFPD's Homicide Detail. He'd seen plenty of gunshot victims in both careers, and he recognized the work of a shooter with talent. Whoever had nailed this victim had known what he was doing. One shot to the chest with a high-velocity round, fired from a fair distance away, using a scope. He took out his phone and called Ryan, the K9 cop. "Hey, Ryan, did you have any luck yet?"

"Yes, Hank sniffed out the exact spot where the shooter fired his weapon," Ryan said. "He was up in a tree just like you suspected. Hank traced his steps to a nearby street, but that's where he lost the scent."

"Good work. Maybe a neighbor saw something." Terrell ended the call and noticed that the news media people were arriving. Yellow police tape kept them at bay.

In his experience, this kind of murder was like a gift-wrapped present for the reporters and their viewers. It was similar to a wreck on the highway; everybody just had to look.

He wondered where Jake was at the moment. He'd checked the Jeep, but it was empty. Terrell shook his head; he was probably off doing something reckless and dangerous—as usual.

Terrell's partner, Sergeant Beth Cushman, had been talking to the Morgue Unit as they'd begun the process of putting the victim into a body bag. Beth raised her voice and yelled at one of the cops, then turned and walked toward Terrell. She had that look on her face that told him she'd figured something out.

Beth had inherited her Scottish mother's pale complexion and blue eyes and had short, flaming red hair and a fiery personality to go along with it. She was a smart, hardworking cop who was good at her job and didn't take any lip from anybody.

Terrell had noticed that Beth had been short-tempered lately—understandable, due to her husband's recent affair and the resulting divorce. She was still adjusting to being a single parent and was struggling to keep it together for her young son.

Beth smoothed the jacket of her dark pantsuit over her pistol and badge. "I got a closer look at the exit wound when they moved the body. The victim was hit with a hollow-point round. He probably died within a minute or two of being shot."

"The shooter knew what he was doing and had a plan," Terrell said.

"That's how it looks to me too. One shot, one kill. He takes pride in his work."

"It could be a professional hit, or it could just be an experienced deer hunter with a grudge."

"Could be anyone in a criminal gang, or someone who just got out of prison after his lawyer failed to keep him from going there."

Terrell nodded. "Or maybe the guy had military training."

Beth looked toward the parking lot, and rolled her eyes. "Oh come on, not these two."

Terrell followed her gaze and saw two plainclothes police sergeants approaching on foot. "Yeah, no surprise."

"Denton and Kirby, butting their noses in again. I bet you they'll say they were just driving by the area."

"Probably, but I think it's your lucky day to deal with them," Terrell said. "I'm going over to the woods to take a look at the evidence Ryan and Hank discovered."

"Okay, I'll handle our shadows, but you owe me."

CHAPTER 7

Beth observed Cori Denton and Ray Kirby walking over to the crime scene. The plainclothes detectives both wore similar black slacks and dark blue windbreakers. Beth wondered if they realized they looked like twins.

Denton was a female police sergeant with brunette hair and a permanent frown on her face. She had a one-sided rivalry going with Beth, and she played dirty. More than once, she'd tried to take credit for Beth's work, and she reveled in spreading gossip in an attempt to make her look bad. Her partner, Sergeant Kirby had a weak chin and was one of those clueless guys who would continue to make passes at a woman even after she'd repeatedly said no. Beth had turned him down half a dozen times.

Denton said, "Hey, Beth. We were nearby and heard the calls on the radio, so we stopped by to see if we could help."

Beth just stared at Denton and didn't say anything in response. She'd recently been "advised" by the chief of police to take some anger management classes. Right now she was trying out their theories, but she still felt like punching Denton in the throat.

~

As Terrell walked toward the wooded area, the crowd of media folks spotted him and started shouting. "Lieutenant Hayes, one quick question."

He was known to some of the local media and easy for them to spot. He was a tall and ruggedly handsome black man who had a body like a professional athlete. He always wore a dark suit, a white long-sleeved shirt, a solid-color tie, and perfectly shined black shoes. The same clothes, every day, without fail. When Terrell was asked why he always dressed that way, he didn't know what to say. For a while he'd said it was because "Chicks dig it." His wife, Alicia, was not amused, so now he said, "Because my wife likes it."

Terrell glanced back at the scene of the crime. One of the media people was doing something risky that none of the rest of them would ever think to do; he'd climbed up on the roof of a wooden pavilion and was observing the terrain from a high vantage point.

Terrell's quick police appraisal pegged the subject as a six-foot-tall Caucasian male with an athletic build, dark wavy hair, "devil-may-care eyes" and a jaded smile. The look on the man's face suggested that he found the world around him both amusing and annoying. Most cops would take one look at Jake and see a potential troublemaker that they should keep an eye on—even though he was similar to them in many ways.

Jake pointed his camera's zoom lens at Terrell, waved, then tapped his mobile phone and held it up to his ear. Terrell's phone buzzed—the caller ID from his list of contacts said Jukebox. In the Marines, Jake had been given the radio call sign Jukebox because he would belt out song lyrics at inappropriate moments. Terrell went by Grinds due to his love for coffee.

Terrell continued walking past the media crowd, nodding to them in acknowledgment but passing by without comment. As he made his way toward the wooded area, he answered the phone with his back to the reporters.

"From your position on that roof, can you see the woods ahead of me?"

"Yeah, I'm doing recon for you, and the woods area looks clear except for your K9 cop and the dog. I doubt the shooter is hiding there under camouflage, or the dog would've found him."

"Hopefully he won't return to the scene of the crime. Some criminals wait until the cops show up, then come back and start shooting again."

"I'll keep an eye on the area for you."

"Thanks for providing cover."

"Just like old times, you know I've always got your back," Jake said. "Although I feel empty-handed without my rifle."

"Any chance you have some coffee and ibuprofen with you?" Terrell said.

"Are the headaches bothering you again?"

"Yeah, and they're worse when I'm working on an empty stomach. This is bad timing. I was just about to go to lunch."

"Only a lawyer could ruin your day after he's already dead."

Terrell laughed. "If he's a divorce lawyer, I hope you have a solid alibi, after the way you and Gwen have been fighting lately."

"My alibi is that I'm not married yet and I'm having serious doubts about going through with the wedding," Jake said.

"When in doubt ... don't."

"Honestly, I've decided to cancel the wedding and break up with Gwen. But when I do, she'll probably shoot me."

"Well, it was nice knowing you. What about the coffee?"

Jake smiled. "I have my thermos in the car. I'll trade you a cup of coffee for a few photos of the police dog and the K9 cop."

"You've got a deal. I also need to take a statement from you about what you saw."

"No problem. What did your K9 team find over there?"

"Our dog sniffed out the tree where the shooter fired his weapon," Terrell said.

"I have a photo of the shooter up in that very tree pointing his rifle at me. Check your phone—I sent all my photos and videos to you."

"Thanks, I appreciate it."

Terrell looked at his phone and saw the photo of the shooter in the tree. The suspect was wearing a ball cap, and part of his face was hidden behind the rifle scope, but the photo was better than nothing. He sent it to Roxanne Poole, the tech officer.

"Doesn't this make you wonder if it's ever morally right to kill some evil dirtbag who totally deserves it?" Jake said.

"You sound like you might actually agree with what the shooter did."

"No, I understand it, but that doesn't mean I agree with it."

"Good, because there is this thing called the law," Terrell said. "You might have heard of it."

"It does sound vaguely familiar."

"Not that you care too much about laws and regulations."

"I used to care, but I take a pill for that now."

"How did you get your ass up on top of that gazebo, anyway?"

"Sorry, but that's a trade secret only my ass knows, and it ain't talking."

Terrell entered the woods, saw Ryan and Hank, and walked in their direction. "I have to talk to the K9 officer now."

"Okay, I'll let you go. Thanks," Jake said.

"No problem, thanks for the intel on the crime scene ... and for covering me. One last thing; Sergeant Denton showed up here uninvited. If she sees you up on that pavilion, she'll probably use that as an excuse to arrest or shoot you. Then if you were locked up or dead, I'd have to fill out some more paperwork and that would be annoying."

"Thanks for warning me. That sociopath is the last person I want to see. And I'm touched by your concern about the paperwork and all."

"Talk to you later, Jukebox."

Jake ended the call, looked off into the distance and saw Terrell walking into the woods. He wrestled with the urge to join his friend as he went into the danger zone.

CHAPTER 8

Jake saw Sergeant Cori Denton and her sidekick Kirby talking to Beth Cushman. He observed them with the critical eye and the knowledge of human folly you gain while working in the news media.

In Jake's opinion, Denton was a scowling nutcase who used her badge to bully people in order to prop up her low self-esteem. Her partner, Kirby, seemed to be a by-the-book choirboy virgin. He looked like he'd never had a good meal, a good bottle of wine, or a good woman in his entire life. Maybe they balanced each other out, bad cop / good cop.

Jake focused his camera's telephoto lens and zoomed in on Denton's angry face for a moment. Seeing her made his heart feel heavy. Some time ago, Denton had shot and killed Jake's pet dog, Gracie—a sweet old black Labrador retriever with gray hair on her muzzle. He'd rescued her from the pound after someone had abandoned the dog in her old age and she'd been a wonderful friend to him. Sometimes he'd taken her to the children's cancer floor of the hospital to cheer up the patients. Gracie had loved every child and nurse she'd met there, and they'd all loved her too.

On the Fourth of July, Jake's neighbors held a block party on their street. Denton and Kirby had driven past, then stopped and yelled at the families to disperse. Gracie had barked at the threatening intruders and when a firecracker had gone off close to her, she'd lunged at

Denton, snarling and showing her teeth. Denton had been far enough away to be out of danger. SFPD policy was to use a police vehicle's fire extinguisher to repel any threatening dogs. But Denton had drawn her pistol and fired three rounds into the beautiful lab, right in front of Jake, his neighbors, and their kids.

Jake had screamed at Denton and had run to Gracie's side. He'd knelt down on the pavement and held his four-legged best friend close while he helplessly watched her die in his arms. Gracie had used her last ounce of strength to lick the tears from Jake's face.

Jake had then stood up and walked directly toward Denton, yelling and cursing and pointing his finger at her. She'd aimed her pistol at him and called for her partner to back her up. Kirby drew his weapon and the two cops ordered Jake to lie facedown on the ground, or be shot. Jake's fiancée had pleaded with him to cooperate and he knew he could be killed, just like his dog. He grudgingly obeyed the police, but continued cursing at Denton. The cops handcuffed him, placed him under arrest on trumped-up charges, and put him in a jail cell.

The neighborhood children had wailed and cried while several of their parents called 911. A television news crew had arrived from Jake's employer and they'd put Denton's angry face on the news for all to see. Protests were held by animal rights groups. The chief of police was harassed by news reporters for months afterward. In the police department inquiry that followed, Denton's official statement had been, "I had no choice other than to shoot the dangerous animal, to defend myself and ensure public safety."

Afterwards, the news had run reports on how there was an epidemic of family pet dogs being shot all across America by over-reactive rookie law enforcement officers. Chief Pierce had publicly apologized and held meetings to make sure it never happened again in San Francisco.

Jake had tried to forgive and forget, but he'd found that he could not forgive the unforgivable. He'd filed a lawsuit against Denton, but the court had dismissed it. He wished she'd move away and torment the citizens of some other city; she'd come here from somewhere far away and Jake wanted her to go back there.

CHAPTER 9

The killer drove several miles away and stopped at a small store. He reached into his backpack for his bottles of meds, but put them back without taking any. "After eliminating the first lawyer on my list, I believe I've earned myself a drink."

In the back of his mind, he was aware that whenever he went off his meds and drank a lot of liquor, all hell might break loose. If he thought too much about the woman he'd loved and lost, he might become angry at the world. He had to avoid dwelling on how she'd died so young, with her whole life ahead of her. The alcohol would serve as another form of medicine, to help dull the memories and the pain that he lived with every day.

He put his pistol in the back of his waistband and covered it with his jacket, then walked toward the store with the feeling he was still in the mood to rid the earth of some unnecessary humans. He talked to himself in a low voice as he walked.

"Every once in a while, I lose patience and I want someone to die. It doesn't matter who or how. It only matters that an irritating life has ended, so the rest of us can live in a slightly better measure of peace."

When he opened the door to the market, he briefly entertained the thought that perhaps if the cashier wasn't properly polite, he would put a bullet in his forehead.

However, once he was inside, he noted the cashier was a cheerful young woman from India. She wore a traditional *salwar kameez* suit of embroidered blue material, printed with a pattern. A child was playing by her side. She was very polite to her new customer.

He was impressed by how the attractive woman demonstrated such grace and poise as he paid cash for a handful of mini bottles of vodka and a cup of ice.

The cashier woman never looked askance at him. She kept a polite, neutral smile on her face and talked about the weather during the entire transaction. The killer noticed she didn't touch the cash register. She only named a round figure. Her right hand remained by her side below the counter most of the time. Was something down there, perhaps a weapon? He also noticed a TV monitor showing four square images of video being recorded inside the store. His face appeared in one of the squares.

He picked up his items and walked toward the door. As he went outside, he looked back at the cashier through the window. He saw her let go of a sawed-off shotgun. It was lying on a piece of canvas that hung underneath the counter like a hammock. It appeared to be shortened at both ends, turning it into a nightmare of a pistol. *Impressive.*

Pulling out of the parking lot, he opened one of the mini bottles of vodka, drank it down in one gulp, and tossed it out the window. "Can't have an open container in the vehicle—that's the law."

The alcohol hit his bloodstream and he began planning the murder of the second victim on his kill list. This next murder would be more of a thrill kill. He would record it on video and put it on the internet so the world could admire his artistry.

CHAPTER 10

Jake put his camera equipment into his backpack, slung it over his shoulder and walked to the edge of the roof.

Dick Arnold waved to one of the uniformed police officers nearby and pointed at Jake. The officer frowned and marched over to the pavilion. Jake sighed. "Here we go again."

"Hey, you can't be up there," the policeman said. "Get down, now."

"Yessir, Officer. Sorry to be up here, but my good friend Police Lieutenant Terrell Hayes asked me to do it." Jake gave the officer a cheerful smile, hung by his arms off the edge of the roof, and dropped to the grass.

The cop pointed toward the media crowd and said, "Get back behind that police tape. It says 'Do Not Cross' for a reason."

Jake made his way to the parking lot and climbed into his Jeep, a black SRT8 model that was several years old with plenty of miles on it, but still ran like a champ. Under the hood it had a HEMI V8 engine that was built in Detroit and could go from zero to sixty in under six seconds.

He exited the golf course, then made his way through neighboring streets until he found the one he'd seen when he'd checked a map on his phone. After driving down to the end of that street, he parked near a bike trail that went through the woods to the golf course. Then he grabbed his camera backpack, poured some coffee from his thermos into an empty Starbucks to-go cup, and walked down the trail, texting Terrell as he went.

I'm in the woods, walking toward you. Tell the K9 cop I'm a friend, and to please keep his dog under control.

~

Terrell stood in front of a tree next to Ryan and his dog, Hank. Ryan had sandy hair and the lean body of a runner. Hank, a Belgian Malinois, raised his nose and sniffed Terrell.

Ryan said, "This is the tree the shooter used as a deer stand."

"I don't suppose Hank found a spent shell casing from that round that was fired?" Terrell said.

"No, the shooter either picked up his brass, or he used a bolt-action rifle."

Terrell nodded. "Right, most dedicated sniper rifles are bolt-action. Nice work finding this tree. Hopefully the shooter left behind some DNA evidence."

"Hank found a note—check it out." Ryan held up a plastic evidence bag containing a piece of paper the size of a business card. Four words were printed on it in block letters style with a felt pen and a ruler.

Terrell read the words and he shook his head. "I've seen some clever criminals in our line of work, but this guy thinks he's special."

A policeman from the Crime Scene Investigations Unit walked past wearing headphones and waving a metal detector over the ground, searching for any brass shell casings the dog might have missed.

Terrell's phone vibrated and he read Jake's text message. "A good friend of mine is approaching our position on foot. I need you to keep Hank on a tight leash so he doesn't react."

"Sure, Lieutenant, no problem. Who is this guy and why is he here?"

"He's a photographer who helped us get some evidence on the crime scene. I'm going to let him take a picture of the tree, and maybe of Hank too if you're okay with that. The chief likes it when Jake runs positive news photos of cops."

Ryan gave some commands to Hank and tightened his grip on the lead. Hank was already sniffing the air and listening intently. His ears twitched and he let out a low growl.

~

Jake walked up and handed the cup of coffee to Terrell, along with a travel-size packet of two ibuprofen tablets.

Terrell took the pills and drank some coffee. "Ryan, this is Jake, we served together in the Marine Corps infantry. You two have something in common. Jake was a dog handler."

"I worked with a war dog named Duke, who was a Mal like your dog," Jake said.

Jake and Ryan shook hands, and Hank sniffed Jake curiously. Jake noticed it and slowly held out his hand in a fist to let Hank sniff him, in a kind of a dog handshake. He noted the surprised look on Ryan's face, and figured Ryan probably thought he was either fearless or crazy. Jake's own theory was that he had a unique smell—that of someone who had no fear of animals. The scent of a former military dog handler who could talk to dogs, understand them, and live with them in a pack, side by side, through hell and back.

Terrell said, "Thanks for the coffee and Vitamin I. My headache is something fierce today."

"Why do you always get headaches?" Ryan asked.

"It's from allergies to … air pollution," Terrell answered. He glanced at Jake.

Jake nodded. "If it's all right with you, Ryan, I'll go ahead and take a quick photo or two and let you get back to work."

"I owe Jake a photo—he gave me one of the shooter up in this tree." Terrell held out his phone and showed Ryan the photo.

Ryan raised his eyebrows. "Jake, you're lucky you didn't get shot."

"I'm part Irish, so lucky stuff like this happens to me all the time," Jake said.

"Or in your case, my brother, it might just be dumb luck," Terrell said, and he smiled.

Ryan's brows furrowed. "He's your brother?"

Terrell nodded. "My brother from another mother."

"One time when we were deployed overseas, I got shot and almost died," Jake said. "But Terrell gave me a blood transfusion, and now we're officially blood brothers. I owe him my life."

Jake began shooting photos of the tree and of Hank.

Terrell received another text. He read the message and said, "The chief says it's okay for Jake to take a photo of the note."

Ryan took the plastic evidence bag out of his pocket. Jake saw a card with words printed on it in block letters.

DEAD LAWYERS DON'T LIE

Ryan held the note while Jake took photos of it, alongside Hank's scowling face.

"I really appreciate this, Ryan. Terrell and I often take a boat out on the Bay to do some fishing. You're welcome to come along on the next trip."

"Sounds good," Ryan said.

"We definitely need to go out on the Bay again real soon," Terrell said, pressing his fingers against his forehead.

"We can take the *Far Niente* out on the water anytime," Jake said. "I just have to let Dylan know I'm going to borrow his boat."

The men said their goodbyes. Jake took the empty coffee cup from Terrell and put it in his camera pack, then walked down the trail.

"I have to go face the media now and give them a statement," Terrell said as he headed that direction. When he came out of the woods area, the media crowd saw him heading directly toward them, pointed their microphones and television cameras at him and began yelling questions. He stopped in front of the crowd, held his hands up for silence, and waited until everyone stopped talking.

"At approximately twelve fifteen this afternoon, San Francisco defense attorney Richard Caxton was playing golf here when he was shot in the chest with one round from a high-powered rifle. He died almost immediately from his wound. We have reason to believe that the shooter was waiting in ambush, in a tree over there." Terrell pointed toward the wooded area and then continued talking. "Our K9

Unit found the tree and followed the shooter's trail to a nearby street, where the scent ended. We believe he got into a vehicle parked there and drove away. When we know anything further, we'll give you an update. That's all for now."

Everybody started yelling questions at Terrell again, but he turned and walked away. He was willing to toss the media a bone at this point, but he was not going to let them demand answers from him.

One reporter's question rang out louder above the rest.

"Who wanted that lawyer dead?"

Someone else in the news crowd said, "Who didn't?"

CHAPTER 11

Jake sat in the driver's seat of the Jeep and turned on his tablet, then used a small wireless Bluetooth keyboard to tap out a short blurb to go along with his photos and video. He was calling the news story "The Attorney Assassination."

He attached the document to an email, along with several of the photos and videos he'd taken, and sent it to his editor's secretary, Debbie.

Hopefully this scoop would help him remain gainfully employed for at least another week or two. His job was hanging by a thread because news organizations were laying off so many photojournalists. The *Chicago Sun Times* had actually handed out layoff notices to its entire photography staff—every single person, including a famous Pulitzer Prize-winning photojournalist.

He started to say something to Gracie, and then remembered she was gone. They'd been a great team. He flipped down the sun visor of the Jeep and looked at the picture he kept there. In the photo, she gave him a toothy grin, the graying hair on her muzzle showing her age.

"Hey, Gracie, I miss you, girl." Jake touched his fingers to the photo and felt a lump in his throat. He closed the visor, took a deep breath and let it out.

His phone vibrated; it was a call from Norman, his grouchy boss at the television/internet news station. He'd probably seen the email and exclusive photos and wanted to complain and criticize as usual. Jake was still angry at Norman for sending him out on the night Stuart had overdosed. "This is never good," he grumbled. "Having a boss sucks."

Jake ignored the call and thought about how he missed the freedom of working as a freelance photographer. There was no guaranteed paycheck, but there was no boss to answer to. He'd also been able to travel the world. Jake liked that lifestyle the best. Today might be the day he had to kick his boss in the crotch and get himself fired. He wondered if maybe he should seek psychiatric counseling for his self-destructive compulsion to kick his bosses in the cojones. No, it seemed perfectly reasonable to him, so why waste time and money talking to a shrink about it? He tapped an icon on his phone to ignore the repeated calls from his boss.

At the crime scene near the first tee, Beth Cushman thought of an idea about how to get rid of Denton and Kirby.

"Look, you two, this is our case, not yours. If you want to loiter here, you'll have to make yourselves useful so I can leave."

"What are you going to do instead?" Denton asked.

"I want to drive over to Brian Tate's place of employment and sweat him. Tate threatened Caxton in court, and now Caxton is in a body bag. I like Tate for this murder."

Denton's mouth hung open for a moment, then her eyes gleamed. "Well, you know we'd like to help you, Cushman, but we were just rolling past here on our way to someplace else. We have to get going." She immediately took off walking toward the car.

Kirby said, "Uhm, Beth I was wondering if you might want to go..."

"No, I wouldn't," she snapped. "I go straight home after work and spend time with my son. Same answer as always, so give it a rest, okay? Don't ask me again."

Kirby shrugged and followed Denton toward the car.

Denton got into the car first and quickly shook a pill out of a prescription bottle she kept in her jacket pocket. She popped it into her mouth and swallowed it with a drink of cold coffee before Kirby could see it. Once he climbed in, they drove toward the printing company where Brian Tate was employed. A few taps on their police vehicle's dashboard computer brought up all of Tate's personal information; he now had zero privacy, and it would remain that way until the case was solved.

CHAPTER 12

The killer reached into his pocket and took out his encrypted phone. He tapped the icon that would scramble his voice and called the British man who was known by the code name "Chairman Banks."

Banks answered on the first ring, as if he'd been waiting for a call from his hired gun, The Artist. "Is it done?"

"Yes, one lawyer down and two more to go," The Artist replied, speaking with a slight Russian accent.

"Any problems?"

"None. It went like clockwork."

"I'm always pleased to hear about a successful performance."

The Artist knew that Banks enjoyed playing God and ordering men killed in much the same way an average person would order a pizza delivered. "That's what you pay me for—my artistic way with weapons."

"Quite nice to have a cleaner working for me who demonstrates a bit of a style as he mops up the dirt and takes out the trash."

"You have a flair for making it sound so glamorous," The Artist said. "What interesting thing are you eating today?"

"How do you know I'm eating?"

"When are you not eating? If it is any time near lunch or dinner, you'll be making the most of it. And you sound as if you might be talking with your mouth full."

"Now that you mention it, you do have a bad habit of interrupting my meals, don't you? But right you are; I have been enjoying a lunch banquet of rare gastronomic delights."

"Why am I not surprised?"

"A man has to eat."

"You eat enough for three men."

"And I *think* enough for three men too. There must be some correlation."

"It's all brain food, no doubt."

"Correct, and besides, I have to maintain my fine figure," Banks said.

The Artist pictured Banks patting his ample stomach. The man had a snobby, condescending manner about him. He always wore proper custom-tailored suits and ties from London's Savile Row. His shoes were handcrafted to fit his feet and his alone. Everything regarding his appearance spoke of old money, elitism and an inherited membership in the pedigreed upper class that looked down their noses at everyone else whom they believed had not benefited from the proper *breeding* to be born into the elite.

Banks was also generously proportioned around the waist, with an impressive stomach that was a result of his gourmet eating habits. And he didn't care if anyone liked it or not. In fact, he pitied the people who ate salad and sipped green smoothies to look thin and starved.

"Years ago in Hawaii, the king was the most heavyset of all people because that was a sign of wealth and leisure. The workers and laborers were all thin and muscular from doing the powerful king's bidding. Those poor overworked pawns were shaped like you, actually."

"They must have been quite handsome, then."

"Perhaps, but the poor drones still worshipped and obeyed the jumbo-sized king and his very big and beautiful wife, the queen."

The Artist enjoyed their verbal jousts, yet each man respected, feared and distrusted the other. Trust and death often went hand in hand. "I'm still curious about what strange foods you might be dining on today."

"If you must know, I am spending my lunch hour enjoying Aztec food delicacies."

"I'm not sure I've ever seen an Aztec restaurant in my travels."

"I'm south of you at the moment, in Mexico City. It's a fascinating metropolis despite the overpopulation and air pollution. I'm having lunch at an authentic Aztec restaurant that serves genuine pre-Columbian cuisine."

"That's a long way to travel for a ... chimichanga."

"I'm here on business, so I may as well enjoy the local delicacies. This isn't your mass-marketed Mexican food smothered in melted cheese that you see in the States. The ancient Aztecs often ate various insects as a source of protein."

"Did you say insects?"

"Yes, we began the meal with an appetizer of *chapulines*, which are grasshoppers. Next, we sampled three different dishes based on fly eggs, beetles, and cockroaches."

"Now I'm sorry I asked."

"Currently, we are devouring the specialty of the house," Banks said, talking with his mouth full. "This prized delicacy is a soft corn taco shell filled with a variety of live insects and a sprinkle of salsa."

"You're eating bugs that are still alive?"

"And while I was biting into my taco just now, a beetle wiggled free of the tortilla, and it is crawling across my cheek. Hold the phone a moment."

Banks was gone a few seconds. "I'm back. A beautiful maiden plucked the beetle from my cheek and popped it into her own mouth, then fed it back to me with a kiss."

"Now it's your turn to hold the phone, I'm going to throw up my breakfast."

"Go ahead and cough up your protein smoothie, or whatever it is you bodybuilders eat for breakfast."

"I had steak and eggs for breakfast so I wouldn't be hungry while I waited for my appointment at the golf course."

"Speaking of your appointment, is the next one going to take place on schedule?"

"Yes, everything is proceeding according to plan," The Artist said. "The next target will die a bloody and painful death very soon."

"Good, we'll talk again after you complete the second job in this series."

"I'll call you then, and meanwhile, enjoy eating your insects." The Artist ended the call before Banks could describe another dish.

CHAPTER 13

Beth Cushman finished her work at the golf course and drove across town to follow up on a lead in the case. She found the address she was looking for and parked around the corner.

The old apartment building was in need of repair. The stairs creaked, the carpet was worn thin, and the walls hadn't seen a coat of paint in many years. On the second floor, the overhead lightbulbs were burned out and one of the apartment doors was marked by several bullet holes. Angry yelling spilled from behind another door, followed by the sound of a heavy object hitting a wall. She felt a tightness in her stomach and gave a quick glance over her shoulder.

Maybe I should have called for backup.

As she walked down the hallway, she put her right hand on the pistol in her holster. Finding the apartment she was looking for, she knocked on the door. Her training told her this could be an ambush, so she stood back from the door and off to one side, ready to draw her weapon at the first sign of trouble.

The door slowly opened and Beth tensed, ready to fight for her life. A middle-aged woman looked out. She had her hair in curlers and was drinking from a chipped coffee cup. Her breath smelled like red wine. The woman confirmed she was the one who'd called the police because she had information about the golf course murder.

As Beth listened to the woman talk, it became obvious she was inebriated, and this was a dead end in the investigation. It was common for people to claim they'd seen something important in a criminal case, but it usually turned out to be nothing.

"You keep your eye on that boy Curtis. He's no good—I've always said so," the woman said. "I heard him complaining that his public defender wasn't working hard enough. Curtis was plenty mad too. I'm sure he's the attorney assassin, right here in our building."

"We'll be watching him. Thank you for your time, ma'am," Beth said.

Beth left the apartment and went down the stairs, shaking her head at the thought that a wealthy attorney like Richard Caxton would've done any public defender work for disadvantaged folks.

When Beth exited the building, she noticed there were now several young males loitering around the steps. The men had gang tattoos and they looked her up and down, appraising her as a potential victim. Beth was wearing a plainclothes pantsuit, and she didn't have her police badge on her belt at the moment. Her suit jacket concealed the pistol on her hip. The low-income neighborhood was a mix of every kind of ethnic group, but Beth stood out like a sore thumb with her red hair and business suit.

One man stepped forward to block her path. He deliberately bumped into her and said, "Hey, Red, I bet twenty bucks the carpet matches the drapes." As he said it, he held up a twenty-dollar bill, then stared her in the eyes and invaded her space as if she was powerless to stop him.

Beth started to reach for her police badge but she felt some pent-up anger rising to the surface. She suddenly lost her temper and threw a vicious right hook, catching him hard in the jaw. He went down like a boxer who had received a knockout punch, leaving him sprawled on the sidewalk and groaning in pain. Beth stepped beside him, leaned down and plucked the twenty-dollar bill from his hand. "You lose, genius." She stuffed the twenty into her pocket, purposely exposing the pistol on her hip as she did.

The man's friends saw Beth's weapon and hesitated for a moment. None of them made any move to stop her from walking away.

Beth went around the corner, got into her car and drove down a side street to prevent them from seeing her police vehicle and possibly filing a complaint. Mostly, though, Beth wanted the group of young men to think that when one of them had harassed a random woman, he'd received an instant and painful lesson in courtesy. And he could have been shot if he'd pushed it too far. That might make them all think twice about harassing someone in the future.

Beth had to admit she was still angry about her husband's affair, and she'd taken out her anger on that punk. Oh well—he could have kept his mouth shut, but he'd disrespected a female who could fight back, and he'd paid the price. She opened and closed her sore right fist as she drove the streets of San Francisco.

CHAPTER 14

The Artist parked his car several blocks away from his luxury hotel and walked the remaining distance. He entered the hotel through a side door near a gift shop and rode an elevator to his floor.

Once inside his room, he peeled off his facial disguise, splashed water on his face and used a towel to wipe off the residual makeup. He sat at the table and resumed drawing a charcoal sketch of the Golden Gate Bridge. Working on art helped to focus his mind, and soon he was ready for some exercise.

He changed into sweatpants and a t-shirt and started doing some plyometric exercises. He constantly trained in the specialized workout that had been developed by Russian scientists during the Cold War to give soldiers explosive speed, power, and agility in hand-to-hand combat. While he exercised, he played music on his phone via a mini Bluetooth speaker. He focused his mind on his plans to kill the next lawyer in a creative, memorable, and artistic way.

After a while, his favorite song came on and it put him into a trancelike state. It was an old song from before he was born—"Behind Blue Eyes," by *The Who*. The lyrics spoke to him of what nobody could understand, how he felt being the lone gunman whose love for Tatiana had now warped into a rabid desire for violence.

As he went through the exercise routine and listened to the song, he saw memories in his mind's eye—flashes of knife fights, gun battles, and carefully orchestrated murders. Some of the killings had gone as planned; some of them had gone wrong. Such was life … and death.

Soon he was covered with perspiration and he felt the familiar anger burning inside him. It was time for a cold shower, or else he might lose his temper and hurt somebody he was not being paid to hurt. He stripped off his clothes and stood there in his black silk boxer shorts as he turned on the shower and adjusted the water to a temperature that would cool his temper as well as his body.

Before he got into the shower, there was a knock at the door. He turned off the water, grabbed his pistol and looked out the peephole. A room service maid was delivering a bottle of their best vodka, along with a martini shaker and a bowl of crushed ice. The delivery was arriving early. Either room service had misunderstood him, or they were incompetent—or this was a trick and someone was trying to kill him.

He set his pistol on a chair and tossed his t-shirt on top of it. Next, he placed a wide-view scope against the peephole viewer that let him see far into the hallway in both directions. Once he was satisfied that the hotel employee was alone, he answered the door. A wide-eyed woman wheeled in the serving cart. After she was in the room, The Artist stepped into the hallway and looked in both directions. Seeing that all was well, he came back inside and closed the door.

The maid tried not to stare at the sexy rippled muscles of the hotel guest's tattooed chest, but her eyes were drawn to him like a moth to a flame. She'd seen a lot of interesting things in her hotel career, but this man looked like he'd stepped out of an underwear advertisement. He had a strange smile, and his cool blue-gray eyes seemed to look right through her and read her mind. She handed him the room service bill, and he added a hundred-dollar tip. Her eyebrows went up in surprise.

"Thank you so much, sir," she said.

"It's worth it just to see your beautiful face, my love," he said, and smiled that seductive yet alarming smile of his.

The maid nodded and left the room. She tried to clear her mind of thoughts about the trouble she could have gotten into with the sweaty, half-naked mystery man. She wondered who he was, where he'd come from, and what all those tattoos of foreign words and symbols meant.

CHAPTER 15

Jake sat in his Jeep near the golf course. He looked through his telephoto lens at each house, hoping to find a home security video cam mounted somewhere.

One home had a wrought iron gate on the front of the driveway. In the fenced front yard was an artistically painted birdhouse on a pole. It was only about six feet off the ground. That seemed too low for a real birdhouse. It was either decorative or…

He got out of the Jeep and walked over to take a closer look. There was a small wireless video camera hidden inside the birdhouse, pointed toward the driveway entrance and the street.

Jake took a picture of the birdhouse with its hidden camera. On the gatepost, there was a button and a little brass sign that said "Doorbell." Jake pressed the button, but there was no response from the house.

He used his phone to access a pay-per-search website that private investigators and skip tracers used to find people who didn't want to be found. If you had a pulse and could fog a mirror, they had your information in their database. They knew more about you than your own mother did. He tapped on his phone screen and entered the home's address into the search form.

The website instantly provided the homeowner's name, Frank Tisdale, along with his income, age, occupation, photos, social media profiles, and a long list of marketing-related data, including his cell phone number. Jake called Tisdale's phone and waited for the unsuspecting man to answer. He stood where the birdhouse cam could see him and smiled, trying to look nonthreatening. His call went to voicemail, but he tapped on his phone for auto-redial and kept calling over and over again. On the third try, the phone was answered.

"What in the world?" Tisdale said.

"Hi, Frank Tisdale?"

"Who is this?"

"Sir, my name is Jake Wolfe, and I'm with the television news. I have a quick question about the hidden video camera you have installed in the birdhouse in front of your home." Jake held up his media ID card at the hidden camera, just in case Tisdale was watching him right now.

"What about it?" Tisdale said.

"Well, sir, we pay fifty dollars cash for information that helps us with one of our television news stories. I only noticed your camera because I'm a cameraman, and I must say you are a genius at camera disguise. Quite frankly, Frank, I'm impressed."

"Fifty is cheap. Make it a hundred and I might talk to you for five minutes. I'm a busy man."

"You drive a hard bargain, but I'll be happy to give a hundred in cash as long as I get the specific information that I'm looking for and get it in time for my rapidly approaching deadline today."

"What kind of information?"

"I just wondered if I could get a copy of your security camera's video recording of the street in front of your house for the past few hours. It would only take a minute."

"Why? What happened on my street today?"

"I'm doing a story about a local celebrity who was playing golf here. I think he might have walked down your street with his mistress by his side."

"Some guy is cheating on his wife, and you want to waste my valuable time?"

"No, sir, I want to give you a hundred dollar bill for five minutes of your valuable time," Jake said.

"Fine, whatever. I'm in the garage, working on a project," Tisdale said. "I'll open the gate and you can come up to the garage door. But be quick about it, only five minutes, okay?"

"Yes, thank you."

The gate clicked and swung slowly open as it hummed on electric hinges. The home had two garage doors and the one on the right rolled up with the help of an automatic door opener. Frank Tisdale was standing there squinting at him in the sunlight. Jake held out his hand.

"I'm Jake, nice to meet you Mr. Tisdale."

Tisdale hesitated, then shook hands. "Call me Frank."

Jake nodded and Tisdale led him over to a computer on a desk. Half of the garage was taken up by an elaborate beer-brewing setup.

Tisdale said, "The video is digital, so you just type your email in here and then click on that icon. It'll send a copy of the most recent twenty-four hours of video to you."

Jake typed in his work email at the TV station and sent a copy there, then sent another copy to his personal backup storage in the cloud.

"What kind of beer are you brewing there, Frank?"

Tisdale turned toward the home brewery and his chest swelled up with pride. "It's my famous double IPA. I make it with four kinds of hops and balance those with a sturdy malt backbone. Everybody who tries it likes it, so I'm going to start my own craft brewery to bottle it and sell it."

Jake pressed the fast-rewind command and kept one eye on the computer monitor as he listened to Tisdale describe the hops and how he used forty percent more malt and did two dry hoppings. The video showed a man walk past, heading away from the golf course and pushing a golf bag on a three-wheeled cart. Jake slowed down the video and saw a clear image of the man's face. One of the golf clubs in the bag looked out of character. It seemed to be a bit too long. The shaft was the color of gunmetal and shaped more like a pipe or … a rifle barrel.

"That's an impressive beer recipe you developed, Frank. How would you describe the taste?"

"My IPA has flavors of pine and floral citrus, hoppy bitterness, caramel sweetness, and some grapefruit on the finish."

As Tisdale went on, Jake fast-forwarded the video to the point where he saw himself walk past the first time, to meet with Terrell and the K9 Unit. He then backed up the digital video and restarted it right at that point, so his own images would be erased by the recording of new video.

"Did you find what you were looking for?" Tisdale said. He appeared at Jake's side and looked at the computer screen.

Jake smiled. "Give me one second while I check my phone to make sure the email arrived." He then took a hundred-dollar bill out of his wallet and handed it to Tisdale.

"Thanks for the video, Frank."

"No problem, thanks for the hundred. What did you say your name was again?"

"Dick Arnold," Jake said as he walked away.

CHAPTER 16

Jake walked down the driveway as the automatic garage door rolled down behind him, then turned and headed up the sidewalk toward his car. As he passed by the birdhouse cam, he ducked his head.

He drove to a coffee shop parking lot and sat in his car as he reviewed the video on his tablet. There were four video segments of the shooter—two of him pushing his golf cart past the camera as he was coming and going, and two as he drove past in an SUV, turned around in the cul-de-sac and passed by again.

Jake used video-editing software to cut and extract the important scenes and then merge them into one short highlight video compilation. He sent a text message to Terrell's phone and attached both videos, along with the background check on Tisdale and a photo of the birdhouse. He followed up with a call to Terrell, but it went to voicemail. "Hey, check your text messages. I sent you some video of the golf course shooter and his vehicle. It's going to be on the news soon. You may want to show it to the chief real quick and get a few points before the whole world sees it."

With that done, he typed up a brief blurb in an email and attached the video, then sent it to his editor's secretary. His email said, "Norman, you wanted close-up images of the shooter's face? You got 'em, boss."

Jake drove toward his office. On the way there, his phone buzzed with a return call from Terrell.

"Thanks for the video evidence. Good work," Terrell said.

"You're welcome, but now you owe me a steak dinner—the shoe is on the other foot. Ha, this is great."

"Yeah, sure, good luck thinking I owe you something. Do the words 'tourniquet' and 'blood transfusion' ring a bell? Remember when you were bleeding to death and all that?"

"Oh, here you go again."

At the same time, they both said, "Instead of putting that tourniquet on your thigh, I should have put it around your neck."

"Seriously, though, I'm calling to warn you that the killer might take a shot at you once he sees himself on your news video," Terrell said. "That's happened to several people who used their phones to take videos of criminals."

"Thanks for the warning, I'll be careful," Jake said.

"Are you carrying?"

"Yeah, I've got my pistol in my camera pack."

They said their goodbyes and Jake continued driving toward the news station. As he drove, he checked his rearview mirror.

CHAPTER 17

The Artist was in his hotel room, planning out an unusual way to murder the second lawyer. After he'd exercised and taken a cold shower, he sat at the room's teakwood table, with a pen and some paper. He began making lists and drawing sketches as he considered every potential scenario and outcome. There were plenty of risks involved in the plan, but he was confident he could pull it off, and the end results would be spectacular. When he finished going over his notes, he burned the papers in the bathroom sink with the overhead fan on.

His thoughts were interrupted when his phone buzzed with an incoming text message. The unique series of vibrations told him it was from Chairman Banks—the highly annoying, highly generous, and highly dangerous man who was going to pay him a large sum of money today. The funds were in payment for the first attorney assassination and would be transferred to one of his many secret bank accounts in the Cayman Islands, Hong Kong, or Singapore.

The text message from Banks said: *Have you seen the news?*

He turned on the television and changed the channel several times until he saw a news video that showed his car driving past what must have been a well-hidden video camera. He could see himself driving the vehicle. The image of his face was somewhat clear, as were the car's license plates.

That was bad enough, but it got worse. Next, he saw himself *walking* past the camera and pushing his golf bag on a three-wheeled cart. Thankfully, he'd been wearing a facial disguise, along with sunglasses and a hat. But if you knew what to look for, you could see the rifle barrel in among the golf clubs in the bag. The video froze when he passed directly in front of the camera, and the image of his disguised face was broadcast to the world. A moment later, that image moved to the left and another image appeared on the right. It was a photo of him in a tree, pointing his rifle at the viewer.

He brought up the TV station website on his phone and scrolled through the page featuring their news teams. In the section listing photographers and camera operators, he found a photo of the face he'd seen at the golf course. Beneath the photo was the name Jake Wolfe.

This was, as the Americans liked to say, really pissing him off. Wolfe was going to die—painfully, and soon.

Yet when he replied to the text message, he reframed the facts of the situation to impress upon the mind of Chairman Banks that he should be pleased with this recent development: *You wanted to cause fear. This will help to cause far more of it. You should pay me an extra bonus for these extra results.*

Banks didn't reply to the text. The Artist gave a fatalistic shrug of his shoulders and said in Russian, "*Pej do dná*," which meant "drink to the bottom." And he tossed back the rest of his vodka in one practiced gulp.

He stood up and looked out the window at the city. Now he'd have to get rid of his stolen SUV and switch it out for another vehicle. He sent a text message and summoned the delivery of a car to a hidden warehouse. The gang that provided these clean cars would charge him an exorbitant fee, but they were professionals and he didn't mind paying their rates.

His next challenge was how and where to deal with this troublesome investigative photojournalist, Jake Wolfe. The man would not simply lose interest and go away of his own accord. His kind never did; they believed in the freedom of the press and the First Amendment and all those American ideals that The Artist didn't understand.

Wolfe had to be eliminated with surgical precision and forcibly retired. It would also send a message to all the other journalists that they should not get too close. In his home country of Russia, journalists were killed under mysterious circumstances every month. The reason he knew this was because he'd killed many of them himself and made their deaths look like an accident or a routine crime such as robbery that had gone badly.

Perhaps he should just kill the bothersome man right now and get it over with. If he was lucky, he might find Wolfe at his office and, since luck favored action, he would take action immediately.

He got dressed and left his room, took the elevator to the ground floor and exited the hotel through a different side door than the one he'd used to enter. After walking a circular route to his car and making sure he wasn't being followed, he then drove the car to a dark, deserted alley and parked. With a quick glance over his shoulder, he opened the back hatch, reached into a duffel bag and took out a new pair of license plates.

The Artist quickly applied strips of thick double-sided permanent mounting tape to the backs of the new license plates. He pressed one of them over the original rear plate and then repeated the procedure for the front plate. The heavy-duty all-weather tape quickly molded itself between the plates and held the new ones on tight.

Next, he got out three adhesive plastic signs, peeled off the backing and stuck one sign onto each of the two rear passenger door windows of the car. The third sign went onto the back hatch window. Now the vehicle had new license plates and advertised a nonexistent tech company on three windows. Hopefully, the disguise would work long enough for him to make the short drive to the hidden location where he would switch cars. Then he'd drive to the offices of the television station that had broadcast the video. If that bothersome man Jake Wolfe was at work, he would kill him. If not, he'd hunt him down. One way or the other, the man would die before the end of the day. This was personal—nobody challenged The Artist so boldly and lived to tell about it.

CHAPTER 18

Jake arrived at the news station and parked in the lot across the street. Before getting out of his car, he used his telephoto lens to look around the area at windows and rooftops and parked cars. He didn't see any threats, so he quickly walked across the street. As he walked, he felt as if there was a target painted on his back.

He entered the building and cut through the lobby, then went down a hallway to his cubicle and sat down at his desk. There was a framed book cover on one of his cubicle walls from a Dilbert book titled *14 Years of Loyal Service in a Fabric-Covered Box*. It showed a drawing of Dilbert in a cubicle similar to the one Jake was in at the moment, and was a reminder that one of his goals in life had been to avoid getting stuck in a cubicle. Where had he gone wrong?

His phone buzzed with a text from his fiancée.

Gwen: *The wedding favor lady is here!*

Jake: *I told you I couldn't get time off work.*

Gwen: *You've disappointed me AGAIN!*

Jake put his phone away. Gwen had recently become an angry alcoholic who treated him with disrespect. He'd fallen out of love with her months ago, and no longer wanted to get married. Last night she'd yelled that she would *never* let Jake adopt another damned dog. Jake had told her he was a dog person, and that was non-negotiable. She'd made the mistake of saying he had to choose between her or a dog. Tonight he'd have to tell her it was over and he was leaving her. She'd go ballistic, but it had to be done. He'd move on and hopefully meet a happy, well-adjusted woman who liked dogs.

He heard Norman ranting and raving somewhere nearby. The voice of doom seemed to be getting closer and louder. Jake grabbed the notes and papers he'd come for and started heading in the other direction. As he went down the hallway, Norman spotted him and yelled, "Wolfe, in my office, now."

Jake sighed, turned around and began walking in that direction. Norman went into his office and started yelling at someone on his phone. Outside the office door in a reception area, an elderly secretary named Debbie sat at a desk with an unlit cigarette hanging from the corner of her mouth. The filter was red where her lipstick had rubbed off onto it.

On the wall behind Debbie's desk was a huge stuffed buffalo head. Jake stared at the head a moment, then looked at Debbie. "That must be new. I'm pretty sure if I'd seen a giant animal head above your desk before, I would've remembered it."

"Nothing gets by you, Sherlock," Debbie said. "That's why you have a corner cubicle."

"They're all corner cubicles, in four-part quads."

"Good at math too. Such a smart boy."

"I don't suppose that's *your* buffalo head on the wall?"

"No, it was just hanging there when I came in to work this morning. I was so surprised I almost dropped my cup of coffee-mocha-latte-frappe-vanilla-foam what-the-heck drink."

"Is it some kind of prank?"

"Norman called it his trophy. He went to a bison ranch and paid money to shoot one of the beasts, then had a taxidermist preserve the head and ship it here in a giant box via FedEx."

"And now you get to sit under it all day."

"I'm looking online at job listings right now. I can't work for this crazy man any longer."

"You can't leave us. This place will fall apart. I'll have to come up with a creative scheme to get Bisonzilla out of your office."

"Thank you. You're a good boy, no matter what Norman says about you."

"Can you tell our great headhunter that I had to leave the office and go follow up on a hot news tip?"

"Yes, and I won't mention that you actually went to your branch office at the Irish pub," Debbie said, and she waved goodbye.

Jake walked quickly down the hallway and toward the front entrance of the building. When he reached the door, a young woman opened it and rushed in as he was hurrying out. In the moment before they collided, Jake noticed she had long dark hair, a nice smile, and cute eyes behind a pair of horn-rimmed glasses. Her black slacks, rubber-soled shoes, and white medical coat suggested she was a doctor. She seemed distracted as she and Jake crashed into each other, and she dropped a file full of papers and a paperback book on the floor.

"Oops, let me get those for you." Jake went down on one knee to gather up the file and the book. The woman bent down at the same time, and they bumped their heads together.

"Ouch." She stood up and held a hand to her head.

Still on one knee, Jake held the file and book up to her. As she reached for them, she gazed down at him over the top of her glasses with an amused look on her face.

Jake smiled at her and stood up. "Sorry about the head butt. I usually just say hello when I meet someone."

She smiled. "That's okay, but now you're on my *list*, that's all."

"Oh, is it a long list, or am I special?"

"No, it's not a long list," she said. "Not the head butt section anyway. So, I guess you're pretty special."

Jake looked into her eyes. "Thanks, I think you're … pretty … special too."

They held each other's gaze for a moment.

"Uhm, well, sorry I ran into you," she said.

"No worries. I hope we run into each other again sometime soon. And I promise—no head butt next time."

She laughed. "Good idea."

"You have a wonderful laugh," Jake said.

She blinked at him several times and started to say something, but then a cloud seemed to pass across her eyes. She took a deep breath and nodded regretfully at him. "Thanks, it was fun bumping into you, literally, but I'm late for an appointment and I've got to go."

She turned away and walked purposefully into the building toward the reception desk. Jake watched her walk away and wished she'd said whatever had been on the tip of her tongue. He found her intriguing. Women who wore glasses and read books were his weakness.

He turned around and walked out of the building, noticing in the glass door's reflection that the woman had stopped, turned, and looked back at him.

She stood there looking out through the big front windows at Jake as he walked away. Her emotions were conflicted, but then the receptionist said, "May I help you?"

"I'm Sarah Chance," she said. "I have an appointment with Jennifer, in the advertising department."

"One moment and I'll page her for you."

While Sarah waited for the salesperson to arrive, she turned and took one last look at the man she'd bumped into, admiring the sexy, confident way he walked. It wasn't every day she met a hot guy with a fun sense of humor. The way he'd gazed into her eyes, like he could see into her soul, had made her heart race.

Sarah looked up when she heard Jennifer call her name. It reminded her why she came here—she was facing a crisis. An attorney had filed a lawsuit against her, and the legal proceedings were scaring away customers and destroying her new business right when it had been starting to grow.

She had her back to the wall, so as a last-ditch effort, she'd decided to try advertising on television. Sarah refused to give up; she'd fight for her career and her future, avoid bankruptcy, and turn her life around. Having a boyfriend would just be a distraction right now because she was a woman on a mission.

Resolved, Sarah took a deep breath and tried to push the charming guy out of her mind. It was just a random encounter that didn't mean anything. Nothing could distract her or stop her from achieving her goals. Not even that hot guy. But damn, his jeans sure did fit him nicely.

CHAPTER 19

Chairman Banks sat in the backseat of his limousine. He pressed the button to roll the privacy window up between the front and back seats. The window appeared to be made of the same thick darkened glass as most were, but this one was also a flat-screen television. The vehicle was also equipped with soundproofing and dark windows. Banks used it as a mobile office to conduct private meetings in person or via a conference call.

He was currently using a sophisticated satellite call software program that was encrypted for privacy. It had been created at great expense solely for Banks and his associates. In order to ensure total secrecy, the software developer had been killed after he'd completed the job; no government agency or criminal organization had penetrated this system so far.

He entered a password and logged in to a secret conference to join other ultra-wealthy members of a private group known as the Council. No member showed his or her face on the screen—only an outline of their country. The person represented by a map of Germany spoke up first.

"*Guten Tag,* Chairman. How are things going with the wet work in San Francisco?"

"You can see the first results of our cleaner's work on the local news here right now," Banks said.

A princess from Belgium spoke next and said, "And when shall we expect the second event to occur?"

"Our man will perform the three kills as quickly as possible," Banks answered. "He works methodically, but also knows we are on a tight schedule and require rapid results."

A Frenchman asked, "How do we know we can rely on this hired gun, The Artist?"

"As I said when I hired him, Ivan Zhukov is one of the most respected and feared assassins in the world."

"Our concern is that we heard a rumor he might lose his temper on rare occasions," a Russian man said. "Once in the past year, his anger caused a problem. Many people died as collateral damage."

"That unfortunate incident was a one-time event. I'm keeping a close eye on Zhukov. We are prepared to have him terminated if he goes off track, makes a mistake, or crosses us in any way."

There was silence for a few moments while every person on the call was apparently thinking about how they could also be killed if they crossed the others in any way.

A woman from Switzerland said, "I'm looking at an online news report right now, and I see that a photojournalist named Jake Wolfe has somehow obtained compromising images and video of our cleaner."

There were murmurings of dissatisfaction among the group. Banks was prepared for it. "That was actually a good thing because it created plenty of news publicity and caused more fear, which applied additional pressure to the individual we hope to persuade."

A man from South Africa said, "I still don't like it. Wolfe should be removed from the chessboard."

"Of course. I'll have Zhukov take care of it."

"If there aren't any further questions, we can adjourn and meet again tomorrow for an update on the second scheduled event," Banks said.

There were no questions or objections. The icon of the map of Switzerland blinked and disappeared. The other maps soon followed suit—Germany, France, Italy, Brazil, Japan, South Africa, Russia, China, Saudi Arabia, India, Canada, Mexico, Australia, and many other countries from around the world.

"Cheers," Banks said, and he too exited the conference.

With that meeting out of the way, he had one more to deal with. He made a call to Ivan Zhukov.

"What can I do for you, Chairman?" Zhukov said.

"Sorry to bother you, but I believe you asked me to keep you informed if any problems might arise on my end of this little project."

"Yes, I did. What's the problem?"

"The other members are worried about this curious fellow named Jake Wolfe."

"Worried enough to want him eliminated?"

"Yes, quite so."

"If you're willing to pay me to make that problem go away, I can take care of it right now," Zhukov said.

"Now would be good; we want the public to know about the lawyer deaths, but we'd prefer to control the flow of information," Banks said. "We don't need that photojournalist acting like a private investigator."

"I'll expect the usual fee for this job, half now and half upon completion."

"Yes, of course. I was calling to offer you the usual arrangements. Since we agree, I'll have a bank wire half of the funds to your account immediately."

"You are a professional, as always. That's why it's a pleasure working with you."

Banks ended the call and breathed a sigh of relief. This was a dangerous business he was in. People died if they made one false move. His guess was that Zhukov had planned to kill Jake Wolfe anyway, but now he'd earn another vast sum of money for work he would've done for free. That was fine with him. Money always greased the wheels of life and he had plenty of it.

He sent word to one of his offshore banks to wire the funds to Zhukov's account. A message came back saying that the transaction would be taken care of immediately. With that done, he lowered the divider between himself and his driver.

"Abhay, be a good lad and find me a Greek restaurant nearby," Banks said. "I suddenly have a craving for grilled lamb riblets, octopus salad, goat stew, and some of those fried zucchini cakes with pickled cucumbers and tzatziki sauce."

"Very good, sir. There is a good Greek restaurant here called Kokkari, over in the Financial District," Abhay called the restaurant and attempted to make a reservation but was turned away. "I'm sorry sir, there's nothing available until tomorrow."

"That doesn't work for me. I want you to stand out in front of the restaurant and purchase a table reservation from a young couple who are walking up to the door and about to go in."

"Offer them a generous sum, as usual?"

"Yes."

"As you wish," Abhay said as he drove to the restaurant.

In the back of his mind, Abhay thought that he was growing tired of answering to Banks. One day he might shoot him in the head, take his money and live like a king. But that time had not come yet—someday soon, perhaps, but not today.

CHAPTER 20

Ivan Zhukov arrived at an old warehouse that was in need of a coat of paint. He stopped in front of the building, pressed a command on his phone and caused a large overhead garage door to rise up at one of the ground-level bays. After driving inside the warehouse, he used his phone to close the door behind him.

He then drove the car up a concrete ramp and out onto the elevated dock. A rat scurried in front of him, but he ignored it. Years ago, when he'd spent time in a prison camp in Russia, he'd seen plenty of rats and sometimes had eaten them to survive. He stopped in front of a bay door and got out of his car, removing his backpack and a duffel bag from the vehicle and setting them aside.

He pressed a button on the wall to open another large garage door. An empty freight truck was parked outside the door with its back bumper up against the loading dock. Zhukov opened the doors on the back of the truck and then drove the Toyota SUV off the elevated dock and into the truck's empty cargo area, where he left the keys in the ignition and set the parking brake. He exited the truck, closed the doors and tapped the button again to make the large garage door descend.

After the door closed, a driver in the tractor-trailer started its engine and drove off. No words had been spoken, no faces had been seen.

Zhukov picked up his backpack and duffel bag and walked down to the other end of the loading dock where he opened another overhead door. A similar truck was parked there, carrying a new Mercedes-Benz inside the cargo box.

He set down his bags and looked in the car's trunk to make sure the unique weapon was there. This was one of his favorites. It was elegant and extra quiet. Few if any people would hear it, except for the one who was killed by it. This custom-made device would create a spectacular, clean kill, and the murder would go down in assassin history as a work of art by a genius of death.

He nodded in satisfaction, backed the car out of the truck and onto the dock, then got out and closed the truck doors and the bay door.

Zhukov got into the car, exited the warehouse and drove through the city, enjoying the ride in his luxurious and anonymous new vehicle. Once he reached the news station where Jake Wolfe was employed, he cruised slowly through the parking area, but didn't see the black Jeep from the golf course. He tapped an icon on his phone to scramble the secure mobile device and called his computer hacker.

A tired female voice, scratchy from unfiltered cigarettes and vodka, answered the call. "What can I do for you?"

"Elena, I need some information," Zhukov said.

"Yes, of course, Ivan," Elena said, suddenly wide awake.

"Find the home address of a photojournalist named Jake Wolfe. He works at a television station in San Francisco. I need it quickly for my ... work."

"I'll call you right back."

Zhukov drove a meandering route through San Francisco as he waited for Elena to find the home of the man who was making things difficult. A cable car rumbled past as he drove alongside a row of Victorian houses with panoramic views of the city and the water. Tatiana would have loved to visit here. His phone vibrated. "Da."

"I'm sending you Wolfe's home address, his fiancée's name, their vehicles and license plates, phone numbers, friends and relatives, all of it," Elena said.

Zhukov watched the data appear on his phone and then double-checked his weapon. The reliable pistol was fully loaded with hollow point rounds, and the suppressor firmly attached. He drove toward the condominium building where Jake Wolfe and his fiancée were living … and would soon be dying.

CHAPTER 21

Jake arrived at his building and drove underneath into the ground-floor parking area. He parked the Jeep and climbed the stairs to the second floor. As he strode down the hall to his condo, he paused outside of his front door and stood there thinking for a moment.

At one time, he'd been in love with Gwen, but her personality had changed until she was a different person. He couldn't go on like this any longer. When he told Gwen he was leaving her, she wouldn't take it well. A few days ago, after drinking too much wine, she'd lost her temper and had started throwing dishes and coffee cups. Maybe he'd say he was postponing the wedding and wanted some time apart to think things over. But he had to say something and get it over with.

He took a deep breath, put a smile on his face, opened the door, and walked inside. The kitchen was on his left, the living room to his right. Gwen was pacing back and forth between them, yelling at someone on her phone. Jake was surprised to see a brand-new large-screen television on the wall of the living room. The receipt on the counter revealed Gwen had charged the big-ticket item to one of his credit cards. There was an open bottle of wine on the kitchen counter that was nearly empty.

He tapped his phone and set it on a small shelf above the sink. If she was already drunk and angry this early in the evening, he wanted a video recording of their conversation, just in case she had another one of her temper tantrums.

Gwen ended the call and came into the kitchen, crossed her arms, and glared at Jake. She was a fashion model in the Victoria's Secret style. Slender, with long legs, a flat stomach, toned curves, and a pretty face seen in countless advertisements. "We need to talk. Why couldn't you be here this afternoon to help me pick out our wedding favors?"

Jake paused a moment, gathered his thoughts, and decided to tell her how he really felt. "Honestly, Gwen, if this arguing every day is what married life will be like, I'm just not cut out to get married."

"You couldn't care less about what I want. That's what you're really saying. Maybe we need to rethink our relationship and whether you and I are meant to be together." Gwen glared defiantly at Jake, lifted her chin, and stared down her nose at him.

A mile away, Ivan Zhukov drove rapidly toward Wolfe's home. He debated between various ways of killing the man. He could park across the street and shoot him when he entered or exited his building or he could shoot him through a window. He knew to fire repeated rounds in that scenario—several rounds to break the glass and several more to kill the target. A third option would be a home-invasion attack. He could wear a disguise, knock on the door under a false pretense, and then force his way inside. In that scenario, if any other people were at home, he'd have to kill them too.

As Zhukov turned his car onto the street where his target lived, he smiled at the thought of shooting the man who had dared to challenge him. His mood swing was moving toward manic, and he was feeling elated at the prospect of seeing the look on Wolfe's face as he died. Getting paid for it was icing on the cake. He started whistling a strange tune.

Jake took a deep breath and let it out. "Gwen, I've come to a decision."

"I've come to a decision too, Jake. I've decided that settling for you as a fiancé might have been a big mistake when there are plenty of better men out there."

"Well, in that case, the good news is you won't have to settle. I've decided to postpone our wedding. I want you to move back in with Marcie, while we think things over."

Gwen slapped Jake hard across the face, leaving a red handprint on his cheek. She put her whole bodyweight into it and hit him with all of her drunken anger. Caught by surprise, Jake reflexively raised his hands to defend himself from the assault.

If a man had hit Jake in the face that hard, Jake might have punched him reflexively, with enough force to knock him off his feet and break his jaw. But he used pure willpower to stop himself from hitting Gwen in self-defense.

Gwen saw Jake raise his hands and then lower them and she said, "Oh, so you want to hit me, is that it? Why don't you do it, then? What's the matter, are you scared of a woman? Go on and hit me, you big pussy. Show me how tough you are. Do it!"

"No. I've never hit a woman and you know it. You're the drunken, abusive partner here, not me."

"Well, I'm going to tell the police you hit me, unless you do what I say. You will go through with this wedding. You will not postpone it and humiliate me in front of everyone I know. If you don't agree, I'll call 911 right now and tell the police you physically assaulted me. I'll have you arrested for domestic violence."

Jake's heart went cold and he stood perfectly still. He'd seen these kinds of false accusations ruin the lives of some of his friends, and he didn't want to be the next victim of the trend. After slowly taking a few steps back, he picked his phone up off the shelf and sent the video to Gwen and Terrell. When her phone buzzed and she looked at the video, she picked up her empty wineglass and threw it into the kitchen sink, causing it to shatter.

"I've also sent that video to Terrell," Jake said, calm. "Now a cop has evidence of you threatening to lie and file a false police report, which is a serious crime that could send you to prison."

She cursed at him and called him every dirty name she could think of, then opened the refrigerator, took out a bottle of Cristal champagne and slammed it down on the counter.

"We were saving this for a special occasion, but I'd say it's pretty damned special when your fiancé postpones your wedding," Gwen said.

He shook his head and touched his face where she'd slapped him. "Sorry, Gwen, but at this point I'm not just postponing the wedding; I'm leaving you. Our relationship is officially over. I gave it my best shot, but if I can't trust you, I can't be with you."

She stopped cursing and stared at him in disbelief, her mouth open. "What did you just say to me?"

"I wish you all the best in your life, but I won't be a part of it anymore. We're done; this is goodbye."

Jake turned his back on her, opened the front door and walked out. He held his phone up with the front-facing video on so he could look at the screen and see behind him as he left.

"Nobody leaves me!" Gwen said. She grabbed the champagne bottle and threw it at the back of Jake's head. The heavy, full bottle slammed hard against the edge of the door as Jake was closing it, nearly hitting him, but he saw it coming and pulled the door shut at the last minute.

He winced when he heard the loud impact of the bottle right near his ear, knowing that if the bottle had hit the back of his skull, it could have killed him. His phone had recorded the assault, and he paused for just a moment in the hallway to send a copy of the video to Terrell. For all he knew, Gwen was calling 911 right now.

Zhukov arrived in front of Wolfe's building, pulled over, and parked illegally in a loading zone across the street. Wolfe's window curtains were open, giving Zhukov an unobstructed view through the sliding glass door and into the living room and kitchen area. He used binoculars to look into the condo and saw a woman there, upset and crying. Her face matched the photo of Wolfe's fiancée he had on his phone. He studied the garage and spotted Wolfe's Jeep in a parking space. The man was home, and it was time for him to die.

Zhukov got out of his car, jogged into the garage and started climbing the stairs two at a time.

Jake stabbed the button for the elevator, but impatience drove him toward the stairs. Just as he turned from the elevator, the doors opened and a woman walked out carrying two bags of groceries. Jake turned around, said hello to his neighbor, stepped into the elevator and pushed the button for the ground floor.

Zhukov stepped out of the stairwell and saw a woman set two bags of groceries on the carpet and dig in her purse for her keys. While she was preoccupied, Zhukov went to Wolfe's door and reached for the doorknob, hoping someone had neglected to lock it. The doorknob turned slowly in his gloved left hand, while his right hand drew the pistol from his shoulder holster and kept it hidden inside his coat.

He was about to ease the door open and step inside when the neighbor woman came back into the hall to grab her other bag of groceries. She looked at Zhukov curiously for a moment, unaware her life depended on what she said or did in the next few seconds.

"If you're looking for Jake, you just missed him," she said. "He went down the elevator a minute ago."

"Thanks, but I'm looking for a unit that's for rent—the realtor told me it was on the third floor," Zhukov said. "Now that I look at the number on this door, I realize I'm on the second floor. How silly of me."

He smiled and shrugged, put his pistol back in the holster, then walked to the stairway door and hurried downstairs. Running into the garage, he looked around for his target. Jake was nowhere in sight and his Jeep was gone. Zhukov cursed in Russian as he ran across the street to his car. He sped around the block, hoping to spot the Jeep as it was leaving. He caught a glimpse of a black SUV on a side street and gunned his engine. When he caught up with the SUV, he saw that it wasn't a Jeep, and he pounded his fist on the dashboard.

Zhukov held his pistol with one hand and steered with the other. He drove in a crisscross pattern through the neighborhood, searching for Jake.

When he'd looked through the condo window and had seen Gwen crying, he'd guessed that the couple might have had a lovers' quarrel. His prey could be somewhere nearby, having dinner at a restaurant with a sympathetic friend or drowning his sorrows with alcohol at a bar.

Zhukov took out his phone and called Elena. "Jake Wolfe left his home a moment before I arrived. I want to know where he is, and I want to know now."

"I've been hacking into their checking accounts and credit cards. Gwen's passwords are a joke," Elena said. "She bought a Samsung smart TV today that's connected to the internet. It has a built-in camera with facial recognition software and a microphone with voice recognition capabilities. It's like voluntarily installing a spying device in your home."

"Access the camera and microphone for me," Zhukov said.

"Working on it now—almost there. A new router came with the TV and ... yes! Gwen left the default factory password on it. Okay, check your phone."

When Zhukov's phone vibrated, he saw a live video stream from inside the condo. Gwen appeared in living color and rich sound.

"Record everything she says and does," Zhukov said. "And dig into Wolfe's recent credit card usage; find his favorite bars and restaurants."

"Yes, I'm on it. And you're welcome."

Zhukov ignored the sarcasm and ended the call. He watched and listened to Gwen for a minute. She was crying and talking to someone on her phone, saying that Jake had canceled the wedding and left her.

Seeing the woman cry brought back sad memories of Tatiana, and Zhukov craved a drink. He told himself that it wasn't like he had a drinking problem—it was just that this killing was such thirsty work and he did so much of it. Nobody else could ever understand his life because they hadn't lived and breathed it. They hadn't walked a mile in his *oboof*, his shoes.

Zhukov gripped the phone tightly as an idea formed. "That woman probably has a bottle of vodka in the cupboard," he muttered. "Maybe I should go back there and offer comfort in her time of distress. She may tell me where Wolfe might have gone."

The neighbor had seen him, but she would only remember the fake glasses and hairpiece he'd been wearing. Gwen's door was probably still unlocked; he could enter quietly and catch her by surprise, turn off the spy TV, and then have a heart-to-heart talk with the attractive woman. The fact that she had recently been his enemy's beloved would make it all the better.

CHAPTER 22

The sun was low in the sky as Jake drove the streets of San Francisco, feeling heartbroken and homeless. After a while, he found himself in the parking lot of Clancy's Irish Pub. He didn't remember driving there. It seemed like his Jeep had gone to the pub on autopilot.

He sat in his car, wondering where he would sleep tonight, instead of in his own bed in his own home. He could always couch-surf in the garage at Terrell's place; "the man cave," as Alicia called it. But then Alicia would naturally want Jake to talk about what had happened with Gwen. And Jake didn't feel like talking about it. He wanted to forget it.

The best choice would be to stay on-board his friend Dylan's boat, moored at the Juanita Yacht Harbor in the small town of Sausalito, just on the other side of the Golden Gate Bridge. Dylan was one of those Silicon Valley software millionaires and currently lived in Dublin, Ireland. All the large American software and internet companies had branch offices in Dublin.

Dylan owned a beautiful sixty-foot Horizon PC60 Motor Yacht named the *Far Niente,* but he never used it. He was always overseas, working on his software empire. The wealthy world traveler and serial entrepreneur only came home to California once or twice a year.

Jake had often borrowed the *Far Niente* for fishing trips. Now he wondered if Dylan would let him live on the boat, for longer than a weekend. He didn't want to wear out his welcome and take advantage of Dylan's hospitality, but Dylan probably wouldn't think twice about it. He was a close friend.

Gwen knew about the yacht and might show up there after midnight, drunk and waving her pistol around while Jake was asleep. On the other hand, she'd been drinking a lot already. Hopefully, she'd soon be passed out asleep in her bed.

Jake received a text message from his sister Nicole. As a psychiatrist, her opinions were usually helpful, sometimes annoying, and almost always right.

Nicole: *Gwen called and left a drunken rant on my voicemail. What's going on, Jake?*

Jake: *This says it all.*

He sent her a copy of the video. After a pause, she replied.

Nicole: *Leave her; she's an abusive narcissist. Walk away and don't look back.*

Jake: *I'm already gone. I'll be spending the night on Dylan's boat, the Far Niente, at Juanita Yacht Harbor.*

Nicole: *Next time, look for a woman who has a beautiful heart, not just a beautiful body.*

Jake: *Truth.*

Nicole: *Love ya, bro.*

Jake: *Love you too.*

He sat there in the Jeep for a moment, thinking things over. Leaving Gwen had been the right thing to do—the only thing to do. But he still felt as if one of his closest friends had died. He took a deep breath and let it out. A drink or two at the pub sounded good right about now. But in his current mood, that could lead to a very long evening, an expensive taxi ride afterward, and a killer hangover in the morning. He thought about his good friend Stuart, who had died so young. Jake was going to Stuart's funeral tomorrow, and he knew that he should honor his friend's memory by being thankful to be alive, instead of feeling sorry for himself. He exited the pub parking lot and drove toward the Golden Gate Bridge, on his way to the *Far Niente*.

~

While Zhukov drove in a search pattern looking for Wolfe's vehicle, he received a call from Elena. "Have you tracked his phone yet?" Zhukov said.

"No, I've been trying to hack into his phone, but he's using some kind of encryption on it," Elena said. "But I was able to hack into his mother's phone and email. Her password is her two kids' birthdays. She just now received a text from her daughter Nicole, saying that tonight Wolfe will be sleeping on a boat named the *Far Niente,* and tomorrow he'll be attending a funeral."

Zhukov's phone vibrated and he received a text with a link to a map that showed the location of the boat. He drove toward the Golden Gate Bridge and used his phone to glance at the details of the yacht harbor on Google Earth. He was thinking he should buy some stock in the company as a way to thank them for acting like a no-cost spy agency.

He would catch Wolfe by surprise and shoot him in the back before the man even knew what was happening. Fair play was for fairy tales. In the real world, only cold brutality and ruthlessness could prevail.

CHAPTER 23

As Jake headed toward Sausalito, his stomach growled and he called a restaurant near the harbor and ordered a pizza to go. "I'll take that combination pizza with all the toppings."

"You mean the kitchen sink pizza?"

"That works for me." He drove across the Golden Gate Bridge and saw an incredible sunset spread across the sky and over the water. Jake felt he was on the right path in life, without any baggage. He was a free man and things could only get better from here on out.

Zhukov arrived at the harbor before Wolfe and checked out the yacht while he waited for his target to arrive. Perhaps if the layout inside the boat was right, he'd hide in there and shoot Wolfe when he came through the door. He walked down to the boat slips and didn't see any visible activity or any lights on in the vessels docked near the *Far Niente*.

When Zhukov got to the boat, he picked the lock on the sliding glass door, went inside and looked around. It wasn't a mega-yacht, but still a large, high-quality vessel that must have cost a small fortune. He wondered how a photojournalist could afford such an expensive boat as this. He must be accepting bribes to run news stories that flattered politicians and criminal organizations.

On the other hand, a smaller-sized pre-owned yacht of this year and type would sell for the same price as many houses and condominiums in San Francisco.

There was a Vincent van Gogh painting on the wall. He had a deep appreciation for the artist and was surprised that he and Wolfe had that in common. Next, he found an end table he recognized as one that housed a large cigar humidor. He picked the lock and saw that it was lined with Spanish cedar and filled with premium handmade cigars, including many brands he knew.

It would have been nice to steal all the cigars, but there were too many of them—dozens of boxes and hundreds of cigars. Right now, he only had the time and the room in his backpack to grab one box. There was a travel-size humidor box that was filled with a mixed assortment of individual cigars and a Boveda sixty-nine percent humidification packet to keep them fresh. He smiled and placed the flat rectangular box into his backpack. Wolfe wouldn't miss these once he was dead, and it was a shame to let them go to waste.

Checking the liquor cabinet, he saw some bottles of top-quality vodka. There was Ocean Vodka from Maui, Square One Organic, and Russian Standard Gold. Zhukov put the Russian Standard Gold into his backpack. It was exotic vodka made from the golden roots of ginseng plants, instead of from grains or potatoes. He wondered if Wolfe had dated a Russian woman with good taste in vodka but poor taste in men.

While opening and closing some more drawers and cabinet doors, Zhukov felt his phone vibrate. Elena texted: *Wolfe is close. I got into his bank account and it shows that he just bought a pizza, right down the street from the harbor.*

Zhukov decided the inside of the yacht was not the right place for his attack. It would be best to shoot the man in the parking lot as he got out of his vehicle, then make a quick getaway. For a moment, he considered pouring the contents of several liquor bottles over the furniture and then lighting a candle that would slowly burn until it ignited everything. But he didn't have time right now, and he could always return and do that later if he was in the mood.

Jake sat in his Jeep in the restaurant parking lot, eating a slice of the hot pizza while trying not to burn his mouth. Then he drove to the harbor and glanced around to make sure he didn't see Gwen's car, or any sign of the attorney assassin. The parking lot appeared quiet and deserted, so he parked and turned off the engine. He reached for his camera bag, and for a moment felt the familiar sense of impending danger. It was the same feeling he'd had at the golf course just before that lawyer had been shot. He wished Gracie was with him now. Her keen sense of smell would have warned them both if any threat was nearby.

Jake got out of the Jeep and slung his camera backpack on his back, then picked up the pizza box and set the small paper bag on top that held the little to-go containers of parmesan cheese and red pepper flakes. He went around the front of the Jeep, staying between the two rows of vehicles as he hurried toward the docks.

Once Jake got to the end of the row of cars, he jogged across the rest of the parking lot and then headed down to the boat slips. He felt better once he had some sailboats and motor yachts blocking him from view. He was out of the line of sight of anyone who might have been watching. Jake went quickly down his own narrow wooden dock toward the slip where the *Far Niente* was berthed. His eyes glanced around and his ears were alert to the sounds of the other boats in the marina. He also looked over his shoulder several times to see if anyone had followed him. All seemed quiet, and he didn't notice anything unusual.

When Jake reached the *Far Niente,* he placed one foot on the gangway and reached one hand for a railing while he still had one foot on the dock. As he held the pizza box in his other hand, it tilted and the small paper bag on top slid off and fell onto the dock.

"Oh, come on; do *not* go in the water," Jake said.

The paper bag stayed on the wood planks, and as Jake dropped to one knee and reached for it, he heard the familiar *snap* sound that a bullet makes when it breaks the sound barrier as it flies past someone's head. Jake had never liked that sound much, or the people who caused it when they took a shot at him. He felt a flash of anger, and his survival reflexes kicked in.

CHAPTER 24

Jake dropped the pizza box on the dock and dove over it and onto the wooden planks ahead of him. He moved just in time to dodge two more bullets that struck a neighbor's power yacht. He stayed low and commando-crawled on the dock, moving past the starboard side of the *Far Niente* to gain some cover.

He took off his backpack and noticed it had a bullet hole in a side pocket where a round had barely missed him. He reached into the pack and took out his pistol, put his backpack on again, and eased into the water. A bullet sizzled past him, but it went high. He held the pistol above him as he swam with a one-handed sidestroke around the stern of the yacht toward the next boat slip.

Jake climbed up onto the dock, hidden from sight by the *Far Niente* and positioned to run and shoot. The sensible thing to do would be to run, hide, and survive, but his Marine training overruled that notion. In his mind, he heard the voice of his drill instructor yelling at him. "Repeat after me, Marines always run toward the fighting!"

He jumped up and ran straight toward the shooter's location, with the pistol held in front of him. He heard footsteps, then the roar of a car engine and the squealing of tires on pavement. Taking a risk, he ran to an open gap between two parked cars.

When he spotted a Mercedes-Benz speeding away. Jake ran to his Jeep, climbed in and took off in hot pursuit.

The shooter began taking evasive maneuvers down side streets and around corners. The man drove as if he'd been trained at high-speed tactical driving. Jake lost him for a moment but then spotted him farther down the road, getting onto Highway 101 to travel back toward San Francisco.

Jake sped down the highway and across the Golden Gate Bridge, then continued in pursuit up and down the hills and streets of San Francisco. The car ahead managed to leave Jake behind again, but he caught up with it on Sixteenth Street, heading toward the Mission Bay neighborhood. Jake's car windows were down and he had his pistol next to him on the seat. He knew he should call Terrell and tell him what was happening, but he couldn't take his hands off the steering wheel to make a phone call while he was driving like a madman.

The Jeep's HEMI engine helped Jake close the distance, as both vehicles were approaching some railroad tracks at the crossing where Sixteenth Street passed under the overpass. There was a train coming toward the crossing from the right; the crossing bells were clanging, the signal lights were flashing, and the red-and-white-striped barrier arms started lowering down across the street.

The shooter in the car ahead didn't slow down. He drove straight at the barrier. The train conductor began blaring his air horn and using his brakes, causing a spray of sparks on the tracks as he tried to slow down.

Jake didn't have a death wish. He knew the stopping distance required of his Jeep at this speed, so he stomped his brakes hard. The Jeep fishtailed, and the rear end of the driver's side of the vehicle started coming around to the left. Jake steered left into the skid to avoid spinning out in a circle, and the Jeep drifted sideways in a barely controlled power slide toward the train tracks.

The fleeing vehicle drove across the tracks right in front of the train and crashed through both barrier arms, barely getting out of the way of the locomotive in time. In the last seconds while Jake was sliding sideways on squealing tires, he took his right hand off the steering wheel, grabbed his pistol and fired one shot out of his open driver's-side window at the fleeing car. A second later, the train roared through the crossing.

The Jeep finally screeched to a stop so close to the passing train that Jake could have reached out and touched it. He took a deep breath and let it out.

"That was close—too damned close."

Through the windows of the passenger cars that were going past, Jake could see the Mercedes had a cloud of steam or smoke pouring out from the engine as it sped away, taking a left and going out of sight. In a moment, the car could disappear into the mixed industrial neighborhoods or escape onto one of the two highway on-ramps.

The train passed by and cleared the intersection, and Jake drove fast in the last known direction of the shooter's vehicle. He crisscrossed the city blocks near the highway but didn't see the car anywhere. Police sirens blared in the distance. The train crossing was close to the main police headquarters; the train conductor had probably called 911. Jake had a concealed carry permit for the pistol, but there was no sense taking his chances that the police would be in an understanding mood about him firing it within the city limits.

Jake hid the pistol under his seat and drove his car in an evasive route away from the area. He saw the flashing lights of two police vehicles coming toward him from the opposite direction, so he pulled into an alley and turned off his lights. He sat and watched in his rearview mirror as the police cars roared past, heading toward the train crossing. Once the cops were gone, Jake exited the alley on the other side, turned on his headlights and drove away.

In a few minutes, Jake was in another area of the city. He thought of going back to the harbor, casting off the lines, and taking the *Far Niente* out on the Bay. But on second thought, the killer might have a partner or some kind of backup shooter waiting at the harbor, hoping Jake would return.

He felt a weight on his shoulders as the reality set in that he was going to have to track down and eliminate this threat.

With that decision made, he thought that for now, a hotel would be a good place to spend the night unless the person who was stalking Jake had access to his banking information. If so, Jake couldn't risk using a credit card to pay for a room. He could get cash at an ATM, but that might also reveal his location to a hacker.

"When in doubt, call a buddy." Jake called Terrell's cell phone, but there was no answer. It was past dinnertime now, and Terrell was a happily married man who followed the philosophy that early to bed and early to rise made a man healthy, wealthy and … a badass. "Sorry, bro," Jake said as he called repeatedly.

CHAPTER 25

Terrell was in bed with his arms wrapped around his sleeping wife, Alicia. He was half-awake and didn't move a muscle, just enjoyed the feeling of her warm body close to his, the oneness of the two of them together. This was where he belonged right now, and she was all that mattered to him.

Tonight, they were finally able to get past their latest fight and kiss and make up. Their lovemaking had been as highly emotional as their current relationship was. It had seemed like a symphony of everything they'd been feeling so deeply. The fight and the forgiveness, the anger and the joy, the pain and the passion. After their song had played out and they were lying in bed, exhausted, wrapped in each other's arms, they felt closer than they'd ever been.

Makeup sex is soooo good, Terrell thought. *Almost worth a big fight … almost.* He loved Alicia so much, he'd probably die if they ever split up like Jake and Gwen had. He'd been sorry to receive Jake's text saying the wedding was off and he had left Gwen. And it had surprised him to see the video attached, of Gwen losing her mind. Those two friends of his were probably feeling heartbroken tonight. It was just sad. Alicia stirred in her sleep, and Terrell held her tighter. She sighed and said, "Mmmmmm," then fell back asleep.

Terrell smiled and thought he was the luckiest man in the world. There was something so special about this woman he was madly in love with. He kissed her beautiful cheek and lingered on her soft black skin, the color of the finest chocolate. He breathed in the scent of her perfume. She was both his greatest weakness and his greatest strength. What a woman, what an angel. He would walk barefoot on broken glass through a burning building just to kiss her sweet lips. At the moment, he couldn't even remember what they'd been fighting about. He was just relieved it was over now.

In the drawer of his nightstand, his cell phone kept lighting up and vibrating. He could see the light flashing through the cracks where the drawer met the sides of the furniture. The buzzing sound was quiet enough that it didn't wake Alicia, but loud enough for Terrell to notice it, since he was half-awake. And he was always half-awake. It was one of the hazards of his job in law enforcement and from his time in the Marines. You were always on call to make sure everybody was safe and could relax, except for you.

After his phone had buzzed for the third time, Terrell realized it must be something important, or else some telemarketer was going to die a slow and painful death when Terrell tracked him down and put a blowtorch "where the sun don't shine." Terrell eased himself carefully from Alicia's arms as he substituted his pillow for her to hug instead of him. She wrapped her arms around the pillow and let out a little moan while her pretty mouth made a pout.

"Sorry, babe, be back soon," Terrell whispered. He kissed her shoulder, and she fell back into a deep sleep. When he checked his phone, he saw it was Jake calling. His friend had probably gone on a broken-hearted drinking binge and needed Terrell to bail him out of a jam ... again.

He found his sweatpants on the floor and pulled them on, then took the phone into the bathroom and closed the door. Broken-hearted binge or not, he knew it was serious for Jake to be calling him repeatedly at night. Jake was a natural-born vigilante and protector of those in need. That got him into all kinds of trouble.

Terrell returned Jake's call, but he gave his friend a hard time. "What is it now? I'm kind of preoccupied at the moment, sleeping between the sheets with an angel, you know?"

"You really do need your beauty sleep," Jake said. "Sorry to bother you, but somebody just took a few shots at yours truly."

"Was it Gwen shooting at you? I saw the video you sent. That girl is acting crazy."

"Gunny Sergeant always warned us to never stick your dick in crazy."

"Maybe you should have listened to Gunny."

"Gwen owns a pistol. I gave it to her, but she didn't shoot at me. Not yet, anyway. It was that attorney assassin, just like you warned me about."

"How do you know it was him? Did he introduce himself when he shot at you?"

"Who else would be shooting what sounded like a twenty-two pistol with a suppressor attached?"

"Good point, that's an assassin's weapon," Terrell said. "Was he driving that same SUV we saw in the birdhouse cam video?"

"No, he was in a brand-new Mercedes."

"What happened? Give me a sitrep."

"The assassin tried to kill me when I was getting onboard the *Far Niente*. I decided to hunt him down like we did to terrorists overseas. I chased him across the Golden Gate Bridge and through the city but lost him when he crashed through the railroad barrier arms at the crossing where Sixteenth goes under I-280. He drove right in front of an oncoming train, but not before I shot his vehicle and damaged it."

"Why didn't you call me sooner?"

"During the chase, my car was barely under control and I couldn't take my hands off the wheel. Besides, I was on a search and destroy mission to eliminate the threat. I still plan on hunting him down. What would your chief of police say about that?"

"Let the police handle it and make an arrest, fool."

"Orders received and ignored, Lieutenant, sir."

Terrell cursed. "I'll call it in now and have our guys search the area."

"Somebody already called. There are cop cars all over the place."

"Did you get his license plate?"

"Thanks for your concern about my well-being," Jake said. "Yes, my friend, in answer to your unasked question, I am unhurt and all my parts are still in one piece."

"The ladies of the world will be glad to hear that all of your parts are still intact," Terrell said. "They are under the mistaken belief that those parts might be good for something. Now, please tell me you got at least a partial on the plate."

"Only a few characters. I think there was some paint on the license plate light, so it was dimmed but still legal."

Jake recited the partial numbers and letters he'd seen and described the vehicle's make, model and paint color.

"Got it, thanks."

"Now that I think about it, when we crossed the Golden Gate Bridge, the toll collection cameras had to have taken a picture of his front license plate."

"That's what I was thinking too. I'm going to call and get a copy of that pic sent to me, then put out an APB on the Benz."

"It was a mistake for him to cross the bridge, but I don't think he expected me to chase after him."

"He probably expected you to be dead."

"True, I almost got shot, but I dropped something and, when I bent down to pick it up, the first round missed me," Jake said. "I'm half Irish-American, so this good luck stuff just happens to me all the time."

"Right, it's not because you're clumsy and you drop things, it's because you wear lucky green shamrock boxer shorts," Terrell said.

"It's pretty cool. I'm not going to lie."

"Where are you now?"

While Jake talked to Terrell, he drove the Jeep in a roundabout way toward Terrell's house.

"Can you send a cop car to park in front of my condo?"

"Why, to protect Gwen? After what she tried to do to you, why would you be so concerned?"

"I guess I just have a protective streak for females who throw bottles at me."

Terrell smiled and shook his head. Women were Jake's blind spot. "Yes, I'll send a car. Now get yourself over here to couch-surf in the garage before somebody else takes a shot at you."

"You want me to camp out in the man cave with all the sports channels on the TV, a pool table, a fridge full of beer, plus the awesome doggie? Who would want to stay in a boring place like that?"

"It would be roughing it, now that you're a yacht captain and all."

"You can call me Captain Mofo," Jake said.

"Do you remember the garage door opener code?" Terrell said. "You know you're welcome anytime—just be sure to send me a text first so I don't shoot you."

Jake drove through Terrell's neighborhood, a few blocks away from his house. "I'll be there momentarily, so I'll let you go now. And, can I use your dryer? My clothes are soaking wet."

"I'm not even going to ask why."

"My bladder had nothing to do with it."

"Hurry up and get your Jeep parked in front of my place with the car cover over it."

"I'm so close, my ass is already there."

"Catch up with it, then."

Terrell ended the call with Jake and called the police station. He reported the partial license plate of the car they were looking for and got someone working on obtaining a copy of the license plate photo from the Golden Gate Bridge cameras. He also sent a black-and-white to check on Gwen.

Then he went back to the bedroom and sat on the edge of the bed while he waited for Jake's text. A minute later, his phone buzzed and the text said, *Opening airlock.* Terrell heard the garage door open and close and his dog Boo-Boo barking hello. The dog was always happy to see Jake. Then he received another text that said, *Mmm, beer,* and replied to it with, *Goodnight.*

Terrell put the phone in the drawer of the nightstand and slid back under the sheets with Alicia. He curled up in the spoon position to her plump round behind and closed his eyes. His last thought as he drifted off was that he'd actually sleep better with Jake in the garage like a guard dog. If there were ever any threats to Terrell's family or friends, Jake would fight to protect them. He would do the same for Jake's loved ones too. That's just how it was and how it always would be, because that's how brothers roll.

CHAPTER 26

Zhukov sent a text message to his dealer in stolen vehicles, and then drove his damaged car down back streets to the same warehouse he'd used before. Once inside, he went to a personnel door and looked out through a peephole to see if Wolfe had managed to follow him.

When he was sure nobody was there, Zhukov got back into his car, leaving his lights off as he carefully drove up the concrete ramp to the loading docks. He moved slowly in semidarkness, guided only by the moonlight coming through a row of dirty windows high above him. Stopping in front of a bay door, he stepped out of his car and removed his backpack and a duffel bag. Then he opened the trunk to retrieve the weapon.

Zhukov exchanged the Mercedes for a Dodge Challenger, placed the weapon in the new car's trunk, and kept his small backpack on the front passenger seat beside him. He exited the building and drove to another area of the city where his hotel was located.

When he'd made his escape, he dwelled upon the fact that the evening had been highly inconvenient. He slammed his fist down on the dashboard. "Wolfe has had a streak of good luck, but it's about to run out. Soon he's going to learn that he should have kept his nose out of my business."

He took a deep breath. For tonight, he'd go to his hotel room and get some sleep. He drove with one hand on the wheel and reached into his backpack for the stolen bottle of Russian vodka. After taking a few drinks from the bottle, he put the cap back on and then lit a half-sized cigar known as a *Hemingway Short Story*.

Soon he arrived at his hotel and drove past the front of the building to do some reconnaissance before parking two blocks away and walking the last part. When he passed by, he saw several police vehicles parked all around the building, and uniformed officers going in and out of the hotel's front doors. Zhukov had no doubt this activity must be about him. That maid might have seen a news report and remembered his tattoos or his foreign accent and reported him to the police.

He drove around the building and saw a light on inside his suite and a man standing on his balcony. Zhukov cursed and thought about his sketches. These people would take his drawings as evidence, and he'd never see his artwork again. He got angry about the injustices that artists had to suffer, and then he felt a mood swing coming on, taking him to a dark place.

Driving away from the hotel, he plugged a small tablet into the vehicle's music system and began playing an old Russian folk song titled "Katyusha." He thought about the words and what they meant in English.

Apple and pear trees were blooming.
O'er the river, the fog merrily rolled.
On the steep banks walked Katyusha,
On the high bank, she slowly strode.

As she walked, she sang a sweet song
Of her silver eagle of the steppe,
Of the one she loved so dearly,
And the one whose letters she had kept.

The evening's troubles, the loss of his artwork, the song, and the vodka, all combined to make his depression even worse. He began to feel melancholy and homesick for Mother Russia, or *Rodina*.

Why he loved his homeland so much, he did not know. It had been a tough place to grow up. His parents had been hungry for most of their lives and living in constant fear of a one-way trip to the prison camps. Terrible things had happened in those camps. Awful, unspeakable things.

The "New Russia" hadn't been much better, after the Americans had bankrupted it via the Cold War. Once the Berlin Wall finally came down and the Russians left the East Germany prison-camp nation, everyone in the world saw undeniable proof that the Marxist experiment had been a miserable failure.

The western side of Germany, aided by America, had been a land of freedom and prosperity. The eastern side, controlled by the Soviets, had been a nightmare police state of slaves imprisoned in poverty.

During his time in the West, Zhukov had discovered a book titled *Death by Government*. It told the truth about how the totalitarian governments of past regimes had killed tens of millions of innocent citizens in Russia, China, Germany, Japan, Turkey, North Korea, Cambodia, Pakistan, and other nations.

Zhukov had a photographic memory and could still remember what the research about Russia had concluded:

"Probably almost sixty-two million people, nearly 54,800,000 of them citizens, have been murdered by the Communist Party—the government—of the Soviet Union. Old and young, healthy and sick, men and women, even infants and the infirm, were killed in cold blood. They were not combatants in civil war or rebellions; they were not criminals. Indeed, nearly all were guilty of ... nothing.

"And part of the killing was so random and idiosyncratic that journalists and social scientists have no concept of it, as in hundreds of thousands of people being executed according to preset government quotas...

"We lack a concept for murder by quotas because we—including the journalist, historian, and political scientist—have never before confronted the fact that a government can and has killed its own people for apparently no reason."

Zhukov knew this was the true and brutal history of his country. In the past, a memo would go out ordering the death of ten thousand "enemies of the people." A memo would come back saying that ten thousand enemies had been *found* and killed.

The murder victims were simply random citizens who were

denounced and falsely accused by their neighbors. People felt compelled to turn on their friends and families in a desperate attempt to save themselves from the insane asylum of death. What had been accomplished by the mass murders? Had it simply been a secret agenda of depopulation?

After the Soviet Union collapsed, the men who had caused over sixty million random murders didn't go away. When many of them and their heirs found themselves unemployed, they simply began participating in organized crime.

First the KGB had made Zhukov into a trained killer, and later the Russian mafia had recruited him as a hired gun. The two organizations had molded him into the instrument of death he was today. He'd spent many years killing people for pay, doing it for his masters like a deadly puppet on a string. These days he no longer killed for his government, or for political reasons, or for organized crime. Now it was done to increase the wealth and power of the shadowy elite, and to line their own pockets.

When Zhukov's life of violence had first started, he'd had little choice. If he didn't follow his master's orders, he would die a slow and painful death. He'd merely been a cog in the machine. Eventually, he'd killed his handlers and become a freelance assassin, working for the highest bidder and with loyalty to none.

However, deep down inside, he was the same as other Russians, who were like most people everywhere else. Most just wanted a normal life with an education, a good job, enough food to eat, a roof over their heads, some friends, and maybe a marriage and kids.

He wondered about the random path in life that had led him to get caught up in this world of secrets and death. Could he ever be completely free of it and have a normal life like the people he saw walking down the street?

He had something in common with former Soviet leader Gorbachev. They were both the descendants of Gulag prisoners, as were millions of other Russians.

He'd felt his life was meaningless until he'd met the one person he'd genuinely cared about ... Tatiana. A single tear ran down his cheek now. Not for the tens of millions of individuals who had been imprisoned and executed, but for the one and only woman he'd ever loved.

He felt a painful nostalgia for those winters when he and his beloved Tatiana had gone ice skating in Gorky Park. He remembered the summer weekends they'd spent at the dacha. Evenings at home where he'd drawn charcoal sketches of her while she cooked the delicious shchi soup and pirozhki pastries. And bedtimes when they'd held each other tight and whispered of plans for their future.

The Organization had said that he needed to prove his loyalty. They'd said he had to be tested. They'd said Tatiana was too curious and she knew too much. His masters had told him he would one day understand why they'd killed Tatiana and that he'd find another woman who was just like her or even better.

They'd said he would soon forget her.

They'd been wrong.

Thinking about Tatiana was always a mistake. It made him angry and sad at the same time. But how could he not think of her? She was in every sunrise, every drop of rain, and every beat of his heart.

Zhukov reached into the black bag and took out an antique snub-nosed revolver that had one round in the cylinder. An end to his pain was only a bullet away. If there was an afterlife, maybe he would be reunited with Tatiana. If not, he would find nothingness and the escape from his tortured memories. Zhukov tried to talk himself out of using the weapon. He told himself that the pain was a part of him now and he would die soon enough anyway. Why be in a hurry?

The self-talk didn't work. It never did when he was in a terribly dark mood. He'd only loved one woman in his life and he would always love her.

With wet eyes and a broken heart, Zhukov spun the revolver's cylinder. He kept one hand on the wheel and used the other hand to hold the weapon to his head in the age-old game of Russian roulette. He kept his finger on the trigger as he listened to the rest of the song about *Katyusha* and drove on alone through the darkness of this strange and foreign land.

Oh, you song. Little song of a young girl,
Fly over the river and in the sunlight, go.

And fly to my hero far from me,
From his Katyusha bring him a sweet hello.

Let him remember this plain young girl,
And her sweet song like a dove,
As he stands guarding his proud nation,
So Katyusha will guard their love.

Zhukov thought of Tatiana's sweet, sad smile as he pulled the trigger.

CHAPTER 27

Early in the morning, Jake had one of his recurring dreams about a battle he'd fought while deployed to the Middle East. The dream unfolded in slow motion with the sounds of gunfire, explosions, and the screams of the enemy.

He had blood dripping into his eyes from a scalp wound, but he kept wiping his eyes on his sleeve and firing his rifle and reloading it. The enemy kept coming at him and his platoon. Although the Marines were outnumbered, each one fought like a fierce killing machine. Slain bodies of their enemies fell dead all around them.

Terrell Hayes yelled something at Jake as a rocket-propelled grenade flew past and barely missed both men. It hit the ground some distance away and exploded with a deafening roar. The shock wave caused Jake to stagger and go down on one knee. Terrell also knelt by Jake's side. The two men nodded at each other and then turned and fought back to back as they kept on firing round after round at the enemy ...

Jake awoke with a start and bolted upright. He reached into his nearby pack, grabbed his pistol and held it in front of him, disoriented. Then he took deep breaths and remembered he was no longer deployed in a war zone. A quick glance at the couch told him he wasn't in bed with his fiancée, Gwen. And this was not the *Far Niente,* where he'd be waking up to the sound of water lapping at the hull of the boat. No, there had been shots fired last night, and a car chase.

A pain in his thigh from an old war wound ached. It would come and go with changes in the weather or his dreams.

A Corgi entered the room through a doggie door and jumped onto the bed and licked Jake's face. Jake smelled good coffee brewing and heard Rihanna's song "Cheers (I'll Drink to That)" playing on a sound system. Alicia started singing along with it.

Oh, that's right, he'd slept in the man-cave garage at Terrell and Alicia's place. He put his pistol away and then petted Boo-Boo. Jake listened for a moment to the song and then began singing along with Alicia at the top of his lungs. Boo-Boo joined in, howling along. After singing a few verses, Jake heard Alicia laughing.

There was a knock on the door and Alicia said, "Good morning, Jake."

"Morning, Alicia, come in."

"Are you decent?" Alicia asked.

"That's what they say about me, but I'm trying to raise my rating to average," Jake said.

Alicia came into the room carrying two cups of coffee. She handed one of the cups to Jake and then sat on a nearby chair. "I played that song for your wake-up call because I remembered you liked how Rihanna sang about Jameson Irish Whiskey."

"Rihanna is obviously a woman of good taste."

"So what brings you to the man cave this time?" Alicia had a knowing look on her face.

"Oh, I just ... misplaced the keys to my condo," Jake said with a shrug, not wanting to talk about it.

"Uh-huh, and that's your story?" Alicia glanced at Jake's keys on the coffee table.

"That's my story and I'm sticking to it." He took a sip from his cup. "Thanks for the great coffee, though. What kind is it?"

"It's from Ethiopia, the birthplace of coffee. But I like how you changed the subject."

"Darn, I never could BS schoolteachers no matter how hard I tried. They are simply too wise."

"You better believe it. Teachers are what make the future generations not suck."

"Please tell me you put that on your business cards."

"I promise to add that on the very next print run."

"Good plan. Seriously, I came by for your wonderful coffee and conversation."

"Speaking of conversations, if you ever want to talk about anything, you can always talk to me," Alicia said.

"Okay, if I ever want to talk, you'll be the first to know," Jake said. He knew that even though Alicia was aware of his breakup and how Gwen had been acting crazy, she probably had no idea that someone had tried to kill him last night. That was not something Terrell would share with her. Terrell tried to shelter Alicia from the disturbing crimes that cops see and hear about.

"Let's go get some breakfast. I'm making bacon and eggs and Terrell is flipping some gluten-free pancakes made with coconut flour."

"I was hoping to have extra gluten in mine," Jake said.

Alicia smiled and shook her head as they walked toward the kitchen. Jake saw Terrell there, wearing a big chef's hat shaped like a white mushroom. Alicia filled a bowl with dog food for Boo-Boo and added a half a slice of cooked bacon, while Terrell delivered three plates of breakfast to the table and sat down.

Alicia smiled and looked at Terrell.

"Now what?" Terrell said.

Jake said, "You can take off the hat now, Chef Ptomaine, you're on a break."

"Oh, sure. You two are just jealous of the hat. Come on. Admit it now. You know it's true."

Jake nodded. "I want to rent a convertible and drive around the city while wearing that mushroom on my head."

It was quiet for a moment while they poured syrup over their pancakes and enjoyed their food. The music mix had ended and a morning television show babbled in the background on low volume.

"Where's the TV remote?" Alicia asked. "Let's turn that off."

Jake saw the remote near his coffee cup, so he picked it up. A commercial came on the TV that featured a young woman wearing a white doctor's coat and black horn-rimmed glasses. She held a

Dalmatian puppy while smiling at the camera and talking about her veterinarian clinic. Jake stopped and stared at the TV while holding the remote in midair.

Alicia smiled. "Oh my, Jake must really like that puppy, huh?"

Terrell looked at the TV and then at Jake and nodded, as Jake continued watching the TV with rapt attention.

The woman said, "You can trust us to take good care of your pets. We're located right across the street from the brand-new dog park. Bring your four-footed family members to our veterinary clinic this week to say hello and get a free chew toy."

She laughed as the Dalmatian puppy licked her cheek, and then she handed a rawhide chewy to the dog and patted it on the head.

"I think maybe Jake got shot by cupid's arrow," Alicia said.

Jake was quiet as he watched the commercial ending, and then he turned off the TV and said, "What?"

Alicia just smiled. Terrell said, "You were in a trance there, hypnotized."

"Well, I literally bumped into that woman at the news station where I work, and she seems so … real and unpretentious," Jake said. "Lots of people you meet these days are fake. Do you know what I mean?"

"Yes, she seems like a genuinely nice person, at least from the commercial, and she obviously loves dogs just like you do," Alicia said.

"And she wears glasses," Terrell said. "Jake seems the happiest when he dates smart, nerdy girls who wear glasses and read lots of books. I keep telling him he should forget about fashion models, join a book club, and start dating a cute librarian."

"You should borrow Boo-Boo doggie and take him to that pet clinic to get a free chew toy—and a phone number," Alicia said.

"Maybe I could say that Boo-Boo needs to be neutered," Jake said.

Boo-Boo howled at Jake and hid under the table.

CHAPTER 28

Ivan Zhukov woke up that morning in a new hotel and an even more elegant suite than the previous one.

He brewed some strong black tea in the carafe of the in-room coffeemaker, then sat at the elegant dining table as he sipped the hot tea and thought about the next lawyer he was going to kill. Today's murder would be more flamboyant and disturbing to the public. A true work of art designed to create panic and to help his employers carry out their latest scheme to make windfall profits.

His morning hangover from the vodka wasn't too bad, considering the amount he'd consumed the night before. He felt grateful that the game of Russian roulette had not killed him just yet. Someday it might, but so far, so good.

On most days, Zhukov valued his life and his plans for the future, so the game was a stupid gamble. He knew that if he would just take his medicine and stop drinking, he wouldn't have so many mood swings. Yet if he did that, he would also give up the intensity of emotion and depth of sensation that made him feel alive. At the moment, he preferred to live dangerously.

Banks had said that it made the Council nervous when they heard rumors that their hired killer was off his meds. Good—let them suffer, Zhukov thought. They were elite, privileged snobs who needed someone to kick them off their high horses. One day he would do just that.

Zhukov watched the sun come up from his view out of the hotel room's sliding glass door. He drank tea and briefly checked the news to confirm the police had been at the previous hotel to capture him. The news reports showed one of his sketches. He felt hatred in his heart for this entire city.

Taking several deep, calming breaths, he sat in quiet contemplation as he worked on some new sketches in charcoal. The latest one was another rendering of the beautiful Golden Gate Bridge. He was infatuated with the iconic engineering marvel. He'd lost his previous drawings, but he would simply create more and better works.

His curiosity about the people who built the Golden Gate Bridge led him to discover Americans also invented just about every other modern miracle.

These facts were never taught in Russia. The schools there always bashed America and taught negative propaganda that criticized the USA. Now Zhukov was learning that the old Soviet indoctrination had all been lies. He still didn't like Americans, but he respected them.

There was a knock at the door and a waiter from room service announced a delivery of breakfast to the room. Zhukov didn't open the door. He called out that he was not dressed at the moment, so please leave the breakfast cart in the hall. He told the waiter to add a fifty percent tip onto the bill for himself. The man was more than happy to oblige.

Zhukov waited until the waiter was gone, then put on one of the hotel's plush bathrobes to cover his tattoos, and a pair of glasses to change his facial appearance. He put his pistol in one of the bathrobe pockets, then opened the door, checked the hallway for threats and brought the rolling cart into his room.

The breakfast tray held orange juice, bacon and scrambled eggs, croissants with butter and preserves, a plate of fruit and a teapot of black tea. He carried the tray out onto the balcony and set it on the patio table, then sat on a padded chair and slowly savored his breakfast as he watched the people of the city going about their lives at the start of a new day. This was not his usual Spartan meal, but life had felt different lately.

He was in the mood to enjoy the small luxuries of the warm croissants, the cool pats of butter and the fresh raspberry preserves. In this business, you never knew if it might be your last meal, so you may as well enjoy it.

Once he'd finished breakfast, he lit up a Perdomo Champagne cigar. It was a light and creamy smoke with a smooth sweetness, and it tasted almost like a slice of toast spread with honey. The thought crossed his mind that perhaps it seemed to taste even better because it was stolen from a man who'd angered him.

As he was smoking the cigar, the sliding door of the room next to his opened and a distinguished-looking man stepped out onto the balcony. He appeared to be in his fifties, and a woman about half his age followed him. The woman had bed-tousled auburn hair.

Zhukov appraised and profiled them, and it seemed obvious they'd spent the night together. They were wearing matching hotel bathrobes, with their bare calves and feet showing below the hems. The man wore a wedding ring, but the woman did not. They looked smug, as if they'd outsmarted others and now felt bulletproof. Zhukov knew better; nobody was bulletproof.

The man glared at Zhukov and said, "I thought I smelled the foul stink of a cigar. The hotel rules say there is no smoking here, so you're going to have to put that thing out, right now."

"Excuse me," Zhukov said politely as he turned his phone so they could see the screen. "Is that your wife there beside you on the balcony in this video, with both of you wearing the hotel bathrobes and perhaps nothing else? Or would it cause you a problem if I uploaded this video to the internet for the entire world to see?"

The man's face paled, and the woman glared at Zhukov.

"That's what I thought," Zhukov said. He set the phone on the table and propped it up against his basket of croissants, where it continued to take video of the couple via the front-side camera, so they could see themselves on the display. Next, he touched the screen of his tablet, took a picture of the man's face and used a facial recognition app to find the man online. In seconds, the man's social media pages filled the screen and Zhukov held up the tablet so the lovers could see it all.

The man stared in surprise at the tablet as it displayed photos of his face from various business and family-related web pages. He closed his eyes for a moment and swallowed in fear.

Zhukov noticed the adulterer's discomfort. "It only took me a moment to find out all about you. I could send this photo to your wife's phone right now. But here's an even better idea. Why don't you apologize to me and then shut your mouth, go back in your room, close the door, and mind your own business? If you do that and hurry up about it, I might just forget that I want to teach you a hard lesson in humility and manners."

"I'm very sorry to have bothered you. My deepest apologies," the man said, red-faced. He retreated hastily into the hotel room and pulled the surprised young woman in after him, closing the sliding door with a thud.

Zhukov smiled and puffed on the fine cigar, pouring himself another cup of tea. He held a sugar cube in his mouth and sipped the tea so it passed over the cube as he drank, the way Tatiana used to do it. That caused him to see her smile in his memories, and the familiar sadness washed over him. For a moment, the thought crossed his mind that perhaps he should jump to the next balcony, enter the suite of the annoying adulterous couple and kill them both, just for practice.

Zhukov's phone vibrated; Chairman Banks calling. He cursed in Russian. "Why can't a man have a moment of peace?" When he answered the call he said, "Good morning. What are you eating now? An insect omelet for breakfast?"

"Good morning. Today you have an important business transaction."

"Yes, and the sun rose in the east. Thank you for stating the obvious. What is your point? Why are you calling me?"

"The additional complication—will you also take care of that today?"

"Wolfe is going to a funeral today, and he will die at the graveyard," Zhukov said.

"That will be convenient for the undertaker," Banks said. "Let's hope it works out better than it did last night, when you failed to deal with him. That made the Council even more concerned."

"Sometimes a fool like that gets a lucky break. Today will be different. He's running on borrowed time. But I do not understand the man. What does he gain by interfering with my plans?"

"I believe that Wolfe is an Irish name. Sigmund Freud said it's no use trying to psychoanalyze the Irish."

"Once he's dead, it won't matter if I can understand him or not."

"If you successfully complete the second transaction today and also the additional complication, you will receive a large sum of money at one of your offshore bank accounts," Banks said. "And we will have dinner tonight so we can discuss the third and most important transaction."

"Thank you, but you're in Mexico City, and there's no need to come up here to San Francisco for dinner. I have everything under control and today will be a very busy day for me. Besides, I don't want to eat insects."

"The third transaction is the most important one. Dinner will be in San Francisco at eight o'clock. I'll send a trusted driver who will take you to the restaurant."

"Sorry, but I don't get into cars unless I know where they're going. If I'm tricked into traveling blind, somebody usually gets hurt. So far that somebody hasn't been me."

"I had to promise never to talk on the phone about the name or location of this very private establishment. However, my driver will tell you the address before you get in the car. You can check it on your phone's GPS. If he deviates from the route, you can express your disappointment to him with your usual extreme prejudice."

"It is not a good career move for drivers or anyone else to disappoint me, surprise me or attempt to cause me harm." Zhukov ended the call without waiting for a reply. He spread some butter and raspberry preserves on a croissant, took a bite, and followed it up with a drink of tea. In his mind's eye, he imagined snapping the chairman's neck like a chicken meant for the soup pot. The time would come for that, but today was not the day, not quite yet.

Banks set his phone down and used a silk handkerchief to wipe sweat from his brow. His hired killer was a loose cannon. That was a fact.

Banks had control of the loose cannon at the moment, but he had to be very careful that the cannon did not accidentally turn around and end up pointed at him. He doubted Zhukov's threat of *autopilot* revenge, and he decided that after this assignment in San Francisco was completed, Zhukov would find himself in a rather inconvenient automobile accident, complete with a flaming gas tank, twisted metal, and a charred corpse.

That thought made Banks feel much better, and he forgot about Zhukov for the time being. He focused on enjoying his gourmet brunch at a private mansion in the hills above Silicon Valley in Northern California.

The two tycoons enjoyed a lavish meal of deep-fried guinea pig on a stick, complete with the head, and side dishes of lamb testicles in cream gravy, and pickled pigs' feet with onions and peppers. They washed these down with a variety of premium wines from around the world. For dessert, they had foie gras baked into a buttery flaky pastry with a touch of vanilla bean, and a bottle of German dessert wine named *Joh Jos Prüm Bernkasteler Badstube Riesling Beerenauslese*. Banks had been told the only hope of pronouncing the name of the wine was to drink several glasses first.

CHAPTER 29

"I'm sorry to eat and run, but I have to go to work," Alicia said as she stood up.

"Couldn't they get a substitute so you could go to the funeral?" Jake asked.

"I got one, but then the school principal decided to schedule me for evaluation."

"I'll give your best to Stuart's parents," Terrell said.

"Thanks. I'll try to make it to the funeral, but if not, I'll see you as soon as I get out."

Terrell went out the front door with Alicia and stood outside on the walkway. Boo-Boo waited inside the screen door and looked out at them while wagging his tail.

Jake drank his coffee as he waited for his friends to kiss and say goodbye. After a few minutes, Terrell came back inside looking dazed.

"It's really nice to see you two getting along so well," Jake said.

Terrell sat down and looked off into the distance. "Alicia has always been the love of my life, but it's dawning on me now that she's like oxygen. I can't live without her."

"Oxygen is good. I hear it's highly recommended by two out of three people who recommend things," Jake said.

Terrell nodded, but his mind was still on Alicia.

Jake poured them both some more coffee and added a touch of Hennessy's cognac to their cups. "Here, drink this. It's like medicine to fortify you after a long night of making up. An Irishman named Hennessy traveled to France and showed them how to make their cognac even better. This is the amazing result of that fateful collaboration of genius. It's so good it's probably illegal in Washington, D.C."

"So it's good for what ails you?"

"It's guaranteed to make rainbows shoot out of your ass."

"Good to go," Terrell said and nodded absentmindedly as he drank some coffee.

Jake slowly waved his hand in front of his friend's face. "Earth to Terrell."

Terrell finally smiled and brought his eyes back from far away.

"What?"

"It's great to see two people who are so happily married. It gives me hope."

"It wasn't so happy last week, but we made it through that mess."

"It was a noble effort."

"I don't know what Alicia sees in me."

"It could be the chef's hat and the pancakes, for real."

"Women go for that, huh?"

"Absolutely, it was in Cosmopolitan's list of top-ten sexy turn-ons. Of course, they suggested you wear *only* the chef's hat."

"I'll put that on my to-do list."

"I'm going to use your guest bathroom for a quick shower before we head out."

"Roger that. You need to wash off your stink as a matter of public safety," Terrell said. He stood up and headed off to the bedroom to get dressed for the memorial service.

Zhukov finished his cigar on the balcony and then went inside to put on his disguise. Once he'd changed his appearance, he left the hotel and walked to where he'd parked the car.

"Time to kill another attorney," Zhukov said to himself as he drove down the street. "This could become habit-forming. But first, a quick stop at a funeral to rid the world of Jake Wolfe."

CHAPTER 30

Jake went out to the Jeep and grabbed a carry-on suitcase that held some clean clothes.

After a quick shower, he changed into black pants, a charcoal-gray shirt, boots and a black leather jacket.

He found Terrell sitting at the dining table, dressed in a dark suit and tie, drinking a cup of coffee, as always. Jake thought the man must be keeping a lot of coffee growers employed with his daily habit. He probably got a Christmas card every year from Juan Valdez.

Terrell looked at his phone and smiled, holding it up so Jake could see the photo he'd received. It was the face of the shooter, caught by a security camera at the south end of the Golden Gate Bridge. "There's our boy. He looks pretty angry."

"That's when I was chasing him. I seem to have made him mad," Jake said.

"You have that effect on a lot of people. I'll text the picture to you. Put his face on the news and tell your viewers he's wanted by the police."

Jake received the photo and forwarded it to his editor's secretary. He added a short blurb.

Hi, Deb, this is probably the real face of the attorney assassin, not wearing a disguise. Meanwhile, I'm still working on that Bisonzilla problem for you.

Jake and Terrell went outside, got into the Jeep and headed toward the cemetery. They rode in silence for a while, on the all-too-familiar drive. The cemetery was located south of San Francisco in the nearby town of Colma, just like most other cemeteries in the area were. Land was so expensive in San Francisco, there were no cemeteries in the city. When Jake turned onto the main road leading to the memorial park, he noticed a Dodge Challenger with darkened windows pull out of a side street and drive in the same direction he was going.

"What were you fighting with Alicia about this time, anyway?" Jake said. "It's none of my business, but I was wondering what dumb man thing you did lately. Maybe I could learn from your mistake and avoid doing it myself."

"She asked me to pick up some bread at the store on my way home from work, and I totally forgot," Terrell said. "Then she got hella mad."

"It's not the bread. It's that you weren't thinking of her. That's the real issue."

"That's how guys are. We're not always thinking of our wives or girlfriends all the time. It's just a fact, a reality."

"Yeah, but it's a fact that bothers them."

"Where's the guidebook about how to be in a relationship?"

"I saw one once. It was titled *Everything Men Know About Women.* The inside pages were all blank."

"Sounds about right. Another thing is, the bread wasn't for Alicia. She rarely eats bread, but started making sandwiches for me to take for lunch because I was eating too much fast food."

"That's really nice of her. Old-fashioned, even. Now I'm jealous. I spent thousands of dollars on a ring for Gwen and I never got one sandwich out of the deal."

"So, my next lunch had a plastic bag with some lunch meat and cheese and lettuce but no bread. There was a note that said B.Y.O.B."

"Writing a to-do list on a yellow sticky note has saved many a man from forgetting things."

"I'll go buy a whole case of those notes, so I won't do something that drives her crazy again."

"The late, great philosopher George Carlin boiled it down to this," Jake said. "*Here's all you have to know about men and women. Women are crazy, men are stupid. And the main reason women are crazy is that men are stupid.* That pretty much sums it up."

"Carlin might have explained the secret of life there."

"The dude should have won the Nobel Prize."

"They should set up a scholarship in his name."

"My theory is that it's all about hormones."

"Why hormones?"

"Testosterone can make men act stupid, and estrogen can make women act crazy."

"You just proved Carlin's theory with science. But how do you know all of this stuff about women?"

"I don't know anything, I'm just winging it and trying to learn from my mistakes," Jake said. "However, I did read that book, *Women Are From Venus and Men Are From Penis.*"

"Are you sure that's the title?"

"Sure, I'm sure. Do I look unsure to you?"

"No, you look like an asshole, since you asked." Terrell raised his eyebrows.

"That's *Mister* Hole to you, pal," Jake said with a grin. "And in that case, I must look good, because mine is a work of art, no doubt."

"Do you study it often, or have you received positive comments?"

"No visitor feedback. Just my best guess."

Jake looked in the rearview mirror and spotted the same late-model Dodge Challenger with darkened windows following behind them. The driver wore a hat and sunglasses. Jake thought about it and realized that the same vehicle had been behind them for several miles. The car might be going to the same cemetery they were, but he mentioned it to Terrell anyway.

"Does that Dodge behind us look familiar to you? It's been there for a while."

Terrell looked in the Jeep's right side mirror. "No, not in particular. I've seen plenty of those cars driving around the city. But if it gets any closer to us, let me know."

As Zhukov followed behind Wolfe's SUV, he noticed the men checking their mirrors. He cursed and turned off at the next street, drove several blocks and pulled over. He'd wait five minutes and get back on the road to the cemetery after a few other cars were in between him and his prey.

He'd been planning to shoot Wolfe when the man got out of his vehicle, but now he'd have to drive by and take the shot while his target was standing around waiting for the funeral to begin. The police report would call it a drive-by shooting and the crime would never be solved.

Jake saw the car behind him turn off onto another street and was glad to see it go. He looked out his window at the cemetery grounds they were approaching, turned the Jeep into the long driveway, and drove through the center of acres of green lawns filled with headstones.

They both fell silent. The time had come to say a final goodbye to their good friend. The mood in the car began to darken like the rain clouds they could see rolling toward them on the horizon.

CHAPTER 31

Jake parked, and Terrell smiled as Alicia got out of her car and walked toward them. When Terrell went to meet her, she was scowling.

"My evaluation with the principal was over quickly," Alicia said. "He gave me a 'U' for unsatisfactory because I make my kids laugh too often."

"Don't let him get on your nerves," Terrell said. "Your kids all love you, and they're learning a lot, too. You're doing a great job."

"The substitute teacher wanted to work the rest of the day and earn some extra money, so I was able to get away and come over here."

A car with dark tinted windows drove into the visitor area behind the group of mourners and parked off to the side unnoticed. Zhukov sat in the car and watched Jake through a pair of binoculars.

He reached into a backpack on the seat beside him and took out his pistol. It would be a difficult shot right now, with all the people moving about. He wished he still had the rifle he'd used at the golf course, but he'd already disposed of that weapon along with the vehicle. At that time, he'd had no idea this idiot would cause so much trouble. But it didn't matter; he'd just wait until Wolfe was apart from the group. Then he'd take him out.

~

People continued to arrive at the funeral, milling around, shaking hands, talking and hugging. Stuart's grieving parents had requested a simple graveside service without any formal chapel ceremony or car procession. The parents had asked Jake to give the eulogy, but he'd said Father O'Leary would be better at it and would give a nondenominational eulogy.

The casket had an American flag draped lengthwise over the top. It sat on the cross straps of a casket-lowering device. There was a short, dark green curtain hanging down below it to disguise the device and the freshly dug grave. Several large bouquets of fresh flowers were arranged around the casket and American flags waved gently in the wind from flagpoles standing in a row behind it.

At the appointed time, Father O'Leary stood in front of the casket to give the eulogy. Everyone in the crowd took their seats on metal folding chairs and focused their attention on him. Behind them, a car with darkened windows drove up slowly and parked even closer to the burial site.

Father O'Leary began the eulogy.

"We gather together here today to say goodbye to our good friend, Stuart Nelson. We mourn his loss and honor his memory. And we pray for the strength to bear our grief and the courage to go on with life, the way he would have wanted us to.

When Stuart was growing up, he was a small-town boy in search of adventure. Always climbing trees, fishing in rivers, and hiking the hills. He grew into a fine young man with a great sense of humor, a real zest for life and a desire to serve his country.

"And he did serve, bravely going off to faraway lands and risking his life. While he was overseas, he also helped an impoverished village in several ways. He worked to put in a well so the women didn't have to hike for miles through dangerous areas to get clean water and carry it back in heavy jugs. He also helped set up solar lights for safety at night in the outdoor marketplace. And it was his idea and hard work that turned a large chow hall tent, filled with dining tables and chairs, into a school for the local children. When Stuart came home to us, he served his community as an assistant coach for a youth soccer team. He worked hard at everything he did, with dedication and integrity. He was a good man, and it was an honor to know him.

"You can talk to anyone about Stuart, and they'll tell you he was a wonderful friend, the kind who stands by you through thick and thin. He was the kind of friend who is always there for you. A friend who laughs at your attempts to be funny and listens to your complaints. Who gives you a push when you need one and cuts you some slack when you've earned it. We were lucky to have had a friend like Stuart, and we should all be grateful we had the chance to know him, although it was for too short of a time. One of his favorite sayings was, 'Don't cry because it's over, smile because it happened.'

"All of us loved Stuart, and our hearts ache with his passing from this world. His death was too sudden. He was too young to leave us so soon. In peace, sons bury their fathers. In war, fathers bury their sons. He is in a better place now, and the memories he shared with us will live in our hearts forever. If we are quiet, we can still hear his voice telling a joke or offering kind words of encouragement. We can still feel his hand patting us on the back, or his arms giving us a hug. And still remember a day we spent enjoying his company, his conversation, and his friendship.

"Hemingway once wrote, 'The world breaks everyone, and afterward, some are strong at the broken places.' It's true, the tragic loss of our beloved friend has broken all of us. But with God's grace, we will grow stronger in the broken places, despite our pain and sorrow. Go forth now and be strong in memory of this brief shining life that touched us all.

"Stuart would want us to carry on. To live, laugh, and love. To make the most of every precious day. We owe that to him, and I want all of you to promise me you will do that in honor of him.

"Lastly, I offer these words from a friend who served in combat with Stuart. 'Rest in peace, Marine. Fair winds and following seas. We got it from here, brother. Semper Fidelis. Until we meet again.'

"In closing I say, may God bless Stuart, and may he rest in eternal peace. Amen."

• • •

The crowd of mourners said, "Amen."

The uniformed Marine Corps color guard fired three volleys from their rifles. Two Marines in dress blues lifted the American flag and held it above the casket as a Corps bugler began sounding taps.

When the final notes of the bugle faded away, the two Marines slowly and respectfully folded the flag into a triangle in a time-honored ceremony. One of them came forward and presented the flag to Stuart's mother and father. The Marine said, "On behalf of the President of the United States, the Marine Corps, and a grateful nation, please accept this flag as a symbol of your loved one's honorable and faithful service."

The Marine slowly saluted Stuart's parents, then turned and walked away. The mother leaned into Stuart's father, overcome by grief, and the father held on to her as they sat side by side.

Stuart's therapy dog sat on the grass next to the father. Cody was a mix of yellow Labrador retriever and golden retriever. The same mixed breed as the world's very first service dog. Cody pulled the leash free from the father's hand, ran over to the casket, leapt on top of it and began howling in sorrow.

CHAPTER 32

Cold raindrops fell on the funeral and blended with the warm tears on the faces of the people there. The sound system played an instrumental bagpipe version of "Amazing Grace." The mourners filed past the parents to pay their respects and then walked to their cars and took their leave.

As the crowd dispersed, Stuart's girlfriend, Taylor, stepped up to the casket, lit a single candle and placed it in front of a flower arrangement. She said some quiet words and blew a sad last kiss to her love, then slowly wandered off like a lost soul, walking aimlessly through the cemetery in the rain.

When the funeral company employees approached the casket to lower it into the ground. Cody snarled at them and showed his teeth. The workers backed away, and one of them made a phone call.

Jake saw what was happening. He walked over to Cody and talked to him in a quiet but firm voice. The rain started coming down harder, and people opened umbrellas as they hurried to their cars. But Jake remained standing there with water dripping off his hair and clothes, like a tree in a storm, speaking soothing but commanding words to Cody.

~

Terrell walked with Alicia toward the parked cars, and they passed a veteran nicknamed Doc. He was a Navy Corpsman who'd accompanied Terrell's infantry platoon into battle. He'd hooked up Terrell's blood transfusion to Jake and had been shot in the arm while doing it.

Doc asked, "How are the headaches these days, Grinds? Getting any better?"

Terrell frowned. "I don't have headaches. You must be thinking of Kowalski."

Doc raised his eyebrows in apparent surprise, but glanced at Alicia and said, "Oh right, my bad. Sorry, bro." He walked away.

Alicia gave Terrell a long look. "Headaches? Is that why we have a giant-sized bottle of ibuprofen that you told me you bought because it was on sale?"

Terrell sighed and thought of some lies he could tell, but he just nodded his head. He could never lie to Alicia and get away with it. Some women had a gift and could guess what you were thinking. "Sometimes I get migraines. It's no big deal."

Alicia put her hand on Terrell's arm. "What's causing them?"

"The doctors at Landstuhl Medical Center in Germany said it was due to the shock waves of an explosion."

"When were you in Germany?"

"Before we met. When our troops get injured in Afghanistan or Iraq or anywhere in the Middle East, they're flown to Landstuhl. It's a US military medical center near Ramstein Air Base in Germany."

"What happened that put you in the hospital?"

Terrell looked off into the distance for a moment while he decided to tell her the truth. Some of it, but not all—never all of it.

"I was injured in battle, along with several other Marines. An explosion gave me a concussion that caused a mild brain injury. Doc, the Navy Corpsman, put us on a helicopter. And then his fellow Corpsmen put us on an aircraft that was basically a flying intensive care unit. That jet flew us to Landstuhl Hospital in Germany."

"Was this the same explosion that gave you all those scars, from being peppered with shrapnel that had to be removed piece by piece?"

"Yes."

"Why didn't you tell me about this brain injury?"

"Lots of veterans have lingering injuries. We just don't talk about them. I thought the headaches would go away, and I didn't want you to worry."

"Look me in the eye and tell me if it was a traumatic brain injury."

Terrell looked her in the eye. "Yes, it was a TBI, but some brain injuries are way worse than others. I survived mine. I just get headaches now and then."

She raised her voice. "Please tell me you don't have a piece of war shrapnel in your head."

"I don't, my helmet prevented that."

In the distance, the dog howled again, a primal, lonely, and heartbroken cry.

Terrell knew it had been a highly emotional week for Alicia, getting their relationship through the recent fight and then making up. Having problems at work, going to this funeral, and now hearing about his brain injury and migraines. When Alicia saw this sad dog with the broken heart, and Jake there trying to comfort him while the rain poured down on them both, she started choking up and shaking. Terrell put his arms around his wife and held her tight.

"I don't know why I've been crying so much lately," Alicia said. "Maybe life is just too much right now."

"That's okay, babe, just cry it all out," Terrell said.

Alicia wept on Terrell's shoulder. He said, "I'm sure I could use a good cry too. I've spent years holding my feelings back, pushing them deep inside, biting down on the emotions."

As they hugged each other, Cody let out another mournful howl. Alicia's breathing started to slow down and become more regular. Terrell looked over at the gravesite at Jake, the man who was born to be a dog handler.

"I think Jake is going to be there for a while," Terrell said. "He won't leave Cody alone when he's suffering."

Alicia looked over at Jake and Cody. "Those two might be good for each other. I wonder what Stuart's parents have planned for Cody."

"Did I ever tell you that you are a very wise woman?" Terrell said. "Let's go talk to the Nelsons before they leave."

~

Zhukov sat in his car and observed Jake alone at the gravesite. The fool was just standing there in the rain, petting a dog. He was obviously an imbecile. Now would be a good time to drive past and put a bullet into him. Zhukov started the car and drove toward the gravesite, keeping one hand on the wheel and holding his pistol in the other. He would try to shoot only Wolfe, not the dog or the casket, but that depended on Wolfe standing still.

Terrell noticed a car with darkened windows coming closer and his cop sense began to tingle. It looked like the same vehicle that had been behind them on the road.

"You go over to the parents, and I'll meet you there in just a minute," Terrell said. "I see someone I need to have a word with."

He walked purposefully toward the car as it approached. He wore his police pistol in a holster on his belt, and as he walked along, his unbuttoned suit jacket flapped open in the breeze and revealed his weapon. When Terrell got closer to the slow-moving car, it sped up and drove off. Terrell took a picture with his phone, then turned and walked back toward Alicia. As he walked, he sent a text to Jake.

I'm riding home with Alicia. Are you going to stay with Cody?

Jake checked his phone and answered the text: *Yes, I'll stay with Cody until he's okay. Then bring him home to the Nelsons. It might take an hour, or it might take all night. Hard to say.*

Terrell: *I saw that car again. The one that was behind us on the way here. It drove slowly past the gravesite. Here's a photo. Stay alert.*

Jake: *Understood. If anyone tries to mess with this casket or this dog, it will be the last thing they ever do.*

CHAPTER 33

Terrell caught up with Alicia and the parents who were standing out of the rain under a small shelter near one of the parking areas.

"Jake told me he's going to stay with Cody as long as it takes to calm him down and then bring him to your house," Terrell said. "Don't worry. Even if it takes until the sun comes up, Jake will stay by that dog's side. I guarantee it."

Mrs. Nelson said, "Thank you. I just don't know what to do with that poor dog. He's been like this ever since …" Her lower lip trembled, and she gazed sadly at the gravesite.

"Something I wanted to share with you is that Jake served as a war dog handler in the Marines just like Stuart," Terrell said. "His war dog was killed in battle and his pet dog Gracie died recently too. He's taken it pretty hard."

"I'm so sorry to hear that," she said.

"Alicia had the idea that maybe Cody and Jake could be helpful to each other by spending time together. At least until your dog gets through this difficult adjustment period."

Both parents looked at Jake talking to Cody. The dog seemed to be ignoring Jake, but on the other hand, he wasn't growling or trying to drive him away. He appeared to respect Jake's authority.

"It's just something to think about," Terrell said. "Stuart might have wanted Cody to be with another dog handler if he was this upset. War dogs and their handlers are meant to be together. Nobody else understands them like they understand each other. It's like they have ESP or something that runs up and down the leash between them."

The parents turned to gaze into each other's eyes for a moment and then looked again at Jake.

Mrs. Nelson said, "Stuart had adopted Cody under the law H.R. 5314, when the dog was retired due to lingering injuries. There was a waiting list for dogs, but as a former handler, Stuart got a special dog. Cody was considered too smart, too independent, and way too much of a handful for a civilian family to deal with. He refused to give up his Marine Corps skills. He needed a former dog handler like Stuart to guide him in his daily duties and provide him with the strong leadership he requires."

She watched Jake and Cody as she talked and saw the pain on both of their faces, the love and understanding, the loyalty, duty, and commitment. Jake reminded her of her lost son, and her heart told her what to do. "Thank you for telling us more about Jake. He never talks about himself. We've gotten the impression he's a bit of a troublemaker, but still a good person."

"Yes, ma'am, I can vouch for that," Terrell said."

Alicia said, "Jake is obviously a tough man, hardened by combat and the things he's been through in life. However, he's also soft-hearted when it comes to somebody who's in trouble and needs help. Just look at him, standing there in the pouring rain, trying to help your dog."

They all looked over at Jake. As he stood there, he appeared like a protective, dangerous bodyguard. But his eyes revealed a hidden gentleness when he looked at the brokenhearted dog who'd lost his best friend.

Mr. Nelson said, "Cody took it hard—really hard. He needs something to do, a job to keep him busy. Stuart adopted him as a therapy dog, and Cody went through that type of training too. He understands hundreds of words, can open doors, turn light switches on and off, and pick up items off the floor. That dog can even open the refrigerator and fetch a six-pack. But the one thing he can't do is sit still for long periods and do nothing."

Terrell and Alicia listened politely and let the man talk. He'd been quiet most of the time, and now he was finally opening up.

"Cody is ornery, too. He'll turn off the TV if you don't take him for a walk or give him his dinner right on time. That retriever is way too smart and dedicated to just sit around the house. He wasn't able to be deprogrammed as much as other former military war dogs usually are. He still searches any bags he sees, and tries to get in front of his pack to protect them from anyone who approaches. Old habits die hard, and that dog always seems to have something on his mind. He has skills and training that he doesn't want to give up. A mission that he can't let go of."

Mrs. Nelson said, "I think Cody got as much therapy from being with Stuart as our son did from him. Maybe Jake could keep him busy and keep his mind off his sorrows."

At the nearby gravesite, Cody howled again. His fur soaking wet from the rain. Jake's hair and clothes were plastered to him.

Alicia said, "Maybe Cody and Jake could keep each other company. They need each other. It's the right thing to do."

Terrell said, "You can go home and rest now. Get out of this weather. Jake will stay with Cody all night and sleep on the grass next to him until sunrise if that's what it takes. He's what we call a dog man. He loves dogs and they love him. Cody is in good hands. There isn't anyone who could take better care of him right now than Jake."

Mr. Nelson nodded at Terrell and Alicia and he said, "Thank you both for coming today. Promise me you'll go on with your life and not feel the survivor's guilt that Stuart's therapists learned he was feeling. He was always asking, 'Why me? Why did I live when so many of my friends died?' Don't let that get to you. Live your life and make the best of it. Do it for Stuart."

"I will, sir, I promise," Terrell said.

Alicia squeezed Terrell's hand and pressed her shoulder against his.

Mrs. Nelson wiped her eyes with a tissue and said, "You two are very kind. We'll talk to Jake about Cody. Thank you. Right now we're going to find Stuart's girlfriend, Taylor."

~

The Nelsons climbed into their car and slowly drove away. The mother leaned her head against the car window and continued looking back at her son's burial place until it was out of sight. "Goodbye, my sweet child."

Toward the end of the landscaped grounds, they pulled up beside Taylor as she walked alone on the grass. She stopped walking and just stood there in a daze, soaking wet from the rain, her eyes focused on something far away.

Mrs. Nelson got out of the car and hugged the girl and guided her into the backseat. She sat next to her and held onto the young woman who could have been her future daughter-in-law and given her grandchildren.

Taylor wept and cried out in pain for the love of her life she'd found and lost, and the wound in her heart that might never heal.

CHAPTER 34

Terrell walked with Alicia to her car and held out his hand for the keys, knowing she understood his need to be in the driver's seat.

Alicia handed him the keys and slid into the passenger seat. "I wish we had an umbrella to give to Jake."

Terrell looked over at the gravesite. "He'll be fine. He's been through far worse things."

Alicia nodded, as if knowing that whatever Jake had been through, her man had been through it too, right by his side.

Terrell started the car engine, but he just sat there looking at the gravesite for a while, not moving. The rain battered the car windows and roof. An old song came on the car radio—Johnny Cash's cover version of "Hurt," recorded a few months before his death. Terrell listened to the lyrics and thought about how people hurt themselves. The pain and the needle. And how you tried not to remember things you wished would go away. His breathing became ragged, and he clenched his hands tight on the steering wheel.

Alicia watched Terrell's face and saw an emotion he rarely let her see ... hate. She put her hand on his arm. "What is it, babe?"

Terrell shook his head. "Why Stuart? Why now? He makes it all the way through the fighting and everything, gets home alive and in one piece, and then he dies from a heroin overdose? I *hate* the people who sold it to him."

Terrell cursed and pounded his fist on the steering wheel violently as he said angry words he usually kept private. This was a side of his personality he kept buried way down inside. It was a good thing the drug dealer who sold heroin to Stuart was nowhere in sight at the moment, or Terrell might have beaten him to death with his bare hands.

Alicia sat quietly and let Terrell vent his pent-up emotions. He knew she wasn't afraid of him. He'd never raised a hand to her, and he never would. Finally, the sadness became too much for him. He slumped forward and pressed his forehead against the steering wheel, gritting his teeth. A rare teardrop rolled down his cheek from behind his dark sunglasses.

A low growl came from deep inside him, and he stopped himself with an effort. He took a deep breath and shook his head. "I'm sorry, Alicia. Sorry to act like a violent animal."

Alicia carefully placed her hand on his leg. "You're not a violent animal, not to me. Let your grief out, just like you told me to. Don't carry it inside you. It will eat you up. Please, baby, it's just us here alone."

Terrell sat there in silence. Alicia unbuckled her seat belt, moved closer, and put her arms around him.

Terrell knew he needed to grieve for his lost friend and for so many others like him. He had too many unshed tears that he'd held inside for so long that needed to be released. It seemed like he either had to cry, or hunt down and kill that heroin-dealing criminal who really deserved to die right *now*. Yet he still refused to weep in front of Alicia. It wasn't in his DNA.

He took several ragged breaths and looked at Jake and Cody. His friend was so loyal; they both were. Alicia was too. Loyalty was why pain could run so deep. If you didn't care very much, life wouldn't hurt very much. People who didn't have deep feelings never experienced deep joy or deep pain. They lived in a trivial, pale shadow of life where nothing was ever a big deal and all that mattered was pretending to be popular.

"Just another day and another dead friend," Terrell said. His eyes wet and his voice thick with suppressed emotion.

Terrell was glad he hadn't wept. Men were not supposed to cry.

Everyone says that to boys when they are growing up. Big boys don't cry. Never show any weakness, or else nobody will respect you. You'll be bullied, beat up, cast out, and ostracized. Girls will think you're weak. Women will not want you. Do. Not. Cry. Ever. Bury it inside and drink it away with alcohol. In fact, a strong drink or two sounded real good to Terrell right about then.

He drove slowly away from the cemetery and began to talk. Slowly and in a ragged voice, he told Alicia about Stuart. Alicia just listened and let him get it off his chest, something he rarely did.

"Stuart had been wrestling with some kind of death wish, doing reckless things that could have caused him harm," Terrell said. "Lately, he'd been driving like a crazy man. As if he was invincible. Everyone had been worried he was going to die in a fiery car accident on some dark, rainy night and he'd have Cody in the car with him when he did it."

"What bothered Stuart the most was that, when he'd helped set up a school in a large tent for the kids in a poor village overseas, the terrorists had tried to stop the girls from getting an education. They hate girls for some reason. Girls are possessions. It's really sad. One morning when a father was walking his daughter to school, the terrorists shot and killed them both. The other girls continued to go to school, with armed escorts, but Stuart felt that the death of the one child and her father was his fault. The guilt stayed with him like a weight on his heart.

"Stuart suffered from back pain due to a war injury. The doctors gave him prescriptions for OxyContin or oxycodone or oxy-something-or-other. Stuart said it was the only thing that could ease his pain, but he quickly became addicted to the prescription opioid. The medicine was overpriced, and that led him to using an illegal but far cheaper drug … heroin. The cruel irony is that the heroin comes from poppies grown in Afghanistan, and it brings in money to buy AK-47s for terrorists all over the Middle East. Stuart was aware of that fact, and it caused him to suffer from additional guilt and shame every time he used the drug. In the end, he either had an accidental overdose, or else his physical and mental pain was just too much for him to bear and he committed suicide."

Alicia listened and nodded her head and wept. Terrell felt that she was crying for Stuart and also for her husband, and Jake, and the grieving dog. She wept for every person who had ever been in a war, and she prayed that someday there would be no more fighting and people could finally live in peace.

Terrell knew that some war veterans engaged in risky behaviors, but he hadn't done that. Not yet anyway. His love for this woman kept him grounded, and it gave purpose to his life. Alicia was his lighthouse and his touchstone and his reason for living. She was his everything. What would he do without her? His head was throbbing worse than usual. He needed a few ibuprofen pills or a shot of Jack Daniels. Preferably both.

As the couple made their way home, any concerns Terrell had about their arguments and fights of the recent weeks were forgotten. He reached out to hold Alicia's hand as he drove. She glanced at him, smiled through her tears and held his hand tighter.

CHAPTER 35

Zhukov recognized Terrell Hayes from one of the photos of Wolfe's friends and family on his phone. He drove away from the cemetery and cursed. He'd been so close to killing Wolfe, but then Terrell had come straight at him like he was ready for a fight. The fearless look on Terrell's face had made it clear the man had prior experience in deadly fights, and he'd survived them all. Zhukov knew a killer when he saw one, and Terrell was obviously a hardened war veteran.

This interference in his plans angered him, but he told himself it was only a minor delay. He would kill Jake Wolfe today. Right now, however, he had to focus on the business of killing the next lawyer target. Business before pleasure.

Zhukov drove across the Golden Gate Bridge and arrived in the wealthy small town of Mill Valley. He bought a to-go cup of black tea from a trendy little coffee shop and then sat in his vehicle in the parking lot. As he poured a packet of sugar into the tea, he studied a file on the tablet in front of him. The screen displayed a photo of his next target, along with all the relevant information he would need to complete the assignment.

According to the detailed background report, an attorney named Maxwell "Max" Vidallen was making a fortune suing doctors for dubious malpractice claims. He was bankrupting many small family physician offices and causing everyone else's insurance costs to skyrocket.

It didn't matter to Vidallen if the claim seemed to be a fake or if the victim had been too lazy to follow the doctor's orders. He was only interested in the insurance companies and how much money he could extract from them. The insurance company lawyers would often settle for an undisclosed sum rather than go to court and risk some unpredictable and astronomical award from a potentially gullible and easily swayed jury that knew nothing about medicine or the law. It was blackmail and extortion, pure and simple, and Vidallen loved every minute of it.

Zhukov read highlights of Vidallen's latest lawsuit against a veterinarian named Sarah Chance. The brakes on a bus had failed and the bus had hit a car crossing an intersection. Sarah had seen the collision, parked her car on the sidewalk, and called 911. Next, she'd stood in a pothole full of water and leaned in through the shattered window of the car to render first aid to a young woman who had a serious bruise on her forehead.

Zhukov thought about when he was a child living in Russia and a kind doctor had saved his life from a fever. The doctor had never made much money, but she'd had the love and gratitude of everyone in the poor neighborhood where Zhukov had grown up. He now felt a personal hatred for this lawyer, Max Vidallen, and looked forward to watching him squirm as he died in pain.

CHAPTER 36

Sarah Chance sat in a courtroom on the witness stand as Attorney Max Vidallen finished up his grueling lawsuit against her. The case had been ugly and ruthless. This was the final day of the court battle. The jury and courtroom crowd watched as Sarah was traumatized by Vidallen's relentless attacks upon every detail of her private life and career.

Sarah felt sick to her stomach. She knew that her insurance company lawyers were also beaten down by the onslaught of legal attacks. They were at the point where they just wanted this problem to go away. It was costing too much money and causing too many headaches. Nobody at the insurance company was concerned whether or not Sarah's life might be ruined by the court case. Their attorneys and accountants simply did the math in private meetings and decided Sarah's fate by the numbers. She was nothing more to them than a statistic on a spreadsheet, one customer out of millions.

This was obviously what Vidallen was counting on, and everything was working out according to his plan. The jury was mesmerized by Vidallen's dramatic cross-examination of Sarah Chance on the witness stand.

Sarah sat there like a deer caught in the headlights, gripped by her fear of public speaking, as she did her best to answer the endless questions.

"Miss Chance, what exactly do you do for a living?" Vidallen asked.

"As I've stated several times, I'm a veterinarian, and I own a pet clinic," Sarah answered.

"Did you attend medical school?"

"I graduated from a veterinary college that is accredited by the AVMA, the American Veterinary Medical Association."

"Do you have a license to practice medicine on human beings?"

"No, I have two licenses from the California Veterinary Medical Board. One to perform animal health care and another to operate a veterinary business."

"So, you are only a pet doctor, you are not licensed to provide medical care to people, is that correct?"

"Yes, that is correct."

"Do you have any training in providing emergency medical care to human beings at the scene of an accident?"

"Yes, I have completed Red Cross First Aid, CPR cardiopulmonary resuscitation training and AED, automated external defibrillator training."

"Did you complete the certified training or the non-certified training option?"

"Non-certified."

"Therefore, you are *not certified* to provide professional emergency medical care to human beings at the scene of an accident, are you?" Vidallen said.

"I am trained, but not certified. That's why I called 911 and requested an ambulance," Sarah said.

"But while you waited for the professionals to arrive, you engaged in amateur efforts at medical care, isn't that true?"

"When Hailey stopped breathing, I provided mouth-to-mouth resuscitation to keep her alive until the ambulance could get there."

"But Hailey is dead now, so you failed in your amateur efforts to keep her alive, didn't you?"

"Hailey survived and lived on for several months, until she died in her sleep from a cerebral ischemia when a blood clot caused a massive stroke. Hailey's physician testified here in court that Hailey skipped her recent doctor appointments that might have found the blood clot in time to save her life."

"But an expert has also testified in this court that her death might be your fault."

"No, it is not my fault. The autopsy found that the blood clot was the result of head trauma in the exact spot where Hailey's head hit the car window in the accident."

"The medical expert said you may have caused further injury to Hailey by moving her head after she was injured."

"I did not move her head. I did just the opposite. I put my coat around her head to make sure it did not move at all."

"Do you believe your coat to be a medical device, or is it an item of clothing?"

"My coat is an item of clothing."

"Your coat is in no way considered an emergency medical instrument or piece of equipment, is it?"

"No, but in an emergency, you might have to improvise."

"Let me ask you a three-part question to see if I understand what you're saying," Vidallen said. "Isn't it true that one: you are not a real doctor, you are a pet doctor?"

"I've already stated that I'm a veterinarian," Sarah said.

"Two: your coat is not an emergency medical device, but a nonmedical item of clothing that was never intended for any medical use whatsoever?"

"I've already answered that question."

"Three: you are not a paramedic or certified in emergency medical care but are an uncertified amateur."

"I've never claimed to be a paramedic."

"And yet you pretended to act like one when Hailey's life was at stake, didn't you?" Vidallen said.

"I didn't *pretend* to do anything. I carefully stabilized Hailey's head with my coat so she would not move and then I gave her mouth-to-mouth CPR when she stopped breathing," Sarah said. "Otherwise, she would have died in her car. I saved her life!"

"Perhaps you meant well, but isn't it true that you are not a licensed medical professional and you only rendered amateur nonmedical assistance with a nonmedical item of clothing?"

Sarah took a deep breath and let it out as she fought to control her emotions. "I only acted as a concerned citizen who helped in a life-threatening emergency, according to California's Good Samaritan laws."

Sarah's attorney stood up and said, "Objection, Your Honor, these questions have been asked and answered. Counsel is badgering the witness."

"Objection sustained," Judge Emerson said. "Move on, Mr. Vidallen."

"Yes, Your Honor, I'll wrap it up right now," Vidallen said, and he turned and looked at Sarah the way a cat looks at a cornered mouse.

"Miss Chance, since you brought up the Good Samaritan laws, are you aware that according to Van Horn v. Watson, the California Supreme Court held that the Good Samaritan statute was only intended to provide legal immunity to trained *professionals* who provided *certified* emergency medical care at the scene of an accident? And it was not meant to coddle amateurs who gave nonmedical assistance?"

"I'm not a lawyer. I just helped an injured girl hold still and keep breathing so she could stay alive."

"No, you're not a lawyer, and you're also not a doctor, and you're not an emergency paramedic, are you?"

Sarah's attorney stood up again.

"Objection, Your Honor, Van Horn v. Watson has no bearing on these proceedings. The current Good Samaritan law covers emergency medical or nonmedical care performed by laypersons."

Judge Emerson smacked down his gavel and said, "Counsel for both parties will approach the bench."

The lawyers had a whispered argument in front of Judge Emerson. He pointed his finger at Vidallen. "The appellate court held that the statute protected an uncompensated layperson from liability for providing emergency medical care at the scene of a medical emergency."

"Yes, Your Honor, but it did not protect from other types of assistance that are nonmedical."

"The current law covers emergency medical or nonmedical care performed by laypersons, except in the case of gross negligence or willful or wanton misconduct."

"Yes, and I believe the defendant engaged in gross negligence and wanton misconduct."

"Then I suggest you stick to that line of questioning. Don't try my patience."

"Yes, Your Honor." Vidallen returned to his table in front of the court and picked up a file, opened it, and consulted some papers as if he'd found a powerful fact of law there. It was just an act for the jury, but their eyes followed his every move and drank in the drama. Vidallen held the open file folder in front of him and pretended to consult it as he spoke to Sarah. "One final question, Miss Chance, but it is of the utmost importance. Is this a correct description of your actions at the time of the accident? You stuffed your coat around Hailey's injured head, and then pressed your mouth onto her mouth. Two actions that could have caused her head and/or neck to move, when they should have held still. Correct or not?"

Sarah's attorney stood up again, but Sarah said, "Asked and answered," and she turned and looked at Judge Emerson.

Emerson took a deep breath to castigate Vidallen, but the attorney said, "No further questions, Your Honor." Vidallen then slapped his file closed as if the case was closed too.

"You may step down from the witness stand, Miss Chance," Judge Emerson said.

Sarah got up slowly, walked on shaking legs and sat down next to her attorney. She could feel every eye in the courtroom staring at her.

Closing statements were made by both lawyers. Vidallen gave the first closing argument. Sarah's attorney followed. Vidallen gave a second "final" argument. In his well-rehearsed story, he explained that California law defines gross negligence as, "An exercise of so slight a degree of care as to justify the belief there was indifference to the interest and welfare of others." He argued that when Sarah had *shoved* her coat around Hailey's injured head it could have applied pressure to the wound. That was proof she had acted with indifference, not with careful forethought.

Sarah and her lawyer had no way to argue with the final argument, and that was exactly how Vidallen had planned it. He reminded the jury that people had testified about how Sarah was a highly emotional person who might have acted rashly and emotionally and therefore with indifference.

Judge Emerson gave instructions to the jury and explained how they were to decide the questions of fact regarding whether Sarah was grossly negligent or acted willfully or wantonly in misconduct. And if so, whether or not Vidallen had proved that Sarah's conduct added to the risk of harm, and that the additional risk was a substantial factor in causing harm to Hailey.

The jury left the courtroom for some time and then returned with a verdict that found Sarah Chance negligent and awarded Hailey's family damages of several million dollars. The family had already received millions from the city government in municipality litigation, but Vidallen had convinced the family to file an additional lawsuit against Sarah Chance too, for millions more, even though it would ruin the life of a woman who'd tried to save their daughter's life.

When the verdict was read, Sarah sat there in shock and looked at the jury with tears on her face. She said only three words, "How could you?"

The courtroom rumbled noisily in agreement as spectators talked among themselves. The members of the jury appeared surprised at the reaction, and perhaps realizing they'd made a terrible mistake.

Someone in the courtroom called out, "You'd better hope that none of your children are ever in a car accident, because nobody will stop to help them, and that'll be your own fault."

Judge Emerson smacked his gavel down and rebuked the crowd, saying, "Order in this court. Remain seated and be silent or I will have you removed."

Sarah's attorney patted her on the shoulder and whispered his condolences to her. She knew he'd fought hard for her, but he saw this kind of thing happen all the time. Honest, hardworking citizens were trampled in court every day of the week.

Sarah stared down at the table in front of her and wept. Her reputation was ruined. She would now be famous for acting with negligence and wanton misconduct that had caused a death. Clients were already avoiding her clinic. If more of them stayed away, she'd soon go out of business.

Judge Emerson read the rest of the decision out loud for the record. Some members of the jury were wringing their hands as they watched Sarah crying, the judge and the spectators glaring, and Vidallen grinning.

At the coffee shop in Mill Valley, Zhukov used his phone to watch the news coverage about Vidallen's court victory. He shook his head in disgust. In his opinion, lawyers held far too much power. And this country was crawling with them, like a plague of locusts that stripped the land clean of assets.

Law schools made lots of money by pumping out more unnecessary lawyers every year. There weren't enough jobs for all of them, and some felt they had to sue anyone and everyone who crossed their paths in an attempt to make a living. Perhaps every adult should go to law school. That way everyone would be an attorney, and who could sue anyone then? Lawyers never sued each other because it would just be an endless filing of papers and motions back and forth. Plus, lawyers almost never went to jail. That fact alone would make a law degree worth getting.

Zhukov thought that there was one sure way to cut through all the legal red tape. Nobody could use a lawsuit to stop a bullet. Now it was time to go and make preparations to kill Max Vidallen. Zhukov wouldn't feel any remorse when he rid the world of the disgusting man. In fact, he almost felt as if he was providing a public service and should receive some kind of commendation, or a letter of thanks from the mayor.

He smiled at his own wit as he drove toward Muir Woods and his next appointment with death.

CHAPTER 37

While Max Vidallen's court case against Sarah Chance was ending, Jake Wolfe was still at the cemetery with Cody. The loyal dog was finally worn out from howling and grieving. They were both wet and chilled from the earlier downpour.

A cemetery employee stopped by and told Jake they'd have to call Animal Control. They were legally obligated to bury the casket.

Jake tried once more to coax Cody off Stuart's casket, but the dog barked and snapped his teeth.

Cody refused to move. Stuart was his alpha and Jake was not; he was just a friend of his alpha. Cody knew Jake from the many times he'd visited Stuart at their den. Cody had nothing against this man. He appeared to be similar to Stuart in many ways. But Jake was not his alpha and he could not give him orders. Cody would stay here by Stuart until he died of hunger and exposure. He was loyal until death.

Jake was trained to understand dog psychology, and he knew what he had to do now. It was best that nobody else saw him do it, however.

They wouldn't understand the power dynamic between the man and dog. Cody was no ordinary house pet. He was a trained war dog, a sergeant in the Marines, and a combat veteran. He was intelligent and dangerous, and would not obey anyone except for his alpha leader. Jake decided he'd have to "alpha-roll" the dog, show him who was boss, and assume command.

The alpha-roll was an extremely dangerous thing to do, even for a trained dog handler. If he made one wrong move, Cody might bite off some of Jake's fingers, or maybe his nose, or one of his ears. In the worst-case scenario, Cody might sink his teeth into Jake's throat. When you trained a dog to fight, you created a double-edged sword.

This is where Jake's training would be severely tested. It was not a move an amateur should ever try, unless that person wanted to risk having their face ripped off by sharp fangs. Jake felt he had no choice, other than to abandon Cody, and his heart would never allow him to do that. He also knew that what he did next would likely require him to take responsibility for Cody for the rest of the war dog's life, no matter the danger to himself.

First, Jake began giving orders to Cody, the way he used to talk to his own war dog back in the day. Cody was accustomed to this kind of Marine talk, and it would put him in the right frame of mind for the surprise that was coming next. After Jake spoke to Cody for a while, he suddenly grabbed Cody by the collar with one hand and wrapped the lead around his snout several times with the other hand. He started turning Cody onto his back while also placing his body close to the dog's body and pinning him down, being careful not to harm Cody's legs.

Cody fought back and tried to bite Jake on the hands and face. Cody's paws raked and scratched Jake's chest and thighs, and Jake was glad he was wearing a long-sleeved jacket. As the two Marines wrestled, Jake carefully pressed his chest down on top of Cody's while holding his collar and yelling in his face. The entire time Jake did this, he used the command voice that he and the dog both knew from their days in combat.

Jake yelled, "Cody, out! Out-out-out! Dammit, out!"

Cody struggled for a while and at one point he almost wriggled his mouth free of the lead and nearly bit off Jake's left ear. Jake felt Cody's hot breath on his ear and realized that this dog was more aggressive than most retrievers, and far more dangerous than he'd expected. Jake felt that when Cody had served as a war dog he might have killed an enemy combatant who'd attacked him and his pack. It could have been a kill-or-be-killed situation and that tends to change anybody's personality some, whether they are a human being or a dog being.

After struggling some more, Cody eventually came to realize he'd been dominated into submission by this man who was a fellow Marine and a dog man. He was very much like a twin brother of his previous alpha. Cody felt that Jake meant him no harm. He had to accept Jake as his new alpha dog, now that Stuart had died. This was the chain of command.

Cody was not happy about losing Stuart, his pack leader and best friend. Yet he was a trained warrior, and he would now accept orders from Jake as his new alpha. The bonding process would take time, but now Cody was partners with Jake and would never try to bite him again. He would instead fight to protect him and his pack and would follow him into hell, and fight and die by his side if necessary. Cody stopped struggling and exhaled a long breath.

Jake carefully unwound the lead from around Cody's snout. With his mouth freed, Cody let out one last heart-wrenching howl. Jake gave orders to Cody as he picked up the exhausted and forlorn dog, set him on his feet, and walked him slowly to the Jeep. Once there, Jake helped him into the backseat. The dog offered no resistance. Jake petted Cody for a minute and spoke soothing words to him.

"Who's the best dog?" Jake said. "You are, Cody. You're the best dog ever."

Jake closed the door and got into the driver's seat. He looked at his phone for a moment, checking the photo Terrell had sent of the car with darkened windows. As Jake drove out of the cemetery grounds and back to San Francisco, he kept careful watch for the car.

He wondered what to do now. Cody wasn't ready to go home to Stuart's parents. They wouldn't be able to handle him when he was this agitated. Maybe a change of scenery might help to change Cody's mood.

"Cody, now that the rain has stopped and the sun is out, I think we should go to the Fort Funston Beach dog park. You can walk on the sand and run at the edge of the ocean surf, bark at seagulls, and then rest in the sunshine. Does that sound good? What do you say, boy?"

Cody made a noncommittal growling sound deep in his throat, as if he was saying, "Maybe, or maybe not." He appeared as if he was still angry at being alpha-rolled by Jake, but was too exhausted to bark.

While they drove, Jake played the classic song "Simple Man" by Lynyrd Skynyrd. It had been one of Stuart's favorite songs. Jake pushed a control and opened the back passenger window. Cody stuck his head out the window and let the wind blow in his face while the song played.

He took Cody to a quiet area of the beach, where there weren't any kids or dogs running around. Cody walked slowly at first and looked around warily. Jake knew that when Cody was a war dog, he'd served in desert environments, so at first the sand might bring back old memories. But retrievers love the water and after a while, Cody perked up some and ran and splashed in the incoming surf.

Jake reached into his backpack and removed a plastic flying disc that had once been Gracie's favorite. He threw it toward the water, and Cody chased after it. He retrieved it and dropped it at Jake's feet with a challenging look in his eyes that seemed to say, "Is that as far as you can throw it?"

After an hour of running up and down the beach, Cody drank some bottled water that Jake poured into a plastic water bowl. Jake then reached into his pack and took out a Kong toy—the treat that Marine dog handlers used to reward their dogs. Cody recognized it instantly and stretched out on a beach towel and chewed on it. After a while, he fell asleep with the Kong toy next to his face. His paws twitched and he huffed in his sleep as his troubled dreams unfolded.

Jake was relieved to see Cody taking a nap. The exercise and sleep would do him a world of good. While Cody slept, Jake called Stuart's parents. "Hi, Mrs. Nelson, Jake Wolfe here. I wanted to let you know that Cody is doing better now. It took some time, but he finally let me take him away from the cemetery. We went to the beach and he played in the surf. Right now, he's worn out and taking a nap."

"Thank you, Jake. It was kind of you to help Cody. We talked it over with Alicia and Terrell, and think it would be best if you would please adopt Cody and keep him with you."

Jake thought about the Alpha roll and how he and Cody had established a chain of command, but he felt guilty for taking the last living memory of their son. "Oh, ma'am, I couldn't do that. Cody was Stuart's dog, and I'm sure you'd want him living at your house."

"No, I think Stuart would've wanted him to live with you, Jake. It'd make you and Cody both happy, and make us happy too. We want the best for him, but we can't get him to obey us or do anything we say. He needs a firm hand and something useful to do."

Jake felt a lump in his throat. "Well, if you're sure about that, then, yes, of course, I'd be honored to have Cody live with me. I promise to take good care of him."

"I know you will. Cody has a veterinarian appointment because he hasn't been eating much of anything lately, so please take him to that. The vet's name is ... let me see here, I wrote it down ... Sarah Chance. When I saw her on TV, she seemed to be a very nice person, so I called her."

"Really, Sarah Chance is your vet? Yes, I'll be happy to take Cody in for his appointment."

What were the odds, Jake wondered. Did Terrell and Alicia have something to do with this vet appointment? They'd obviously had a hand in how the parents decided to let Cody live with him. They were good friends, and he felt lucky to know them.

"Cody also has a slight limp on a hind leg, from a lingering combat injury," Mrs. Nelson said.

"Yes, I noticed that while we were here at the beach."

"Nobody has been able to do anything for him. Dr. Chance said she could try holistic medicine, a change of diet, and acupuncture."

"That sounds kind of woo-woo, but I'll ask her about it."

They said their goodbyes and Jake ended the call. Cody was awake now, and he licked Jake's hand. That was a good sign. Jake gave him some dog biscuits he found in his backpack that were still good. Cody scarfed them down. He seemed to be getting some of his appetite back.

"Nobody could ever fill Gracie's paws," Jake said, "But I think we'll get along just fine, Cody."

Cody barked once and took Jake's hand in his mouth and held it—not biting it, just holding it. This was a new behavior Jake had not seen with any other dog and one he guessed that only a retriever might do.

"What are you trying to tell me, Cody? Don't worry, I'm not going anywhere. We're partners in crime now, big guy. You're stuck with me. And I'm glad you like the water, because your new home is floating on it. Are you okay with bunking on a floating bachelor pad?"

Cody looked Jake in the eye, let go of his hand, and barked once as he wagged his tail. Jake thought it was almost as if the dog had nodded his head yes at him too, but that was impossible, wasn't it?

CHAPTER 38

Max Vidallen was thrilled with his court victory against Sarah Chance. Afterward, he drove away in his red Porsche and decided to celebrate. He made a phone call to a high-priced matchmaking service.

It was a very discreet "arrangement" service that specialized in matching up female models and actresses with rich and famous men for ongoing relationships. The men paid ten thousand a month to help support their girlfriends, and the matchmaking service kept ten percent as its fee.

With more than a hundred clients at the present time, the service was grossing over a million dollars a month. The woman who ran the company was taking in over a hundred thousand dollars a month and over a million per year. Most of that was pure profit because her only overhead costs were a website and a phone. She ran the business from the living room of her penthouse apartment, on the top floor of a luxurious high-rise building.

It was all perfectly legal too, because this kind of arrangement constituted an ongoing relationship between two consenting adults, not one evening of sex for cash. Vidallen had checked into the laws to make absolutely sure it was okay. The legal documents involved were similar to the "girlfriend agreement" that many of Hugh Hefner's female houseguests had signed in years past at the Playboy Mansion.

While most of the paying customers were men, there were also many female clients who sought out the special arrangements. These were wealthy and powerful alpha women who were far too busy for dating. They enjoyed having a ridiculously handsome and hot "boy toy" in a fun relationship they could begin and end whenever it was convenient for them. Each hard-bodied male escort acted incredibly charming and chivalrous as he catered to the female client's every whim and desire.

Max Vidallen had recently ended a six-month long arrangement with a woman named Belinda. He called and spoke to the madam. "Hello, Crystal, it's Max Vidallen. I still miss Belinda, but as you said I have to move on and find someone new. Do you have any recent members that might be available to visit my home for a first date?"

"Hello, Max, darling," Crystal said. "Yes, I have several new young women that you might like. Let me take a look at the member site for you."

Crystal was pleased to hear from Vidallen. She knew his money well. He should have logged into the private website, but he expected Crystal to choose the perfect companion for him. Although Vidallen was somewhat of an annoying jerk, money was on the line. She had to send a woman who was highly independent, and wouldn't let him boss her around. She scrolled through the profiles until she came upon the photo of a Swedish girl who was able to wrap men around her little finger.

"Max, there is a new and absolutely stunning actress who joined our matchmaking service recently. You might have seen her in a billboard ad on the side of a cable car, advertising a tanning salon. She's wearing a pink bikini and pink heart-shaped sunglasses and she's blowing a kiss."

"Yes, I've seen that ad. She's a real beauty."

"Her name is Kelli Ivarsson, and she's even more impressive in person. Kelli is a Swedish import, a blue-eyed blonde with a delightful accent and a fun sense of humor."

"Kelli sounds like someone I'd like to meet."

"She's looking for a relationship with a successful, charming and *generous* gentleman."

"I'm sure Kelli would be a fun person to be in a relationship with.

I'd like to meet her as soon as possible. Is she available tonight, by any chance?"

Crystal heard the desire in his voice and smiled. "Kelli is rarely free on short notice, but a famous athlete who had reserved a date for tonight was called out of town unexpectedly. His loss is your gain. As you know, the fee for our matchmaking service is paid in advance and nonrefundable."

"Please charge the monthly fee to the same American Express Black Card I've used before. Tell Kelli she can pick up her favorite liquor on the way here, or anything else she wants, and add it to my tab."

"Of course, and the charge will appear on your credit card bill as the usual advertising agency business expense. Have an enjoyable evening. I hope this is the beginning of a beautiful relationship for both of you."

Crystal disconnected and then charged Max's card. Once the fee was paid, she placed a call to Kelli.

When Kelli Ivarsson got the phone call, she logged into the matchmaking website to learn more about this guy who was asking her out. She looked at his photos, read details about him, and checked the reviews left by previous girlfriends. He seemed like a bad guy to get into a lawsuit battle with, but his former girlfriends said he spent money like water, and he could be quite charming if he wanted something.

Some people would call Kelli a gold digger, but she felt that she was only being practical and logical. Her mother had always said, "There are millions of men in the world, and it's just as easy to fall in love with a rich man as a poor man."

Kelli was new at this, and she wanted to be careful about any potential relationships. All of the men were screened, but she'd rejected two of them so far. One was an egotistical blowhard who talked about himself nonstop. The other was a heavy drinker who had wanted her to spank him. Thanks, but no thanks. Maybe the third try would be the charm.

Kelli's finger hovered over the display on her phone and moved back and forth between the "Accept Date Proposal" icon and the "Decline Date Proposal" icon.

"Oh, well, I didn't have anything interesting planned for this evening anyway," Kelli said. She went ahead and pressed "Accept."

That opened another screen, and she saw some more private details about the man and his home, and their date for this evening. There was a note that said he wanted to relax in the hot tub before dinner and he'd asked her to bring the pink bikini and sunglasses. That made her laugh. Men could be so simple-minded and predictable at times.

Kelli dressed in the pink bikini, matching pumps and a little black dress that stopped at mid-thigh. She put on lipstick named Hot Pink Candy Yum-Yum, and of course, the infamous heart-shaped sunglasses.

The matchmaking service sent a limousine to pick Kelli up at her front door. Mano, the same bodyguard-sized Hawaiian guy as usual, was driving. He got out and held open the door to the back seating area for her.

"Hello, Kelli, you look lovely today," he said. "Do you want to stop at any stores or restaurants on the way?"

"Thank you, Mano. Yes, I'd like a bottle of Krug champagne. And maybe some chocolate-dipped strawberries, if a store has any."

"I can stop at a special market I know of in Mill Valley. They always have all kinds of amazing foods ready for takeout."

"You're so good to me, Mano. Be sure to get something for yourself. The client will be billed for it."

"Don't mind if I do. A top-shelf bottle of scotch would be very nice. Thank you."

Kelli could tell that Mano loved his job, driving models and actresses from place to place and getting free liquor and gourmet food in the process. Plus, there was the very rare occasional secret date with one of the women, when they got bored with Mr. Moneybags and were in the mood to give a bad boy a good time.

On the way, Mano called the market and told them what he wanted. He didn't ask how much it would cost.

Kelli relaxed in the luxurious backseat of the limo. She was looking forward to meeting someone new. Like most of the women who belonged to the matchmaking service, she actually enjoyed these arranged romantic relationships. The wealthy boyfriends took their dates to the best clubs and restaurants, to plays, the opera, on vacations, and to private parties of the rich and famous. Gifts of jewelry and other expensive luxury items weren't uncommon, either.

Kelli was curious about Max Vidallen. She looked at his website profile again. It said that he earned a fortune and had inherited a fabulous house on Mount Tamalpais in Mill Valley. The multimillion-dollar-home was paid off, but Max bragged that his monthly property tax bill was higher than what many people paid for a monthly house payment.

Ivan Zhukov approached Vidallen's home from another direction that would take him to the redwood forest behind the house and to the back deck.

CHAPTER 39

Zhukov knew there were fifty miles of trails on Mount Tamalpais and some of them wandered past the majestic redwood groves of Muir Woods. But today he was only interested in the trails that ran below Max Vidallen's property. As he drove his car along the Panoramic Highway, the thought crossed his mind that maybe he should have driven a Beemer. They were so common here in Marin County that the local people claimed the letters BMW stood for "Basic Marin Wheels."

He pulled into a small open area on the side of the road that he'd scouted earlier. Several cars passed by, but no one paid any attention to him. If they had, it wouldn't have mattered, because he was wearing a facial disguise and sunglasses. Once Zhukov was parked, he opened the trunk and grabbed his backpack that held a unique weapon.

A short walk into the trees took him out of sight of the road and into a beautiful forest. These trees were Sequoias, coast redwoods, the tallest type of trees in the world. Some were thousands of years old. They were spectacular, and Zhukov appreciated their majestic beauty. They didn't grow anywhere else except in Northern California and Southern Oregon. He'd never seen these amazing trees before and felt the desire to draw some charcoal sketches.

Zhukov reached the part of the trail that approached the back of Max Vidallen's property and saw the lawyer's beautiful home, nestled among the old-growth redwood trees. He recognized the house from Google Earth.

If the beautiful home was any indication, the business of suing doctors was paying Vidallen well. Once he was in sight of the back deck, he went off the trail and deeper into the woods, taking out his binoculars to look around for anyone who might be watching. He didn't see anyone out on the decks of the few homes that were in sight of the tree he had in mind for the job. The homes here were few and far between and were mostly shielded from their neighbors by the size of their properties and by the large trees.

He looked through the binoculars and saw Max Vidallen's back deck with its hot tub, tables, and chairs. A few redwood trees grew through carefully constructed holes in the redwood deck boards. He found it hypocritical and shook his head.

Vidallen's deck and hot tub offered spectacular views of Muir Woods and, further away, San Francisco. Zhukov was sure that the lawyer would bring his date out there to impress her and to get her into a bikini or less. He knew all about the date because Elena had bugged the lawyer's phone via spyware attached to a photo of a cute woman with a flirty message.

Zhukov climbed the bushy tree he'd scouted out previously and found the branch he planned to use for mounting the weapon. The thick green branches of the tree provided ample cover for him to hide in, out of sight of any neighboring homes in the distance. He opened his backpack, quickly assembled the device, anchored it to the branch with adjustable Velcro straps, and pointed it at the hot tub. There was a red laser sight mounted on the weapon, along with a small wireless video camera with a zoom lens. The weapon sat on a gyroscopic device that could swivel up and down, turn left and right, and tilt at an angle. His phone could display an image of what the camera saw, and it could adjust, aim and fire the weapon.

His phone vibrated with a message from Elena, saying that the target was almost home and a woman was on her way in a limousine. That made Zhukov smile. Everything was going according to plan. He climbed down and hiked back along the trail the way he had come.

As he walked, he glanced at his phone display and saw Vidallen appear, go onto his deck, and turn on the hot tub jets. Next, he fired up some patio heaters that were similar to what restaurants used for their outdoor seating areas. The camera was working perfectly. Zhukov would wait to kill Vidallen when he was in the right position and sitting still.

~

Vidallen went inside the house to pour himself a drink. He received a text message from Crystal, along with a link to a web page that gave him more information about Kelli.

According to the profile page, Kelli liked Krug champagne so much that she'd be bringing a bottle with her. One of her favorite dinners was filet mignon and lobster tails with Caesar salad. He was pleased to read that she was open-minded about nudity and would hook up on a first date if the mood was right and she was enjoying herself. Kelli's bio also said that she had dated two men from the matchmaking service so far and had rejected both of them as relationship material. However, both men said she was a fun date with a great sense of humor and she was unbelievable in bed.

Vidallen wanted the mood to be perfect, so he called his personal chef and told him the menu Kelli preferred. Next, Vidallen got out a champagne bucket, filled it with ice, and added two upside-down champagne flutes to the ice to chill.

With that done, he poured himself a Laphroaig thirty-year-old single malt Scotch. He put on a pair of board shorts and went back outside to relax in the hot tub.

Soon he heard the limousine pull into his driveway and a car door open and close. The intercom buzzed, and Max greeted her on the speaker. "Hi, Kelli, come on in. I'm out on the back deck in the hot tub. It's just through the living room to the sliding glass door."

~

Kelli went inside the house and walked through the living room, admiring the incredible view through the windows and slider. She stepped out onto the deck and said in her actress voice, "Well, hello there, Mr. Vidallen. Wow, I think this is one of the most beautiful views I've ever seen."

"I was just about to say the same thing about you, Kelli, and please call me Max."

Kelli smiled sweetly at his predictable comment and walked slowly toward him, doing the runway model walk she'd practiced—heel in front of toe, heel in front of toe. She had a bottle of Krug champagne in one hand. She saw an ice bucket on a stand. "For me?"

Max smiled and nodded, "Anything for you, my dear. I must say, you look even lovelier in person than on your billboard."

"You saw my ad? I hope you liked it."

"I loved it. You were perfect."

"Did you like my bikini?"

"Oh yes, and those cute sunglasses."

Kelli opened her purse, took out the pink sunglasses and put them on. Then she pulled the tie on her wraparound dress and let the front fall open to reveal the pink bikini.

"You mean these old things?"

Max raised his eyebrows. "You should be in Hollywood, honey. You are a star."

"Thank you, Max. I hope to be there soon. Now if you would be so kind as to pop my champagne."

"I'll be happy to pop anything you'd like."

Kelli laughed politely and handed him the bottle. If this was his effort at being clever and charming, he was off to a slow start.

Max sent the champagne cork flying over the deck rail with exaggerated flair, adding litter to the forest. Some of the expensive champagne bubbled up and out of the bottle, going to waste. Max took a chilled champagne flute out of the bucket and poured some of the bubbly for her.

"Would you care to relax in the spa until my chef arrives? He's going to prepare a dinner for us—your favorite, I believe. Filet mignon, lobster tails, and a Caesar salad."

Kelli smiled and let her dress slip off her shoulders and draped it on a nearby wooden chaise lounge. She was aware that Max was watching her every move. The time she'd spent on her appearance was paying off.

Max handed the glass to her. She took a sip and let out a sigh. "That's wonderful. Krug has the best bubbles."

"You can relax in warm bubbles while you sip cold bubbles," Max said, motioning to the hot tub.

"I like that plan," Kelli said. "But first, I want to take in your beautiful view for a moment."

Kelli walked across the deck, letting Max get a long look at her from all angles, like she was in a Victoria's Secret fashion show. She was reminded of something Jessica Alba had once said: "Guys are stimulated easily, and they are easy to manipulate. All you have to do is wear a sexy outfit." That was a fact of life, and she didn't mind it as long as she was in control.

Kelli paused and leaned her elbows on the deck rail, looking at the view and posing there to give her date some eye candy. She thought it was funny, because at home in her apartment, she usually just wore tattered sweatpants and a faded t-shirt.

Max couldn't take his eyes off her beautiful face and lithe, ripe body, glowing with Viking sensuality. He was totally enchanted with her and said so.

She walked back toward him, moving with the practiced grace of a movie star on the red carpet. As she got closer to the spa, she saw a red dot of light appear on Max's chest. It moved around and settled over his heart. Next, she heard a strange slicing sound, like a sword being swished through the air. That was followed by a loud thud, then something strange and terrible was protruding out of Max's chest.

Kelli's mouth opened in shock as blood began to pour from Max's body into the bubbling spa water. She let out a scream and fainted.

Max tried to scream too, but only a hoarse croak and foamy blood came out of his mouth. He was pinned to the side of the hot tub by a graphite hunting arrow. His mouth opened and closed like a dying fish on a hook as he gasped his last breaths and flailed his arms in spasms, splashing them in the bloodstained water.

Zhukov sat cross-legged inside of a hollow burned-out redwood, near where he'd parked his car. The inside of the tree was quite large, and although it looked to be recently burned, it hadn't been in a fire for nearly two hundred years. The tree was a survivor, much like Zhukov himself. He felt at one with nature while sitting there. And he smiled as he looked at his phone's video feed, which showed Vidallen dying exactly the way he'd planned it. The lawyer's career of filing lawsuits against innocent doctors was officially over.

Zhukov saw the woman lying unconscious on the deck. It was fortunate that she'd fainted, because now she wasn't doing any hysterical screaming to alert the neighbors. The best part was that her bikini-clad model's body would cause a useful distraction when the police arrived.

He turned the crossbow cam back toward Max and saw the lawyer's head drop forward as his arms stopped moving. "So many lawyers, so little time," Zhukov said, smiling.

He walked back to his car, started the engine and was about to pull onto the road when he felt an odd desire to take one last look at the scene of the crime. He used his phone to access the weapon's video cam, then rotated it back and forth on its gyroscope mount. First to the far right … then to the far left.

At another house, some distance away, there was an older man on his deck. He was standing next to a telescope on a stand and was talking frantically on his mobile phone while putting his eye to the telescope, which was pointed at Vidallen's patio. He turned the telescope until it was pointing at the weapon on the tree branch. Zhukov saw his face turn pale and then the man backed away from the telescope and ran into the house.

Zhukov couldn't help but laugh at the look on the man's face when he'd noticed the weapon was no longer pointing at Vidallen, but had turned and was pointing at him. Zhukov smiled as he drove the car back toward San Francisco. Once he was on the Golden Gate Bridge, he began thinking about the spectacular way he would shoot his next victim, the female attorney. But first, he *must* rid the world of Jake Wolfe.

CHAPTER 40

Jake climbed aboard the *Far Niente* and fed Cody some dog food he'd borrowed from a neighbor. He then checked the video recording from the boat's onboard security camera, as was his habit. The video showed a figure that appeared to be a tall, slender man creeping onto the boat and picking the lock on the aft sliding door. He moved lithely on his feet. The man wore a black stocking mask and gloves. The only parts of his anatomy that could be seen were his eyes and mouth. Jake paused the video and zoomed in. Gray eyes and thin lips.

It was surprising how fast the intruder had opened the locked door of the boat. That was a top-quality lock, so the man was no amateur.

Jake's phone buzzed and he saw that it was his editor calling him. He answered and said, "Sorry, you have the wrong number."

"Listen, we just picked up some chatter on a police frequency scanner," Norman said. "Another attorney has been assassinated. This one at a home on Mount Tam."

"Let me guess. Since I'm in Sausalito, I'm closer to Mill Valley at the moment than anybody."

"Obviously. Why else would I give the story to you, when you're such a wiseass?"

"That's better than being a dumb ass. And it's so nice to be appreciated by my boss. I'd tell you to kiss my wise ass, but I was heading in that direction anyway."

"Sure, you were. What kind of a fool do you think I am?"

"I don't know. How many kinds are there? Is it like Baskin-Robbins thirty-one flavors?"

"Listen to me, you—"

"I'm driving into the tunnel under the hills. You're breaking up." He made static sounds and whooshing noises.

As Jake ended the call, he heard Norman say, "Sausalito is already on the other side of the tunnel."

Jake laughed and said to Cody, "The heck with that guy, right, buddy?"

Cody barked once, grinned and panted Ha-Ha-Ha.

"Attaboy."

Jake and Cody got into the Jeep and drove fast toward Muir Woods. Jake arrived at the house and parked on the street, then grabbed his personal DSLR camera as well as the lightweight handheld video camera that belonged to the TV station. He told Cody to stay in the car. Cody didn't like that one bit. Jake left the Jeep's windows and moonroof open a couple of inches to give Cody some fresh air. The sun was setting and the air was cool. Cody wouldn't get overheated in the car.

Cody started growling, but Jake said, "Cody, I know you're able to unlock and open these car doors. But do *not* open them. Remain inside the vehicle for your own safety. That's an order. Do you hear me, Marine?"

Cody huffed in acknowledgment. He sat up straight, and watched the people outside the Jeep.

Jake got the feeling Cody would obey the order, unless he decided that Jake needed his help. Then all orders were forgotten.

Jake got out of the vehicle and was challenged by a Mill Valley police officer. The cop checked Jake's press ID and driver's license. He said, "Okay, but stay behind the police tape. This is a crime scene."

"Yes, sir, no problem, Officer," Jake said and smiled like a compliant sheep.

Jake stood there and innocently fiddled with his video camera until the cop looked away at someone else. He noticed that the cops were questioning a man who was wearing a chef's outfit. They had the chef assuming the position against a van with a catering logo on the side.

While they patted him down, Jake quietly made his way around the right side of the home, then went down a wooden walkway to the far end of the deck. He was technically still behind the yellow police tape. The cops had run it along the side of the house and across the entrance to the back deck.

A police officer stopped him at the place where the wooden walkway met the back deck. "Stay behind this tape, understood?" The officer's tone of voice changed when he recognized Jake. "Hey, Jake, what brings you to our neck of the woods?"

"Just slumming it here in Mill Valley today, Craig. How's life been treating you, buddy?"

"Same old, same old. I can't complain. Not much crime in this sleepy town of rich folks. Until today, that is."

"I guess I wandered into this deck area by accident. But I won't interfere with your work or the crime scene. I just want to get some pictures with my telephoto lens."

"Okay, but stay put and be quiet. Don't cause any trouble."

"You've got it, Craig, no worries."

Craig got a call on his phone and walked away to talk in private. Jake peered through his telephoto lens and got a closer view of the deck area. The murder scene was surreal. He saw a man who appeared to be dead, sitting in a hot tub filled with blood-red water. And there were two uniformed police officers who had a bikini-clad blond woman standing at attention with her hands handcuffed in front of her.

Jake shot some still photos and then switched back to the TV camera and started taking video. He set the camera on a lightweight telescoping tripod then plugged the camera into a small tablet. He could either borrow somebody's Wi-Fi or use his phone's network to send the live video to the news station.

Jake looked again at the dead man in the hot tub and saw an arrow shaft protruding from his chest. By the angle of the arrow, it was clear that the woman hadn't shot the man up close. The shot must have come from a distance. Jake swiveled the video camera away from the house and used the zoom to search for clues. He saw another home some distance away that had a deck. There was a telescope on a stand pointed toward the forest area. Jake followed its trajectory until he found a tree with a well-concealed weapon on a branch. Looking at the weapon with his zoom lens, he saw that it appeared to be some kind of crossbow with a small video camera attached.

Jake waved at his police friend, Craig, and when he came closer, Jake pointed at his tablet. "Take a look at this video feed, Craig. There's a weapon in that tree. And over at that house, there's a telescope on the deck that's pointed right at that tree. Somebody there may be a witness."

"Nice find. I'll tell our guys who are searching the area." Craig gave Jake a fist bump and then made a call on his phone.

Jake turned and looked over at the woman in the swimsuit. She certainly didn't look like she was carrying any concealed weapons in her tiny bikini. Jake felt that the use of handcuffs on her was somewhat overzealous. On the other hand, he knew that cops were trained to secure this type of situation.

One cop was as tall and muscular as an NFL linebacker. He was asking questions and looking the woman up and down. It was hard not to; she'd made every effort today to get a man's attention. But she wasn't answering any of his questions. She just stood there crying. This was neither the man nor the attention she'd had in mind. The woman looked familiar to Jake; he turned his camera toward her and zoomed in on her face.

She had her back to him, but when she turned her head for a moment, he saw the side of her face and recognized her. She was a model-actress named Kelli Ivarsson, a good friend he'd done photoshoots with. He was fond of Kelli, they got along well and he thought she was a nice person—smart, happy, and easy to talk to. Not stuck up like some actors and models were.

Jake looked at the other cop. She was a female who was acting polite and professional. As he stood there thinking he should call a lawyer for Kelli, a distinguished-looking older gentleman appeared next to him.

The man was wearing a well-made Italian suit, expensive shoes, and a nice overcoat that all spoke of money and success. Jake recognized the man as a powerful attorney named Gregory "Bart" Bartholomew. He'd known Bart for many years. His daughter had held her wedding at the winery in Sonoma that Jake's parents owned. The silver-haired man spoke in a cultured voice he'd picked up at Harvard Law School.

"Well, hello, Jacob, my good man. Would you please be so kind as to record my work here on video? You'll be generously compensated by my law firm, of course."

"No problem, Bart, I'd be happy to. Also, that woman right there is a good friend of mine. I hope you're here to act as her attorney. If not, I'd like to hire you to represent her, starting immediately."

"That's quite noble of you, young man, and far beyond your budget. But don't worry about your friend, a client of mine asked me to represent the young lady. I'll use every power at my command to have her free of custody as quickly as possible."

"Thanks, Bart. Those two have been trying the good cop/bad cop thing, but Kelli hasn't been saying a word."

Jake showed Bartholomew the tablet that was recording the scene. He flicked his finger across the screen, which showed the website of the news station where he worked. The video could be seen playing on the news in real time. There was a superimposed square in the corner that displayed a woman's face as she commented on the situation.

The "bad cop" pointed his finger at Kelli. Jake had the camera on mute, but now he turned up the volume on the powerful microphone and they heard the cop say, "You could go to the electric chair for murder, do you hear me?"

Jake was broadcasting it live, and everyone viewing the news online heard what was said. Kelli had her eyes closed and was crying.

"I ... want ... my ... attorney," Kelli said as she sobbed.

Bartholomew noted the storm cloud passing across Jake's face and thought that perhaps he'd arrived just in time to prevent the occasionally hot-blooded young man from stupidly attempting to rescue yonder fair maiden and getting himself arrested for interfering with a murder investigation. Bart made a gesture toward his ear and also at the video camera. He mimicked turning down a volume knob. Jake muted the microphone.

"Easy now, Jake. When the cop threatened her with the death penalty he might have helped her to beat him in court. Involuntary confessions are prohibited by the federal constitution's Due Process Clause and by Article I, Section 15 of the California Constitution."

"Go tell him that," Jake said.

Bart nodded. "Now that Kelli has requested her attorney on a live internet news feed, it's time for me to intervene. The Mill Valley chief of police might call or show up here soon. I talked to the chief and the mayor while I was in my car. They want to avoid having the news media say the words 'Mill Valley' in the same sentence with 'high-priced prostitute,' if that can be avoided."

"FYI, the murder weapon is a crossbow, mounted way over there in that tree. You know Kelli didn't put it there. She wouldn't know a crossbow from a CrossFit class."

Jake showed Bart some video of the crossbow weapon up in the tree. Next, he took a small wireless microphone out of his pocket and attached it to Bart's tie. The mic looked like a tie bar. Jake then stepped back, turned up the audio volume, focused the TV camera on the attorney, and counted with his fingers. Three, two, one, go.

CHAPTER 41

With the TV camera focused on him, Bartholomew politely announced himself to the nearest police officer. He stepped over the police tape and held up his business card and driver's license for identification.

"Gregory Bartholomew, attorney at law, here to see my client, Miss Kelli Ivarsson, the witness to this crime."

As the officer took his time inspecting the ID and the gold-embossed business card, Bartholomew said, "The witness requested her attorney, and it was broadcast on the news. If you have any problem with my ID, we can get your chief of police and the mayor on the phone right now, and you can explain your delay to them personally."

Bart held out his phone and displayed a photo of the chief of police on the screen, standing next to himself and the mayor. One tap of his finger and a call would be placed to the officer's boss.

The officer recognized the well-known and powerful attorney, and he knew that the man rarely ever lost a case. This was not a guy he wanted to be on the wrong side of. He handed the ID back to Bartholomew and said, "Proceed."

As Bart passed by the officer, he pointed at Jake and said, "That man is working for my law firm in an official capacity to record details of this scene for our legal case. His name is Jacob Wolfe and his camera holds evidence that is admissible in a court of law."

The officer looked over at Jake and frowned.

"Neither he nor his camera may be interfered with in any way, or it will be considered tampering with evidence," Bartholomew said. "That is a serious crime with serious penalties. Is that understood, my friend?"

The look on the officer's face indicated he was fighting to control his urge to punch the lawyer in the mouth. But he just spoke into the radio to inform the two officers detaining the suspect that her attorney was approaching them and that his ID had checked out.

Bartholomew's eyes quickly took in more details of the crime scene as he walked directly up to Kelli. "Gregory Bartholomew, attorney at law. This young lady is my client." Bart took off his long overcoat and placed it over Kelli's shoulders to cover her up. Her hands were still cuffed in front of her, and Bart placed the front edges of the coat between her fingers so she could hold it closed.

Kelli sighed in relief to have the coat on. She'd felt so exposed and helpless, all alone, locked in cuffs. Bartholomew quietly whispered some reassuring words into her ear. He asked her if she'd said anything to the police and if they'd explained her legal rights. When she shook her head no, he said something further, and although she continued crying, she nodded her head in understanding.

Kelli felt lucky that Crystal had sent her attorney here so quickly, before the police could make her say things she'd regret. They were skilled in the art of getting confessions out of people. For the first time since she'd fainted, Kelli began to feel some hope of getting free of this nightmare. If only she'd pushed the "Decline Date Proposal" icon.

Bartholomew put his hand protectively on his client's shoulder and turned to the two officers. "As Ms. Ivarsson's attorney, I wish to go on record that my client will not be answering any questions at this time. It would be improper procedure since she has been drinking champagne and is also in a state of shock."

The male officer said, "Your client was present at the scene of a murder and was handcuffed as part of an investigative detention."

Bartholomew scowled. "I demand she be released and allowed to leave at once to seek medical care. If you place her under arrest, she will say nothing and I'll follow you to the police station, bail her out immediately, and have a long talk with your chief about all the mistakes in leadership I believe you've made here today."

The officer glared at the lawyer as if wishing the best of luck to whoever was shooting the bastards.

A uniformed officer escorted the elderly neighbor to them. "This is the neighbor who called it in. He says he witnessed the murder through his telescope and claims the woman had nothing to do with it. He also saw some kind of crossbow weapon mounted on a tree branch."

The older neighbor man nodded in agreement. He started to speak, but the cop cut him off. "According to this witness, it looks like the young lady was telling the truth. She'd been standing over there by that broken champagne glass. That's where she fainted. She'd gone to look at the view before walking back toward the hot tub. That probably saved her life. For all we know, if she was in the tub, she might have been shot and killed too."

Bartholomew said, "Now do you plan to handcuff this other important witness and make him stand at attention in his underwear while you yell and threaten him too? Or are we done here and free to go, Officer?"

Another cop walked up and said, "We found a note, pinned to a tree." He held up a plastic evidence bag and displayed the note.

DON'T BOTHER CALLING A DOCTOR.

The officer in charge was about to say something when his mobile phone buzzed. He glanced at the screen, groaned, and answered the call. "Yes, Chief. What? On TV and the internet? Understood, sir. I'll tell Ms. Ivarsson she's free to go." He removed the handcuffs from Kelli's wrists.

"Thank you," Bartholomew said.

The officer gestured at Kelli. "The chief asked if you'd bring the *witness* down to the station tomorrow for an interview. She is now released on her own recognizance."

Bartholomew nodded. "You have my word she'll be there. And now there's the matter of Miss Ivarsson's attire. Has anyone bothered to look for her clothes? I'm sure she didn't arrive wearing a swimsuit, and I'll be damned if she'll leave that way."

The officer's face turned red in embarrassment and was broadcast on live television.

Bartholomew had never been popular among the police in the Bay Area; now he was even less so.

CHAPTER 42

Zhukov drove his car over the Golden Gate Bridge and into San Francisco. He felt curious about the crime scene back at the home of Max Vidallen, so he pulled over and parked. He used his phone to view the live streaming video, which showed that the neighbor's deck was empty, the telescope sitting there deserted.

Moving his finger across the phone display, he turned the camera toward the deck of the dead lawyer and saw that the police had arrived. He panned the camera further and saw Jake Wolfe standing off toward the far end of the deck pointing a video camera at the tree. He cursed at how this lowly newsman kept showing up at the scene of his carefully orchestrated murders. Zhukov moved his finger back and forth on his phone to make the camera move on its gyroscopic mount from side to side, as if it was an animal shaking its head. He then turned on the red targeting laser and pointed it at Wolfe.

Wolfe gave the middle finger salute to the camera.

Zhukov gritted his teeth. At that moment, he would've gladly paid a million dollars if the crossbow could fire another bolt to kill Jake Wolfe. He decided that in the future, he'd add a redundant weapon to this setup. Perhaps one of those M203 single-shot 40mm grenade launchers, the kind designed to attach under the barrel of a military rifle. He imagined the immense satisfaction he'd feel at firing a live grenade at the photojournalist's smiling face and blowing his head to pieces.

Zhukov took a deep breath and let it out. He wouldn't let Wolfe get to him. He'd done a masterful job of killing Vidallen. It was time to collect the other half of his money for this second murder. He called Banks to give him a report.

"Do you have good news for me?" Banks said.

"Yes, the second assignment has been completed, and it all went well, exactly as I planned it," Zhukov said.

"Brilliant. What about the additional problem that has developed, with that nosy photojournalist, Wolfe?"

"That problem will be solved in conjunction with the third target."

"That is good news. It will be a relief to be rid of the cheeky bugger. And speaking of the third target, when are you going to shoot the woman?"

"Very soon. I'm taking care of things in their logical sequence."

"I don't understand your methodology, I must admit."

"No one does. It's the work of a misunderstood artist. Perhaps I should file a patent on my creative techniques."

"Always the flippant one, but you still deliver the results. I interviewed others in your line of work and asked if they would shoot a woman, but they all said no. I appreciate your open-mindedness about that."

"Maybe I believe in true equality."

"Very amusing. You believe only in money… and art, of course."

"Without money, there wouldn't be as much art in the world."

"What about the starving artists?"

"They are all doing just that—starving. But well-fed artists like Michelangelo and Leonardo da Vinci had wealthy patrons. We might not have the Mona Lisa or a statue of David if their respective artists had to dig ditches to pay for food."

"I understand. Just imagine how many more paintings Vincent van Gogh might have produced if anyone had been his patron or bought a single one of his artworks," Banks said. "But nobody ever did. Not one of his paintings was purchased while he was alive."

"That is a travesty. The great man died far too young," Zhukov said, and then his voice began to rise. "Van Gogh received no appreciation or support for his art. Now his unsold paintings are auctioned for millions, if they ever go on sale at all. Thinking about that always makes me angry."

Banks heard cursing and the sound of something shattering. Zhukov was known to smash furniture, break windows, or do damage to cars upon occasion. He decided to pay him a compliment. A little flattery couldn't hurt.

"Speaking of artwork that never goes on sale, is there any chance I could procure one of your charcoal sketches? Ever since you showed me photos of them on your phone, I've wanted one to hang in my office."

Zhukov didn't say anything.

"I'd pay an outrageous sum for one of your fine representations of Yosemite, for example. That one you showed me was reminiscent of the black-and-white photography of Ansel Adams."

Zhukov paused for a minute while Banks waited … and then replied, "That is an unusually polite thing for you to say. You must want something from me."

"Yes, I want one of your works of art."

"My sketches were lost, but I'll draw new ones and you can take your pick."

"Thank you. I'll have the sketch framed and hung in my office in London, in a place of honor."

"You're welcome. I'll see you at dinner."

Zhukov ended the call and looked at the dashboard of his car. The leather was ripped and the molded plastic was shattered. His hunting knife was stuck into the stereo and there were broken pieces of the dash on the floor. He must have attacked the dashboard with his knife while talking about van Gogh, but he had no memory of the violent act. He realized he was at a very low point in his withdrawal symptoms. Tomorrow would be an unpredictable day.

CHAPTER 43

At the crime scene, Kelli pointed at the deck furniture and said, "I'm going to go put on my dress."

The policeman nodded in agreement, and Kelli turned and walked across the deck to the chaise lounge. When she picked up the dress, she glanced toward the police tape and saw a guy she knew named Jake Wolfe, operating a TV camera. A group of other media people began to crowd in behind him. Jake smiled and waved at Kelli, and she rushed over to him.

"Jake, I'm so glad to see you. Thank goodness you're here," Kelli said. She dropped her dress and reached up with both arms to give Jake a hug over the yellow police tape. As she raised her arms, the overcoat on her shoulders fell off, leaving her wearing just the bikini.

Jake returned Kelli's hug, and several of the media began taking photos and video of the blond model in her pink bikini, hugging their colleague Jake, with the police "do not cross" tape between their two waists at crotch level. Jake noted the news crews were all grinning because this was a classic image destined to be on the front page of various news sources, and go viral on the internet. They lived for this kind of stuff, and they would tease Jake about it for years to come. He'd never hear the end of it.

He wanted to say some friendly profanity to his colleagues, but he ignored them instead. Kelli didn't seem to want to let go, so Jake gently released himself from her hug, but held her hand. He made an effort to look her in the eyes when he spoke to her, instead of staring at her body that had won the genetic lottery.

"Hey, Kelli. I hope you're doing okay after all you've been through here," Jake said.

"I don't know if I'm seriously hurt, but I fainted from shock and got a bruise on my hip," Kelli said as she turned to the side and pointed to a small bruise near her right butt cheek. More cameras flashed and video was broadcast.

Jake just nodded and acted as if this kind of thing happened to him every day, and it was no big deal. He'd practiced this detached demeanor while doing photography for bikini catalogs and NFL Football cheerleader calendars.

"Let's get you dressed and out of here, okay?" Jake said. He lifted up the plastic police tape and stepped under it, then picked up the black dress from the deck near Kelli's feet. He held the dress up for Kelli so she could put her arms into it. She tied it around her waist.

Craig saw him step past the police tape and stared hard at Jake. A look passed between them that said Craig wanted Jake to get back on the other side and make it quick. Jake nodded in agreement and held up one finger to indicate it would just be one minute.

"Jake, could you please give me a ride home?" Kelli said.

"Sure, I'd be happy to."

"Thank you so much. Let me grab my things."

While Kelli was retrieving her purse and putting on her shoes, Jake picked up Bart's long overcoat off the deck and held onto it. Kelli returned and said, "Okay, I'm ready. Can we please get out of here?"

"Yes, and if you don't mind my saying so, that was the fastest I've ever seen a woman get ready to go anywhere."

Kelli nodded at his attempt at humor, but she didn't laugh. He helped her put on the long coat and then he lifted the police tape again, holding it up for her before crossing under it himself.

Craig nodded in thanks at Jake for getting behind the tape. Being friends with a cop didn't mean you could do whatever you felt like doing. This was a crime scene, and the police were in charge. You had to respect the badge and the uniform.

Jake tapped an icon on his tablet that sent a signal to

Bartholomew's tie-pin mic and caused it to vibrate repeatedly, like a mobile phone getting a call. Bart noticed it and he joined them.

Jake said to Kelli, "The way to handle this media circus is to look straight ahead, hold your head up, keep a neutral expression on your face, and don't say a word, okay?"

She nodded.

"And you might want to put on those sunglasses. They'll hide your eyes and make you look like a Hollywood celebrity," Jake said. "Close the long coat, and tie the belt. When they yell questions at you, block them out as if you have earplugs in your ears. Do not react and don't turn your head. Think about your favorite celebrity and pretend you're her."

"Can you hold my purse for a minute?" Kelli said.

"No, sorry, I'm not a guy who holds purses, but you can set it down next to my camera bag on the deck right there," Jake said.

Kelli raised her eyebrows in surprise. Apparently not used to men saying no to her. She set the purse down, closed the coat and tied the belt, then picked up her purse, took the sunglasses out, and slid them on.

"Why would you hold the coat for me, but not hold my purse?" Kelli said.

Jake smiled. "If I hold your coat, it means I'm a gentleman, but if I hold your purse, it means I'm pussy-whipped, and I'm not, so I won't."

"Is that some unwritten law of guys?"

"Yes, I believe it's on page 101 of the Guys' Handbook." Jake put his cameras and telescoping tripod into the backpack and then whispered to Bartholomew that he'd give Kelli a ride back to the city and, if needed, to the hospital. She was also borrowing Bart's coat but would return it tomorrow.

Bartholomew nodded his head in agreement, and the trio began walking the gauntlet of media people. Jake reached into his jacket pocket for a pair of sunglasses and put them on. Kelli held tightly onto Jake's arm above the elbow.

The news cameras began to flash in earnest now, and Jake got a taste of what it was like to be on the receiving end of far too much photographic attention. Some of the photographers behaved in a professional manner, but others started yelling at him and getting in his face, just like the worst of the paparazzi. Jake felt the urge to punch one or two of the pushy ones, but he kept his cool, faced straight ahead and ignored everything around him.

The street in front of the late Max Vidallen's home was jammed with news media vehicles, reporters, and television cameras. Bartholomew walked in front of Jake and Kelli. One reporter held a microphone up to Bart's face and yelled, "Did that woman kill her lover?"

Another reporter said, "Was it a crime of passion?"

A third said, "Is she the attorney assassin the police have been looking for?"

The cameras took close-ups of Kelli's tear-streaked face and the heart-shaped sunglasses hiding her crying eyes. She looked like a pop music star who had just become a widow. The photos and video clips began to appear on news websites and went viral all over the internet.

Bartholomew cleared his throat, straightened his tie, and started his speech to the news reporters, similar to the version of events he'd told to the cops. He again spoke like an actor on the stage, similarly to the way he did in the courtroom. Soon most of the cameras and microphones were pointed in his direction.

"My client is a witness to a shocking murder," he said. "She's lucky to be alive."

Jake and Kelli got into the Jeep, and Cody stuck his face between the two front seats and gave them a toothy grin. Jake scratched Cody behind the ears. "Kelli, this is my dog, Cody. And, Cody, this is Kelli. She's our *friend,* and she's under our *protection.* Say hi and be friends, Cody."

Cody barked once and nodded his head, then rubbed his nose against Kelli's shoulder. Kelli patted Cody on the head. "I feel safe with Cody here."

Jake drove away from the house and passed by several police vehicles. Kelli stared straight ahead and took deep breaths. The relieved look on her face indicated she was thankful to be leaving the house in Jake's car instead of a police car.

CHAPTER 44

After driving for a few miles, Jake said, "Where to, mademoiselle?"

"I don't think I really need to go to the hospital," Kelli said. "But I'm kind of scared to go home and be alone right now."

"You're welcome to hang out with me and Cody for as long as you want. We'll protect you from harm, I promise."

"Thank you. That's sweet of you, Jake. Do you think maybe we could go to a quiet restaurant? As long as it's far away from here."

"Yes, and I'll even let you supersize the fries."

Kelli appeared shocked for a moment, until she saw his grin. Then she gave him a playful punch on the shoulder. "You know what I mean."

"There's an excellent Italian place in North Beach where we could relax for a while. Sit in a cozy booth and have some wine and pasta, comfort food. The people that own the restaurant would be very protective of you, too. Nobody in their right mind would ever mess with that *family*."

Cody barked twice and shook his head. Jake smiled at him in the rearview mirror. He knew that Cody wanted to do his job to help guard this person against harm. She was under his protection.

"Italian is always good; I'm a big fan of meatballs," Kelli said.

"That's right, you're Swedish. We could go to IKEA and have some of their Swedish meatballs. Maybe look at some shelves that are impossible to put together."

Kelli smiled and shook her head at him. "Any restaurant you like would be fine. But no sushi, that stuff scares me."

"Uncooked sea animals aren't your thing?"

"Ewww."

"When you live on a boat, you call that bait."

"Oh, that's right. I'd heard you were living the single life on a yacht now," Kelli said. She spoke the word yacht with reverence. "Maybe we could stop by your yacht for a while instead of going to a restaurant. I'd love to have a drink by the seashore, with Cody there to watch out for us. That would really help to calm my nerves."

Cody barked once and pressed his nose against Jake's arm.

"Uhm, sure, of course," Jake said. "We could even take the boat out on the water if you really want to get away from it all."

Kelli's shoulders relaxed and she stopped clenching her hands.

"Yes, please, that sounds wonderful."

"Let's do it. What do you like to drink?"

"Do you have any champagne?"

"Let me think. I'm pretty sure I saw a bottle of Veuve Clicquot Brut Yellow Label in the fridge."

"I love Veuve Clicquot. Didn't I see on the news that they found some priceless old bottles of that champagne in a shipwreck?"

"Yes, but the bottle in my fridge is not one of those, sorry."

Kelli laughed and then put her hands over her face and took some deep breaths. When she took her hands away, she sighed. "Thanks for making me laugh, Jake. I'm so stressed out right now. I could use a few laughs—either that or I'm going to have to scream."

"I'm sorry that one cop was tough on you. The Mill Valley police are among the finest officers you'll find anywhere, but that one guy was overdoing the bad cop act a little bit. I've never seen him before, so he must be new. Maybe he was just having a bad day."

"Yes, the rest of the police were very professional, but he was frightening, especially when I was in shock."

"I think it's his job to frighten suspects, but thankfully that's all over now."

"I was so relieved when we drove away from that house," Kelli said. "You are seriously my knight in shining armor."

Jake shrugged. "Maybe a knight in rusty armor."

"If it wasn't for you and Crystal's attorney, I might be sitting in a cold jail cell right now, shivering in my bikini." Kelli crossed her arms and shuddered at the thought of it.

Jake decided to change the subject. "By the way, you were very kind to send flowers when Gracie died. Thank you. It meant a lot to me."

Kelli's face softened. She reached over and put her hand on Jake's shoulder. "When I heard what had happened to Gracie, it broke my heart. But I'm glad you got another dog. Cody seems so nice."

"He's a good dog for sure. Except it looks like when I left him in the Jeep, he chewed up my flip-flops that were in the backseat."

Kelli laughed again, and this time it came a little more easily.

When they arrived at the harbor, Jake opened her door and held her hand as she stepped out in high heels. He looked around the lot and was relieved that he didn't see Gwen's car. He wished now that he'd never given her that pistol.

Kelli took off the overcoat, folded it, and set it on the car seat while Jake opened the back passenger door so Cody could get out. They walked across the parking lot, Kelli holding on to Jake's arm.

"Sorry to cling, but I'm having problems walking on the pavement in these ridiculously high heels," Kelli said.

When they reached the wooden dock, Jake knew that the spiked heels could get stuck between the boards. He spoke in an officious voice and said, "Kelli, this is your yacht captain speaking. We will be on a barefoot cruise, so please take off those shoes and proceed barefoot down the dock and onwards to the *Far Niente*."

Kelli smiled, stood at attention and gave Jake a saucy salute. "Yessir, Captain, sir."

"I could get used to hearing that," Jake said. "Let's go have some of that champagne. It's calling our names."

Kelli stepped out of her pumps, picked them up in one hand, and walked down the smooth wooden dock in her bare feet. Cody trotted ahead of her, leading the way. Kelli didn't do the model walk. It appeared she felt comfortable being herself with Jake.

Jake smiled at the sight of her walking barefoot and looking in wide-eyed wonder at all the boats and the sparkling blue water. He was seeing the more innocent, happy, and real side of her. And he hoped that the yacht and the seashore would help her forget about everything else for a while.

As he watched her walking barefoot in that black dress, she reminded him of the lead singer from the Swedish band Roxette—when she'd performed a live concert version of the classic song "Listen To Your Heart."

Boarding at the stern of the *Far Niente*, Jake unlocked the weather-tight sliding glass door and they all went inside.

CHAPTER 45

Terrell Hayes had the afternoon off after the funeral. He spent it at home, curled up on the couch with Alicia, talking, kissing, and watching movies. This rare moment was so good it made him ponder his life and how he might arrange it so he had more afternoons like this with his sweetheart. It occurred to him that the truth in the saying "work sucks but I need the bucks" was the reason this afternoon was such an unusual treat. He was a cog in the machine like everybody else and had no idea how he could rise above it.

As it got closer to dinnertime, they were talking about having a pizza delivered or getting some takeout food. But Terrell got a call from work telling him to report to Chief Pierce about going on an impromptu undercover assignment.

After the call ended, Terrell groaned and said, "Oh, man, not that gang-related homicide thing again—not tonight."

Terrell apologized to Alicia, but she told him not to worry. She was worn out and planning to go to bed early to catch up on some much-needed sleep. They'd had a wonderful afternoon together, so they were more than fine.

Terrell knew that when his wife said things were "fine," she might mean they really were fine, or she might mean they were nowhere close to fine. He wanted nothing more in this world than to join his wife for dinner and an early bedtime—but duty called, and he had to answer.

Terrell kissed Alicia goodbye and drove toward the police station, feeling the old familiar tug-of-war between love and duty.

Arriving at the Public Safety Building, he headed to the chief's office. The door was open and Terrell knocked and went inside.

Chief Pierce looked up from his papers, nodded at Terrell and said, "Come in and have a seat, Hayes. Thanks for volunteering to work on your day off."

As Terrell sat down, he raised his eyebrows at him as if to say, "I didn't volunteer, so please cut the ridiculous BS." But he remained silent and stoic.

The chief smiled a tired and knowing smile, and pushed a file toward Terrell. "Take a look at this and give me your thoughts."

Terrell opened the file, grunted, and rubbed his five-o'clock shadow. "This guy again?"

"Yeah. William T. Farmington, otherwise known as WTF."

Terrell flipped through the photos and reports. "We know he's killed people, but the guy is Teflon-coated. Nobody has been able to get anything on him and make it stick."

"Maybe tonight you can change that and show him he isn't so slick after all."

"I'm ready to give it the 'old precinct try,' Chief," Terrell said, but he yawned.

"Try to curb your enthusiasm, Hayes. Let's not get carried away here."

"Where is Mai Thai when I really need coffee and a donut?"

"Short and sweet? That nice girl was just here a while ago, and she delivered a box of good stuff to the second shift. Go get yourself a coffee and donut and come back for the rest of the briefing."

"Thanks, Chief. Be right back."

Terrell checked his text messages as he walked down the hall. He'd been ignoring them because he'd wanted to give Alicia all his attention. If the text didn't repeat over and over, he figured he could let it wait. There was one text from Jukebox that had come in a while earlier.

The text said: *The assassin shot another lawyer, this time with an arrow.*

It happened in Mill Valley. You might want to suggest that the chief send Ryan and his dog Hank there to help the MVPD search the woods. Make you all look good.

That was a great idea to send the K9 Unit over there to work with the neighbors. Jake was always trying to help his friends in law enforcement. The guy could be annoying at times, but he was also a really good friend, at least when he wasn't causing all kinds of trouble. Jake had sent a link to a news story. Terrell scanned the news for details.

He went to the breakroom coffeemaker and filled two cups, then picked out two donuts. He hadn't asked the chief if he'd wanted anything. The chief always said no. Terrell just brought him a coffee and a powdered jelly-filled donut anyway, and set it down without saying a word.

Terrell told the chief about the poisoned arrow shot from a tree on Mount Tam, and put out the idea that maybe Ryan and his dog Hank could help the Mill Valley cops search the woods for clues. Those guys didn't currently have a K9 unit over there, so they'd appreciate the gesture.

Pierce nodded. "Good idea, Hayes. You're a team player and have leadership ability. I'm thinking you could be our next captain, so try to avoid getting shot tonight."

"Your pep talks need some work," Terrell said with a jaded smile.

CHAPTER 46

In the parking lot of the yacht harbor, Gwen sat in her car and watched the *Far Niente* through a small pair of opera binoculars that she often used at sporting events.

She could just barely see into one of the boat's windows, through a narrow spot between two curtains that were not fully closed. She spied on Jake and Kelli and watched them drink champagne and then slow-dance to some music. It wasn't long before they began kissing each other. Now they were making love on the couch. As Gwen watched them, she began talking to herself.

"So, you can afford to pay thousands of dollars a month to support a playmate girlfriend. You've probably been doing this since the day we met. I'm glad I had an affair during that photo shoot in Jamaica, now that I see who you really are, you jerk."

Gwen took some deep breaths and felt a panic attack coming on. Opening her purse, she took out a three-by-five photograph in a frame behind a piece of glass. The photo was of Gwen and Jake in happier times. She also brought out a razor blade and a small piece of folded paper that was about the size of a packet of sugar, but was filled with a very different kind of white powder.

She carefully unfolded the paper and tapped out some of the powder onto the glass. She used the razor blade to chop the powder up into a fine dust and form it into two lines, then rolled up a twenty with practiced ease and snorted the cocaine up her nose. One line of powder disappeared up the left nostril, and the other line went up the right nostril.

The car stereo played a mixed collection of sad breakup songs and as Gwen listened to the lyrics about the suffering and regret of lost love, she began to accept that she'd made a mistake beyond repair when she'd wrecked her relationship with Jake. There was nothing she could do to take back the things she'd said and done to him. He might forgive her, but he would never love her again like he once had. And he'd truly loved her, so much—she realized that now. Another woman would take her place, and he'd forget all about her. Why had she done all those awful things to him? What had she been thinking?

Tears came to her eyes as she slowly moved the razor blade toward her wrist and pressed it against her flesh. One slash across her veins, and all this would be over. That might make Jake feel bad, like he'd made a mistake in leaving her. Maybe it would ruin his life forever. Gwen felt the cold, sharp steel touching the thin veil of skin that was the only thing between her and death. Then she closed her eyes and felt her body shudder as she pressed harder on the blade. Seconds passed, but Gwen took a deep breath and realized she couldn't go through with it. The thought of the painful sawing across her skin and the resulting spray of warm blood made her queasy. She started crying and cursing Jake and that evil tramp Kelli.

Gwen reached into her purse and removed the pistol Jake had given her for protection. A bullet into the roof of her mouth would end things faster. One click of the trigger and it would be done. Jake would find her here in the morning … and then he would be very sorry. Her death would haunt him forever.

The irony was that Jake had given her the pistol after a frightening night when a stranger had tailgated her car, trying to run her off the road. She'd called him on her phone, afraid for her life. He'd rushed to find her and slammed his car into the man's bumper, sending his car spinning into a ditch. Jake had gone into a rage and beaten the man, saying that if he ever threatened another woman, Jake would find him and kill him. After that night, Jake had insisted that she learn to fire a pistol and carry the weapon with her at all times.

Gwen's heart ached when she thought of how Jake would never

protect her again, never hold her in his strong arms, never listen to her or understand her like no man ever had before. He would never again make her laugh, or sing to her, or make sweet love to her the way only he could. And although there was no way to get him back, it just wasn't fair that another woman would have him now, especially her modeling rival, Kelli.

The pistol felt cool in Gwen's shaking hand, and in a moment of clarity, it occurred to her that if she was going to die tonight, then Jake and Kelli should die too. They could all go out together.

As the drug coursed its way through her nervous system, the bitter taste of the cocaine dripping from her nasal passages into the back of her throat was making her gag a little. She twisted the cap off another single-serving bottle of white wine and gulped down the whole thing in one long drink.

"If I can't have Jake, nobody can have him," Gwen said, slurring her words, as she opened the car door and stepped out on shaky legs.

Gwen walked slowly toward the *Far Niente*, holding the pistol in her right hand. She gritted her teeth and almost fell down. Everything was clear to her now. She would surprise Jake and shoot him first, before he could stop her. Next, she'd make that slut Kelli get on her knees, beg for her life, and then put a bullet in her pretty face anyway.

This was right, this was good, and it would straighten everything out. Gwen stumbled in a daze down the wooden dock, getting closer and closer to the boat. In a few minutes, everything would be okay. The world would stop spinning and she could be at peace at last.

Gwen saw some movement near her right side, a shadow passing nearby. She waved the pistol, and a dog appeared out of the dark, like a ghost.

The dog quickly took her right hand in his mouth and bit down on it, not hard enough to cause any damage, but enough to cause her pain and make her drop the pistol and jump back in fright.

The dog moved forward and stood over the pistol, protecting it with his body, one paw on either side of it. He looked deeply into her eyes and growled low in his throat while showing his sharp teeth. He then began slowly walking toward her, with the fur on the back of his neck standing up in warning.

Gwen backpedaled quickly away from the dog, but he followed her closely, growling all the while. One of her feet slipped on a wet board on the dock and she fell backward on her rear. The dog continued coming toward her, and she felt panic rising in her throat as she got up and ran for her life. She could hear the panting of the dog close behind her, but she made it to her car, got inside, and closed the door.

Gwen started her car and drove straight at the dog, trying to run over the beast from hell. The dog dodged out of the way and stared at her with those unnerving wise eyes. Gwen drove off into the night, cursing and wiping tears from her face while she played more sad songs on the car stereo and drank another small bottle of wine. Driving erratically, she crossed the center line on the road several times, almost causing head-on collisions with other cars.

"The hell with Jake and that backstabber Kelli," Gwen said. "Someday they'll all be sorry, and they'll pay for this. It's not over yet."

~

Outside the yacht, Cody padded quietly along the dock, holding something in his mouth. He went onboard the stern of the *Far Niente* and placed the item off to the right side of the sliding glass door. Gwen's pistol glinted in the moonlight as it sat there.

Cody could have torn off Gwen's hand with his teeth, but he'd felt there was something wrong with her ... she was a sick puppy who needed help. He wouldn't hesitate to kill anyone who threatened his alpha or his pack. He would also defend any people he'd been ordered to protect, such as the floral-scented woman who was on the boat at the moment. However, he was an intelligent dog, and in this situation, he'd made his own decision based on training, instinct and something more ... something unexplained.

Cody sat and watched the harbor area as he sniffed the air and listened to the sounds of the night and the ocean. This life by the water was much better than his previous tour of duty in the hot and dangerous desert, far away from the land of his birth. He was glad to be back home in America and to be living with the alpha named Jake, the man with the dog eyes that looked into his own eyes and understood his thoughts and feelings.

On most days, Cody missed his former alpha, Stuart, but a war dog sometimes lost brothers and sisters in the fighting. Cody felt in his bones that this was where he was meant to be at this time in his life. He knew that Jake also missed their mutual friend Stuart. That was a bond the dog and man shared.

Cody stretched out prone, rested his head on his paws, sighed and closed one eye, keeping the other eye partway open and trained on the dock. If anyone else approached the boat, he'd be ready for them.

CHAPTER 47

Zhukov was holed up in his luxurious hotel room, where he exercised, drank black tea, and plotted out the complex plan for his next murder. As the dinner hour approached, he went to the closet and selected some clothes. He changed into a charcoal-gray suit with a tailored shirt, a silk tie, and calfskin shoes. Looking in the mirror and approving of what he saw, he headed out for his dinner meeting wearing a pair of soft black leather gloves and pulling a small suitcase on wheels.

A uniformed doorman saw Zhukov going out through one of the hotel's side doors. "Good evening, sir, may I hail a cab for you or assist you with your bag?"

"No, thank you," Zhukov said. "My driver is picking me up." Zhukov handed a large bill to the man and smiled as he passed him. He walked two blocks away and turned down an alley. Halfway down the alley, there was a row of large trash dumpsters he'd seen earlier. He entered a code into the combination lock on the suitcase, and a sizzling sound started coming from the inside. Small wisps of smoke began escaping from the zippers. He lifted the lid on a dumpster, tossed the suitcase inside, and closed the lid. Inside the dumpster, the suitcase continued to sizzle and smoke as another acid packet burst open and melted the suitcase's contents.

Zhukov walked farther down the alley and saw a homeless-looking man step out of an alcove. The man appeared to be in his early twenties and was wearing a filthy red-and-black checkered flannel shirt and threadbare, dirty jeans. His long black hair had not been washed for some time. He was holding a rusty knife, and his hand was shaking, either from fear or from the desperate need of a drink.

"Hand over your wallet and nobody gets hurt," the man said. Then he coughed hard, and his eyes watered.

Zhukov smiled calmly at him and said, "You have it backward, my friend. Somebody gets hurt, and nobody hands over their wallet."

The man's eyebrows furrowed in confusion and Zhukov leapt at him like a tiger. Zhukov's knee crashed into his groin and he grabbed the man's knife hand and twisted his wrist. The man dropped the knife and started to scream in pain, but Zhukov threw a controlled punch to the man's throat, and the only sound that came out was a high-pitched wheezing. The man fell to the ground, gasping for breath, with his one un-sprained hand holding his crotch.

Zhukov dropped a few twenty-dollar bills next to the man and then calmly walked to the end of the alley. As he walked, he pulled and straightened each of his shirt cuffs. He saw no reason to kill the unfortunate fellow who was down on his luck, although it would have been a simple thing to put more weight and follow through on that blow to the throat. He only killed people he was paid vast sums of money to kill, or anyone who might make him angry. This thirsty bum had merely been a slight inconvenience, not someone who deserved his full fury and creative genius.

Looking to his left and right, Zhukov stepped out onto the street, walked another block and hailed a cab in front of a hotel he'd never visited before. He gave the taxi driver the address of another hotel a few miles away. Once there, Zhukov called Banks and told him where his driver could pick him up. Banks said it would be a black limousine with a red ribbon tied to the antenna. Banks gave Zhukov the mobile phone number of the driver in case there was any need to talk to him. This was the worst part for Zhukov. He was at a known location and had to loiter there waiting for the car. He called the driver's phone.

"Yes, sir?"

"When you pick me up, arrive alone, put your windows down and pop the trunk. If I'm attacked by *anyone* tonight, my secret backup team will kill you and your family and everyone in your hometown—do you understand?" Zhukov said.

"Yes, sir, understood sir."

"Good man."

Zhukov ended the call, crossed the street and went inside a small convenience store. He picked up a newspaper and pretended to flip through it as he looked out the window.

Minutes later, Zhukov saw the car pull up to the curb. The windows were darkened and he couldn't see if anyone else was in the car. He called the number of the driver again and said, "Go around to the back of the hotel and park there."

The driver started to say something, but Zhukov ended the call. He left the small store and went around the corner and down a side street, then called the number again and told the driver to leave the hotel and drive down the side street slowly with all of his windows rolled down. When the car passed by the dark doorway where Zhukov was waiting, he stepped out and pointed his pistol close to the driver's face.

The driver stopped the car and appeared unfazed as he felt the barrel of the weapon press against his ear. He said, "Good evening, sir. Feel free to inspect the vehicle before entering."

The driver moved his hands slowly and carefully as he pushed a button that popped the trunk. Zhukov looked into the car and the trunk, and did a quick check underneath. He pulled out the backseat and looked below it before he sat down. Once he was seated, he kept his pistol barrel pressed against the back of the driver's neck.

The driver remained calm as he asked, "Shall we go now, sir?"

Zhukov nodded at the driver in the mirror and said, "If I hear any odd noise or feel any slight bump, my finger will pull this hair trigger, and your brains will spray all over the windshield."

"Yes, of course, sir," the driver said. "In that case, I'll turn off the music and try to avoid running over any potholes."

The driver had nerves of steel. Zhukov had to give him credit for that. As they drove off into the night, Zhukov thought the driver appeared to be from India, speaking English with a British accent. He was dressed in an expensive suit and had a stylish haircut. Zhukov was mildly impressed with this kid. He would bet money the man was well armed and trained to kill.

No words were spoken as they made their way into Chinatown. When they arrived at the address of the dinner meeting, Zhukov looked up and down the street but didn't see any restaurants ... only apartments and shops.

His cell phone buzzed, but the caller ID didn't show any number. He knew by the time on the clock that it must be Banks checking in. He didn't much like Banks or his little group of ultra-wealthy sociopaths. However, the man and the organization paid extremely well and gave him a lot of latitude to carry out his assignments, so he politely put up with them, for now.

Zhukov answered the phone. "I'm here at the address, but I don't see a restaurant."

Banks said, "It's a very private restaurant with no sign outside, and no menu; located in the building with the round red-and-gold door."

"I see the door."

"That's the entrance. Now be a good man and please don't shoot my driver. He is quite a valuable asset and virtually irreplaceable."

"Are you observing me right now as I'm pointing my pistol at your driver's head?"

"No, I simply know you well enough by now, and it was a reasonable assumption."

Zhukov smiled and glanced around at windows and rooftops, looking for any possible threats. He got out of the car and nodded at the driver, who then drove away. Zhukov thought he could use a driver like that on an occasional assignment.

While Zhukov walked over toward the round red door, he spoke into his phone. "So, are we having some fancy chow mein for dinner?"

"Come in and see for yourself."

Zhukov ended the call and came close to the round door. He heard heavy locks unlatching and the door swung slowly open on silent brass hinges. The door had a small peephole at eye level and a square metal plate at waist level that looked like a gun port on an armored car.

Zhukov casually crossed his arms and slipped his hand under his suit jacket and onto his pistol in its shoulder holster. He watched the empty space between the door and the frame grow wider as the door opened. He was prepared to kill anyone and everyone inside the door if they made the slightest threatening move against him.

CHAPTER 48

At police headquarters, Chief Pierce explained the plan for the evening. Terrell was to go into the city's Tenderloin area and attend a party where several drug dealers would be present. This went far beyond the drug squad's problem. One of these gangs was murdering the competition on a weekly basis, and it was up to the homicide division to stop the killing.

"You'll be playing the part of a man recently released from prison," Pierce said. "You resemble him except he's a lot better looking than you."

Terrell nodded and smiled, unfazed at the typical friendly insult from his boss.

"The parole officer has the man on ice in a safe house for some fabricated violation. Nobody knows where he is."

Terrell frowned. "I won't railroad people with false charges."

"He'll be released tomorrow … cleared of all charges, a free man."

Terrell listened as Pierce explained his role, the hotel he'd be staying in, and the pistol he'd be carrying. "That's the building they call the Heroin Hotel, right?"

Pierce nodded. "There are drugged-out people sleeping in the halls and nonresidents coming and going at all hours making drug buys. The rooftop is known as the shooting gallery. Every morning it's littered with used needles from people shooting up drugs the night before. There's always a lot of other trash there too. Condoms, underwear, empty booze bottles, you name it. Watch your step."

"I remember when a junkie was murdered there last year. The place had leaky toilets, a broken elevator, mice, cockroaches, and bedbugs. It was a real fleabag."

"I'm glad you've seen it already. That way it won't be such a shock to your sensitive nature."

Terrell nodded his head, pretending to agree. He liked it when Pierce ribbed him. It reminded him of his days in the Marines. "One question, Chief. How come all I get to carry is a Saturday night special pistol, while the criminals are probably carrying assault weapons like TEC-9 machine pistols converted to full-auto?"

"You have to carry a typical dime-a-dozen gangbanger pistol because that's what everybody else has. But we'll load it up with hollow-point rounds for you."

"But don't you think these druggies expect me to be heavily armed, or else I look like I'm a pussy or an outsider? I should have a serious weapon on me."

"Look, I understand that gang types expect you to show your manhood with your firepower. But I don't want to risk having them take a Mac-10 or something similar away from you, that they might use to shoot at our people in the future."

Terrell was insulted. "Nobody can take my weapon away from me unless they kill me first."

"And you being killed is a very real possibility," Pierce said. "This is a dangerous assignment."

"Which is exactly why I need a serious weapon."

"You can carry a Saturday night special in your pocket like every other criminal. That is the most common weapon. In spite of all the publicity about assault weapons, a plain old cheap handgun is what almost every criminal uses, day in and day out. You know that's true."

Terrell nodded resignedly. Day to day on the job, Terrell carried one of the standard sidearms issued by the SFPD, the SIG Sauer P229. It was manufactured in Exeter, New Hampshire, and it truly lived up to its "To-Hell-and-Back-Reliability" claims. It was super reliable, accurate and concealable. It fit his hand like a glove and was the best damned pistol he'd ever fired. His firearms instructor called it "the

Cadillac of pistols." Plenty of Special Forces teams all over the world used SIG pistols. Carrying anything less caused Terrell's heartburn to flare up.

"Yessir, Chief," Terrell said. "I'll go sign out the Saturday night special pistol now and get to work on my disguise."

As Terrell walked down the hallway, he mumbled profane complaints that he wished he could say to the chief but never would.

CHAPTER 49

In Chinatown, Zhukov watched as the red door opened to reveal a large, muscular Chinese man who was dressed in a well-tailored suit and tie. He bowed silently at his guest, gesturing with his big calloused hands and a tilt of his head to please come inside.

Zhukov gave the man an appraising glance and recognized someone who could easily kill you with his bare fists. The man had a handsome face, except for a nose that had obviously been broken at least once and maybe twice.

The man returned the same kind of appraising glance at Zhukov and gave a formally polite smile in recognition of a fellow member of the private club to which all violent killers belong. With the understanding of the potential for high-level deadly force having passed between them, the two men entered a beautiful foyer and the big man closed the door.

Zhukov slowly stepped up a wide red-carpeted stairway with shiny brass handrails on both sides. At the top of the stairs, he saw a reception area with a large crystal chandelier above. On the left was a four-foot-tall, painted porcelain vase that featured pastoral scenes from China's five thousand years of history. On the right stood a breathtakingly attractive Chinese woman with a face like royalty, wearing an embroidered silk dress and gown in the ancient traditional *Hanfu* clothing style of the Han nobility. She bowed her head and greeted Zhukov in Mandarin. Her musical voice sounded like she was reciting poetry, and although Zhukov didn't understand a word, it was clear that she was inviting him to go with her.

The woman moved with the grace of a ballerina as she led the way through the room with Zhukov following behind her. They passed some low tables that were about the height of a coffee table, where well-dressed and wealthy Chinese guests sat on flat pillows on the floor.

Zhukov was taken to a corner where Banks was seated on a pillow waiting for his arrival. It was apparent there were not going to be any chairs provided for him or anyone else, only seats on the floor. He was intrigued and decided that if Banks was content to sit on the kind of pad you'd see on a hardwood chair, he was too. Plucking at the creases in his expensive slacks at mid-thigh, Zhukov squatted down on a pillow across the low table from his current employer.

"Thank you for getting here a few minutes early," Banks said. "If you are late to this dinner, they don't open the door and you lose your hard-to-get reservation and high-priced prepayment. Once per evening, Monday through Saturday, every guest at this restaurant is served the same meal, all at the same time. I am told it is quite a delicious feast."

"I'll take your word for it, you being the food expert," Zhukov said.

Another intriguing Chinese woman approached the table who appeared as if she'd stepped out of a thousand-year-old painting of a warrior princess. She placed a small porcelain cup of clear liquid in front of each of the guests, bowed her graceful head, and retreated.

Banks picked up the small shot-glass-shaped white cup. "This is a strong alcoholic drink to begin the meal and promote digestion. It is called *baijiu,* and is distilled from sorghum grain. The Chinese usually share toasts at feasts and fine meals such as this."

Banks raised his cup. "After I say the toast, the custom is to tap the bottom of your cup on the table and then drink the shot in one gulp."

Zhukov raised his cup in the same manner.

"*Gānbēi,*" Banks said. "In translation, that means dry glass, or what we would refer to as bottoms up."

Zhukov repeated the toast, and they both tapped their cups on the tabletop and drank the shot of fire water. It burned going down and made Zhukov feel warm all over.

Banks said, "This powerful drink is an example of why this establishment is poetically named the *Eat and Drink Too Much, Live Fast, Die Young, and Leave a Good-Looking Corpse* dinner club—or some such, roughly translated."

"That name really rolls off the tongue," Zhukov said.

"We are the only non-Chinese guests here tonight, so we want to be polite and follow their traditions," Banks said.

"You know me—I'm always the quiet and polite one," Zhukov said.

Banks raised an eyebrow, shook his head, and smiled. Zhukov smiled too. He enjoyed bantering with Banks. The man was well read and world-traveled and had a good sense of humor, unlike so many of the other contractors.

"I'm intrigued by the attractive people that work here," Zhukov said. "What is their story?"

"These men and women come directly from China and are descendants of various people who worked at the royal palace of a famous emperor from long ago," Banks said. "The emperor selected the best and brightest men and women to serve him, those with long ancestries of noble bloodlines going back thousands of years. They say that some of these people look similar to famous historical figures seen in paintings and books. And that is because they are indeed direct descendants of those historical figures."

A gong sounded and the kitchen doors opened. Out came waiters and waitresses all dressed the same way in matching blue pants, white silk shirts, and blue silk brocade Mandarin jackets with gold buttons. They pushed chrome metal carts on wheels, the kind you'd see in a dim sum restaurant, but these carts each held a silver platter featuring a mountain of steamed white rice.

"Ah, here comes the first appetizer now," Banks said. "The meal will begin and end with a bowl of white rice. Never eat all of the rice in your bowl, it is considered rude. They will refill it for you if it gets low. Also, at the end of the meal, they will serve a full bowl of rice. Leave it all in your bowl to show that you are full and satisfied."

Zhukov nodded his head and glanced around the restaurant, his interest piqued. As the appetizer cart approached, he said, "If I didn't know better, I'd say that mountain of rice almost looks like it has scorpions crawling all over it."

"You have a good scientific eye for arthropods. Yes, those are deep-fried scorpions and they are very popular at Beijing's Donghuamen Night Market. You've got to try them."

"No egg rolls, huh?"

"None, I'm afraid. We'll start off with these flash-fried scorpions and then enjoy all kinds of exotic meat and seafood dishes."

A male waiter with a noble, handsome face parked a cart next to the table. There were a half dozen of the crispy creatures swarming lifelike on the tall mound of steamed white rice. The waiter gave each of the men an individual bowl of rice and used chopsticks to expertly pluck two scorpions off the mound of rice and place one on top of each of their bowls. Next, he set down a variety of small dishes filled with savory dipping sauces and left the guests to enjoy their food.

Banks picked up his rice bowl and held it near his mouth with one hand while he used the chopsticks in his other hand to pick up the scorpion. He bit off one of its front pincers and chewed it as he set the rest of the scorpion back in the bowl. He smiled and nodded at Zhukov as he ate, then smacked his lips. "It's quite good; try it, you'll like it."

CHAPTER 50

Police Sergeant Cori Denton sat on her couch, drinking a gin and tonic. She received a text message from a cop friend linking to a news story featuring a video of Jake Wolfe. He was at a multimillion-dollar home on Mount Tamalpais, where another attorney had been murdered, this time with a crossbow arrow. There were videos and photos of Jake with a blond woman.

"There he is at the scene of the crime … again," Denton said. "And he saves a near-naked damsel in distress. How convenient. This guy is looking more like a suspect in these murders every time I see him."

Denton sent a text message to Kirby. He didn't reply, the lazy bum. It was in the evening hours during his time off, but so what? She drank down the rest of her gin and tonic in one long gulp and went to the kitchen to get another. This time she skipped the tonic and drank from the bottle. The straight gin burned her throat and lit a fire in her belly. She took another drink and wiped her mouth with the back of her hand.

Her phone buzzed again—her mother. She cursed and answered the call. "What do you want now, Mother? Are you out of cash again?

"Just enough to pay my electric bill," her mother said.

"Every time I give you money, you spend it on booze and smokes."

"Life has been hard for me, ever since your father left us."

"Well, I hate him as much as you then, because if he'd stuck around, maybe he could have stopped you from hitting me. And I remember every time you hit me. Every. Single. Time."

"I just wish I'd taken my birth control pills that night you were conceived," her mother said.

"Thanks, Mom, love you too. Have a heart attack, okay?" Denton ended the call. There was a sharp knife on the kitchen counter. She picked it up in her right hand and held it against her left bicep. Her skin was scarred from previous cutting sessions. "I hate everyone," she said and started to cut her arm. Blood dripped down to her elbow, and drops fell onto the countertop.

Denton saw her reflection in the kitchen window, and it looked like the image of someone else, someone she didn't know. Who was she now, and what was she turning into? She blamed everyone but herself, and her eyes darkened as she thought of the people she hated—her mother, her boss, and especially Jake Wolfe. She couldn't stand the sight of his face.

"Damn them all," Denton said.

She cut her arm again … and again.

CHAPTER 51

At the restaurant, Zhukov looked at the fried scorpion on top of his bowl of rice, then shrugged his shoulders and picked up his set of chopsticks. He was somewhat awkward handling the chopsticks, but he managed to get the scorpion near his mouth and bite off a pincer. He chomped on the crunchy item and then took a drink of tea.

"These are quite large, crunchy and salty—and surprisingly tasty," Zhukov said. "They are like ... dark meat lobster. If lobsters had dark meat."

"They really are delicious," Banks said. "Thank you for trying them. We need to at least taste a portion of every dish or we'll cause great insult to our hosts. It would be unfortunate if the chefs were offended and decided to poison us or use their meat cleavers on us."

"These scorpions really do seem unusually large and dark. What kind are they, do you happen to know?"

"They are black Asian forest scorpions. Usually, they're simply deep-fried and salted, much like French-fried potatoes. But these are special because the chef bought only the largest of the large scorpions, quickly flash-fried them in very hot peanut oil infused with garlic, then dusted them with a seasoning of herbs and spices and served them with these rare and delectable dipping sauces."

They both tucked in and started biting off scorpion arms, legs, heads, and tails, dipping the morsels into some of the sauces and making low growls of approval with each one they tasted.

"So why did you invite me to this dinner meeting?"

"Simply to make you an offer; I was wondering if, when this job is complete, you might consider working for me exclusively."

"Work for you alone, not for your business group?"

"Yes, I have plenty of *jobs* that would keep you busy and well paid. You'd make even more money than you are already."

"I'll give it some serious thought and get back to you."

"Splendid, and perhaps after dinner we can enjoy a nightcap of brandy and cigars. I'd like to have a private meeting and discuss a few details of the current project. My associates have been asking some questions."

Zhukov, the inscrutable Russian, said nothing and his face revealed nothing. He did not agree nor disagree.

A waiter returned to clear their dishes, and then another waitress brought out two plates full of what appeared to be prawns.

"These are called drunken shrimp," Banks said. "And you may notice that the wiggling sea creatures are still barely alive, writhing in agony."

"And do we wait until they expire, or eat them while they are alive and suffering?"

"Oh, alive and in pain, of course. The only challenge is picking them up with chopsticks while they are squirming around in their death throes. I imagine I can hear their quiet cries, so sad." Banks deftly picked up a wriggling shrimp and popped it into his mouth, then chewed happily.

Zhukov looked at the shrimp on his plate for a moment and then made an effort to pick one up. It took a few tries, but he managed to get a grip on one and set it on his bowl of rice. He lifted the bowl to his face and scooped the wiggling shrimp into his mouth. Once he'd chewed and swallowed the squirming sea creature, he said, "Somewhat disturbing, and yet quite delicious."

The dishes that followed included starfish fried in shark oil, duck's foot webbing, fish air bladder, bird's nest soup, goat lungs with red peppers, pickled snakes, seahorses on a stick, and dog brain soup.

When the last dish was served, Zhukov said, "Dog brains? No, I don't think so, that's just wrong."

A waiter removed the plates from the table, and another waiter appeared with a platter of fruit.

Banks helped himself to some Mandarin orange sections. "When they serve fruit, it is a signal that the dinner has come to a conclusion and it is almost time to leave."

"That's one way to solve the problem of guests who don't have the sense to know when to leave a party. Will they bring us the check or is it all prearranged?"

"The thousands of dollars per person for this rare dinner must be paid in advance when the reservations are made."

Zhukov raised his eyebrows. "That was quite an investment in cuisine. Thank you for inviting me to dine with you."

"I enjoyed sharing the experience with someone who is open-minded enough to try interesting foods."

An astonishingly attractive cocktail waitress appeared, wearing a beautifully embroidered cheongsam-style, red-and-gold silk dress. She set down two small curved cups, then bowed politely and walked away.

"This after-dinner drink is a one-hundred-year aged Yanglin Feijiu liqueur that was invented by a famous herbalist doctor in China," Banks said. "The recipe is a secret, but it is rumored to include jujube, chrysanthemum, dried orange peel, cloves, and raisin tree fruit. It gets its green color naturally during fermentation from bamboo leaves, fennel, and pea leaves."

Zhukov held up his cup of liquor and nodded.

"*Gānbēi,*" Banks said.

They banged their cups on the table and tossed back the exotic drink in one gulp. Zhukov tried to act casual, but this was a new experience. His throat was burning and his head was spinning from the rare concoction. After a minute, the roaring in his ears faded and he was able to stand up and follow the crowd on their way out. The staff of handsome and beautiful servers all lined up and bowed deeply at the guests as they walked past and headed down the stairs to the round red door.

At the bottom of the stairs, the large and dangerous-looking man stood next to the open door and didn't say a word. However, when Zhukov passed by him, they made eye contact for a second and each gave a slight nod—a message of mutual respect between deadly fighters.

Once outside, Banks and Zhukov saw dozens of men dressed in black suits, standing in positions up and down the street to ensure the safety of the people who were leaving the restaurant. Banks gestured to his limousine parked at the curb with the driver standing next to it, waiting. As they walked toward the limo, Zhukov said, "I could use a well-trained driver like that at times."

"In London, there's a special school for these drivers, males and females from many nationalities, but mostly English, former SAS military men," Banks said. "I'll give you the contact information if you'd like. But right now, let's enjoy some brandy and cigars and the discussion of business in my limousine."

"I'm sorry, but I don't wish to discuss my work at this time," Zhukov said. "I appreciate the fine dining, and I will think about your generous offer of exclusive employment, but I will not reveal my plans to anyone."

Banks looked thoughtfully at Zhukov. Out of the corner of his eye, he noticed the assassin's right hand poised as if it was ready to draw a weapon.

"I understand ... I'll explain that to the Council," Banks said.

"I'm glad you grasp the importance of secrecy in my work, and you're not making the mistake of pressing me for answers."

"No worries, I wouldn't do that to you. Now my driver will take you wherever you wish to go. Good evening."

Banks made a motion with his hand, and the driver of a similar limousine parked nearby got out of the car and held the back door open. Banks walked over to the limo and got inside. The driver then closed the door, got into the front seat and drove away.

Zhukov looked around at the windows above him. There could be a shooter in any one of them but he wasn't worried; he was wearing the latest high-tech bulletproof vest under his shirt. He raised his eyebrows at the driver. The man nodded his head in understanding and lowered all of the windows and popped the trunk.

Once Zhukov had completed his inspection of the vehicle, they began driving on their roundabout journey through the city, with Zhukov's pistol barrel pressed against the back of the driver's neck.

CHAPTER 52

After midnight, inside the building nicknamed the Heroin Hotel, Terrell was doing his best to act like he was a criminal. He drank from a forty-ounce bottle of malt liquor, smoked some cannabis, and gambled with dice, along with the rest of the fine folks there.

He tried in vain to listen and pick up clues about the recent murders, but so far he'd wasted his time. This angered him because he could be home asleep in his own bed, curled up next to Alicia. He knew she was unhappy about it too. She'd shared her feelings about his job many times during their arguments. Alicia would say yes, somebody had to do it, but why did it have to be him? She had a valid point, but there was something about working in law enforcement that had a strong draw for a particular kind of person. Terrell couldn't explain it, but he knew it when he saw it. People who worked in law enforcement and first responder positions in public service were the ones who couldn't turn away when they saw something bad happening. They were the type of men and women who ran toward the twin towers in New York while everyone else had fled toward safety. What kind of people did that? His kind of people—men and women like him.

Terrell was just not able to put his head in the sand like an ostrich and pretend there weren't bad people out there doing terrible things … people who needed their asses kicked hard. That was what had caused him to join the Marines, and it was also what had made him want to be a police officer. But working in law enforcement was often a stressful, difficult, and thankless job. No wonder the divorce rate and alcoholism rate were so high for cops compared to so many other professions.

His thoughts were interrupted when someone said, "Here, do a line of coke."

"No, thanks, I'm good," Terrell said.

"Come on, what's your problem?"

"How do I know it's really coke? That could be meth, or roofies."

The man cussed him but Terrell just shrugged. His head was hurting, so he went outside to have a cigarette. He replied to the text from Jake that he'd received earlier—Jake was probably asleep, but they texted each other at all hours of the day or night.

Jake was sleeping in bed next to Kelli on the *Far Niente* when his phone made a unique series of vibrations that only occurred when Terrell was texting him. He sat up in bed and looked at the text.

Thanks for the K9 tip. Chief liked it. Ryan and Hank will help the MVPD search. Meanwhile, I'm on undercover duty in the Tenderloin, drinking a 40-oz.

As Jake looked at his phone, Kelli got out of bed and went into the head. Jake sent a text to Terrell.

You're living the dream.

When Kelli came out, she was wearing her dress, holding her purse and smiling fondly at Jake.

Jake wasn't exactly sure what was going on, why the rush. He smiled. "Got a really early manicure appointment?"

Kelli laughed softly and shook her head at him. Cody started barking and growling in a way that warned Jake there was a stranger approaching. A few seconds later, a security system speaker beeped.

Jake pulled a pistol out of a thick hollowed-out constitutional law textbook about the Second Amendment. He moved so suddenly that Kelli let out a little shriek.

"Don't worry, Kelli, this is simply for your own protection." Jake gave her a reassuring smile as he pulled on a pair of pants.

"Please be careful, Jake. I texted my limo driver to come here and pick me up. Don't shoot him."

Jake nodded, then turned on the TV and adjusted it to show a night vision video feed of the dock. A large Hawaiian-looking man wearing a suit was walking slowly toward the yacht with his hands held out to his sides in plain sight, quite purposely and politely.

"Is that big island bruddah guy your driver?"

"Yes, that's Mano Makua, one of the nicest guys you'll ever meet … as long as you don't make him angry."

"I'll keep that in mind. He's a big, solid guy. Was he a wrestler or something?"

"He told me he used to be a ukulele player in a Hawaiian group that played live music for hotel luaus at Waikiki Beach, but then a foreign corporation bought the hotel and switched to cheaper recorded music. He moved to the mainland and got this job as a limo driver."

As Jake moved about, he noticed Kelli staring at all of the scars on his bare chest and back. He grabbed a t-shirt and put it on as he walked through the salon area and out the sliding glass door at the stern of the vessel. Cody followed him and snarled at the approaching man. Jake commanded him to stand by and wait for a threatening move from the intruder. Cody stopped barking and stayed by Jake's side, but he kept his eyes on the visitor, ready to attack him at the slightest provocation.

"What can I do for you?" Jake said. He held the pistol in his hand but didn't point it at the man.

"Mano Makua, limo driver, here to pick up Miss Kelli."

"Do you play the ukulele?"

Mano stared at Jake for a moment and then glanced at the pistol and the growling dog. He took a breath, raised his eyebrows and said, "Why do you ask?"

Jake smiled then and put the pistol away in the back of his waistband. "Kelli said you do. I play the guitar, so maybe you and I could jam to some Hawaiian songs."

Mano finally smiled. "Sure, we could jam sometime if you've got good beer."

"I've got some Longboard Lager and Pipeline Porter from Hawaii."

"Well, all right, then."

"Mano is a Hawaiian name, isn't it?"

"Yeah, it means shark," Mano said, and he smiled, showing his teeth.

Kelli stepped onto the dock, put her arms around Jake and gave him a long kiss. Mano took several steps down the dock to give them some privacy.

"Jake, you'll always be my knight in shining armor," Kelli said. "But I can't be tied down right now. I have to go to Hollywood and put my blond ambition to work on my career. I hope you understand."

"Of course, but if you ever find yourself in a bikini and handcuffs again, you know who to call."

She laughed and kissed him again, as if one of them was a sailor going off to sea for a year. Then she set off, walking barefoot up the dock toward the parking lot, with Cody trotting along protectively beside her.

Mano and Jake waited a moment before following Kelli. Mano said quietly, "I don't think I've ever seen her act this way. Just FYI, if you were to break her heart, I'd have to break your neck." He gave Jake a big smile.

Jake returned the smile. "The same goes for you."

When they reached the parking lot, Jake opened his Jeep and took out Bart Bartholomew's long overcoat. He held it up for Kelli to put on, and she kissed him again. Cody put his head under Kelli's hand and she petted him.

The two men shook hands and exchanged business cards. "Hawaiian beers and a ukulele jam on the boat," Jake said.

"I'll look forward to it, and I'll bring the Maui Wauwie ganja," Mano said.

Kelli patted Cody on the head one last time and said, "Cody, you take good care of Jake for me, okay?"

Cody barked once and nodded his head.

Mano opened the limousine's door for Kelli, and she got into the backseat. When they drove off, Kelli looked back at Jake from behind the darkened windows.

It occurred to her that Jake was the only man she'd made love to in recent memory where she hadn't closed her eyes and fantasized about a movie star. She wondered about the days to come. If she made love to some famous actor in Hollywood, would she close her eyes and fantasize about Jake?

~

Jake stood there and watched the limo take Kelli away. He had a lot of mixed feelings, but he was sure of one thing—he'd never met anyone quite like her before. In retrospect, he realized that she'd "loved him and left him," in a way similar to what many men did to women. He smiled and shrugged. That was okay; she'd helped him break free of his past with Gwen so he could move on with his new life.

Jake called to Cody, who was sniffing around the area. The dog trotted over to him and the two of them walked back to the *Far Niente*. Cody went inside, walked in a circle three times, and curled up on the floor near the couch. Jake started to follow Cody inside the yacht, but he stopped when he saw something on the deck, off to the side of the sliding door, in a shadow. The dark shape looked like the purse-sized pistol he'd given to Gwen some time ago.

He took a small Swiss Army knife out of the coin pocket of his jeans, opened the blade, put it through the pistol guard and picked up the Glock 26. Going inside, he locked the door behind him and brought the pistol to Cody. "Did you leave this by the door for me?"

Cody sat up, sniffed the pistol, and then barked once and nodded his head.

"Let me guess, you caught Gwen coming to the boat to shoot me with this and you disarmed her without injury," Jake said.

Cody growled at the pistol and then flopped back down onto the floor and exhaled loudly. He raised one eyebrow at Jake as if to say, "Duh."

"Nice work, buddy. Thanks."

Jake walked to the stateroom, put the pistol in the drawer of his nightstand and climbed into bed. Cody stood up and followed Jake, got onto his dog bed, stretched out, and closed his eyes.

While Jake slept, he dreamt that he and Kelli were living on the *Far*

Niente and sailing around the Hawaiian Islands. She was wearing the pink bikini and heart-shaped sunglasses. He was in board shorts and flip-flops. They drank cold beers and Jake played the ukulele while Cody sat on the deck and occasionally barked at passing dolphins. Off in the distance, dark storm clouds were gathering over rough seas, and Jake was heading straight toward them.

CHAPTER 53

Zhukov drove the car around in the dark, crisscrossing the streets of San Francisco and scouting out an escape route relating to the attack on his next target, the female lawyer. He'd had to change the plan and improvise a bit, due to Jake Wolfe's meddling. That fool was a distraction and a pest that needed to be exterminated.

His phone vibrated with a text from Banks. He didn't want to communicate with the bothersome snob right now, but it was probably best to just get it over with. He was passing by a quiet parking lot, so he pulled in and read the text.

Banks wrote, *Sorry for the late hour, but the Council has formally requested that you and I have a quick meeting tonight. I propose that we do it while we enjoy the cigars and brandy that I'd mentioned earlier.*

The words *formally requested* were a code that meant it was a condition of Zhukov's employment contract and he was required to do it if he wanted to get paid.

Zhukov texted a reply. *It's bad timing right now. I'll text you in a few minutes.*

For a moment, Zhukov debated about where to meet with Banks and his driver. He could go park the car at a hotel and then walk or take a taxi to another hotel. But this parking lot was quiet and he'd seen a taxi stand a few blocks away. With a fatalistic shrug, Zhukov parked the car in a numbered space, got out and walked over to the old-style pay kiosk. The lot was the type that didn't have a full-time attendant; someone just stopped by a few times a day to collect the cash. Zhukov put some bills into the slot and walked several blocks away to the taxi stand, where he caught a cab.

After changing taxis and locations twice, as was his habit, Zhukov sent a text to Banks and met up with the limousine, driven by the same Indian man with the British accent. The driver pushed a button and all the windows rolled down and the trunk popped open. Banks was sitting in the backseat, bemused at this precaution and how quickly Zhukov had trained his driver to do it for him. Zhukov checked the trunk and then got into the backseat next to Banks. The windows went up and the limousine drove off. When they were underway, Banks pressed a button that raised the privacy partition up between the driver and the backseat.

"May I offer you some cognac and a cigar?" Banks said.

"That will do nicely, thanks," Zhukov said. "Speaking of cigars, I happen to have a couple of special ones with me if you'd like to try them."

Zhukov reached into the inside breast pocket of his suit jacket and produced a slim black leather cigar holder. He opened it and took out two 97-rated Padron 1926 cigars.

"Those are fabulous cigars. I'd be honored to take you up on the offer," Banks said. "And allow me to provide you with a snifter of Hennessy XO Extra Old Cognac."

"Good choice—one of my favorites," Zhukov said.

They lit the cigars and poured the cognac. Banks puffed and exhaled and said, "Ah, the characteristic Padron flavor. These cigars are hard to find. You must have paid a premium for them."

"I got what you might call a real *steal* on them," Zhukov said.

"The reason for this talk is that the Council is getting concerned," Banks said. "They are asking you to give them an exact time that the woman will be shot."

"Tell them they should not push me," Zhukov said. "It will be done very soon, at a time and place of my choosing."

"I tried to explain that to them."

"Tell them I was planning to kill Jake Wolfe in his sleep tonight, but you and your Council interrupted my work with this impromptu meeting."

"Sorry about that. I'll ask the Council to avoid meddling in your work. They are a demanding group of individuals and they lose patience quickly."

"I'm losing patience with them as well."

"My concern is that they could vote to have you replaced with another contractor, and if I'm outvoted there is nothing that can be done about it."

Zhukov gazed at Banks for a long moment. "Let me show you something."

He tapped his phone screen several times and held it up so Banks could see it. The phone displayed the live feed from a video camera. A man was standing in a landscaped garden with his back to them, smoking a cigarette.

"See that person facing away from us?" Zhukov said. "Now watch the back of his coat."

Banks looked at the video on the phone and saw a round green circle with crosshairs appear on the man's back, the type a sniper would see while looking through a rifle scope that had an illuminated reticle.

Zhukov moved his finger over the phone's touchscreen and the crosshair reticle roamed over the man's back and then settled on his head.

"That targeting crosshair is from one of my remote-controlled weapons, similar to the crossbow that killed Max Vidallen from afar," Zhukov said. "This crosshair is inside the camera lens and is not visible to anyone but us. The man and his bodyguards have no idea I'm pointing a weapon at him."

Banks saw the crosshair image vanish, and then the man turned and walked a dog on a leash. When the man faced to the right, Banks recognized him as one of the Council members from France. He was a dealer in priceless paintings, a multimillionaire, and a supposedly untouchable man.

Banks felt himself beginning to sweat as he realized that Zhukov could kill the man right now by remote control from the other side of the world. He could probably kill any of the Council members just as easily, including Banks himself.

"That man goes out to that garden on his property at all hours of the day and night," Zhukov said. "He smokes his Gauloises and walks his dog. Sometimes he makes a phone call and I can hear his side of the conversation. He must be an insomniac, because he is there regularly, no matter what time it is or what the weather is like."

"Quite amazing, I must admit," Banks said as he made an effort to keep his composure.

"Perhaps I should kill him right now as you watch, just to send a message to your Council," Zhukov said. "If I press my fingertip right *here*, with one touch on my phone screen, I can blow his head off."

"That won't be necessary. This has been demonstration enough, simply more proof that you are the absolute best in the business," Banks said. "No need to send the message. I'll tell them you are following your plan and they need to be patient."

"I have many other surprises like that, installed all over the world, just waiting for a signal from me," Zhukov said. "Or if I should unexpectedly die or disappear and not check in for a set amount of time, the signals will come from an automated computer system on a botnet that I have set up to avenge my death. Modern technology is truly frightening, isn't it?"

"Indeed, and ingenious. I'm impressed," Banks said. A drop of cold sweat trickled down the back of his neck, and his hand shook as he took a much-needed drink from his snifter of cognac.

CHAPTER 54

On the *Far Niente,* Jake's phone vibrated with a text message, pulling him from his dreams. Cody opened one eye and gave Jake a tired look. Jake groaned in protest, but then he thought it might be Kelli or a friend in need, so he grabbed the phone. Surprisingly, the text message was from his favorite taco truck. "I wasn't expecting a text at this hour from my taco and burrito connection, but let's see what Luis has to say," Jake told Cody.

The text said, *I think I just saw the murder suspect from your news story.*

Jake texted back: *Is he there now?*

No, he parked a car nearby and walked away on foot.

Did he see you?

No, should I call 911?

No, stay out of sight. I'll bring the police.

Gracias.

De nada.

Jake made a call and got Terrell on the phone.

Terrell was smoking a cigarette in the hotel parking lot. He answered the call. "You're up late."

"My friend Luis at the taco truck sent me a text," Jake said. "He thinks the attorney assassin parked a vehicle near their truck and walked away. I told him I'd bring the police, and that's you, super-cop."

"I'm sure he just imagined he saw the guy, the same as so many of the false sightings we get," Terrell said. "But let's go check it out. There isn't anything happening here at the Heroin Hotel except for folks pissing their life away. It's pretty sad. I'm outside right now because my room is what could be more accurately described as a condemned outhouse. I took a taxi here and walked the last several blocks, so you'll have to drive by and pick me up."

"I've heard of that place; it sounds like some fancy accommodations for sure. I'll get my shoes on and head in your direction."

Jake was tired from a long day, some good champagne, and a great amount of physical and emotional exertion with Kelli on his couch and again in his bed. He felt like he could barely walk, but he'd made a promise, so he and Cody got into the Jeep and drove off. Once Jake was on the road, he called Terrell again. "Okay, I'm on my way. What's the address?"

Terrell recited the address, and his room number.

"So, you don't like your sweet room, or roomy suite, or whatever it is?" Jake said.

"It sucks, big-time," Terrell said. "I went back inside and I'm sitting on the disgustingly filthy bedspread right now. Get me out of here, and hurry up. I'm hungry."

"What are you doing there anyway? Did Alicia kick you out of the house for smoking?"

"No, fool, I'm on a stakeout, trying to get evidence for a homicide investigation. I've spent hours drinking and gambling with killers and pimps and hoes."

"Drinking forties with shorties, huh, player?" Jake said.

"Chillin' like a villain; someone has to do the tough jobs," Terrell said.

"The taxpayers thank you for partying for the public good."

"These druggies sleep all day, make more money in a month than I do in a year, and they don't pay any taxes. It's just wrong."

"Until they get killed or get sent to prison."

"I'm not cut out for the gangsta life. I just want to go home, curl up to my woman and get some sleep."

"You sound drunk if you ask me," Jake said.

"Well, I didn't ask you, did I?" Terrell said. "But of course, I have been drinking and smoking quite a bit. You have to play the part here, or you're a dead man."

"Good thing you have lots of practice at that drinking thing—you'll fit right in."

"I knew it would come in handy someday. You were always a big help with all my practice drinking too, so thanks for the assist with the near-endless homework."

"Happy to help; plan ahead, that's what my mom always told me."

"You should have listened more to your mom. Maybe then you could be here, living the dream at the Heroin Hotel."

"I'm always missing out on opportunities," Jake said. "Like if only I had gotten that college degree where I'd have majored in weather prediction in the Mojave Desert."

"It's too late now. Some other weatherman got the easy job you could've had in the Mojave," Terrell said. "Every day the same forecast: dry and hot as hell. You could just phone it in, actually be living someplace nice like Colorado."

"I love Colorado. Just thinking of that awesome lost career makes my balls hurt."

"Try buying a larger size of boxer shorts. Maybe that'll help."

"Maybe that's what my balls have been trying to tell me."

"Have talkative balls, do you?"

"Yes, in fact, they never shut up."

"Kind of like you," Terrell said. "But speaking of balls, that reminds me—I've got to piss a river after drinking that forty of malt liquor, or was it two forties?"

"My bet is on two forties, and double-strength alcohol malt liquor hits you kinda like … twice as much," Jake said.

"But double-strength beer means half as many trips to the bathroom."

"There you go with the mathematics again. Okay, go make a river and I'll be there in five minutes."

"Five minutes is cutting it close."

There was the sound of water splashing and Terrell said, "I'm hanging up now so I don't drop my phone in the toilet … again."

CHAPTER 55

When Jake arrived at the address, he stopped the vehicle and looked around. The building appeared as if it should be condemned. Terrell should have been standing out in front. That was the plan, and Terrell usually stuck to the plan, yet he was nowhere to be seen. Jake sent a text message to Terrell's phone. No reply. He tried calling him, but the call went to voicemail.

Maybe Terrell was still in the bathroom. Jake gave the horn one good toot and waited. Someone looked out a window and seemed to wave something, maybe a pistol. Jake ignored him. He'd seen way worse things pointed at him out of windows—such as AK-47s and shoulder-launched rockets. He told Cody to stay put. Cody growled, but he obeyed. After locking the Jeep, Jake walked over to the room that Terrell had mentioned.

It was a good thing the room was on the ground floor and not up on one of the higher floors. Climbing those flights of stairs was not on Jake's list of fun stuff to do right now. Jake quietly knocked on Terrell's door. No answer. He knocked louder, trying not to wake up the entire building while he was at it. Not that everyone was sleeping anyway. There were many rooms with lights on in the windows, and he could hear music and laughter coming from up on the roof. He called Terrell's phone again; still no answer.

This situation was highly unusual. You could say what you wanted about Terrell, but he was as reliable as a Swiss watch while doing his job. When he and Jake had been a team, they'd worked together like a well-oiled machine.

Jake wiped the layer of dust and grime off a small section of the window and peeked in through a slim opening between the drapes. There was Terrell, sitting on the couch, his chin down on his chest. He'd actually nodded off like sleeping beauty. Terrell was only in his late twenties, but he was getting civilized and couldn't hold all that booze like these younger gangbangers who did speedy drugs half the night and then slept until noon.

He tried the doorknob. No good, it was locked. He banged on the door, hard. Terrell just snored away. Jake called and texted his friend on his cell phone again. No answer, no movement. He tried to open the door with a credit card. No luck. He wrenched the doorknob back and forth and up and down. It didn't release. Terrell must have had a long bar lock jammed up against the doorknob and braced against the floor. Smart man, good for him, but now what?

Jake tried pressing on the sliding window and getting it to jump the track. It didn't work. Someone had stuck a wooden dowel on the track, and it was holding the window very tight against the frame. *Note to self,* Jake thought. *Never try to break into the hotel room of a police officer. It's not going to happen.*

He went to the Jeep and got his trusty aluminum baseball bat out of the back cargo area. He always carried it, along with a first baseman's glove, a softball, and an SF Giants hat. The equipment was just a cover story for him to carry the metal bat, in case the time came when he needed to hit something hard—really hard. Right now was one of those times.

Jake thought it might be a mistake, but he didn't care. He swung the bat down in a controlled arc onto the doorknob and broke it clean off on the first try, making a loud pinging sound. Then he hit the knob area of the door again with a horizontal home run swing, and the door burst open and slammed against the near wall.

Jake was feeling impatient right about then, and without thinking things through he yelled at his best friend, "Wake up and get your tired ass out here, fool!"

Terrell had already awakened with a start when the bat had first hit the doorknob. He'd pulled his pistol and taken cover behind the bed. Now he yelled, "Hands where I can see them, or I'll shoot!"

Jake had quickly stepped back behind the wall next to the door. He said, "Grinds, it's Jukebox, hold your fire."

"Dammit, Jukebox, I almost shot you."

"That's why I'm not standing in the doorway."

Meanwhile, other doors in the building began to open. Angry residents stepped out onto the balcony walkways. One giant of a man spoke in a drunken voice and said, "You better have a good reason for yelling at me to get my tired ass out here."

It occurred to Jake that perhaps yelling in the middle of the night in front of this fine establishment was not the best idea he'd ever had. It was time to beat a hasty retreat to the safety of the Jeep. As Jake walked briskly in that direction, more doors opened, and additional men stepped out. Some of them were holding bats, golf clubs, pool cues, tire irons, and similar types of blunt implements. People of all races, colors, and creeds came toward him and they all had one thing in common: they wanted to beat him to a pulp.

Other residents looked out of windows and laughed at the spectacle unfolding below. This was going to be an entertaining show.

"Not good," Jake said. "When will I learn to keep my big mouth shut?"

Jake would've liked to stay a while and cheerfully apologize for the unwanted wake-up call, but he was almost to the Jeep, and decided it would be a wiser course of action to simply leave immediately. How did he always seem to get himself into situations like this?

He got into the Jeep, locked the doors, revved the engine and put it into reverse, then backed up next to the door of Terrell's room. Terrell recognized the vehicle and came outside. Jake saw him appear next to the front passenger door, waving a cheap-looking pistol around. Terrell pointed the gun at Jake and yelled at him loudly enough so everybody could hear. "Fool, open the door to my ride before I pop a cap in you. You're the worst driver I've ever had working for me."

Jake unlocked the passenger door so Terrell could open it. Then Jake put his hands up and said loudly, "Okay, boss. I apologize for yelling. Don't shoot me."

Jake heard shouts from the building's tenants, saying such things as "Shoot him anyway," and "Let me whack him with this golf club."

Fun stuff like that.

As Terrell climbed into the front passenger seat, he called out again. "I'd shoot him, but he's my only driver at the moment. Not worth a damn, but you can't find good help these days."

There was more yelling from the balconies. One man said, "Let me bust open the fool's head and my nephew Darren can be your driver. That way he can have a job and pay me back the money he owes me."

One gang member with a shaved white head who had taken some money from Terrell in a card game said, "You're leaving before you try to win back some of your losses?"

"I've got to go collect some cash from my bitches and then I'll be back to win everybody's money," Terrell said.

Jake hit the gas pedal and pulled away before Terrell even had his door all the way closed.

"Not worth a damn?" Jake said.

"Home, James." Terrell snapped his fingers twice.

"Collect some cash from your bitches?"

"Don't tell Alicia I said that. I was playing the part of some strange pimp guy I supposedly resemble."

"Okay, but I don't give rides to strangers."

"You are mighty strange, but we're not strangers."

"Oh, really, have we met before?" Jake said.

"No, but I took a dump once that looked kind of like you," Terrell said.

"That must have been a good-looking dump."

"I gotta tell you, Dale Carnegie, you really know how to win criminal friends and influence criminal people."

"Yeah, well, you were a lot of help there, passed out like a college frat boy at his first beer pong party."

"Thanks for blowing my cover, too."

"No, you are well known but not blown."

"Kind of like your love life?"

"Now they just think you're a pimp."

"I hate pimps," Terrell said.

"Me too. Let's go find a pimp and beat his pimp ass until he stops his pimpin' ways," Jake said.

"I stayed up late soaking up cheap malt liquor like a sponge, and now my head is splitting," Terrell said. "This career path I'm on sucks."

"That's all you have to say for yourself? You could have shot me by accident back there, waving that cheapo pistol at me."

"What gratitude, after I saved your worthless self from those rudely interrupted criminals. If you had half a ball, you wouldn't have needed my help anyway."

"And if you hadn't passed out, it never would have happened in the first place."

"Why do white people have to be so dramatic? You're a friggin' drama queen. Besides, there wasn't even a round loaded in the chamber of this pistol, see?"

Terrell pointed the handgun out the open window in the direction of a dumpster they were driving past and pulled the trigger.

Instead of a quiet click from the pistol of Terrell "it's not loaded" Hayes, it boomed as it fired a round of ammo. When the bullet hit the dumpster, it caused an incredibly loud clang and made Jake imagine what the biggest gong in Asia must sound like—at two in the morning.

Car alarms began to wail in vehicles parked nearby. Dogs started barking. Lights went on. People shouted. Somebody shrieked. A man pointed a shotgun out of an apartment window. A homeless man who'd been asleep in the empty dumpster lifted the lid and looked out in a daze. He was wearing a red-and-black checkered flannel shirt and he had unwashed long black hair. His mouth formed the words, "What the hell?"

"Nice shooting, cowboy," Jake said as he broke the speed limit in the empty streets. He grabbed a tall cup from the cup holder and gave it to Terrell. "I brought you some cold coffee. Drink it."

Jake thought it was probably a good thing he hadn't shared any of his exploding nitro bullets with Terrell. He had a few of those that he'd been given by some guys he knew in the Kidon Unit of the Israeli Special Forces, when he'd done them a favor during a deployment. The hollow rounds weren't actually filled with nitroglycerin—it was too volatile. But they'd been nicknamed "nitro rounds." They were similar to the Mk 211 high-explosive incendiary/armor-piercing ammunition (HEIAP) used by Navy SEALs in their XM107 .50-caliber sniper rifles. Except that this particular ammo contained a new and secret explosive compound, only known to the intelligence community and a few of their black ops friends. It was highly illegal for Jake to have them, and that was 'nuff said about that.

Terrell stared at the smoking gun and frowned at it like somebody had played a trick on him. "Apparently, the loaded chamber indicator on this junky pistol is not indicating squat."

Terrell then carefully clicked on the safety and placed the gun on the dashboard.

"Shooting a dumpster is going to look really good on your resume," Jake said. "What have you been smoking?"

"I suppose I may be just a bit sobriety-deprived at the moment," Terrell said. "And your driving is not helping my headache. In fact, now that I think of it, maybe hanging around with you is the cause of my headaches."

Jake spoke in a voice like a television drug commercial and said, "If you are experiencing these symptoms, ask your doctor if *four-twenty* might be right for you. Side effects include getting the munchies and not giving a—"

"Shut up and step on the gas," Terrell said.

CHAPTER 56

When the Jeep approached the lot where the taco truck was parked, Terrell reached for his pistol and coffee cup, taking one in each hand. He stared at them and said, "Let's see, pistol goes in pocket, coffee goes in mouth. All set."

"Glad you got that straight," Jake said. "Nothing gets by you, even with a hangover."

"That's why I get the big bucks. I am a highly trained professional," Terrell said. "And for your information, I can't be hungover if I'm still drunk."

"Words of wisdom."

"Okay, maybe I do have a blistering hangover and I'm simply asking the media to respect my privacy during this difficult time."

"Are you feeling any better now that I bought you a cup of gourmet coffee?"

"I have the feeling of impending doom that comes from hanging out with you, but otherwise, I'm okay," Terrell said. He took a sip of coffee, made a face and said, "Tastes like ass."

"You know what ass tastes like huh?"

"Even worse than ass, if that's possible."

"Artificial ass flavor number five?"

"So where did the perp go? My head hurts and I just want to shoot him and be done with it."

"I like your plan; keep it simple. My buddy's text said the suspect parked here and then walked away. Maybe he's at a nearby hotel."

"Or he just abandoned the car and isn't coming back. That would be okay, because it would mean I can go home to my fine woman and my comfortable bed."

Terrell's phone vibrated. Someone on the night shift had sent him a link to a news video of Jake getting hugged by a woman who was wearing a bikini. Terrell watched the thirty-second video clip, then played it again and held the phone up so Jake could see it. "What is it with you, anyway?" Terrell said. "Do you use Jedi mind tricks to make women like you?"

Jake shrugged. "What can I say? One woman told me that she dated me because I could make her laugh."

"With the way you seem to attract women like a babe magnet, why did you put up with Gwen's angry tantrums for so long?"

"Uhh ... because I really believed I was in love with her?"

"Another case of positive thinking gone wrong," Terrell said. "Better to think negative—that way you're never disappointed."

Jake pulled over near the parking lot and texted his friend Luis in the taco truck to let him know he and a policeman had arrived. He got a text in reply saying the wanted man had left a Dodge car in the lot. He'd walked away going east and had not returned so far.

Jake texted: *Thanks, Luis.*

The return text said: *This is Guadalupe. Luis and Maria's daughter. My parents are not here. I'm the one who has been texting you, not my father.*

Jake: *Oops, sorry, have we met?*

Guadalupe: *No, I've been away picking crops. Earning money to pay for college.*

Jake: *We're going to search the area now.*

A flashlight went on and off twice inside the taco truck window, with the light pointed toward the Jeep.

Jake and Terrell exited the vehicle, with Cody following along by Jake's side. They quickly scanned the surrounding street, windows and rooftops for threats. Jake clipped a leash onto Cody's collar and they all walked toward the taco truck.

The truck's door opened and a college-aged Latina woman stepped out wearing a faded t-shirt and yoga pants. Her hair was mussed and she wasn't wearing any makeup. It appeared that she'd been sleeping in the truck. Jake's guess was that it was probably illegal, as everything else was nowadays, but her secret was safe with them.

The young woman said, "I'm Guadalupe. You must be Señor Jake. My parents told me you were a friend and if there was ever any trouble, I should contact you."

"Yes, I'm Jake. Nice to meet you, Guadalupe. Where are your parents? Are they okay?"

"They were taken by *la policía*. An officer came and told my parents their restaurant permit expired a week ago. When my parents argued that they already paid the annual fee and were waiting for the sticker to come in the mail, they were accused of *resistirse al arresto*. My mother and father are in the San Francisco County Jail right now."

"That's not good. I'll see what I can do to help them. What was the name of the officer?"

"*Señora* Denton."

Jake felt his heartburn flare up at the mention of Denton.

Terrell said, "Is she saying her parents got arrested? All I know how to say in Spanish is enchiladas and cervezas."

"Denton came here and handcuffed her parents and took them to jail," Jake said.

"That's ridiculous. Why was Denton here? She's supposed to be working on homicide cases, not arresting burrito-making working mothers."

"*¿Por qué la policía vino al restaurante?*" Jake said.

Guadalupe looked at Jake sadly and pointed at him. "The police woman came here because of you. She knew you bought food here with your debit card. She wanted my parents to tell bad lies about you and sign a statement. But they refused to betray you. Señora Denton got very angry."

Jake sighed. "I promise you I'll get your parents out of jail. I give you my word."

Guadalupe didn't believe him. The look on her face made that clear but she nodded politely at him. "When Denton pressured my parents to lie about you, they just kept shaking their heads and saying *thou shalt not bear false witness against thy neighbor*."

"Your parents are good people; they're like family to me now. I'll keep my promise to gain their freedom, you'll see."

"I'm sure I saw that bad hombre you're looking for. I recognized his face because I'd seen it on the news. The photo of when he was driving on the Golden Gate Bridge."

"Your text said he parked a Dodge?"

"Yes, that's the car right there." Guadalupe pointed at a Challenger. "Then he walked in that *dirección*." She gestured at the street that went east.

"Good work. We're going to find him."

Guadalupe still appeared skeptical. She gave Jake a quick appraising glance up and down from head to toe and back, then tossed her dark hair and closed the door. As the door was closing, Guadalupe looked Jake in the eye. She gave him a small, tentative, curious smile. She hadn't lost hope, not yet.

Terrell said, "I'll take a quick look at the vehicle while you and Cody scout around the parking lot."

"Good to go."

"Cover my six."

"Roger that."

Jake and Cody covered Terrell's back as they did a quick walk around the lot. Jake held his pistol close by his thigh as he did recon. Cody sniffed the air and the ground, searching for a scent trail.

Terrell carefully approached the Dodge. It was backed in with the front facing out, presumably for a quick exit. He carefully looked inside, then got down on one knee and looked underneath. It appeared to be free of booby traps, so he made a hand signal. Jake saw the signal, and he brought Cody close to the car. Cody alerted to something explosive near the driver's door. Jake studied Cody's body language and reached into his pocket for a tiny but very bright flashlight on his keychain. He shined it inside the car and looked around.

"Based on Cody's reaction, my best guess is there might be some grenades under the driver's seat," Jake said.

"But no C-4 and not rigged to explode I hope?" Terrell said.

Jake shook his head. "Probably a stash of frag grenades."

"Probably? That's very reassuring, professor."

"Don't touch the door."

"Wow, good advice."

"Is this the same car we saw on the way to the funeral?"

"Yeah, it looks the same. Order Cody to search for the driver. If we lose the trail, we can come back here and conduct a stakeout."

Jake leaned close to Cody and gave him a command to track the enemy.

Cody did as he was trained to do and sniffed the car door handle and the ground nearby. He let out a low growl and then sniffed the air. He looked at the street and pulled on the lead while holding his tail straight out.

"Seek, Cody. Seek, seek, seek."

Cody followed the scent trail out of the parking lot and down the sidewalk in the direction that Guadalupe had pointed out. Jake walked right behind Cody, holding the lead while Terrell followed them and covered their backs.

CHAPTER 57

Banks sat in the backseat of the limousine and sweated in fear because of what Zhukov had shown him on his phone. It was diabolical how Zhukov had set up a remote-controlled weapon, targeting one of the Council members.

Zhukov said, "Of course I have no reason to want *you* dead, Chairman, so there's nothing for you to worry about. You are my benevolent employer and the payer of generous sums of money, which I appreciate."

"Yes, of course. You and I have a good working relationship," Banks said, forcing his voice to remain calm. "I value your services, and you value how well I reward you for a job well done. It's only business, after all."

"It's a pity that not everyone on the Council is as appreciative, businesslike, and patient as you are," Zhukov said.

"I'll explain to them that you can't rush a great artist at his work," Banks said.

"Exactly, and I'm glad we had this little talk, even though it interfered with my plans to kill Jake Wolfe tonight."

Banks lowered the screen between the front and back seats and spoke to his driver. "Abhay, our meeting is successfully concluded. Please take our honored guest anywhere he wishes to go now."

"Yes, sir. My pleasure, sir." Abhay glanced in the rearview mirror at Zhukov.

"Abhay, is it?" Zhukov said. "I believe that's a Hindi name meaning brave and fearless. It suits you."

"Very good, sir, thank you, and where to now, sir?" Abhay said.

The limousine drove in a roundabout way, as was routine by now, and Zhukov told the driver to stop in front of a hotel he'd never visited before.

Zhukov got out of the car and said to Banks, "The thing you desire will happen very soon, I promise you."

Banks nodded, and his face showed his great relief at this reassurance. He was caught between the powerful council members and this killing machine of a man who could take your life from afar with a touch of his phone.

Zhukov walked away into the fog and darkness. He switched taxis several times and was soon within walking distance of the lot where he'd parked his car. He planned to approach the lot slowly, and if there was the slightest sign of trouble, he would slip away in the dark and steal another vehicle. Car theft was like child's play for him. But for some reason, he was feeling a fondness for the powerful Dodge at the moment. It was mostly the game that beckoned to him, matching wits with the smart people who worked in law enforcement. They were the only ones who really understood him and could offer him a challenge.

When he got to the parking lot, everything looked the same as when he'd left it. He was walking up to the car when he heard the sound of running footsteps rapidly approaching from down the street. It was then that he noticed a black Jeep parked nearby.

Zhukov pulled out his pistol and ran the remaining distance to the car. He pressed the remote control on the way, in case the car had been rigged to explode when the door was unlocked. There were no explosive surprises, so he approached and quickly checked underneath the car, and then under the driver's seat. As he was getting into the vehicle, he saw two men running in the darkness, along with a golden-haired dog. The men appeared to be carrying pistols and they were coming straight at him. They would soon be within firing range.

He needed to improvise a plan of escape. If he drove away from the armed men, they could open fire and shoot him in the back of the head as he tried to escape. That left him few options.

"When in doubt, go on the attack and kill the enemy," Zhukov said, quoting his former Spetsnaz Special Forces military instructors.

CHAPTER 58

On the way back to the parking lot, Cody alerted to a man up ahead of them who seemed to fit the height and weight profile of the suspect. He was heading straight toward the Dodge.

"Bogey at two o'clock," Jake said and held tight to Cody's leash as he started running alongside his dog.

"Roger that." Terrell ran off to the left to flank the target.

The suspect noticed them and sprinted to the parked car. Headlights came on and the car drove straight at them. The driver's arm appeared outside the window holding a pistol, and he fired several rounds at Jake.

"Something tells me that's our guy," Jake said.

"Oh, you think?" Terrell said.

Jake and Cody ducked into the gap between two parked cars to avoid becoming hit-and-run casualties. Terrell fired a round at the driver, and Jake got off a shot at the rear tire as the car roared past. The attack was over in a few seconds and it didn't appear that anyone was injured. Terrell had shot a hole in the car's windshield, but the driver smashed the glass out of his way with his pistol and kept on driving.

"Those must be run-flat tires," Jake said as he took off running toward the Jeep with Cody by his side. "I'm sure I put a round into one, point-blank."

Jake pressed the button on his car remote which started up the Jeep's engine.

"Maybe you missed point-blank," Terrell said as he ran beside Jake. "You had the driver and he's still driving."

"My SIG would have got him, but this junk pistol is worthless."

"Sure, blame it on the equipment."

"It's made by the lowest bidder—oh, wait, that's in the Marines."

They all climbed into the Jeep and drove after the escaping car. Terrell leaned out the passenger window with his pistol in hand, ready to fire at the escaping vehicle.

Jake drove the Jeep like he'd stolen it. The HEMI engine roared and they gained on the car ahead. "Shouldn't you call for backup?"

"I will in a minute," Terrell said. He pressed a button and opened the moonroof in the vehicle's ceiling. "Turret gunner time." He stood up on his seat with his upper body out of the moonroof. The wind blew in his eyes as he fired a round at the car ahead and missed. He yelled at Jake, "Give me your pistol. This piece of junk can't hit a thing."

Jake was taking a corner, and he said, "Wait a second, I've got both hands on the wheel."

Jake's pistol was tucked in between the driver's seat and the center console, but Terrell gave Jake an impatient look and then sat back down and rustled through the glove box in front of his knees. He saw a Smith & Wesson Model 500 Magnum, a .50-caliber revolver with a long barrel. It was the largest and most powerful production-made double-action revolver in the world. And highly illegal to own in the state of California.

"Ha, I knew you'd have an extra weapon in here, and this thing is *psycho*," Terrell said. He grabbed the pistol and stood back up in the moonroof.

"No, no, no," Jake said as Terrell leaned out through the moonroof again. "Stop, Terrell, those are exploding rounds!"

Just as Jake yelled, Terrell pulled the trigger, and there was a flash of bright light as the trunk of the car in front of them exploded in a ball of flames. The trunk lid blew completely off the car and flew through the air like a flying disk—right at their heads.

Jake yelled, "Get down!"

Cody and Terrell both ducked and Jake swerved the Jeep to the right, running up on the sidewalk, mowing down a parking meter and just barely missing a fire hydrant. The flying trunk lid shot past them, sizzling hot and leaving a smoke trail. It smashed into a Volkswagen, ripping the top off the car like a can opener and making it into a convertible. Jake drove on the sidewalk and then wrestled the Jeep back into the street through a gap between parked cars.

After the fleeing car's trunk had exploded, hundreds of green pieces of paper came flying out of the trunk like confetti, and some were on fire. Terrell sat down next to Jake in surprise as they drove through the green cloud. "Is it my imagination, or is that a whole lot of money?"

"Looks like major cashola, mister asshola," Jake said. "Let's stop and pick it all up so you can hire a good lawyer for shooting that illegal ammunition."

"You could have said something sooner, fool."

"I tried to, but you're just a trigger-happy police mofo."

Terrell growled something unintelligible.

Jake thought that the man just had no sense of humor when it came to stupid things he had to deal with through no fault of his own. Some hundred-dollar bills blew in through the Jeep's open windows and moonroof. Jake grabbed one of the bills and stuffed it into Terrell's shirt pocket.

"You're buying beers later," Jake said.

"Oorah," Terrell said.

Jake glanced over and saw the look of anger and violence on his friend's face. He'd seen that look several times before in bloody lands far from home. He knew there was no point in trying to talk logically to his buddy right now.

Up ahead of them, the fugitive took some more wild shots at the Jeep. Terrell said, "I'm really starting to hate this guy."

"Time for plan B or what?" Jake said.

"That *was* plan B ... It's time for plan F."

"What is plan F?"

"Go F-ing crazy," Terrell said in his combat voice. "I'm going to blow him away with these exploding rounds."

Jake knew that voice well. "Get down, Cody. Trigger-happy Terrell is going ballistic."

~

Cody barked once and hunkered down in the foot-well behind the passenger seat, where he could still see Jake. He kept his trained eyes on his alpha, watching him closely and waiting for orders. He was glad to be back in action with his Marine brothers. The smell of gunpowder made the fur on the back of his neck stand up. He showed his teeth and let out a deep growl. Cody wanted to sink his teeth into a terrorist, any terrorist—just point him in the right direction and he would do his job.

~

Terrell stood up in the moonroof again and fired at the car ahead. The driver of the fleeing car was now doing evasive maneuvers, after the surprise of the exploding trunk lid. Despite the fact that Terrell was drunk and high and both vehicles were jockeying for position, some of his shots actually hit pretty close to the intended target.

The first shot missed and blew a parked Vespa motor scooter into the air in a fiery explosion that sent sizzling scooter parts flying off in all directions. Another shot went high, flew past the car ahead and hit the window of a wholesale piano store. It made a deafening sound as the huge window shattered and a concert piano exploded, seeming to hit all of its keys at once, very hard. The resulting piano and percussion crescendo was enough to make Beethoven turn over in his grave.

"Shoot him when he turns," Jake said as he wrestled with the steering wheel. "You're wasting my boom-bullets, and you only have two left of the five. Get him broadside."

The car up ahead had turned a few times, but Terrell had been trying to line up a shot on the back of the driver's head when he was going straight, hoping to blow his brains out. Terrell bit down on his anger and kept his aim steady, and when the car ahead of them took a wild, fishtailing turn to the right, he was ready for it.

Jake yelled, "Brakes!" And he stomped on the brakes, trying to make the turn. That caused Terrell to lurch forward and slam hard against the roof, which knocked the air out of him. But he held tight to his pistol and kept his footing. He just grunted and used the pain to help him steady his aim. That's what made Terrell such a good shot. The power of focus. The wind on his face made his eyes water, and he wished he was wearing his shooting glasses as he lined up a shot at the car's passenger door.

When the car ahead of them turned, Terrell fired twice and the last two rounds hit the passenger door of the fleeing vehicle, directly in the center panel below the window.

The Jeep skidded sideways as Jake tried to make the sharp turn while going too fast. At that moment, he saw the car they were chasing implode in a cloud of fire and shattered glass, like a spectacular fireworks display.

The two exploding rounds caused the passenger door to be rammed inward and all the windows in the car to burst outward in a cloud of glass splinters. The car itself went up on the two left wheels and scraped against a row of delivery vans parked along the street, trailing sparks as it continued racing forward, out of control and on fire.

The side of Jake's vehicle slammed against a parked car and then sideswiped several more as he fought to keep the SUV upright during the turn.

The Dodge came to an abrupt stop when it ran into a parked truck. The front airbag deployed, and moments later, the driver got out, staggering on his feet with blood dripping from his nose and right ear. A chorus of car alarms started going off all along the street.

"Yes, I owned him!" Terrell yelled. "Who's the man?"

"Get some, you magnificent bastard," Jake said.

They saw Zhukov duck down out of sight behind the smoking wreck of his car and then reappear with a small backpack in his hand. He began throwing round-shaped objects in the path of the oncoming Jeep, one after another.

"Grenades out!" Terrell said.

"Going bootleg, hang on," Jake said.

Jake slammed on the brakes and screeched to a stop, put the Jeep in reverse and punched the gas as he gave his best effort at doing a J-turn in the tight area he had to work with. The wheels were smoking and hopping, and the Jeep's rear end fishtailed to the left as the front end lurched to the right.

Terrell just hung on for dear life.

Jake kept one foot on the brake and one on the gas as he cranked the steering wheel. This situation was reminding him of combat, where everything was always going ass-backwards and FUBAR, but you had to win anyway.

Jake could tell they weren't going to be able to spin completely around and reverse course, so he steered and drifted sideways toward an alley between two closed businesses. It didn't look like the Jeep could fit in the gap between buildings, or straighten out in time to even try. But Jake let off the brake, shifted from reverse into drive, and pinned the gas to the floor as he purposely sideswiped a parked car to help direct his drifting.

The Jeep shuddered, burned rubber, bounced off the impact and almost flipped over … but Jake purposely hit another car on the other side and straightened the trajectory in time to thread the needle and drive into the alley.

"Keep your arms inside the ride, kids!" Jake said.

Terrell yelled some creative profanity, dropped back into his seat and made sure his right arm was inside the open passenger window as Jake scraped both sides of the Jeep against the brick buildings on either side of the narrow alley.

The grenades behind them began to detonate one after another in the street and sent hot shrapnel tearing into everything within range. Cars got ripped apart, storefronts were destroyed, and windows exploded into clouds of razor-sharp glass. One grenade was a flash-bang, and when it went off it caused a flash like lightning and a bang like thunder. But it exploded out in the street, and the Jeep was spared the brunt of it in the alley.

"Reminds me of a nice Sunday drive in the MRAP, when we were overseas," Terrell said.

Jake didn't reply. He focused on racing the Jeep down the alley like a bullet going down the barrel of a gun, ripping off both side mirrors as he went, barely fitting between the buildings as they escaped the grenade shrapnel.

There were two plastic trash cans near the middle of the alley, and Jake crashed right through them, sending a blizzard of recycled plastic containers and empty beer cans flying into the air. A garbage dumpster had been left blocking the alley across the street up ahead, where Jake had been planning to go.

"I'd rather not die tonight, Jukebox," Terrell said.

"Don't worry, Marines never die, they just go to hell and regroup."

"Stop. The. Car. Now."

Jake pulled up on the emergency brake lever while stomping down on the brake pedal and deliberately scraping his side of the Jeep against the brick wall to slow it down. Sparks flew off the side of the Jeep, the tires squealed, and the vehicle came skidding out of the alley.

Jake took a hard left turn onto the street to avoid crashing head-on into the dumpster, and the Jeep drifted as it turned left and slid sideways. The right rear bumper scraped the brick wall and slowed the vehicle some more as Jake continued to pump the brakes.

The Jeep finally came to a stop while it was sliding sideways, but Jake couldn't prevent the right side of the vehicle from slamming up against the metal dumpster. It wasn't a life-threatening impact, but the small airbag to the right of Terrell's head inflated and smacked against his face. Terrell cursed and pulled out the knife he had strapped to his left forearm, then stabbed the airbag and deflated it.

"Stupid airbags," Terrell said. "Why is there one by the side of my head anyway?"

"Five-star crash safety rating, that's why," Jake said, and he hit the gas and drove down the street.

"This situation is really starting to get on my nerves."

"Cheer up; it will probably just get worse."

The Jeep's engine roared like a rocket as Jake drove full speed in the direction of the last known location of the shooter.

Terrell stood up again in the moonroof, waved the empty pistol and yelled like a drunken man in a bar fight.

"That's right, fool, don't mess with the SFPD or I'll put a nitro cap up your tailpipe."

Jake said, "Get down; you're out of ammo."

Terrell wasn't listening, so Jake punched him hard on the thigh. "Sober up and stay alive, Marine."

"Pfffffft, that didn't even hurt. You hit like a punk, but I'll sit down if it will calm your fragile nerves."

Terrell's thigh felt like it had been kicked by a mule. He turned to his right, looked out the window and made a pained face for a moment, and then turned back. "Got any more of those exploding bullets? Hand them over right now. I've still got an itch to scratch with this guy."

They came upon the scene of destruction and saw the smoldering wreck of the getaway car, but there was no sign of the shooter. Jake thought it was a good thing the streets in this business and warehouse area of town were deserted at this hour of the night.

"No, I don't have any more rounds for that, but take my pistol," Jake said. He patted his hand at where he'd stashed his pistol, and then he pulled over and stopped the Jeep.

"We lost him," Terrell said. "But he's on foot, so let's hunt him down and put a bullet in him."

"Roger that. I'll grab my shotgun out of the back and Cody can pick up his scent trail."

Terrell grabbed Jake's pistol while Jake got out of the Jeep and opened the back hatch. Jake kept a Remington 870 Wingmaster twelve-gauge pump shotgun stashed inside a long cardboard box that had a big picture of a leaf blower on the outside. He took the shotgun out of the box and then opened the passenger door to let Cody out. The dog quickly picked up the scent trail of the shooter and the three combat veterans jogged up the street. As Cody followed the scent, the men followed Cody, pointing their weapons in front of them and scanning doorways for motion.

CHAPTER 59

As the trio ran up the street, a Corvette drove out of a parking space with its headlights off and came roaring straight at them. An arm reached out of the driver's window of the car and started firing a submachine gun.

"Take evasive action and return fire," Terrell said.

"Roger that." Jake ran along behind a row of parked cars, firing rounds of buckshot over the tops of the vehicles. When he reached the last car, he crouched on one knee and commanded Cody to take cover. Cody sat behind the car while Jake leaned across the hood and fired another blast from his shotgun at the escaping Corvette. Terrell stood across the street and fired Jake's pistol.

As the Corvette was heading for a corner, about to turn out of sight, its rear windshield exploded, and its right rear tire blew out. Terrell and Jake fired additional rounds that riddled the Vette's trunk as it turned and roared away into the night. The car continued moving fast with its lights off and with the driver repeatedly ducking low to his right and then popping back up for a quick look ahead.

Jake ran up to the corner, reloading the shotgun with some hollow-point deer slugs from a web ammo holder on the stock. He looked around the corner and saw a street that went into a gated industrial area with lots of delivery trucks parked all around. The gate was a checkpoint, without easy access in or out. One truck up ahead on the inside was backing across the street at an angle so it could park at a dock. The truck would soon block both lanes, and the escaping Corvette would disappear as the truck cut off the view. Jake knew that a cloud of buckshot would not do here because a stray double-ought pellet could hit a bystander, but the deer slugs would work in this situation. Each round was a fat slug of lead the size of your thumb with a hollow core.

Jake rapidly fired and pumped the shotgun again and again. In his last glimpse of the escaping car, Jake saw it drive up onto the sidewalk out of control, bounce off a building and then regain the road. The freight truck then finished backing up and blocked the view.

"There's no other way into the gated area from this end," Terrell said. "Grenade boy will probably drive to the other end and carjack a delivery van or truck, and then disappear if he hasn't already."

"It looks like we might be hosed," Jake said. "But maybe you could try flashing your badge and telling that truck driver to move his rig so we can get past here and go inside."

Terrell shoved the pistol into the back waistband of his pants and was reaching into his pocket for his badge when a uniformed security guard came running out the door of a building and pointed his pistol at them.

"Drop that shotgun and put your hands above your head," the guard said. "And you ... take your hand out of your pocket, very slowly."

"I'm a police officer, lower your weapon," Terrell said.

"Yeah, sure, you cops must have changed the style of your uniforms, huh?" the guard said, looking at the gang-like undercover clothing Terrell was wearing.

Another truck drove up and stopped at the gate, blocking off the space between the security guard and Terrell, Jake, and Cody. The three veterans took off running to the corner and went around it, then ran fast to the Jeep. They drove away from the industrial complex, heading in the direction that shooter had been going.

"Maybe we can find one of the other entrances to that fort of a place," Jake said.

Terrell was looking at Google Earth on his phone while Jake drove, and he pointed his finger at a blinking beer advertisement on the roof of a tavern far off in the distance.

"Head toward that blinking sign way down there," Terrell said. "That may be the direction grenade psycho went."

"Good to go," Jake said and drove dangerously fast down the dark street that ran alongside the walled compound of warehouses.

Cody's ears twitched and he started barking. A moment later, his two human pack members heard the sound too. There were at least a half a dozen police car sirens off in the distance but approaching fast from all different directions.

"I don't suppose you ever made that call to HQ?" Jake said.

"I forgot to; it slipped my mind," Terrell said. "I was kind of busy *shooting*, you know, while all you did was drive like some dickhead on a Disneyland ride. You were supposed to remind me, anyway."

"Oh, so now it's my fault, malt liquor man?" Jake said.

"It's dawning on me that we're in a somewhat screwed legal situation here," Terrell said. "Not to mention I need a cigarette and I have a headache, and I need to take a piss like a river."

"Plan F didn't work, so we need to think of plan Z while we're driving," Jake said.

"I'll think, you just drive, because if you try to think and drive at the same time, we might crash."

"Okay, we're approaching the bar with the blinking beer sign. Where to now, tavern tour guide?"

"Turn left down that sketchy-looking street."

Police sirens continued to wail in the night. Nobody spoke as Jake drove blindly at frightening speed through the deserted area, and Terrell pretended he wasn't scared of dying due to Jake's test of his driving-while-blind capabilities. When they finally reached an area with streetlights, Jake slowed down a bit and glanced at Terrell. He was glad he didn't see any wounds or blood on his friend.

"You doing okay, Grinds?" Jake said.

"I make a living," Terrell said.

"No, I mean healthwise."

"I smoke too much and I have high blood pressure, but all in all I'm fit as a friggin' fiddle."

"What. I. Mean. Is. Did you get hit by any glass or shrapnel, maybe a bullet?"

"Oh, that. No I'm good."

"At least nobody is injured except old Betsy here," Jake said, patting the dashboard of his Jeep.

The roar of a helicopter flying overhead sounded through the Jeep's open moonroof. The sound got louder and louder, and soon they saw a police helicopter fly over their vehicle and hover above the main scene of destruction, shining a powerful spotlight down on the area. Police car sirens kept getting closer, and flashing lights were approaching from all directions like moths to a flame.

"Here comes more cavalry," Jake said. "Prepare to explain yourself, and make it good."

"The chief is not going to find this amusing," Terrell said.

Jake scratched his head like he often did when he started making up some blarney to bamboozle folks in authority. When Jake was growing up, he'd always been the guy the other kids had counted on to BS the teachers, parents, and adults as he tried to explain their way out of whatever mischievous but mostly harmless trouble they'd gotten into. That had made Jake the lightning rod for the fury of many uptight adults who liked to bully kids just because they could.

"When you were standing up in the moonroof, you tried to call HQ, but you dropped your phone and it fell in the backseat," Jake said.

"Right ... and maybe earlier when you called me to say hello, I told you to pick me up at the Heroin Hotel because my fun new criminal friends were not buying my cover story," Terrell said.

"Your life was in danger."

"I actually was in danger the entire time. What if, on the way home you wanted to drive past the taco truck and show me where you eat most of your meals?"

"And when we drove by there, we just happened to see the perpetrator, so we gave chase. We had to, didn't we?"

"He started shooting at us, so I had no choice but to officially commandeer your taxpayer vehicle and give chase, and then I stood up in the moonroof to return fire in self-defense. Maybe at that juncture, I tried to call it in, but I dropped my phone."

"Did you just say juncture?" Jake asked. "You really did get your money's worth at the hotel."

"I took one for the team," Terrell said.

"So you dropped your phone, and the next thing we know, the perp started tossing grenades out the window," Jake said.

"Grenade dude with an attitude had bags of frags," Terrell said.

"Call it in now, say we're in pursuit, need backup, code seven-eleven and all that cool cop stuff."

"But I shot illegal exploding bullets, how do I explain that?"

"No, you didn't. We can blame the exploding stuff on that weasel who tossed the grenades. That's what took out the Vespa scooter and the piano store."

"You media types are good liars," Terrell said. "That's something I've always secretly admired about you."

"Who would believe there was even such a thing as exploding bullets?" Jake said. "All that destruction was caused by grenades that the crazed perpetrator tossed out of his moving vehicle at us brave heroes."

"This is sounding better by the minute," Terrell said. "I like that heroes part. What was in those exploding rounds, anyway?"

"They're like the Mark 211 ammo our snipers used in the sandbox, but the explosive and incendiary stuff is way stronger. It's kind of like C-4 mixed with material from a phosphorous grenade, combined with a new pyrotechnically initiated fuse in the point."

"I'll take your word for it, Professor Boom-Boom."

"Get a wet wipe and some latex gloves from the first aid kit in my glove box."

Terrell opened the glove box and took out the gloves and wet wipes. "What now, wipe my butt with these so the folks in prison will appreciate my hygiene after the chief throws us in jail?"

"Use those to clean off that pistol and then give it to me," Jake said.

Terrell rolled his eyes at the obvious advice; he already had the latex gloves on and was cleaning off the pistol with one of the wipes.

"Why do you carry an illegal pistol loaded with illegal explosive rounds anyway?"

"I'm realizing now that it was not one of my brightest ideas. If you must know, I was saving that to fend off the zombie apocalypse."

Jake took a pair of leather gloves from the console and put them on. He tried to snap his fingers impatiently with the gloves on, but it wasn't happening, so he gave up and just held out his gloved hand to Terrell and shook it at him. Terrell slapped Jake's hand away and then finished wiping the zombie pistol clean. It was a revolver, so all the empty shells were still in the cylinder. Terrell pulled all five of the shells out of the pistol one by one and wiped them clean, then put them back into the cylinder. The shells were so large, he figured they were nearly two inches long.

"I cleaned off the shells too," Terrell said.

"No live rounds left in there, I hope," Jake said.

"No, the rounds were all fired so there's no live ammo."

"Those things can blow off important body parts."

"And you might need those parts later."

Jake turned the Jeep and drove down a dark alley, stopping halfway through near a steaming sewer vent. After Jake and Terrell did a quick look around for CCTV cameras, Jake opened the Jeep door and dropped the pistol down the drain along with the wet wipes and latex gloves. He heard a splash as the pistol sank underwater.

"That was a waste of an amazing pistol," Jake said.

"You're better off without it, unless you want to get arrested," Terrell said.

CHAPTER 60

While driving out of the alley and back onto the street, Jake said, "How about that phone call?"

Terrell called police headquarters. He took a deep breath and then spoke in a loud emotionless cop voice and acted like the action was still happening. *In pursuit of the suspect in the lawyer killings. Shots fired, grenades exploded, officer needs assistance.* The dispatcher informed Terrell of some related facts, and Terrell ended the call.

"He's long gone. Dispatch said a security guard at the warehouse area called in a report that somebody stole a truck and left behind a shot-up Corvette."

Terrell's phone vibrated. It was Chief Pierce calling. Terrell groaned, showed the phone to Jake and answered the call.

Pierce asked some tough questions. One thing led to another. Soon there was no denying the fact that Terrell had been drinking and had smoked some extra-strong cannabis. Jake was there with him, driving the Jeep. They'd been involved in some headline-making street violence and Terrell had no arrests to show for it. Pierce told Terrell to meet with him at 8 a.m. for a full report.

"I tried to tell you I wasn't the right guy for this undercover thing, but we'll laugh about this someday, Chief," Terrell said.

Pierce had already ended the call.

"We laughed, we cried, we blew things sky-high," Jake said. "I can't believe we let grenade weasel get away."

"I'm in deep weeds. The chief wants to see me in his office at oh eight hundred," Terrell said. "And he's mad at you too, wonder boy. You fired all those rounds from the shotgun and you missed grenade weasel, how?"

Jake shrugged as he continued to drive toward the scene of destruction. It was clear now that the new nickname for the shooter was going to be *grenade weasel*. Most of the time, these things just happened naturally. It was the work of some unknown science.

"Tell the chief you can't be there at that time. You have a breakfast appointment with, uh, your psychic."

"Sure, that could probably work. Nights like this make me wonder why I ever wanted to be a cop. The criminals can do any crazy thing they want, but I have to follow all these rules of engagement. And if I bend the rules the slightest bit, some committee gets all butt hurt."

"Is butt hurt covered by your cop health insurance?"

The helicopter above them flew in circles; when it passed by, it shone a spotlight down on the Jeep, blinding Jake for a moment.

"Not helping," Jake said and put a hand to his forehead to shade his eyes.

They were getting close to the street where the grenades had exploded. Terrell patted his front left shirt pocket again and shook his head. He drummed his fingers on the dashboard, obviously feeling the nicotine oppression upon him.

"I'm out of smokes. Could you just shut up and find me some tobacco before I punch you in the thigh like you did to me?" Terrell let out a loud breath and pressed his fingertips against his forehead.

Jake looked at the center rearview mirror and saw a police car coming up from behind them. He tried to glance at the side mirrors, but both of them had been broken off in the alley.

"We have a cop car gaining on us," Jake said. "Get that shiny badge out and on display in case we get pulled over."

Terrell took the badge out of his pocket, clipped it onto a lanyard and put it around his neck.

"Do I have a police cover in this hillbilly Humvee?"

"You put one in the pocket behind your seat."

Terrell reached back and found a black ball cap with the word POLICE on the front and put it on his head. It was not a regulation SFPD uniform cap, but it got the message across.

The police car roared past them on the left, with lights blazing and siren wailing. The driver had no idea who or what had caused the flames and destruction but was racing to the scene and ignored the Jeep. Jake looked over at Terrell and they both just shrugged. Jake noticed the look on Terrell's face and knew his friend needed some coffee and tobacco.

"Come to think of it, I might have a couple of those Macanudo Café Robusto cigars that are sealed in fresh packs," Jake said. "Check in the center console there, under a bunch of useless papers like my registration and insurance and stuff."

"You'd better not be playing," Terrell said.

"Nope, I remember there was at least one cigar left over from the last tailgate party. I kept it in the Jeep because I just knew you'd need a smoke one of these days."

Terrell rummaged in the console under his left elbow and found two cigars in foil pouches.

"Foil-sealed freshness without a humidor, you've got to love that."

"Yup, it's pure genius. Give me one of those, since there are two."

"I thought you didn't want anybody smoking in the Jeepzilla and you quit cigars to be all healthy and pure as the Virgin Mary."

"I may be a virgin, but don't call me Mary," Jake said. "Cigars can stain your teeth, raise your blood pressure, and give you mouth sores. But what the heck, it's a special occasion."

"What kind?"

"We didn't die."

"Okay, that is kinda special."

Flashing police car lights swept the street up ahead. Terrell used his razor-sharp knife to cut a thin slice off the end caps of both cigars. He handed a cigar to Jake and they both lit up.

The two men puffed on their cigars in the comfortable silence that best friends share, and Terrell drank the leftover cup of coffee.

They approached the scene of the explosions, holding the cigars out the car windows and blowing the smoke out there too, so as not to bother Cody.

Jake said, "I'm going to hunt down the guy who tried to kill us, if it's the last thing I do."

Terrell nodded. "I agree. Did I ever put that police light in your rig like I kept saying I would?"

"I think you said you were going to put a bubble under that seat."

Terrell reached under his seat and pulled out a dashboard beacon light that suction-cupped to the windshield. He set it up and turned it on, and the light began flashing in a similar pattern to that of the SFPD vehicles.

When they arrived at the wholesale piano outlet, Jake pulled over and parked. Terrell reached behind his seat, took out one of his police parking permits that he kept there with his hat, and tossed the permit onto the driver's side of the dashboard.

When the Jeep came to a stop, Terrell stepped out into the street, let out a loud burp, clenched the cigar in his teeth and then unzipped his pants and peed on the pavement. Every cop within shouting distance stopped what they were doing and started clapping in applause and whistling. One cop called out, "Nice work, Hayes. Did you catch the perp or just blow up this street for fun?"

Jake lowered his visor and sat still. He knew that after Chief Pierce was done chewing out Terrell, he'd give Jake a turn. The thought crossed his mind once again—you're damned if you do and damned if you don't.

There were times when Jake thought of just sailing away in the *Far Niente* to a quiet spot in Tahiti or Fiji where he'd find a happy, smiling, suntanned island girl to live with him on the boat. This was definitely one of those times.

CHAPTER 61

At sunrise, Ivan Zhukov woke up in his hotel room, ate breakfast and took a shower. After the steam cleared from the mirror, he applied the facial disguise he'd wear to attack the third attorney. Turning his head left and right he studied his reflection. It was perfect.

Zhukov left the hotel via a side door and walked several blocks to where he'd parked his latest vehicle—a plain white commercial van. A quick glance in the back of the van confirmed that the special weapon was there where he'd left it, hidden inside a large cardboard box. It was a thing of beauty. No one had ever been shot with such an ingenious device before.

Today's shooting would be his best performance yet. One shot from a special weapon for a special lady. He smiled at the thought. Every attorney in San Francisco was frightened right now and carefully watching their backs. But this one thought she was safe. Untouchable. Special.

She was wrong.

Soon she would find out just how wrong. The entire nation would find out when they saw it on television.

First, though, he needed to kill an innocent bystander. Any man who was close to his own height and weight and currently disguised hair color would do. He just needed a body double to make his scheme work as planned.

Zhukov got into the van and drove around San Francisco looking for an unlucky victim. He cruised the city streets, death on wheels, passing dozens of people who never knew how close they were to becoming a murder statistic. He coldly observed the people going through robotic motions to fritter away another day of life. Many never stopped to think about what they were doing or why. Or how easily it could all come to a sudden, bitter end.

Finally, he saw a promising target. A man in his twenties was walking along with earbuds in his ears, looking at his phone. It was a perfect combination to render someone totally unaware of their surroundings. The man was also close enough in height and weight and hair color for Zhukov's purposes. He followed the man from a distance, not letting the van get too close, yet never losing sight of his target. The opportunity came when the man cut through an empty alley. There were no security cameras or other people in sight, and Zhukov decided to make his move. He pressed on the gas pedal, quickly drove toward the oblivious man and pulled up right next to him.

The man jumped in surprise when the van appeared. The look of surprise was frozen on his face when a suppressed .22 pistol was fired from the driver's open window. A hollow-point round entered his heart, mushroomed inside and killed him instantly. Zhukov put the van's transmission in park, jumped out and opened the sliding side door, then picked up the dead body off the pavement, shoved it inside the van, and closed the door. Fifteen seconds after the moment he'd pulled the trigger, he was back behind the wheel and driving away from the scene of the crime.

Now it was time for the main event: the shooting of the female attorney. And the collection of a very large payment, wired to one of his offshore bank accounts. His mood swing took him to a manic state, and he whistled a strange tune as he drove the van.

CHAPTER 62

Jake woke up on the *Far Niente,* and for a moment he wondered if he'd only dreamed of the crazy car chase of the previous night. He got out of bed and opened the sliding door at the stern of the boat so Cody could walk up the dock to the garden area. Then he went to the galley and made some coffee. His phone buzzed with a call from Debbie.

"Good morning, Debbie, how's my favorite person today?" Jake said.

"This is Pam. I just started working here," a woman said. "Debbie is in a meeting. Norman asked me to tell you that your assignment for this morning at the Moscone Center is canceled. Instead, he wants you to go get some pictures of people enjoying today's nice weather at the Marina Green."

"What, like people jogging and flying kites and walking their dogs on the grass—that kind of stuff?"

"Exactly like that. Photos for a lifestyle piece about things to do in the city that are free or don't cost much money."

"That's more important than a presidential candidate and his wife giving talks about the *Literacy for the World* campaign?"

"The boss assigned someone else to do that. Sorry, I don't make the decisions. I just pass them along and do what they tell me."

Jake had a strange feeling about this woman. "Could you send this info to me in a company email? I like to keep a record because the boss has a way of forgetting he told me to do something, and then later he says I must have been mistaken."

"Yes, of course, I'll send it in just a minute. I've got to go now. Nice talking with you, Jake."

A minute later, Jake's phone buzzed with the email. It came from his editor, at the company email address, just like all the others he'd ever received. He still had an odd feeling about this, but his boss was probably just punishing him for his rebellious attitude.

Jake ate some breakfast, took a quick shower, and got dressed. He called a college student named Caleb who sometimes assisted him on photo shoots and asked him to meet him at the Marina Green. Next, he called an actor friend named Russell, who performed in a local theater group. The group was great at staging elaborate pranks.

"This prank is not exactly legal," Jake said.

"That makes it all the more fun," Russell said. "What shenanigans are we up to this time?"

"I want you and a friend to visit the news office where I work. You should both be wearing official-looking coveralls. One of you should be carrying a clipboard while the other one is pushing a hand truck loaded with an empty cardboard box. The box has to be large enough to hold a clothes washer or dryer. See a woman named Debbie about removing a stuffed bison head from the wall above her desk. Put the head in the box, take it away and load it into a van. Then drive away quick."

"I've always wanted to steal a buffalo head—truly I have."

"The next step is for you to take the thing to the rival news station and mount it on the wall above the desk of a TV reporter named Dick Arnold."

"I'd love to. That guy is so annoying."

"Once the buffalo head is on the wall, take a photo showing the head and the desk, and email the pic to my boss Norman. Use an anonymous email account. Add a note saying, 'Thanks for the head,' and sign it with Dick Arnold's name. Post the photo on various social media websites and change Arnold's name to *Benedict 'Dick' Arnold*, in hopes the online media will think that's his actual name. Maybe they'll start calling him Benedict Arnold from now on."

"Oh, this is very good mischief," Russell said. "One of my friends can even hack into Arnold's email and send the pic from there, but it's going to cost you some cash, you know."

"Of course, and it will be worth every dollar. Can you get it done today, by any wild chance?"

"Sure, we can start on it right now. This kind of thing really brightens my day. Keep thinking up stuff like this."

Jake ended the call, and then he and Cody left the boat and walked up to the marina parking lot. When Jake saw all the damage to his Jeep, he let out a sigh. Both mirrors were torn off the doors, there were deep scratches all down the driver's side from grinding along the brick wall, and the passenger side was dented from slamming into the trash dumpster. The front and back bumpers both needed to be replaced, and the windshield had a long crack across it. On closer inspection, he found several bullet holes here and there. He called a friend of his in the auto body business and left a voicemail saying he wanted to drop off his Jeep for major repairs.

Jake and Cody got into the vehicle, and Jake lowered his window. A man approached the Jeep on foot with a large manila envelope in his hand. Jake drew his pistol, and just as the man reached his car door Jake pressed the control to lower Cody's window.

The man shoved the envelope in Jake's face and said, "You've just been served with legal papers."

The man then noticed the pistol that Jake was pointing at him and his face went pale. At that moment, Cody stuck his head out the window and started barking and snapping his teeth close to the man's face. The man took off running, got into a car, and raced away.

Jake took a look at the papers and saw that Gwen had falsely accused him of domestic violence, and she'd filed a restraining order against him. Even though the accusations were unsubstantiated, Jake was now legally required to do several things.

First, he had to stay away from Gwen and avoid all contact, even by phone or text or email. Second, he was required to move out of his own home and not return. Third, he had to sell or turn in any guns or firearms in his possession to the police and provide a receipt to the court from a law enforcement agency within forty-eight hours. Fourth, Jake had to pay all of Gwen's bills and debts. And fifth, Gwen had checked off the box that required Jake to attend fifty-two batterer-intervention classes, once every week for a full year.

According to the paperwork, Jake was legally bound to do all of this before he even got a hearing in court to deny the false accusations. And if he lost his case at that future hearing, the order could keep going for up to five years. After that it could be renewed for another five, for a total of one full decade. It would also be entered into a statewide computer system to let the police know about it, and they would consider Jake a danger to all females.

Jake felt like the rug had been pulled out from under him. All of his life he'd been a good man who was protective of women, but what was the point if the only thanks you got was to be stabbed in the back?

He used his phone to take pictures of several pages of the restraining order and sent the pictures along with a text message to his attorney, Bart Bartholomew. Next, he forwarded the video of Gwen hitting him in the face, threatening to file a false complaint against him, and then throwing the champagne bottle at his head.

"Fun way to start off the day, huh, Cody?" Jake said.

Cody barked once and leaned in between the front seats, sniffed the paperwork and let out a low growl. Jake got out of the Jeep and let Cody out. He walked to the compost pile next to the garden and tossed the papers down.

"Cody, pee now—pee there," Jake said, and he pointed at the papers.

War dogs are trained to empty their bladder on command, and Cody obediently peed on the papers. He then grinned at Jake and breathed Ha-Ha-Ha.

"You're such a good dog," Jake said.

Jake had taken a picture of Cody peeing on the lawsuit papers and sent that pic to his lawyer too. Bart could use a laugh in his line of work. Hopefully, he'd know how to put a stop to this problem. Jake used a garden shovel to toss dirt onto the papers and bury them. The symbolism was not lost on him. The relationship had been dying for some time and now it was officially dead and buried. Sad but true.

"Who wants to go to the park?" Jake said.

Cody barked once and wagged his tail. He trotted by Jake's side to the Jeep. They drove to the Marina Green and began enjoying a picture perfect day by the Bay. People were flying kites, walking their dogs, having picnics on the lawn, jogging and exercising, sitting and holding hands, and enjoying life.

The scene reminded Jake of something the poet Dylan Thomas had once written: "San Francisco is incredibly beautiful, all hills and bridges and blinding blue sky and boats and the Pacific Ocean. I am madly unhappy, but I love it here."

Jake smiled as he took pictures of the pleasant scene, not knowing that someone was going to try to ruin his life in the next few minutes.

CHAPTER 63

At the Moscone Center's South Ballroom, the assassin smiled as he closed in for the kill. Zhukov squinted through his scope at the presidential candidate up on the stage and focused the crosshairs right between the congressman's eyes. At this range, he simply could not miss.

His weapon was hidden inside a professional television news camera that was mounted on a stand. The facial disguise that he wore matched up perfectly with the photo on his forged identity badge. It was that of TV news cameraman Jake Wolfe, who was conveniently absent and would be blamed for this crime.

With his foolproof disguise and identification, Zhukov blended right in with the other photojournalists and television news crews that had been cleared by the Secret Service for this news event.

As Congressman Anderson made his speech in front of the crowd and the cameras, Zhukov carefully entered a numeric code into his smartphone, which served to activate the weapon's remote trigger. There was a one-second delay and then…

Click.

Zhukov was rewarded with a thrilling but quiet click of the firing mechanism inside the unloaded camera weapon. With so much activity around him in the media section, no one heard the muffled sound.

"I am *so* good," Zhukov whispered to himself. "Next time it will be loaded. I was only testing it on you. Such a pity it's not your day today, you lying politician."

Zhukov smiled as he thought of that future day and how satisfying it would be for him to fire a bullet into the troublesome man. But he'd made a deal with Banks, and the congressman wasn't part of the deal.

With a careful turn of a control knob on the camera, Zhukov secretly loaded a round of very special ammunition into the chamber of the disguised weapon. Now he was ready for the real job at hand.

He waited patiently for his actual target: the congressman's pregnant wife, Katherine, who was hoping she would soon be the next First Lady of the United States. He saw her face peek out from behind the stage curtain.

"Yes, that's it, come out here now … so I can *shoot you,* my darling," Zhukov whispered.

~

Katherine Anderson peered out from behind the curtain toward the stage and the crowd. The ceremony to benefit her favorite new educational program was well attended. Her husband's talk was reaching the point where Katherine would walk out to join him in front of the microphones and give a speech of her own.

She watched her husband make a passionate speech. Secret Service agents stood in various places around the auditorium, watching the crowd. The agents had been assigned just recently, when the candidate had reached a particular level in the polls and raised a pre-determined amount of campaign money.

Katherine couldn't help but smile as she saw the powerful man standing there, the man she loved. He was going to make such a wonderful father for their baby. She put a hand on her round tummy. A baby at long last. How many years had they tried to conceive … and waited and hoped? It seemed like an eternity. Daniel had been so patient and positive, blaming himself and fate, never her. She knew the fertility issue was her own medical problem but had never told Daniel about the painful secret buried in her past, and she never would. No one would ever know, except for her trusted personal physician and good friend, Dr. Rachel Brook.

The media was going wild over the possibility that if the couple won the election, there would be a baby born in the White House. Today the reporters and photographers were in full attendance. She saw some now-familiar faces of journalists and cameramen that followed Daniel around, plus some local news teams.

As she waited, her hands rested on her swollen belly, and she let her eyes roam over the spectacle before her. It was a madhouse, just as it usually was when she and her husband appeared in public. Fame was turning out to be a royal pain in the neck, but there was no way to regain her privacy now. Those days were over. Anonymity was like virginity—once you lost it, you never got it back. Today the media circus appeared to be the same as usual, except she had an odd sense that one detail was out of place. What was it?

Looking around, she noticed a cameraman talking to himself and grinning like he'd won the lottery. There were some eccentric, creative types of people in the media, she knew that. But this man was more than eccentric; he seemed ... strange. Katherine had a funny feeling about him. Although she was sure she'd seen him at other public appearances, he'd never acted in this way before. Maybe he was simply high on back pain medication or something similar. Still, no one was allowed near a candidate if they were under the influence of any substance. She should probably ask a Secret Service agent to take a closer look.

In Washington, D.C., a top-ranking Secret Service agent named Shannon McKay was at work in one of the situation rooms located beneath the White House in a maze of tunnels aptly nicknamed *the Catacombs.* This situation room resembled the inside of an air traffic control tower, but instead of large windows, it had six large flat screen television monitors.

As always, McKay wore her trademark charcoal gray suit, crisp white shirt and plain tie. She watched the faraway *Literacy for the World* ceremony on the various monitors, and she cycled through a variety of viewpoints from cameras mounted in strategic locations. There was a similar situation room full of monitors and agents very near to the scene, right there in San Francisco's Moscone Center. McKay was providing them with an extra pair of seasoned eyes on the situation, whether they liked it or not. She had a high level of authority and was also curious about this new candidate, Congressman Anderson.

McKay's eyes flicked from TV screen to TV screen. Everything seemed to be going fine, except that Katherine had looked for a long moment at one television cameraman in particular, and then she'd looked directly at a Secret Service agent and waved her hand to get the agent's attention.

McKay sat up straight and studied the cameraman. Why did he have that manic grin on his face? The more she studied him, the more she got a funny feeling in her stomach. There was just something odd about that guy. McKay didn't like odd, she didn't do odd, and she would not tolerate odd anywhere near the protected people that she was responsible for.

You could scoff all you want at so-called women's intuition, but some women had it. That was a fact. Besides, McKay knew that Katherine was a former prosecuting attorney. Katherine just knew things about people that the general public could never know. McKay respected that wisdom and experience. And McKay had been trained to look for anything that seemed out of place or suspicious in any way. That was all it took to make her take action, and she didn't hesitate. She would protect "Kat and the Big Guy," as she called the couple, with the same zeal as she protected the current president and his wife. She hurriedly typed command codes on her computer keyboard.

First, she alerted the agent closest to Katherine that the woman wanted to get his attention, and he should go to her and see what she had to say. The man was wearing a small earbud speaker, with a thin wire leading down into his collar. He turned and began walking toward Katherine.

Next, by McKay's request, her view on TV screen number three changed as the live feed from one of the remote-controlled Secret Service surveillance cameras came under her direct control. She focused it on the odd cameraman's face. His smile was very strange indeed and, in the magnified close-up, his complexion appeared very pale and pasty. Was he wearing some kind of TV makeup? It took only a few seconds to run the man's facial image through the computer's FRP—the facial recognition process that matched it against the faces of hundreds of thousands of known terrorists, criminals, and a group called *persons of interest*.

There was no match.

The computer also checked the approved media list and guest list, and it came up with the probable identification of Jacob "Jake" Wolfe. Details of his life began to scroll across one of the TV screens. Jake had served in the Marines and was currently working as a photojournalist for one of the local television stations there in the San Francisco Bay area. Previous to that job, he'd worked as a freelance photographer and shot news photos for the Associated Press, National Geographic, and various news websites.

Wolfe looked okay so far, but McKay wasn't through yet. She ran a quick criminal background check and a news story search via a special software program on her computer. She was glad to see that Wolfe had no criminal conviction record. That was reassuring. But wait a minute, what were these two arrest records about? One for possession of a controlled substance, and a later one for setting off some kind of … explosion?

On the Moscone Center stage, Congressman Anderson was finishing up his speech. Below and to the right of the stage, Zhukov licked his lips in anticipation and checked the time on his phone to be sure everything was running on schedule. He was feeling impatient, but it wouldn't be long now until Katherine stepped into his weapon's target zone.

The congressman ended his speech by saying, "And now, let me introduce the real heart and soul behind this ambitious project. The face you've seen on the news. My wife and best friend. Soon to be the mother of our child. And with your support, the next First Lady of the United States … Katherine Anderson!"

Katherine was about to talk to a Secret Service agent about the strange cameraman, but now she had to walk out onto the stage. She appeared right on cue and was greeted by thunderous applause and a standing ovation. The polls said Katherine was even more popular than her congressman husband. She smiled and nodded left and right while waving "the princess wave," as she'd been taught by the publicists and modeling coaches.

As she smiled for the crowd and the media, Zhukov was smiling too, and he focused his special camera weapon on the "Future First Lady's" forehead, right between the eyes.

The audience ended their applause and took their seats. Daniel remained next to Katherine for the moment. Whenever the two of them shared the stage, they typically traded some witty banter at the podium, and today the congressman was in a rare mood. The prospect of Katherine having a baby after all these years had him both elated and flustered. Katherine wanted to tell him to relax; he wasn't the one with a baby growing inside of him. Instead, she just smiled the false, calm smile of someone who was living with the stress of life in the media spotlight, knowing that your every move was being recorded and broadcast so the restless crowd could judge you.

Daniel put his hands on Katherine's upper arms, held her at arm's length and looked into her eyes.

"Promise me, Katherine, no more of these speeches and meetings until after you have the baby."

"Just this one last speech," Katherine said sweetly. "And then, well, there is that fundraising dinner with the major donors next week." She couldn't help pushing his buttons. It was too easy. She tried not to laugh while anticipating the result.

Daniel dropped his hands to his sides in exasperation, but he made an effort to keep his voice calm. "I thought we agreed you were going to let the governor fill in for you on that luncheon so you could stay home and get some rest."

Katherine smiled and reached out her right hand, grabbed the lapel of his suit jacket and slowly pulled him closer to her, well aware that the media was recording and broadcasting her every move.

"No, handsome, you're mistaken. We agreed I'd think it over. I did, and I decided on doing it myself. It's my project, my idea, and my hard work. I'm doing it, so please get used to the idea ... Mister Congressman."

Daniel scowled like a judge, squinted one eye and exhaled loudly, shaking his head.

Katherine loved the way he was so uncomplicated yet powerful. He could be charmingly old-fashioned. Meanwhile, she was current with the modern world and the latest ideas and trends. She knew the congressman valued her opinion of what his voters were thinking. And his total love for her was one of the few things in life she could count on unconditionally. He was her anchor in the storm. He was a rock.

"All right," Daniel said, with his voice rising. "One final lunch of rubber chicken, and then you'll go home and follow your doctor's orders to the letter. Agreed?"

"Agreed, of course, darling," Katherine said, smiling cheerfully after her victory.

"And just so we're absolutely clear on this—you agree you'll do exactly what your doctor says. Not that you'll think it over."

"My goodness, I'll sit by the window and knit baby booties if it will help you calm down, big guy. Of course, I'll also run the *Literacy for the World* campaign from my home office. That means I'll need an assistant or two, phones, and computers."

Daniel held his hands out by his sides with palms up and looked heavenward for help that didn't appear. The audience chuckled and commented to one another. Dozens of news cameras captured the couple's chemistry and camaraderie on television, websites and publications. People all across America and the world were smiling and laughing and nodding their heads at this now-familiar peppery banter between the popular duo.

But there was one individual in the media area who had other ideas about the couple's future. Zhukov stood behind the TV camera and watched Katherine on the display screen. He wished the rich attorney would stand still and begin her speech so he could shoot her and get it over with. Some mafia criminals and wealthy business oligarchs in his home country had caused his beloved Tatiana to suffer. And now, with this act, he would send a message to his former colleagues in Russia: "Someday I'll come for your loved ones too. Nobody is safe from me."

As he looked at the former prosecutor, he whispered to himself,

"Ah, the beloved Madonna and child." Then, with a start, he sucked in his breath and whispered, "Of course, the *child*. That's even better."

He moved the crosshairs of his camera-weapon away from Katherine's face and lowered it to focus on her rounded belly. His heart began to beat faster in anticipation of what he was about to do. He watched Katherine as she continued bantering with her husband. And then Daniel bent at the waist and placed his ear on the top of her pregnant belly, hamming it up for the cameras.

It was the *perfect* shot. Zhukov *had* to take it. Aiming at Katherine's stomach, right under the congressman's nose, a thrill ran up his spine as he reached into his coat pocket and placed his fingers on his smartphone. Daniel moved his head and temporarily blocked Zhukov's aim.

"Oh, come on, you *kopoba*, you cow," Zhukov whispered to himself. "Move your fat head up and back ... just a little higher ... just a touch more ... almost there."

CHAPTER 64

Agent Shannon McKay typed on her keyboard as she brought up Jake Wolfe's arrest records. Her fingers flew over the keys, and she had data appearing on three of the six flat-screen monitors in front of her.

A quick look showed her that neither arrest had ended in a conviction. In the arrest for possession of a controlled substance, the record said he'd been a passenger in a car, and the driver had been stopped by law enforcement. The driver was found to be in possession of drugs, but Wolfe had not been in possession or under the influence. However, the sheriff had arrested Wolfe simply for being a passenger in the car, along with his friend Dylan. That was ridiculous, but it happened every day. Many of the women who were in prison now had ended up there because they'd been riding in a car when their boyfriend had been arrested. But soon after Jake's arrest, the charges had been dropped by the prosecutor. Dylan, however, had spent hard time in prison.

Wolfe's second arrest had occurred several years later, after his military service. It was for allegedly detonating an "improvised chemical explosive device" on the Fourth of July. A cop named Denton had arrested him, but he'd gone to court and been found not guilty by a jury. The so-called explosive device had been a soda pop bottle filled with vinegar and baking soda that caused it to burst. A teenage boy had popped the bottle as part of a science experiment that he'd seen on

YouTube. Wolfe hadn't participated; he'd only seen it happening and had supervised, to make sure no kids got hurt.

"Innocent or not, how did this guy get on the approved media list?" McKay said to herself. "And is he dangerous, or just an irresponsible man who likes to make loud noises on Independence Day?"

McKay used her security clearance to quickly tap into Jake Wolfe's military service file. He'd served in the Marine Corps as an infantry rifleman and then had volunteered to be an IED detector dog handler, going through a training course. And upon graduation, he'd become what is called an improvised explosive device detector dog handler.

Her eyebrows went up when she noted that he'd been wounded by the enemy in battle and had almost bled to death. He'd been awarded a Purple Heart and also received a Bronze Star for acts of heroism. Duke, his faithful dog, had not survived. The psychologist said that Jake had never gotten over the loss of his four-footed friend. He was carrying anger and resentment on his shoulders, always looking for some criminal to take it out on. McKay had great admiration and respect for the troops and their war dogs … and that made her sorry for what she felt she had to do now.

"Better safe than sorry," McKay recited from her training. She hit keys on the computer and alerted the Secret Service to quietly but immediately pull Jake Wolfe aside to answer questions in private. If he resisted at all, he was to be arrested and subdued with any force deemed necessary.

Two Secret Service agents nodded at her command and started to walk purposefully toward the camera crews where Wolfe was working. To be thorough, McKay also notified a Secret Service sniper named Adams who was secretly located in the lighting area above the stage. Her orders were for him to focus a weapon on Jake Wolfe and keep him in the crosshairs until he was detained. She'd give the order to have Wolfe shot with a tranquilizer dart if he made the slightest move that she didn't like.

McKay typed a command that made her phone system begin calling all known phone numbers for Wolfe. At the same time, she ran a computer program to try a little-known technology that used thermal imaging to scan someone's entire body through their clothing. This was just to eliminate the chance that the cameraman was wearing a disguise or hiding a weapon. It was experimental technology, and it might make the person being scanned feel sick for an hour or so. But she was willing to make a photojournalist vomit if that's what it would take to protect the people she was responsible for.

While the computer was scanning, one of the phone calls was answered.

"Hey, this is Jake," a man said.

The man McKay was watching on the TV screen was not answering a phone.

"Hello," he said again, "Can you hear me?"

The voice recognition software quickly compared the voice of the man who answered the phone with the voice records in a secret NSA computer file of every voice in America that had ever spoken on a mobile phone. The NSA also had a copy of every driver's license photo in their facial recognition database, and an image of almost every car license plate, photographed by license plate reader cameras mounted on police cars and installed next to highways and streets.

The software made an exact match; this was the real Jacob T. Wolfe on the phone. If the technology was working correctly, the person manning the camera at the speech was someone else in disguise. Her skin crawled as she saw the grinning cameraman mumbling to himself. This new technology had a few false positives, but her stomach lurched. The potential impostor had to be dealt with immediately.

"Jake Wolfe?" McKay said. "This is Shannon McKay, I'm a federal agent. This is an important call, stand by one moment."

McKay typed an emergency alert message that would be read immediately on the smartphone of every agent in the vicinity of the congressman. She also sent a message that gave the sniper the go ahead, for any reason he felt necessary, to shoot cameraman "Jake Wolfe" with a tranquilizer dart, or a bullet in the heart, at his discretion.

Adams was armed with both a tranq gun and a sniper rifle with a suppressor. He could use either one, depending on his discernment of the threat level and whether innocent bystanders were nearby that might be at risk as collateral damage.

McKay spoke into her phone. "Jake, this is Agent Shannon McKay of the United States Secret Service calling from the White House in Washington, D.C."

"Oh, sure, of course you are," Jake said. "You telemarketers are really getting creative."

"Listen to me, Jake. Right now, I'm looking at a man with your exact same facial features and ID. At this moment, he's manning a TV camera at a congressman's press conference. The computer has checked your voice as we're speaking and it seems to match your records. Where are you right now exactly?"

"This sounds like a prank call, but if you must know, I'm at a giant lawn by the San Francisco Bay, known as the Marina Green. It's about seventy acres of grass and it has a great view of the water and boats and the Golden Gate Bridge. I'm taking photos for a lifestyle piece that will be seen on the news."

"And yet I'm looking at you on live video from the Literacy for the World speech."

"Impossible. I was supposed to work a television camera at that event today, but my employer reassigned me to something else. Can't you ping my phone and confirm my location?"

"Yes, but phones can be cloned," McKay said.

"You can look at me on live video here too if you tap into the CCTV camera on top of the memorial flagpole. I'm in the area of the lawn right in front of it. I'll be the guy waving at the flag as if I think the flag is waving back at me."

Jake looked toward the flagpole and waved. The flag waved too. Some people nearby watched him and started gossiping about the strange man. Jake found it ironic that one of the countless CCTV spy cameras in the city that he hated so much was now helping him prove his innocence. He took out his driver's license and held it up next to his face.

McKay rapidly tapped keys on her computer. "I'm in, and I have eyes on the green. I see you, and I'm zooming in on your face. Stop waving and hold still. Damn, you are the identical twin of the man at the Moscone Center."

"I don't have a twin. Are you serious that a man is impersonating me there? How close is this impostor to the congressman? Get your people on that guy and handcuff him right now."

"I've already alerted the agents. The impostor should be in custody within sixty seconds."

"Sixty seconds is too long. You need to tackle him, take him down. Hell, just shoot him in the leg or something."

A chime sounded from McKay's computer. The software had a partial match to the thermal scanning composite. The shape of the cameraman's face, his body language, and his physical posture suggested that he might be a murder suspect who was wanted by Interpol and various governments around the world. Classified orders from the CIA noted that he was to be arrested or, if deemed necessary, shot on sight. A file from MI5 in London said much the same thing. The secret codes McKay was reading told her that if this suspect really was a Level One threat, their sniper should shoot him, right now.

The body-reading technology was not perfect, but it had proven to give a fairly good guess of an identity. It went far beyond facial technology and worked similarly to the way the human brain can spot a friend in a crowd and recognize him or her by the familiar way he or she stands, walks or gestures. Right now, according to the new technology, a potentially dangerous man had his hand in his coat pocket and appeared highly animated, possibly high on something. McKay was faced with the decision to possibly kill someone. She didn't hesitate.

"Talk to me," Jake said.

"Stay on the phone, and stay where you are. Don't move. I'm giving the order for this impostor Jacob Wolfe to be captured, or shot and possibly killed. I suggest you lie low for now, to avoid an accidental death."

McKay punched the keys to enter an emergency code. Her computer sent the name and photo of the target, Jacob Wolfe, to every agent's smartphone at the scene, along with the order saying, *Imposter, wearing a facial disguise: Code NCT. Neutralize, Capture or Terminate.*

She also barked orders into her phone as she fought back the bile that was rising in her throat. Her trained eyes watched the flat-screen TVs, and she saw the disguised killer lick his lips and grin.

"Act on the order," McKay said. "Act now!"

CHAPTER 65

Zhukov was planning to go to a nearby restroom and trigger the weapon from there with his phone. He noticed men and women in black suits coming toward him. It was time to leave, immediately if not sooner. He held one hand on his stomach and bent over slightly as if in pain. He said to a photographer next to him, "I must have food poisoning or something. I need to run to the restroom and throw up again. Don't let anyone touch my camera, okay?"

The other photographer wrinkled his nose at the words "throw up." He nodded and grimaced in sympathy, but quickly turned his attention back to the entertaining scene on the stage. Zhukov's television camera was positioned near the end of the media area, close to the doors, so he was able to hurry out of the auditorium in only a few seconds.

~

Adams received a message from McKay: "All personnel, Code One immediately on news cameraman Jacob Wolfe. That is actually an impostor wearing a disguise."

Adams already had his sniper tranquilizer rifle aimed at the target. Now he had permission to neutralize or kill. He intended to attempt one time to neutralize, and then to kill after that if necessary. But suddenly the target bent over and held his stomach as he moved among the crowd of media people. A second later, the target went through a doorway and into the hall. Adams was tempted to fire through the space of the closing door. But it was no good; he might miss and take out civilians as collateral damage. The tranq dart could kill if it hit someone in a vulnerable area. Thankfully, the target was moving away from the people the agents were protecting. Adams let out a frustrated breath and then spoke into the tiny radio on his wrist. "Target is on the move. He exited the auditorium through door B into the hallway. Team Delta Five, Code NCT."

Zhukov hurried to the nearest men's restroom. Once inside, he used a janitor's master key to lock the deadbolt. Next, he pulled a micro syringe out of his pocket, stuck the applicator needle into the keyhole and injected liquid "lock-out drops," rendering the deadbolt inoperable.

He looked at his phone and the video feed from his TV camera. Anderson was standing next to Katherine, listening to someone in the audience asking him a question for the baby. He bent over again to talk to his wife's stomach and relay the baby's answer. His head was blocking the shot. Secret Service agents were moving quickly toward the couple.

There was a loud knock at the bathroom door. Zhukov cursed himself for not following his original plan and exiting the auditorium sooner. He could have then shot Katherine by remote control while he was driving away in his car. But it was just so much more *artistic* to do it with the congressman and the unborn baby as part of the masterpiece. His training told him he should make his escape, but he intended to fire the shot, no matter what. Great sums of money and his professional reputation depended on it. The knocking at the door became louder and more insistent. Zhukov made himself focus his attention on his phone screen. He had to hurry and fire the weapon *now*.

The congressman turned his head to grin at the audience, giving the camera weapon a clear shot at Katherine's abdomen. Zhukov was thrilled. After stalking Katherine and studying her every habit and scheduled speech, it was the perfect moment. He tapped his phone, activated the camera weapon's trigger and said, "Bye-bye, baby."

~

Inside the auditorium, one of the Secret Service agents was in a balcony, searching the crowd with his binoculars, and he saw Wolfe's unmanned camera appear to move up and down slightly.

"What the hell?" He felt a chill go down his spine, and he spoke into the microphone in his shirtsleeve cuff. "Code One on the television *camera*. It might be a remote-controlled weapon. Take out the target's camera, knock it down, shoot it, do it now!"

There were cries of alarm from the crowd as two agents ran toward the camera, one from each side, neither one knowing if it might explode in his or her face, but each doing their duty in spite of the risk. Several other agents were seconds away from placing themselves in front of the congressman and Mrs. Anderson, directly in the line of fire.

On the balcony, Adams aimed his tranquilizer rifle at the television camera. The dart had a powerful impact that could knock it over. However, the dart might ricochet and hit someone in the eye. He had to make a perfect shot. Quickly focusing on the camera, he inhaled a breath and let it out as he squeezed the trigger.

At that same moment, the camera weapon fired. The two weapons were triggered almost simultaneously. Adams was looking through his scope, and he felt his stomach sink as he saw the camera kick and emit a puff of vapor. His dart hit the camera a second too late. The dart knocked the camera flying backward, but not before it had fired its projectile.

Adams cursed and picked up his other rifle, which was loaded with live ammunition. He scanned the crowd with his scope, hoping to put a real bullet into the head of Jacob Wolfe or anyone else who might pose a threat.

The agents who had been running to put their bodies in harm's way heard the muffled shot from the television camera, just as they leapt in front of the couple in an urgent attempt to protect them. Each one of these brave men and women of the United States Secret Service was trying to get in front of the bullet and be shot by it, sacrificing their bodies in defense of the protected. That was the way they'd been trained, and it was what they were sworn to do.

The single round shot out of the camera and barely missed the agents. The strange projectile flew past within an inch of one agent's rib cage, and lightly grazed the underside of the coat sleeve of another agent's raised arm. It flew past and hit Katherine Anderson directly in her stomach. The impact was right under Congressman Anderson's nose as he was posturing for the cameras.

A bright red stain appeared on Katherine's maternity dress and splashed up onto the congressman's face, dripping down his cheek. This horrific imagery was broadcast across the nation by dozens of media cameras. Hundreds of people in the audience and millions more across America who were watching on TV and on the internet all cried out in unison at the sight of it.

Katherine screamed, fainted, and fell to the floor. Daniel got down on his knees on the stage next to her and held her head in his arms, calling her name. Men and women wearing dark sunglasses and armed with automatic machine pistols surrounded Daniel and Katherine, forming a human shield in a circle around them. Other agents blocked the doors of the auditorium so no one could go in or out. One agent approached the microphone and yelled orders for everyone to put their hands on top of their heads. Several people in the audience fainted; others were crying.

Adams pointed a red laser targeting light at the chests of any people in the audience who did not put their hands on their heads fast enough. He blamed himself for not shooting the camera a split second sooner, and now he wanted to shoot a terrorist, any terrorist.

On stage, Katherine was semiconscious and moaning. Daniel was calling for a doctor. The two Secret Service agents who had run to the location of the camera were now pointing pistols at the closest news reporters and demanding to know where Jacob Wolfe had gone.

One of the frightened cameramen said, "He told me he was sick with food poisoning and had to run to the bathroom."

~

A broad-shouldered and steely-eyed agent named Easton nodded and spoke orders into the small microphone on his wrist. Easton was aware that the Moscone Center was made up of over one million square feet of space, and the fugitive could be hiding anywhere. The agents needed to move fast if they were going to apprehend him before he escaped.

Easton heard a report that an agent had found the nearby men's restroom to be locked. Someone matching Wolfe's description had been seen entering. He hadn't come out yet, despite the agent banging on the door. Security was bringing a key. Easton said, "Do not wait for the key. Break down the door with any means necessary. Open it immediately." Next, he called any available agents to go outside and look for open windows and suspects on the side of the building where that restroom's window was located.

Easton took off running toward the locked restroom, intent on shooting the lock off if necessary. When Easton arrived and saw the door still locked, he cursed, went to a fire response box on the wall and removed the fire axe. "Stand back," he said. He swung the big axe down, smashing its six-pound polished-steel head onto the lock of the restroom door. And again, and again, and again ... like a man possessed.

From inside the restroom, Zhukov heard the screams arise from the crowd in the auditorium. He grinned and felt a thrill run up and down his spine. There was a loud crash against the outside of the door and then another and another. He was cutting it very close, and he knew he had to run for it now.

Standing in front of the mirror for a moment, Zhukov quickly peeled off the facial prosthesis mask that looked like Jake Wolfe's face. He removed the brown contact lenses, took off his local news station sports coat and his shirt and tossed all of it into the trash. Underneath the shirt he'd removed, he wore a white tourist t-shirt that said *San Francisco* on the front and showed an illustration of a cable car.

Zhukov unlocked the window with his master key, climbed out and dropped onto some juniper bushes below, then stepped onto a walkway. He began running, and he sent a quick text on his phone that ignited a small firebomb he'd previously hidden in the bathroom trash can.

Smoke began to pour out of the bathroom window as Zhukov ran down the walkway toward the side street where his latest car was parked. He took a few quick glances at the live news video on his phone, still being broadcast by one of the cameras of a local TV news website. He heard the blood roaring in his ears and felt his heart thudding in his chest as he witnessed the terror that was unfolding on the stage. Terror that he'd created with the push of a button. The feeling of power was almost too much for him to bear.

Zhukov reached the car, got inside and drove toward a busy cross street. As he began to merge with the other cars on the road, he looked in his rearview mirror and saw several agents running out of the conference center.

He'd cut things too close. It was time for another distraction.

CHAPTER 66

Jake stood on the grass at the Marina Green. "McKay, are you still there? What's going on?"

There was no answer. Jake stared at his phone and wondered what to do next. Agent McKay had told him to hold on, and she'd started frantically yelling orders into other phones and radios. Then her call had ended abruptly. Jake guessed McKay had momentarily forgotten about him because she had more urgent problems to deal with.

"This is crazy. I'm not going to just stand around here while someone is impersonating me."

Jake got another call. It was from his laid-back stoner friend, Tanner, who worked as a bartender in a touristy hotel lounge. "Dude, I'm at work, right? And all of a sudden, your face is on the television? Above the bar? News lady says you're wanted? By the police? What's up with that bro?"

"That's not me. That guy is an impostor wearing a face mask to look like me."

"Looked pretty realistic, man. Had me fooled."

"I'm at the Marina Green right now doing a photo shoot, nowhere near where that stuff is going down."

"Well, you'd better tell that to the cops," Tanner said.

"Thanks, Tanner. I plan to."

Jake ended the call. This situation was totally surreal. Moments ago, he'd been minding his own business at this beautiful park, just taking some pictures. There were people having picnics, jogging, flying kites, tossing Frisbees, walking dogs, watching the sailboats and playing with their kids. Life was good. Now a moment later, he was being impersonated and falsely accused of who knows what. And his face was being shown on the news as a wanted criminal.

He turned to his college student assistant and said, "Caleb, I have a bit of an emergency to take care of, something I have to do right now. Can you finish up the photo shoot and put the equipment away?"

"Sure, I'd love to, boss man," Caleb said.

"Get a few dozen more shots, and if I'm not back in an hour, you can stow the camera equipment in the trunk of your car and grab some food." Jake picked up his camera backpack that held his personal DSLR camera, but he left the other equipment bags for Caleb to use. He called to Cody, who was watching him while resting on the grass. He jumped up, and they jogged over toward the parking area by the water.

As Jake got closer to the Jeep, he pushed the remote start button on his key fob, as he often did, to start the engine and the heater or air conditioner. This time, however, the moment the engine started, a small explosion blasted some kind of round projectiles up through the windshield and roof. The driver's side of the vehicle now looked like Swiss cheese, with a pattern of buckshot-size holes right where Jake would have been sitting if he hadn't used the remote.

Every person within earshot turned and looked at the Jeep with the shot-up windshield and smoke coming out of the holes. Jake stopped in his tracks when he saw what had happened and spoke to Cody. "It looks like the explosive must have been planted under my seat. My butt hurts just *looking* at that. I guess we're taking a different way out of here, Cody."

Jake was not amused to be on the receiving end of this kind of creative ordnance. He pulled his camera backpack around in front of him to get access to his pistol through a zippered slit in a pocket. The pack was also modified with a lining of Kevlar and would act as a makeshift bulletproof vest in a pinch.

Cody let out a fierce growl, his hackles bristling.

Jake understood the fight-hungry look in Cody's eyes. It'd been a while since the dog had bitten a chunk out of a terrorist, and today would be a fine day for it, but sometimes you had to choose your battles. No further shots or explosions were heard, so Jake flipped the pack around to his back again, clipped the leash onto Cody's collar, and then headed back across the grass, away from the water and toward the city.

When Jake got to Marina Boulevard, he crossed to the other side of the street and then snuck a quick glance at his reflection in the glass of a large bay window on one of the homes there. In the reflection, Jake saw a motorcycle cop drive past. The officer turned off Marina Boulevard and rode his Harley-Davidson Road King motorcycle right up over the sidewalk curb and onto the grass. He turned on his lights and siren and zoomed across the big lawn toward the parking area as the crowd parted and people moved quickly to get out of his way.

"Don't look in this direction, Officer," Jake said under his breath, "Just keep your eyes on the smoking wreck of my Jeep. By the way, that is one badass motorcycle you've got there, boss."

Jake and Cody walked down the sidewalk, while Jake made a conscious effort to smile and look like he was just walking his dog and getting some exercise. He turned the first corner he came to and walked up a side street away from the Bay, then headed in the direction of a trendy sidewalk café.

"Cody, stand post." Jake pointed to a spot just outside of the velvet rope that ran along the side of the outdoor dining area. Two other dogs were sitting there, patiently waiting for their family members to finish their meals. Cody went to the spot and stopped there, looking back at Jake as if this was total nonsense. Jake nodded at him knowingly and gave the hand signal for *sit, stay.* Cody sat, and one of the other dogs barked at him, but he just stared at the dog, growled and showed his teeth as if to say, "Seriously? Come at me if you really want a piece of this, fool." The other dog backed down and stopped barking.

Jake entered the bar area and spotted an ATM machine. He had one credit card Gwen didn't know about, and he withdrew the largest cash advance he could.

He went out the back door and then into a gift shop next door, where he paid cash for several prepaid cell phones and cards with minutes, along with a Giants baseball cap. He exited the gift shop, stuffed the phones into his camera backpack and put on the new baseball cap along with his sunglasses. The moment Jake stepped out onto the sidewalk, a police car pulled over and parked nearby and two officers got out. Jake turned his head away from them and ducked into a waiting taxicab.

"Where to, friend?" the driver asked. He spoke with an accent and had a beard.

"Pull up there by the end of the block, I'm waiting for someone."

"One block, are you kidding me?"

Jake waved a twenty-dollar bill and said, "Once we pick him up you'll earn a nice fare. Or I could just give my money to one of these other taxi drivers." He opened the door partway.

"Relax, my friend, you got it."

The man drove his taxicab down the street and parked at the corner. Jake gave him the twenty and asked him to wait just a minute.

The man nodded and smiled, "Sure, pal, twenty bucks a minute is okay by me."

Jake walked quickly along the sidewalk until he could see Cody from a half a block away. He let out a low whistle in a pattern that Cody recognized, and the dog trotted right over to him. They went to the taxi and got in the backseat. The driver gave Cody a skeptical look until Jake showed him another twenty and said, "There are lots of other taxis here if you don't like my dog or my money. Any taxi will do, you're not a special snowflake."

"No worries, I was just admiring your dog … and your money. Where to now, big spender?"

"Head east, toward Fisherman's Wharf," Jake said, naming the first place that came to mind.

"Okay, and it costs double for the dog."

"No, it costs the same. Don't push your luck."

The taxi driver looked at Jake in the mirror and pushed his luck anyway. "Okay, only twenty dollars more for the dog."

Jake lost patience. "If you mention my dog again, I might tell him to bite you. He's got rabies. Right, boy?"

Cody growled and huffed his hot breath on the back of the driver's neck. The driver said nothing, but his face paled when he looked in the mirror and saw Cody showing his teeth. He made a few turns until he was on Bay Street, heading toward the Wharf area.

CHAPTER 67

The police department was receiving hundreds of phone calls about possible sightings of Jake Wolfe.

The media was still naming Wolfe as the perpetrator. Their colleague had done the unthinkable. The story was on every news program—on television, the internet, and radio.

Chief Pierce was in his office, yelling into his phone. "And get Lieutenant Hayes on the radio or the phone, right now." Pierce was going to have to put every cop in the city on the task of apprehending Jake Wolfe. It rubbed him the wrong way to think that Terrell's friend could be involved in anything like this. Jake had always seemed like a stand-up guy, even though he bent a few laws now and then. But reckless or not, Jake was always on the side of the good guys. In fact, just last night, Jake had nearly gotten himself blown up by grenades while trying to help the police catch a serial killer. This didn't add up. Something wasn't right. He wondered if the Secret Service had any clues. He was about to call them but was interrupted when his phone rang for the umpteenth time. "Chief Pierce."

"Chief, this is Dr. Lang. We have a problem with one of the officers."

"I've got bigger problems right now, so if it can wait—"

"It's about Sergeant Cori Denton. I have reason to believe she's a ticking time bomb, sir," Lang said. "We need to help her before she causes an incident."

"Put that in writing for me, along with your recommendations for vacation time, anger management, or whatever would help Denton."

"I'm working on it, and I want to meet with you today. Denton might be a danger to herself and to her fellow officers and to public safety."

"We'll have a meeting as soon as you're ready." Pierce ended the call and started ordering more cops to make their way to the Moscone Center area as fast as possible.

Terrell stopped at Starbucks for a cup of coffee to go. As he was walking back to his car, he received a text message from Beth.

Beth: *Anything going on?*
Terrell: *Getting coffee at Starbucks*
Beth: *What's the coffee of the day?*
Terrell: *Caffè virgin*
Beth: *Awkward*
Terrell: *Damn autocorrect. I meant caffè vagina.*
Beth: *WTH?*
Terrell: **Caffè Verona! V-E-R-O-N-A*
Beth: *Ha ha*
Terrell: *How do you turn off autocorrect?*
Beth: *You could read the instructions*
Terrell: *That's just crazy talk*
Beth: *Oh sure, blame it on autocorrect*
Terrell: *I blame everything on technology*
Beth: *Probably a case of asphalt*
Terrell: *Meaning?*
Beth: *Your ass—your fault*
Terrell: *You're nooooo help*
Beth: *I'm getting one of my intuitions*
Terrell: *Uh-oh, fertilizer gonna hit the fan?*
Beth: *Maybe so, stay frosty*
Terrell: *Going to my rig, check the computer*

Beth: *Me too, touch base in a bit*

Terrell: *Roger that, out*

Terrell got into his vehicle and looked at the dashboard computer. He saw the face of Jake Wolfe on the monitor. The all-points bulletin said Jake was wanted for shooting a congressman's pregnant wife in the stomach.

"This time Jukebox is really up the creek without a paddle," Terrell said as he called Jake.

~

Jake's phone vibrated—it was Terrell calling. Jake didn't want to talk with the taxi driver listening, but he didn't have much choice.

"Turn on the radio," Jake said.

"Sure, buddy," the driver said and turned on a news talk radio station. The topic of discussion was a criminal named Wolfe who had shot a pregnant woman.

"Can you put it on sports or music?"

"In a minute, I want to hear this news."

Jake cursed under his breath and answered Terrell's call. "I guess your coworkers are eager to interview a certain person."

"This is a nightmare. Someone at the Moscone Center shot the very pregnant former prosecutor Katherine Anderson right in her stomach," Terrell said. "And the shooter looks just like you. He could be your twin brother."

"Current medical condition?"

"I don't know, but right now the threat to yours is growing worse by the minute."

"You know I would never do that. Plus I have an alibi and witnesses."

"There's an APB out on you. Everybody with a gun and a badge is after you. Federal, state, city, and county law enforcement of every kind. Let me pick you up in my police vehicle for your own protection."

"Okay, I'm loitering at the Marina Green, just like Secret Service Agent Shannon McKay told me to."

"Liar. Two of my fellow cops are at the Marina Green right now, questioning your assistant, Caleb. They found your Jeep there, shot full of holes."

"Yeah, that's true. Somebody doesn't like me."

"I'm using your cell phone's GPS to track you," Terrell said. "The phone data tells me you're driving away from the area, traveling in a vehicle at approximately thirty miles per hour, heading east on Bay Street."

"You're good. I'm going to have to switch to one of the throwaway prepaid phones I bought."

"Just pull over and you won't need the burner phone because you'll be safe in my car."

"I can't sit around in custody. Nobody should be able to shoot a pregnant woman and get away with it, especially when they're wearing a mask to look like me. I'm going to find him and put a bullet in him."

"Stand down, Jake. Every cop except for me believes you did this. They won't hesitate to draw their weapons. Pull over right now and wait for me to pick you up."

"I want the shooter to go down for this just as bad as the cops do. Let me help. I'm an investigative photojournalist, and I can investigate."

"No, you can't; you need to go into hiding until we get this straightened out."

"If your guys are talking to Caleb, he can verify my whereabouts at the time of the incident. I was also caught on video by the CCTV camera on top of the Marina Green's flagpole. Call Agent McKay of the US Secret Service at the White House, she's my new best friend."

"I'll pass that along, but the cops are in no mood right now to hear you say they're wrong."

"No cops ever want to hear they're wrong. You guys all have confirmation bias. Hang on, I'm getting another call. I'm going to put you on hold."

"No, do *not* put me on hold," Terrell said as he turned on his flashing lights.

"I'll be right back," Jake said and he answered the other call.

CHAPTER 68

Zhukov steered the car with one hand and used his phone to view a live feed from a video camera inside the white van he'd been driving earlier. He could see the body of the man he'd killed. The man was now wearing a mask of Jake Wolfe's face. He'd been posed on his stomach, holding a rifle.

Zhukov reached into his pocket and took out a stolen radio that was patched into the Secret Service channel. He tried to sound like an agent as he said, "The suspect Jake Wolfe has been spotted in a TV news van parked near the north corner of the building. He appears to be armed with a rifle."

From memory, Zhukov recited the van's license plate number and the names of the cross streets at the corner. The van he'd stolen was a similar style to the other media news vans, and Zhukov had stuck a sign onto the side of the vehicle featuring an out-of-town news station's logo.

Next Zhukov entered a code into his phone that turned on a proximity detector inside the van. If someone approached close enough, it would trigger a surprise.

After driving several blocks away from the scene of the crime, Zhukov drove the car into a hotel's underground garage and parked in one of the few corners he'd scouted out earlier where no CCTV cameras were watching. He got out of the car, leaving the keys in the ignition and all the windows down. With luck, someone might steal the vehicle and cause more confusion.

Earlier, he'd left a red Audi parked a few spaces down so he could switch cars. He used the key fob to pop the trunk, grabbed a small duffel bag and got into the car. He opened the bag and used the contents to change his appearance once again. Moving quickly, he put on a woman's blond wig and added a long-sleeved red blouse that was a similar color to the car. He smeared concealer cream onto his face, applied bright red lipstick and put on a pair of red-framed sunglasses that also matched the car and blouse.

Zhukov lit up a long, thin cigarette, drove the Audi to the exit and put his prepaid ticket into the card reader. The barrier gate arm lifted up and he drove through the toll gate. One of the parking lot guards glanced over and noted an unusual-looking woman who apparently liked the color red. The woman blew a cloud of smoke at him and drove away. The guard shrugged and went back to looking at his phone.

Zhukov drove the Audi in an evasive pattern to be sure that nobody was following him. He laughed at how clever he'd been, and felt the sudden urge to make a spontaneous phone call to a number that Elena had given him. He knew he shouldn't do it, but he was having a wild mood swing, so he used a throwaway phone to make the call and smiled when he heard the person answer.

"Jake Wolfe."

"Hello, Wolfe, you imbecile," Zhukov said. "How does it feel to know that *you* just shot Her Highness, the congressman's wife, right in her fat little baby bump?"

Zhukov laughed loudly, delighted with himself, and then ended the call. He removed the battery from the phone so it couldn't be used to triangulate his location.

Jake cursed, checked his phone, and saw that Terrell had ended the call. He wondered what to do now. When in doubt, call in a favor. He thought for a moment about who might be the most powerful person he knew, and then called FBI Special Agent Knight. Jake had often given Knight tips about federal crimes that he'd come across in his investigative journalism work. On more than one occasion, the information Jake had provided led to arrests and made Knight look good to his bosses.

"Come on, Knight, answer your phone," Jake said. "Please be there when I need you." The phone went to voicemail and Jake left a message. "Agent Knight, this is Jake Wolfe. I just got a phone call from a man I believe is the one who shot Katherine Anderson. He sounded like he had a Russian accent. If you hurry and trace the phone that just called my phone a minute before my call to you, it might help you locate the fugitive. I hope that makes sense. Thank you."

Jake recited his phone number just in case he hadn't been clear or the caller ID hadn't worked. He ended that call and sent a text message to Terrell, Beth Cushman, and Agent McKay with a short version of the same message. McKay's text came back as undeliverable. She must have called him on a landline phone.

Beth got into her car and looked at the computer display. She saw the APB about Terrell's friend Jake Wolfe. Her eyebrows went up in surprise. This didn't make any sense at all. Last night, Jake had risked his life while helping Terrell and the SFPD on a homicide case.

Beth's phone buzzed and she checked her text messages. A cop had sent her a short video clip taken from a police vehicle dashboard camera when backup had arrived to help Terrell last night. In the video, a parked car was blown to pieces and a fire hydrant was flooding the area. Terrell was standing next to Jake's Jeep in front of a destroyed piano store, dressed like a gang member, smoking a cigar and taking a piss on the street. There were hundred-dollar bills and fifties and twenties scattered on the ground, and people were running around picking up the cash while officers tried to stop them.

Beth shook her head at the thought of the shenanigans her partner had been up to while she'd been asleep last night. Next, she saw a text from Jake Wolfe. She stared at the screen for a moment in surprise, reading the text and thinking it through. Probably best not to reply to that text from a wanted fugitive just yet. Sorry, Jake. She did want to help, though. Especially since she knew Terrell was in deep weeds right now because of the night before and because his friend was a wanted man.

She thought of an idea that might do some good, so she started the engine and got back on the road and sped toward the police station, with the siren wailing and the lights flashing. She called Terrell's mobile phone, but it went to voicemail.

"Answer the phone," Beth said. "Answer now!"

CHAPTER 69

Sergeant Cori Denton sat at her desk at the station, looking at the APB on Jake Wolfe on her computer screen. According to the APB, he was wanted as a suspect in the shooting of a former prosecutor who was the wife of a congressman and presidential candidate. Next to Jake's face was an image of a note that had been left by the shooter.

The note was on paper the size of a business card, with words printed on it in block letters, and was signed by Jake Wolfe.

THE PROSECUTION RESTS

Denton pounded her fist on the desk and stood up. "I *knew* it! I knew Wolfe was dirty. Look at that. What did I tell you?"

Kirby shrugged. "Looks like you were right, Dent."

"Of course I was right. Ever since I busted Wolfe for that improvised chemical explosive device, I knew that sooner or later he was going to commit another crime."

"It seemed like you were padding his file with a lot of BS just to make him look bad."

"And you said I was wasting my time, but now I have this thick file jacket to give to the chief."

"Well, it's your case. You had the previous arrest, and you've been working on fabricating ... I mean, building his jacket," Kirby said.

"That's right, it's my case. Jake Wolfe is *mine,*" Denton shouted so everyone could hear.

Nobody objected, and Everett, the squad boss, came over to give orders. "Take the ball and run with it, Denton. Show me what you can do. The rest of you, do your best to assist Denton on the case and nail this guy quick. The entire nation will be watching us. Let's show them how we kick ass on crime."

A sergeant on the other side of the room said, "I have a woman on the phone who saw Wolfe's face on the television news. She claims he walked up to the outdoor patio of the restaurant where she works and asked for a table for two, but went inside to wash his hands and never came back out."

"Get a unit to that restaurant," Denton said. "Search the nearby shops and businesses."

Another sergeant said, "Now I have a call from a man who claims Wolfe was in his gift shop next door to that same restaurant, buying several prepaid cell phones with cash."

"If there are records of the phone numbers of those prepaid phones, I want them right now," Denton said.

Kirby tapped on the computer keyboard. "I'm looking at Wolfe's financial information. He used a credit card to take cash out of the ATM machine in the cocktail lounge attached to that restaurant."

"Good work. Did you get access to his emails?"

"Yes, I'll go through them now."

"What's happening with his phone?"

A cop called out, "Wolfe just used his phone a few minutes ago to talk to ... Lieutenant Terrell Hayes? Right now his phone is currently traveling east at vehicle speed on Bay Street toward Fisherman's Wharf."

"Get me into his OnStar so we can hear every sound inside his vehicle," Denton said. "And access the LoJack so we can pinpoint his exact location and turn off his engine when we pull up behind him."

A female cop said, "The OnStar and LoJack in his vehicle seem to be disconnected. Also, one of our motorcycle cops just found his Jeep at the Marina Green parking lot, shot full of holes. He may be riding with an accomplice or in a taxi."

Kirby looked up from his computer. "An email says he's living on a boat at a harbor in Sausalito. But for all we know, he may have the boat berthed over by Fisherman's Wharf today, ready for a fast getaway."

Denton paced back and forth. "Alert harbor security."

"I've sent the police speedboat there too," Kirby said.

"Good. What's their estimated time of arrival?"

"ETA is ten minutes."

"Get them there in five."

"You've got it."

"Alert all of the taxi companies that a fugitive may be riding in one of their vehicles going east on Bay Street."

"Working on it," a man said.

"Somebody get me on all patrol car radios."

"Patched in; your mic is hot," a woman said.

Denton stopped pacing and grabbed the mic, "All units, be advised. Suspect Jacob Wolfe is in an unidentified vehicle heading east on Bay Street toward Fisherman's Wharf. He may attempt to escape on a boat."

An image of Wolfe's face and a map of the moving cell phone's progress were shown on every police car's dashboard computer screen. Underneath Wolfe's photo, the caption read, *Wanted Fugitive. Considered Armed and Dangerous.*

Denton purposely left the microphone on as she said, "And Terrell Hayes better have a good explanation for why he was talking on the phone to his friend, the *perpetrator*, a few minutes ago. Otherwise, Internal Affairs will crawl up his butt and camp out there while they investigate him forever."

She then turned off the microphone and smiled at the thought of her rival getting into trouble. Now the whole department knew about it too. If anyone was going to get promoted, the events of last night and today were certainly tilting the odds squarely in her favor. And putting that dirtbag photojournalist Jake Wolfe in prison was going to be icing on the cake.

Denton paced back and forth again as she plotted her next move.

Under her shirtsleeve, the fresh cuts on her left bicep throbbed with her elevated heartbeat. She told herself she liked the pain. It helped her focus on destroying her enemies.

~

As Jake watched out the window of the taxi, he turned the situation over in his head. If Terrell could track his location using his phone signal, then so could anyone else with the same technology, including the criminal who just called him. Jake thought about that for a minute, then looked up ahead and saw an airport shuttle in front of a hotel. An idea started to form in his head right as his phone vibrated. "Talk to me."

"Hi, Jake, this is Nevaeh at Dr. Fleming's office. I'm calling to follow up on your recent naturopathy appointment."

"I'll have to call you back later, Nevaeh, I'm kind of in the middle of something right now," Jake said.

"The X-rays show you have over a dozen metal fragments in your body."

"I know, that makes it extra fun at the airport checkpoints, but I've got to go now."

"Okay, just be sure to drink the liver detox tea every day as the doctor recommended."

"No problem; that tea isn't bad if you add a shot of brandy to it."

"Wait, what? The doctor says you're drinking too much alcohol."

"Tell the doc I only drink on days that end in a *Y*."

"Dr. Fleming also wants to know if you are getting more exercise."

"Does horizontal exercise count?"

"Horizontal?"

"Sorry, Nevaeh, but I have to run. Talk to you later."

Jake ended the call and then started putting his idea into action. He made sure his phone was set on mute, and then spoke to the driver. "Hey, my friend, I'd like to get out at that hotel. Here's some extra cash, and I apologize for any inconvenience."

The driver quickly got over any ill will when he saw the additional money. "Okay, sure. You're the best customer I've had all week—except you have that scary dog."

Cody grinned at the man in the rearview mirror and panted Ha-Ha-Ha.

The driver pulled the taxi into the hotel's loading zone, and Jake and Cody got out. Jake walked up to the airport shuttle and asked the driver, "Does this airport shuttle go to the San Francisco Airport?"

The shuttle driver sighed and looked as if he wanted to slap Jake across the face. "Yes, sir, this San Francisco Airport shuttle goes to the San Francisco Airport."

A man waiting in line to board the shuttle said, "What airport did you think it went to … the Miami Airport?" He pointed at the sign on the side of the van that said "San Francisco International Airport."

"That would be a long drive to Miami," Jake said, and he smiled and laughed at himself right along with everyone else. When all eyes were looking at the sign on the side of the van, Jake slipped his muted phone into a shopping bag held by a woman in a tourist t-shirt. Moments later, she took her turn and got onto the bus.

Jake told the driver, "Thanks, I'll be catching a ride with you later."

The driver looked at the dog and then nodded and smiled the frazzled smile of someone who deals with the public on a daily basis. He got in his shuttle and drove toward the airport, taking Jake's phone along for the ride.

Terrell Hayes set his phone on the seat as he drove his car and waited for Jake to come back on. A truck stopped and blocked his side of the street. He couldn't pass it due to oncoming traffic, so he took an alleyway to go around. When he got back on the street, he noticed that his phone display showed the call had dropped. He looked at his dashboard computer screen to check the GPS route of Jake's phone and was not happy with what he saw.

"The airport? Not a good idea, Jake."

Terrell also noticed that he had an unread text message from Jake and a voicemail from Beth.

Special Agent Knight was sitting at his desk in the FBI headquarters receiving orders for a full-scale manhunt. Initial reports were brief, but one thing was certain; someone in the news media had shot a congressman's pregnant wife. That man was now public enemy number one in the city of San Francisco. The man's name and the image of his face were going out to every FBI agent and police car computer in the area. The data would appear on Knight's computer and phone any moment now.

Knight wanted to get in touch with a special asset he had within the news media. That guy always seemed to know what was going on. In the past, he'd proven himself to be a helpful friend of the Bureau. On more than one occasion, he'd tipped off the FBI about information he'd gathered as part of his job. Those tips had aided investigations and resulted in the arrests of violent criminals. Other times, he'd agreed to keep confidential items out of the news and had protected Bureau secrets and sources.

Even though Jake Wolfe was a bit of a rebellious nonconformist, he'd proven to be one of the most helpful average citizens Knight had ever met. Jake might even be working at the Moscone Center today as a cameraman. That would be lucky. If he had witnessed the crime, he might've noticed something that could help the investigation.

Knight had Jake's phone number stored in his phone. He took the phone out of his coat pocket so he could call him. At that moment, the photo of the shooter suspect appeared on his phone and his computer. The printer started spitting out paper copies. Knight stared at the image in shock and disbelief. He felt like someone had slapped him across the face. It was a photo of Jake Wolfe, grinning like a madman. Impossible.

Looking at his phone, Knight noticed that Jake had tried to call him a few minutes ago. That was surprising under the circumstances. Knight was going to have to explain to the brass why a wanted suspect had called him moments after a crime. Maybe Jake wanted to turn himself in to someone he trusted.

Knight returned Jake's call, but there was no answer. He tried the call again and again.

CHAPTER 70

The Secret Service agents at the auditorium had the crowd under control. People were crying and agents were shouting orders. The doors to the large room were sealed off. The agents had all the television cameras knocked over and all the camera operators lying face-down with their hands handcuffed behind their backs. They were holding everyone else at gunpoint with their hands on top of their heads. One agent walked through the crowd asking everyone to be calm, patient and disciplined, for their own safety. He apologized for the inconvenience and promised that this would be over soon.

An agent named Len Gannon was kneeling next to Congressman Daniel Anderson, shouting something to him again and again.

"It's *not* blood, sir," Gannon said.

Daniel grabbed Gannon's arm and yelled, "Get a doctor!"

Gannon looked the congressman in the eye. His arm was being crushed in the man's grip, but he spoke in a calm, professional voice. "A doctor is on the way and will be here in a moment," Gannon said. "But, please, listen to me. It was *not* a bullet. It was a *paintball*. This is not blood. This is only red paint."

Daniel stared at Gannon for several seconds and blinked his eyes. He then rubbed the red liquid between his fingers, looked at it closely and smelled it. He checked his wife's stomach and realized there was no wound, not even a hole in her clothing. Katherine had been hit by a hard plastic paintball. It had created a wet splash of red paint when it burst open as it was designed to do. She'd fainted, probably suffering from shock, but she was not wounded or bleeding.

Now Daniel felt like he might faint too, with relief. His shoulders slumped, and he felt a massive wave of adrenaline coursing through his body. He gritted his teeth as his stomach lurched and he almost vomited. He let go of Gannon's arm and then clenched and unclenched his fists and took deep calming breaths. He nodded his head and spoke slowly and deliberately.

"Understood. Thank you, Agent Gannon."

Daniel then whispered soothing words to Katherine. He told her it was only a paintball. She was not injured, nor was their baby.

A Secret Service doctor arrived and knelt by Katherine's side. He treated her for shock and then spoke quietly to Daniel. "I want to get her to a hospital immediately, to make sure there's no chance she might suffer a miscarriage."

Daniel's face went pale, and his nostrils flared. "Let's go right now."

While several agents put Katherine onto a stretcher, Daniel glared toward the media area. The look of animal fury on his face was enough to turn Agent Gannon's blood cold.

"Whoever did this is going to pay dearly for it, I swear to you," Daniel said.

Gannon felt the truth of the threat in the sound of the congressman's voice. He had no doubt that whoever had done this was a walking dead man, or would soon be wishing he was dead.

Zhukov drove along the highway and saw cars ahead of him slowing down and stopping. When he looked further up the road, he noticed a police roadblock. He wondered if it was a standard procedure or if it was happening because of his reckless phone call to Jake Wolfe. He wouldn't be so careless in the future. What had he been thinking? What was it about Wolfe that angered him so?

He was prepared for a roadblock contingency, and he pulled over onto a side street to a touristy area that he'd seen on the map earlier.

He parked the car, took a large handbag out of the trunk and walked across the street. When he reached the sidewalk, he heard the sound of tires squealing and saw the flash of lights from a police car coming around the corner. He quickly stepped into a clothing store and pretended to look at some jackets while he glanced out the window and watched the police car pass by. When the car was gone, Zhukov left the store and went through a doorway leading to the retail building's parking area. He hid behind a garbage dumpster, took off the sunglasses and wig, and tossed them into the trash.

Zhukov reached into his handbag for a variety of items and put on a starched gray shirt and a baseball cap with the word *Security* stenciled on them. He strapped on a black web belt that held a pistol in a holster and a walkie-talkie police radio. To complete the costume, he clipped a photo ID onto his shirt pocket that said he was employed by a well-known security company.

He used a wet wipe to clean the makeup off his face while looking in a pocket-sized mirror. The last item in the handbag was an official-looking clipboard that held a pad of business forms printed with a calendar-like schedule of weekdays and times. He put a few checkmarks next to various entries, as if he'd been keeping track of his rounds.

The average person wouldn't suspect anyone who wore a uniform, carried a clipboard, and looked like he or she was in charge of things. Many people were unthinkingly obedient and compliant to anyone in authority. A lab coat, a uniform, even a clipboard or a name tag along with a commanding tone of voice could make them obey in a response similar to Pavlov's dog. However, cops could smell criminal activity from a mile away. Their BS detectors were always on high alert.

Zhukov tuned the handheld radio so he could listen to the police channel. Standing there in the open-sided parking area, he got decent reception and could listen to what was happening. And all the while, he appeared as if he worked there and was a part of the establishment.

He listened to some chatter on the radio. The police were not talking about him, only about Jake Wolfe, "the suspect." He smiled at the thought of the useful fool he'd impersonated. Wolfe was close to his same height and weight, and he was now the subject of a manhunt while he, *The Artist,* walked away free. Such is life in the world of instant news, quick judgments and the unthinking viral sharing of popular memes that have no basis in reality.

"I wish I could have stayed to watch more of the spectacle," Zhukov said out loud. "I was only being paid for one target, but I got three. The Madonna, the baby, and I also framed Wolfe at no extra charge. That's because I'm the best."

Zhukov knew he should call Banks and give him a report, but right now he wasn't in the mood to talk to the elitist, privileged oligarch. Banks could use a lesson in humility. Someday, Zhukov would deliver the lesson. He smiled at the thought.

CHAPTER 71

Jake had memorized Secret Service Agent McKay's phone number, and he punched it into one of the prepaid phones.

"Shannon McKay."

"It's Jake Wolfe. The shooter just called my phone to laugh at me. I'm sure he used a throwaway phone, like the one I'm on now. But if you hurry and put a trace on his phone that called mine, you might get lucky."

McKay typed on her keyboard. "Thanks, I've assigned an agent to do it. And you're heading to the police department to turn yourself in, right?"

"Yes, ma'am."

"Liar."

"Bye now."

"Wait."

"Okay I'm waiting, but I can't stay on the phone for long. You understand why," Jake said.

"I'll be brief. I'm currently the one and *only* person who believes that you were impersonated. Right now, I'm trying to get the police and the FBI to listen to me, but they're like sharks that smell blood in the water."

"I can understand how they would react that way. They saw my evil twin with their own eyes."

"Right. I have a video of you at the park, but they have video of you committing the crime. I have voice recognition of you on a call, but they have dozens of your media peers as witnesses against you. My evidence could be faked, theirs appears to be iron-clad."

"I look guilty, I have to admit, but more importantly, how are Katherine Anderson and her baby?"

"You're more concerned about them than you are for yourself?"

"Of course. I'm not pregnant, and I haven't been shot."

"Katherine and her baby are both alive and well. She was shot with a red paintball, not a bullet."

"That's so … bizarre. You're absolutely sure?"

"Yes, absolutely."

"That's a relief. But why would someone do that?"

"Unknown, but everybody in San Francisco with a gun and a badge is hunting you down."

"I'm sure they're just following orders, but it would be nice if they went after the real criminal with the zeal they're going after the innocent man. Meanwhile, they're letting the guilty person get away. This happens all the time—just ask the folks at the Innocence Project."

"That's what I've been trying to explain to everyone. But I work for another agency, I'm from out of town and I have breasts, so they aren't listening to me so far."

"Talk to SFPD Sergeant Beth Cushman. She's my buddy Terrell's partner and is super smart. She'll listen to you and then talk to the chief."

"I'll do that. And I've already sent photos of the real suspect to the FBI and the SFPD. But the man is a master of disguise, so the photos might not be much help."

"Who is this guy? I want to find him and make him sorry he was ever born."

"This information is on a need-to-know basis—but I saw in your files that you have top secret clearance."

"Yeah, when I served in the Marines, I did some work that was classified."

"My theory is that the suspect is a hired killer named Ivan Zhukov who works for the highest bidder, often wealthy multinational corporations and financial conglomerates. He almost always operates in disguise as part of his standard operating procedure."

"Your theory? You can't prove it was him?"

"No, and I can't prove it wasn't you."

"What kind of corporation would hire a killer?"

"Secretive cartels that control vast empires of food, drugs, energy, and commodities all around the world. Most companies would never do such a thing. But there are a few criminal organizations pretending to be businesses. Does that surprise you, being in the news media?"

"Nothing surprises me any longer. Who does this guy kill for his bosses, and why?"

"We suspect he recently killed an inventor who was developing a hovercar that floats on four fans instead of rolling on four wheels," McKay said.

"Like a quadcopter, but way bigger and with a seat in the middle?"

"Yes, the hovercar looks similar to other cars, but it floats a foot off the ground and runs on electricity. It's made out of hemp fiber, which is lightweight like plastic but has an unbreakable kind of shock-absorbing quality like thick rubber."

"Henry Ford invented a car made out of hemp. I saw an old film clip of it on YouTube."

"This scientist took Ford's idea to the next level and made it into a hovercraft vehicle that costs half as much to buy and maintain as a regular car, and it doesn't burn any gasoline."

"That would disrupt a lot of industries—car makers, tire manufacturers, oil and gas companies, auto parts suppliers, steel mills, plastic conglomerates—you name it."

"None of those industries were aware of this invention. Somebody who was invested in their stocks found out about it and decided the world was not ready for such a breakthrough."

"Did a major investment firm or a super wealthy individual have the inventor killed?"

"I believe a particular group of rogue investors hired Zhukov to kill the inventor," McKay said. "The genius died in a hit-and-run car accident, and the prototype for the hovercar disappeared from a highly secure laboratory on the same night."

"If the hovercar caught on, the stock of that company would shoot way up. Meanwhile the stocks of those other companies would go down, and the investors would lose millions."

"So the inventor had to go. Someday these wealthy individuals will patent his hovercar idea and sell it, but that's almost impossible to prove."

As Jake was walking, he saw two police officers drive up on Harley-Davidsons and begin a search pattern. "Sorry, McKay, but I'll have to call you back on another burner phone. This one has been traced by the police."

"Jake, stay with me. I need to tell you something else. It's important."

But Jake was already gone.

CHAPTER 72

At the Moscone Center, Secret Service agents searched the perimeter and found the white van reported as Jake Wolfe's hiding place. Agents surrounded the vehicle with their weapons drawn, ready to fire.

One agent spoke into a megaphone and said, "You are surrounded by federal agents. Drop your weapon and come out of the van with your hands above your head."

There was no response. Agent Adams, the sniper, took aim at the van from his vantage point in an upstairs window. The sun reflected on the van windows, but he could just make out a man lying down in the back. He appeared to be holding a rifle.

Adams focused the rifle scope's crosshairs on the target and spoke with Agent McKay over his radio. "McKay, this is Adams. I have *eyes on target*. He's lying prone inside the van. Please advise if you want the target taken alive for questioning, or if I should shoot to kill."

"I want him alive for questioning. Please stand by for further orders," McKay said.

"Roger that, standing by."

McKay spoke to one of the agents on the ground. "Easton, this is McKay. Our sniper has eyes on target. The suspect inside the van is lying prone and holding a rifle. I'd like to bring him in alive for questioning. I have a feeling he's not the shooter but is an accomplice or a decoy. The shooter seems far too intelligent to be there."

Easton said, "Understood, McKay. One question, can our sniper's *tranq* dart break through the window glass?"

"No, that's the problem, so I'm hoping you can break a window to clear his line of fire," McKay said. "Or pull open one of the front doors and toss a flash-bang grenade inside the van."

"We could send the robot to open the van."

"Negative, the suspect might start shooting, and then so would all our agents. You have to take him by surprise."

"Roger that, I'm on it." Easton decided that if he shot a window, it could kill the person inside the van, because the man would probably stand up and start firing his rifle. He took a stun grenade from the agent who was carrying the special weapons. Holding it in his right hand, he crouched down behind some parked cars and snuck up on the van. If any of the doors might be unlocked, the driver's door had the best odds. When he reached the parked car closest to the van, he spoke into his collar microphone. "Moving in on the target."

He pulled the pin on the grenade but held tight on the trigger while he ran to the van and yanked on the door handle. It was locked, and a proximity detector picked up the van's movement. It sent power to another device that ignited a string of firecrackers inside the van. Easton heard what sounded like a rapid series of gunshots.

Another Agent yelled, "Shots fired, get down!"

Easton dropped to the ground, still gripping the grenade, and he yelled, "This is Easton, I'm all right. Shoot out the back window so the sniper can use the tranq gun."

His order came too late, as the rest of the agents reacted the way they were trained to do. They opened fire with their automatic weapons, riddling the van with bullets.

Adams, the sniper, had also seen what appeared to be weapon fire from inside the van, threatening his fellow agents. He fired one expertly aimed, steel-jacketed round, which went through the window, hit the target above the ear, and blew off half of his head. After taking the shot, he spoke calmly on the radio. "Shots fired from inside the van. Target one is terminated." His voice sounded cool and professional, like a Navy Top Gun pilot landing a fighter on an aircraft carrier in the ocean, at night, during a storm, with one engine on fire. No problem.

Agent Easton signaled the others to hold their fire and approached the back door of the van. He took a quick peek in the window and saw the bullet-riddled body of a Caucasian male with half of his face blown away. "Stay clear, the van could be rigged to explode. Keep a safe distance while the K9 does its job."

Easton signaled to a uniformed Secret Service agent from the canine unit, who approached with his dog and the two of them walked around the van in a slow circle.

"Seek, girl; seek, seek, seek," the agent said.

The dog seemed uncertain and growled at the van as she circled it. She stopped near the back door, sniffed there for a while and sat down.

The dog handler spoke to Easton, "She's indicating this back door as a probable location of explosives. It might be that she smells the gun smoke from inside. But she's good, real good. If she doesn't like the van's back door, I'll bet money there are explosives behind it. The question is whether or not they're rigged to go off."

"Nice work," Easton said, "Now we're going to use the robot to open the door. Can your dog find the pin I pulled out of this grenade? I'm getting tired of holding it in a death grip."

The dog handler looked at the grenade in Easton's hand, and his eyes went wide. "Yeah, we might want to locate that pin."

Easton signaled for the man with the remote-controlled robot to go ahead. Everyone took cover behind parked cars as the robot rolled toward the van on small tank treads. At the van, the robot's arm extended and pulled on the door latch. There was a small explosion and the door flew open with a burst of flames. It smashed into the robot, broke its arm and sent it flying backward. Burning metal shards from the explosion flew through the air, leaving smoking trails behind them.

"Send the robot back," Easton said. "Use the working arm to open the other door."

Easton had his pistol drawn and pointed at the van, ready to shoot anything that moved. In his other hand, he continued to hold the grenade in a tight grip. The robot handler set the device right-side up on its treads and sent it back to the van. This time, when the robot opened the other back door, there was no explosion. Easton was grateful that he hadn't tried to open the rear door instead of the driver's door. He might be in an ambulance on his way to the emergency room, possibly missing a hand or an arm, maybe blind from the shrapnel.

The dog and handler found the pin to the grenade, and Easton carefully inserted it back into the mechanism. He let out a sigh of relief, then held his pistol in front of him and approached the open back doors of the van to look inside. The dead man with the rifle looked stiff, pale-skinned, and had his mouth open. He appeared to have already been dead for several hours. Easton also noted some leftover firecrackers that hadn't gone off. The criminal who had set this up probably thought he was a funny fellow. Easton wanted to find him and shoot him. "Clear! Get a fingerprint kit over here."

One agent fingerprinted the dead man and took a DNA sample. Another took photographs and then found and peeled off the facial disguise from the half of the face that remained.

Easton saw the mask of Jake Wolfe's face being removed, revealing a different person beneath. He spoke to Agent McKay on his small microphone. "McKay, your instincts were correct. This man is a decoy. He was wearing a mask to look like Jake Wolfe. It appears that he's been dead for several hours. We're running his prints and DNA through the system now."

"Understood. The actual shooter is on the run, and I doubt if he's still disguised as Wolfe. Send me the video of the dead man's mask being removed."

Easton spoke into the microphone in his fist, alerting the other agents of the current situation. He knew that in the meantime a picture of Jake Wolfe's face had been sent to every police officer's in-car computer screen all over the state of California. Every cop was hoping to take him down and be a hero.

Easton sent the video to McKay. She forwarded it to the SFPD and the FBI, explaining again that she believed the suspect had disguised himself as Jake Wolfe; by now he probably had a new disguise.

When the update arrived at police headquarters, it was routed to the person in charge of the case. Sergeant Denton took a brief look at the half-baked conspiracy theory, shook her head in disbelief and ignored it.

The reporters at the dedication ceremony were all furious at Jake Wolfe. He was one of their own, and they felt sick at heart about what he'd done. They wanted him to go down hard.

Jake's media rival, Dick Arnold, was especially thrilled with this bad news. Arnold was dedicating all his time and effort to this news story, and was regularly updating an ongoing special report about Jake. Arnold called the police officer he'd briefly talked to at the golf course shooting, the one named Denton. His call went to voicemail and he left a message.

"Hello, Officer Denton, my name is Dick Arnold. I'm a television news reporter. We spoke recently at the Paradise Golf Course crime scene. I'm doing a story about this Jake Wolfe criminal and I'd like to include a quote from you in the news story. Please call me back at this number."

Secret Service agents were out in force at the hospital where Katherine Anderson was being treated. They guarded the hallways, staked out the rooftop, and secured the surrounding buildings.

Katherine had suffered from shock, but she was in stable condition and resting. Her friend, Dr. Rachel Brook, was in the room. Daniel was there too, holding his wife's hand and not leaving her side. Dr. Brook had a nurse take an ultrasound of Katherine's abdomen and send the images to the computer on her desk. She then went out of Katherine's room and down the hall to her office to view the ultrasound in privacy.

Dr. Brook closed her office door, sat at her desk and studied the reading. Judging by what she could see, the baby appeared unhurt. And as she looked closely, she also noted that it appeared to be a girl. Dr. Brook was about to go back to Katherine's room and tell her the good news, but she stopped when she saw the rest of the test results regarding Katherine's overall health.

Dr. Brook leaned closer to the computer screen and read the report, again and again, not wanting to believe what it said. After confirming the findings, she felt her heart sink. A drop of cold sweat dripped down the back of her neck, and she clenched her fists so tightly that her fingernails dug into her palms.

"Please no, it can't be," she whispered. "Please, not *that*. Not now."

CHAPTER 73

In the Homicide Detail squad room, Sergeant Denton was in her element, hunting down a man she hated. "Get me cell phone tower dumps from every tower near Wolfe's condo, the yacht harbor and his place of employment. I want all the phone company's stored data from those towers for the past year."

"Working on that now," Kirby said.

"And somebody give me updates on Wolfe's phone," Denton said. "What is his current location and who is he talking to right now?"

A man sitting at a nearby desk said, "I'm logged in to his phone company's private portal for law enforcement, and I'm pinging his device. His phone is changing direction and moving south on Highway 101 toward the airport."

"Alert the TSA and airport security. Call the taxicab companies, tell them to be looking for Wolfe, and ask them which cabs are en route to the airport right now."

"Half the taxis in the city are going to the airport and back all day."

"So what? Tell the companies to call those cabs and ask who they're transporting. If it's a man and a dog, we've probably found our suspect. That other taxi driver called in and said Wolfe had his stupid animal with him. What kind of idiot fugitive brings their pet along when they're on the run from the police?"

An officer said, "The electronic surveillance van has been in pursuit of the signal from Wolfe's phone. They think he's riding in an airport shuttle, and they're closing in on it right now."

"Do we have backup for the surveillance van?"

Everett, the squad boss, was monitoring unit movements on a tablet computer he held in his hand. "Two units are close. One is ahead of the shuttle, and the other is coming up fast from behind."

The police undercover surveillance van came alongside the airport shuttle. Sergeant Roxanne Poole used a homing device to track Wolfe's phone. She spoke to her driver. "Suspect's phone location confirmed onboard the airport shuttle."

The driver spoke into his mic. "We have confirmation on the shuttle, units may proceed."

The cop that was coming up from behind the shuttle moved his car close to the van's bumper and turned on his lights and siren. The police car up ahead started slowing down, which forced the shuttle driver to press on his brakes. The surveillance van driver turned on his lights and drove so closely alongside the shuttle that it almost bumped up against it.

The frazzled airport shuttle driver was being boxed in by three police vehicles. The only place to go was to his right, onto the shoulder of the highway. The driver looked to his left at the van and saw a window go down, revealing a police officer pointing an assault rifle at him.

The police car behind the shuttle turned on its speakers, and a cop said, "Airport shuttle driver, this is the San Francisco police. Pull over to the right, turn off your engine and put your hands on top of your head."

The shuttle driver was sweating in fear as he pulled the shuttle off to the side of the highway and parked. Several police officers ran to the vehicle with their guns drawn. Two cops wearing body armor and high-tech helmets came into the van. One of them put handcuffs on the driver and made him get out and lie facedown on the ground. The other cop shouted, "Everybody in the shuttle, put your hands behind your heads and interlace your fingers."

He had his pistol in one hand and was holding a device in the other that looked like a typical handheld GPS, but it could "ping" any mobile phone and determine its location. He walked up and down the aisle of the shuttle and stopped in front of a frightened woman. He waved the device over her and her possessions. A low tone emitted from the device when he pointed it at her shopping bag.

The cop's Plexiglas face shield muffled his voice when he said, "Dump out the contents of your bag. Slowly, no sudden moves."

The tourist began sobbing and nodding her head as she carefully upended her shopping bag onto the empty seat next to her.

The cop saw the mobile phone and held his device close to it. There was a fast tone from the device, and he picked up the phone in his gloved hand. "Where did you get this?"

She looked at the phone as if it was a poisonous snake and she shook her head. "I've never seen that phone before in my life."

Her husband just sat there, confused and slightly panicked, looking back and forth between the phone and the cop.

The officer took the phone, exited the shuttle and went to the electronic surveillance van. He handed the device to Roxanne.

Roxanne was the Computer Forensics Unit technician and was referred to as Rox by her friends, and "box of rocks" when being teased. She was a geek genius when it came to anything high-tech. She used one finger to push her glasses higher on her nose, looked at the phone and then at her colleague. "Is the suspect in custody?"

"No, he sent his phone on a ride."

"Clever son of a gun; you've got to give him credit for that."

Several black SUVs with federal government license plates raced up to the scene and stopped with a screech of tires. Men and women in dark suits and dark sunglasses got out and waved their FBI credentials at the police.

"FBI, we'll take it from here," one agent said, as several other agents surrounded the bus.

The police officer in charge of the scene said, "This is a city case, we can handle it ourselves."

"No, the FBI has jurisdiction."

The SFPD officer called headquarters and was advised to hand over the crime scene to the FBI, but to continue following up other leads in the investigation.

Rox looked out the window of the surveillance van and saw what was happening. She picked up a CelleBrite Universal Forensic Extraction Device (UFED) and plugged it into Jake Wolfe's mobile phone.

In a few seconds, Rox had cracked the phone's password and downloaded a copy of the entire memory. She extracted all the phone's existing and hidden phone data, including call history, text messages, contacts, photos, videos, internet browsing history and GPS data. The device even found everything that had ever been deleted, and it copied all of that too. Rox put the phone back into the plastic baggie and spoke to the other cop. "Can you give this phone to the FBI agents? That way, if they ask you about it, you can honestly say you don't know anything."

The officer nodded and took the evidence bag from Rox. He got out of the police van, gave the phone to the nearest FBI agent, and explained that it was Jake Wolfe's phone. Rox saw the FBI agent say something, but her driver only shrugged his shoulders and walked away.

Rox was happy for once to give away a crime scene to the feds.

The cops drove away with grins on their faces. They were looking forward to seeing the FBI agents on the news being asked to explain how the phone was on the shuttle, but the suspect wasn't.

While her partner drove them back toward the police headquarters on 3rd Street, Roxanne called in and gave Denton her report on the situation. As Rox was talking, she plugged the forensic device into her vehicle's police computer and sent a file of Jake Wolfe's phone data to Denton as an email attachment.

Denton cursed at Rox when she heard about Wolfe's trick of sneaking his phone onto the shuttle, as if it was the technician's fault somehow.

"Get everything Wolfe has. His online purchase history, his Google searches, his deleted emails, and any images from his phone that are stored in the cloud. None of that is ever fully erased. They keep a copy forever."

"Working on it as we speak," Rox said, tapping on her computer keyboard as the van moved through the streets. Rox rolled her eyes. She was well aware of how to do her job and didn't need some uptight sergeant telling her how. "I'm also getting his internet service provider and his antispyware software company to give me his web browsing history for the past several years," Rox said. "They both track you the entire time you are online."

Denton ended the call abruptly and started scanning through the electronic file that Rox had sent. It was obvious that the suspect was a photographer. Wolfe had an amazing number of pictures on his phone. She quickly scrolled through the photos, looking for sexy selfies. But she was disappointed when she didn't find any nude photos.

"Someone get the post office to do a mail cover," Denton said. "Their mail imaging computers take photographs of the exterior of every piece of mail sent in the United States. Request the stored images of all mail received by Wolfe for the past three years."

A cop said, "No problem, making the call now. Most people have gone paperless, though, so there probably won't be much to look at except junk mail."

"Where are the phone numbers on those prepaid phones Wolfe bought?"

"I've been trying to get them, but the gift shop people can't seem to find the records," Kirby said.

"Oh, really? Send a uniformed officer there, a big scary guy like Randall, and see if it helps jog their memory. If they still don't cooperate, have Randall start searching the place inch by inch and asking everybody for ID."

"I'll call Randall right now."

"Does Wolfe have any emails or online purchase activity going on?"

"He just paid his electric bill with a travel points credit card—why would a fugitive on the run care about that?"

"You've never heard of automatic bill pay?"

"Oh, right. Other than that, he's receiving lots of text messages and emails asking him WTF, but he hasn't sent out any texts or emails himself in the past few minutes. His most recent phone calls and texts in the past hour went to SFPD officers Hayes and Cushman, a local FBI agent named Knight, and an unknown number in Washington D.C. that is not listed in any database."

For a moment, Denton felt a twinge of doubt about Wolfe's calls to the mysterious D.C. phone number but her hatred overrode her doubt and she shrugged it off. That filthy criminal had to go down, and she had to get promoted so she could protect this city from lowlifes like him. She wanted that lieutenant's shield. It would help her destroy more criminals. That was all that mattered right now. She had to win at all costs.

Denton began to pace back and forth again, clenching and unclenching her fists. She noticed Everett, the squad boss, watching her.

CHAPTER 74

Jake's new throwaway phone buzzed, but it didn't display a number. It only said "Unavailable." Jake answered the call. "I'm sure popular today."

"Jake, this is Agent Knight at the FBI. What the hell is going on?"

"How did you get this number?"

"I got it because I'm in the FBI and we know what you're going to do before you even think of doing it. We know where you were last night and what you had for breakfast this morning. Now tell me your side of the story, and it better be good."

"Yes, sir. In a nutshell, a woman called me from work to say I'd been taken off my photography assignment at the Moscone Center. I was sent to do a lifestyle photo shoot at the Marina Green instead."

"Who called you? What was her name?"

"She told me she was a new hire named Pam. Next, when I used my remote to start my car, there was a small explosion that blew out the windshield."

"An explosion inside your vehicle?"

"Yes, somebody set me up to be the fall guy. Now my goal is to find the man who is impersonating me, and beat him to a pulp. That's about it ... so how's your day going?"

"You have no idea," Knight said. "The perpetrator left a body in a media van and the Secret Service shot a few dozen holes in him.

Everybody is so jumpy they'll shoot anyone who even looks like you. If you have a twin brother, tell him to stay home and hide under the bed."

"My only twin is the guy impersonating me."

"Turn yourself in to one of our FBI agents so we can keep you safe in protective custody while we figure this thing out."

"Everyone is giving me that same advice, and I wish I could follow it, but I don't feel like disappearing into the witness protection program."

"You'll only be going to our FBI headquarters in the federal building here in town. And you don't have any choice. I'm not asking you, I'm ordering you to stop running and to let an FBI agent bring you in."

"Sorry, but I can't let this guy get away with shooting Katherine Anderson."

"No, Jake, the last thing we need is you acting as an angry vigilante. Several agents are converging on your position and they're going to bring you in."

"Okay, G-Man, you win," Jake said. "Tell your people that I'm thinking of giving myself up into their custody." Jake ended the call and took the battery out of the phone.

He told himself that he hadn't lied to a federal agent. That would've been a crime. He'd said he was *thinking of* giving himself up. He did momentarily think about it, but he decided against it. Jake felt that the FBI was an impressive organization and he tried to help whenever he could, but he had no desire to be taken in for questioning. Federal laws were so incredibly broad that you could be sent to prison simply for talking, for saying a few words. Next year, the feds would probably start arresting anyone who passed gas.

Agent Knight continued speaking to Jake, but the call had ended. He hoped Jake would turn himself in; if his story was true, the man had been framed and nearly murdered so far today. If a rookie police officer found him, he might end up being shot by mistake, but if Knight took Jake into custody, he could make sure his friend got a fair hearing. Jake was already being smeared in the news media. His life could unravel fast, and he might never recover. Right now, his best hope was to trust Knight.

He looked at a framed quote he kept on his desk to remind him to use his FBI power wisely. The quote was by an FBI agent named Gary Aldrich, who had worked at the White House. Knight read the words every day.

> The mere existence of an FBI investigation can lead to an individual's personal, professional, and financial destruction. An actual indictment is like dropping a house on someone. FBI agents, at least senior ones, are well aware of this, and they use their power wisely. We have seen how businesses can go under, banks fail, marriages dissolve, prosecutors become famous, and defense attorneys become wealthy as a result of a single visit from an FBI agent.

Katherine Anderson rested in her hospital bed with her eyes half-closed. She'd asked to be released so she could go home, but had been told there were a few more tests to be done. Various doctors and nurses and Secret Service agents came into her room and went out again. Daniel sat next to her and held her hand while he talked quietly on his phone.

Down the hallway, Dr. Rachel Brook was in her office studying Katherine's chart. Her prognosis was that the mother and baby both appeared to be uninjured by the paintball, thank goodness. Dr. Brook's concern was what she'd seen on a routine ultrasound of Katherine's breasts. She stared closely at the image. The sight of it gave her a knot in her stomach. The ultrasound could be wrong, but in the image, it looked as if Katherine might have a mass in her left breast. It could be a harmless lump related to pregnancy, or it could be a tumor … breast cancer.

Many women who were surprised with a prenatal diagnosis of cancer were then faced with frightening decisions about their own health and their baby's health. It was doubly challenging to save both lives. Sometimes the mother opted to have her breasts removed in a double mastectomy.

Dr. Brook knew that Katherine had tried for years to get pregnant, and this baby was greatly wanted and hoped for and loved. She felt a weight on her heart, but reminded herself they couldn't be sure of any diagnosis based on this hurried exam. They'd need to do a biopsy.

CHAPTER 75

At the SFPD Homicide Detail squad room, Kirby looked up from his computer screen. "We got the numbers of the prepaid phones. Wolfe was just now using one and talking to … wait … the FBI?"

"He must be talking to the feds because he's scared of the SFPD. Where is he right now?"

"He's near Fisherman's Wharf. That makes sense because his phone went on the shuttle near there. The wharf was his last known location. We have two cops searching the area."

Denton cursed at herself for assuming that Wolfe had boarded the shuttle, hidden the phone, and then exited at one of the next stops. "Send more cops, double up on the search. Do we have any CCTV cameras at the wharf? Can we see if there's a man with a dog? Hopefully Wolfe is still taking his stupid pet along for the ride."

"Some of the tourist shops have security cameras in their windows. We can start calling them."

~

At the wharf, Jake pretended to be a blind man wearing dark sunglasses and walking carefully along the sidewalk with a golden-haired guide dog by his side. All Jake needed was a white cane to complete his disguise. It felt wrong to be impersonating a blind man, so he'd have to atone by making a donation to charity. Cody, however, was a certified service dog and the vest he was wearing was the real thing.

Jake wanted to hunt down Zhukov, but first he had to dodge the police dragnet and get free of this crowd of tourists. As he walked down the crowded street, he was surrounded by people, yet he still felt alone.

He stopped and bought a souvenir. It was an inexpensive garden flag attached to a white wooden dowel. He asked the seller what the flag said. The woman told him it said, "Grandma's Garden." Jake walked a block away, removed the flag and set it on a park bench. He then used the five-foot-long white dowel as a makeshift cane, tapping it in front of him as he walked along with Cody.

He noticed a lot of sudden activity in the tourist shops along the street. People came out of doorways and looked around, talking on phones and adjusting storefront CCTV cameras. The citizen snoops were eager and willing to hunt down a fellow citizen and a neighbor, as long as someone in authority told them they had to do it because he was one of "the bad people."

Time was running out—he had to go into hiding. Too many law enforcement organizations were on his trail. There was only one other organization he knew of that could possibly help him now. He was going to have to call in a powerful favor, but he couldn't use his current phone to do it. His guess was that Agent Knight must be really fast at tracing calls, or else the cops had discovered the numbers of his prepaid phones. Either way, it was time to dump the phone he'd just used.

Jake walked toward a trash can, but then noticed the line of people waiting to get onto the ferry boat to Alcatraz Island for a tour of the old abandoned prison. A smile crossed his face as he thought of the previous phone he'd sent on a journey to the airport. He put the battery back into the burner phone and set the volume on mute. He then passed close by the line of tourists, gently bumped into a man who was wearing a camera bag on his belt, and dropped his prepaid phone into the man's bag. Jake apologized for bumping into the man. When the tourist turned and saw the dark glasses, white cane and guide dog, he said, "That's okay, man. No problem."

Jake and Cody walked away. "That trick might not work twice, but it's worth a try, huh?"

Cody barked once and panted Ha-Ha-Ha.

Jake went down a side street away from the wharf and the crowds and activity. He'd been walking in this direction because there was a quiet little bar here he knew of that still had an old-fashioned pay phone in the back near the restrooms. When Jake went inside, the bartender said, "Hey, you can't bring a dog in here."

Jake turned in the general direction of the voice but looked off to one side as if he couldn't see the man. "I'm sorry, but he's my seeing-eye dog. I have a permit to take him anywhere. It's the law, my friend. If you don't comply with the law, this place will be shut down, and you'll be out of a job. We'll be gone in just a minute after I make a phone call."

"Why is that dog giving me a strange look?"

"Maybe he thinks you look strange. He's trained to bite your nuts off if you seem like a threat."

"Go on and use the phone, but make it quick."

"Thanks, and I'll put in a good word with my dog about your nuts."

Jake walked away, tapping his cane. When he got to the pay phone, he was glad to find that it was still in working order. The very few pay phones that were left these days were often vandalized and broken. One day soon, they would become as extinct as the dinosaurs. The only reason this phone was still here was that it helped mitigate the legal liability of the bar owner. This way the owner could say he'd provided a phone for patrons to call a taxi if they were too drunk to drive. It wasn't his fault if they got in a wreck.

Jake placed a call to the Italian restaurant where he'd worked years ago, when he was in high school. A woman answered, and Jake said, "I have a case of Montepulciano d'Abruzzo to deliver to Anselmo Amborgetti, but I'm having car *trouble* and I need someone to pick me up. Please tell Big Mo I'll be in debt to him and it is *a matter of honor*."

There was a long pause, and then the woman said in Italian, "*Un momento, per favore*."

An older man came on the line, his voice raspy from grappa and cigars. "Who is this?"

"Hey, Big Mo, it's me, Jake the Knife," Jake said, using his old nickname from his restaurant days. When Jake was a restaurant cook, he'd once gotten into a heated argument with a waiter, and he'd thrown a kitchen knife in anger and stuck it into a wall. Hence, the nickname that would forever be his on the Italian side of his family tree.

"Where are you, little buddy?"

"I'm in a bar near Fisherman's Wharf," Jake said and recited the name and address.

"I know that place. I've got a man and a car close by there right now. He'll pick you up out back in the alley in a few minutes. How is your mother? We all love her and miss her here."

"Mom's doing great. She misses all of you too. Tell your driver I've got a dog with me."

"That's good you got a dog. I'll call my guy right now."

"Thanks, Mo. You are a man of honor."

"And you are family to us here. You can always call, day or night, and we will stand by you. *Capisci?*"

"*Capisco.*" Relieved, Jake hung up the pay phone with a surge of gratitude for the loyalty of his Italian friend and the entire Amborgetti family. He was related to Anselmo by a cousin or two. Jake's mother, Rosabella, had worked at the restaurant for many years. Eventually she'd changed their lasagna to her own grandmother's handwritten recipe that had been brought across the ocean from Italy.

The members of the Amborgetti family were some of the most trustworthy people Jake had ever known. Just don't ever break the *famiglia's* trust. They could be fearsome people, and they had *long* memories. They never forgot a friend or an enemy—never. If someone double-crossed them, the next thing you heard was that his dead body had floated up to the piers with a canary stuffed in his mouth.

Jake walked out the back door with Cody and they hid out of sight in the doorway alcove. Soon, a black limousine drove up the alley from Jake's right and stopped next to him. The driver's window went down. An amused but dangerous-looking Italian man gave the two of them an appraising look and then nodded his head. The locks on the passenger doors popped open, and Jake and Cody got into the backseat.

CHAPTER 76

Sergeant Kirby studied his computer monitor and said, "The prepaid phone Wolfe recently used is now heading out onto the water in the Bay."

"He's trying to escape on a boat, just like I thought he would," Denton said. "Get me the SFPD Marine Police, hurry."

"You're patched into patrol boat SF Marine 1, on line three."

Denton put the desk phone on speaker. "This is Sergeant Denton in Homicide. We're tracking a phone used by the fugitive Jake Wolfe. It is currently moving out onto the water."

A deep, gravelly voice said, "This is Captain Leeds. We're receiving your data on our computer. It appears the device is moving in the direction of Alcatraz."

"Maybe he thinks he can hide out on the island. Pursue and intercept. Be advised the fugitive is considered armed and dangerous. He also has a military dog with him. The dog is trained to kill and is suffering from PTSD. Do not hesitate to fire at will on either the man or the dog. Both of them are a serious threat to public safety."

"Affirmative, Sergeant, we're engaging in pursuit now."

The police boat's computer-controlled diesel engines roared and its siren wailed as it charged across the water of the San Francisco Bay. Leeds stood tall in the bridge, looking ahead through binoculars. Marine 1 was the SFPD's largest boat—a police version of the forty-seven-foot US Coast Guard motorized boat known as a USCG MLB.

As the boat got closer to the location of the phone signal, Captain Leeds made positive ID of the vessel up ahead and reported it on the radio.

"Sergeant Denton, the phone we're tracking appears to be riding on the Alcatraz ferry that takes tourists to the island."

Denton cursed. "Understood, Leeds. FYI, the last time we closed in on the suspect's phone on public transportation, it turned out that he'd sent it for a ride on an airport shuttle while he went in another direction."

Leeds and his police shipmates heard that on the speaker and they all started laughing. Leeds took his thumb off the transmit button on his radio to prevent Denton from hearing them. He laughed along with his crew for a moment, then held his hand up for silence and pressed the button and said, "Roger that, Denton. We'll assume the suspect is on board, but if all we find is his phone, we won't be surprised."

As the ferry got closer to Alcatraz Island, another SFPD patrol boat, a smaller and faster M2-37 twin-engine aluminum Moose Boat, raced ahead to pass the target vessel and cut it off from the other direction. The powerboat soon overtook the ferry and pulled in front of it. The lights and siren came on, and a voice boomed from the loudspeakers. "This is the San Francisco police. Turn off your engines and stop your vessel. Everyone on board, put your hands on top of your heads and do not move. Prepare to be boarded." A uniformed officer stood on the deck of the police boat, holding a high-powered rifle so the passengers and crew on the ferry boat could see him.

Marine 1 came up behind the ferry boat, and Captain Leeds studied the ferry with his binoculars. When the ferry powered down its engines, the police boat pulled up alongside it. Leeds hailed the ferry boat captain on the ship-to-ship radio. "San Francisco Police patrol boat Marine 1 hailing The Hornblower."

"This is The Hornblower. Captain Foster speaking. Go ahead, Marine 1."

"Captain Foster, this is Captain Leeds. Do you happen to have a yellow Labrador dog or a golden retriever on board your vessel at this time?"

Foster was puzzled by the question, but he recovered quickly. "No, sir, Captain Leeds. Although we do allow service animals on board, there are currently no dogs on the vessel."

"Understood. We are now going to board The Hornblower and search your vessel, passengers, and crew. Your full cooperation will be appreciated."

"Yes, sir, understood."

"Stand by to be boarded."

Leeds made it his business to know all about the various boats in *his* Bay. The Alcatraz ferry boat named The Hornblower was the nation's first hybrid ferry. The sixty-four-foot eco-friendly vessel was powered mostly by solar panels, wind turbines, and grid electricity. Leeds was impressed by the effort that went into it.

Leeds switched on the loudspeakers and said, "Attention, passengers and crew of the ferry boat Hornblower. Stand by to be boarded by the San Francisco police. Keep your hands on your heads and sit very still to avoid arrest or possible injury. Your full cooperation is appreciated. We are looking for a specific individual. If you have nothing to hide, you have nothing to fear."

The passengers on the ferry boat had their hands on their heads. Some were frightened while others were thrilled to see the police boats and the officers in action. The police boat came up alongside the ferry, and several armed police officers boarded the ferry. Captain Leeds walked into the control area. Captain Foster stood at attention and saluted.

"Captain Foster of The Hornblower," Foster said. "The vessel is yours to command, Captain Leeds."

Leeds nodded in appreciation of the man's professional manner and said, "You're a good captain, Foster. Thank you for your cooperation."

The police boat didn't have the same high-tech equipment used by Roxanne in the surveillance van, so the officers searched everyone the old-fashioned way. They made the passengers empty out their pockets and purses, searched their belongings, and frisked them one by one.

An officer named Maltz found Wolfe's prepaid phone in a tourist's camera bag. "I've got the phone," Maltz said, and he put the device into a plastic evidence bag.

Maltz showed the phone to the man who had been carrying it and said, "Where did you get this?"

The nervous man said, "It's not mine. I swear I've never seen it before. You have to believe me."

"Have you seen or talked to a man who had a golden-haired dog with him?"

"Yes, sir, a blind man with a white cane and a Labrador retriever guide dog bumped into me when I was in line to board the ferry."

Maltz nodded and walked over to Leeds. "We've finished searching the vessel, Captain. The fugitive and his dog are not on board, only his phone. The man who had the phone in his camera bag said a blind man with a guide dog bumped into him as he was boarding the ferry."

"Good work. We're done here, let's return to the boat," Leeds said.

The police officers began to disembark The Hornblower and return to the police boat.

Leeds turned to Foster. "We found what we were looking for, Captain. That phone was slipped into someone's camera bag. The suspect did this same thing on an airport shuttle earlier today."

Foster looked visibly relieved that no one on his boat was being arrested at gunpoint. He nodded his head politely at Leeds.

Leeds handed his police business card to Foster and said, "One of these days we should have a beer after work."

Foster gave Leeds his card in return. "That would be great, Captain Leeds. I'll look forward to it, thank you."

The men shook hands, and then Leeds and the remaining police exited the ferry boat and reboarded Marine 1.

CHAPTER 77

In Brussels, Belgium, the members of the Global Assets Council were conducting a secret meeting. Belgium had more castles per square mile than any other nation, and one of the castles was owned by a powerful woman in the pharmaceutical business. She was an actual princess, and her fourteenth-century palace was surrounded by forty private acres of immaculate grounds, including a rose garden with over ten thousand rose bushes in two hundred different varieties. Her estate was often used as a secure location for Council meetings. She provided her fellow members with luxurious and elegantly decorated suites, beds made up with the finest linens, and food prepared by top-rated chefs.

Several men with high-powered rifles and trained dogs walked the perimeter of the estate. Electronic jamming equipment ensured that no one could eavesdrop. The business that was being discussed here included billion-dollar deals and life-and-death decisions that could affect millions of people around the world. Brussels was home to over two thousand international corporations, scores of them owned by Council members. The secretive, private group rarely accepted new members, and then by invitation only. If anyone declined the invitation, they soon died in an "accident" or from "natural causes."

The Council's official address was a small office in a nondescript building, on the second floor above a bank. The bank was on the Isle of

Man, off the coast of England. No one ever showed up for work at the office. No one ever answered the phone. All calls went to a voicemail system. There were no visitors, except for one time when a private investigator had picked the lock. The only things the PI had found in the office were an empty desk, a chair, and a computer monitor. The monitor had turned on without him touching it, and a female voice had spoken to him. The voice had the sound of an artificial intelligence system, much like SIRI.

"You are trespassing. Your face has been recorded on video. Police are now en route. Please sit in the chair and wait. Cooperate peacefully with the arresting officers, to avoid injury to yourself."

The PI had fled the scene. A week later he was walking across a street in London and was struck by a car and killed in an unsolved hit-and-run accident. No one ever visited the office again after that.

The purpose behind the Council's secret work was to create a private investment group. An association designed to enable its members to buy and sell at a better advantage by avoiding middlemen, government regulations, and taxes.

The members considered their group to be a sovereign entity, above the law. Not liable for taxes or lawsuits, and not loyal to any nation or government. Their only loyalty was to profits and power. Billions of dollars of their ill-gotten gains were secretly stashed away tax-free in offshore banks in the Cayman Islands and Bermuda. A numbered account in Switzerland held their substantial accumulation of gold coins.

The international group's members included dictators and other political leaders, billionaire business tycoons, arms dealers, and heads of organized crime groups. Plus a few high-ranking military officers and intelligence agency operatives from various governments around the world. Each year the members elected one person from their group to act as the leader, and each had their own code name, rarely ever mentioning their real names. The current leader went by the code name "Chairman Banks." Every member contributed millions of dollars to the Council's trust fund each year, for use in advancing their cause around the globe.

A deadly secret differentiated this business group and trust fund from others. The members wouldn't hesitate to pay generous sums of money to have someone killed if he or she got in their way. It was only mathematics to them. Why allow a problematic person to cost them fifty million dollars in lost profits when that person could be eliminated for a paltry one million dollars or less?

A recent Council project was designed to profit from a potential ecological disaster. They used sabotage to make it happen and caused it to be even worse than projected. Next, they profited from the millions of dollars spent on cleanup and restoration efforts—in spite of the fact that the chemicals used for clean-up caused additional toxic pollution.

Another project was a potential war conflict they had influenced and caused to escalate between two third-world dictatorships. They profited from the resulting sales of Russian AK-47 assault rifles and ammunition, and sales of armed drones manufactured in China.

A regularly implemented plan was to manipulate news stories in order to drive stock prices up or down. They would then profit from the moves by selling short or placing bets on stock option "calls and puts." Insider trading and market manipulation were illegal in the United States, although members of Congress often profited from nonpublic information. However, the Council did these stock trades through a Nigerian bank with a corrupt manager who accepted bribes and looked the other way. The US lawmakers and EU regulators were not aware of the transactions and had no control over them.

The Council's latest project involved a company that was developing a new medicine that could help save the lives of children all over the world. It promised to be twice as helpful as the drug that a competing company was currently selling, and would only cost half as much. The problem for the Council was that this new corporation was privately held, and the Council was not able to buy stock in it and profit from its success. Their plan was to put a stop to the progress of the new wonder drug and thereby protect their investments in the competing company and continue to earn windfall profits. Meanwhile, a great number of children who would die. The Council members believed that the deaths were just a cost of doing business in their line of work.

The current chairman of the Council was not in attendance at this meeting. Chairman Banks was busy in the United States, dealing with a problem. The other members had grown impatient with his leadership and with the current situation in San Francisco.

If the group decided that the current chairman was either incompetent to lead or was not being completely loyal to the group and its goals, they would have him killed immediately and without hesitation. That was the sworn agreement they all made when they joined the Council. Once a member, always a member—until the day you died of natural causes, or were eliminated due to a vote by the other members.

The Belgian princess called the meeting to order and said, "The first order of business is a vote regarding our current chairman."

CHAPTER 78

In San Francisco, Chairman Banks used his encrypted phone to call Zhukov.

"Are you calling to compliment me on my work?" Zhukov asked.

"I want to know why you failed to carry out our agreement," Banks said.

"What do you mean? Haven't you seen the news?"

"Yes, and I'm extremely angry, along with the rest of the Council."

"Explain."

"You and several other contractors were asked if you would shoot a woman. The others said no, but you said yes. Now you've pulled some kind of stunt here that I don't understand."

"I said yes, I would shoot the woman, but I didn't say I would *kill* the woman. And I did shoot her, so I honored my agreement."

"But you shot her with a paintball, not a bullet. That wasn't what the Council had in mind when we paid you a fortune to do this job."

"You paid me to neutralize the congressman so he'd be absent from his job in Washington for several days. You have achieved that result. The congressman is currently at the hospital with his wife. He's staying close by her side. Your goals have been realized, albeit in a more elegant and artistic fashion than the heavy-handed way you had envisioned."

Banks was not accustomed to having anyone talk back to him. He was almost ready to verbally abuse the hired help as he usually did, but he stopped, took a calming breath, and looked around for any targeting lasers that might be painting a dot on his body by remote control. "Very well, as long as the man stays in San Francisco tomorrow and doesn't fly back to Washington, D.C., I'll consider this mission accomplished. I'll try to convince the rest of the Council to do the same."

"Yes, it would be wise of them to be as understanding as you are," Zhukov said.

"You have no idea of the position you've placed me in, my friend," Banks said. "If I should die in a random car accident this week, you may want to disappear for a while, for your own health reasons."

"If you are killed, I will avenge your death in a suitably bloody fashion."

"Well, now, I feel so much better with that comforting news. Death no longer holds any fear or regret for me."

"You're very amusing. Tell your friends that if Congressman Anderson tries to get on a flight to Washington, I will kill him, no matter what. I guarantee that."

"What about the photojournalist who is causing problems?"

"Stalin said that death solves all problems; no man, no problem. If Wolfe gets in my way again, I'll start killing his family and friends, one by one, until no one is left alive. I already know where his parents and his sister live. I know the school where his friend Alicia works as a teacher. And I know where Sergeant Beth Cushman lives with her young son. There are many ways to get to Wolfe."

"I'll pass that information along to the rest of the Council, but in the future, we want you to let us know your plans so there are no surprises."

"You can assure the Council that I want the same results that they want. I've invested my own money, betting on their desired outcome. I'm not stupid. I figured out why you want to tamper with what the congressman is doing in Washington. I'll be profiting from the results in the same way you will."

Banks used a silk handkerchief to mop his brow. This Russian fellow was too smart for his own good. If the Council learned that he'd uncovered their secret plan, they'd have him killed immediately. "I'll hold off telling the Council that for now."

Zhukov laughed. "Yes, I imagine that's something you've never heard from one of your hired guns."

"Quite so, I'm afraid," Banks said and ended the call.

CHAPTER 79

In an alley behind a tourist bar near the Wharf, a well-hidden CCTV camera recorded video of a black limousine stopping and picking up a tall man and a golden-haired dog. The video was sent electronically to the police station computer system.

Kirby saw the camera footage and he said, "Denton, we've got something on video near the Wharf."

Denton stopped pacing and looked at the computer. "That's Wolfe, get a car over there."

"That looks to me like a blind man and his guide dog."

"Just the kind of cheap trick a criminal like Wolfe would use. That's him, I can smell him. Did we get his face on the camera? Let's run it through the facial recognition software."

"No, he was wearing a baseball cap and sunglasses and kept his head down and never looked up."

"What about the license plate?"

"It isn't clear. It seems to have some kind of reflective plastic over it. Maybe if we take screen shots and magnify them, we can read the plate."

Denton tapped some keys on her computer and magnified the video, but she couldn't see the man's face or read the car license plate. Seeing the man she believed to be Wolfe, she said, "Our long lost dynamic duo. How sweet it is." She silently added, *My promotion is a done deal thanks to you losers.*

Denton stood up and called out to the cops in the room, "We've got positive ID of Wolfe on CCTV. Damn, I'm good."

The video appeared on all their displays and went out to the computers on the police car dashboards. Kirby raised his eyebrows because Denton had lied about the positive ID. She was gambling and betting on this, but since he was her partner, he went along with her.

"Now to close the net on those criminals," Denton said. "Their asses are mine. Maybe Wolfe will resist arrest or pull a weapon. That would make my day." The cuts on Denton's arm throbbed as she imagined shooting the evil man and his filthy animal.

Police cars converged on the six-block area around the bar. Their orders were to find a black limousine. However, there were always dozens of limos crisscrossing the city at any time of day.

Kirby worked on the computer for a bit and then said, "I've got some of the plate."

"Send it out to all units."

A few minutes later an officer driving an unmarked car passed by a limousine. His automatic license plate reader camera got a positive ID. He did a U-turn and radioed in. "I'm following a limo that matches the partial on the license plate."

"Keep them in sight, but don't get too close or pull them over. We want to get them surrounded," Denton said.

"Copy that. Here's my current location." The officer recited the cross streets and direction of travel.

Denton grabbed her jacket. "Let's roll. Wolfe is close by and I want to take him down myself." She ran out the door with Kirby following close behind.

Everett, the Homicide Detail squad boss, scratched his chin in thought for a moment. He then followed Denton to the parking area. This was an important arrest. Everyone in America would see the news about it. He'd tag along and make sure it was handled correctly.

~

In the limousine, Jake sat in the backseat, hidden behind the dark tinted windows. "Thanks for giving me a ride," he told the driver. "I appreciate it."

"No problem. If Big Mo says to pick you up, that's what I do."

"Where are we going?"

"We'll drive to an oil change business. You'll get out while the car is parked in the service bay, and you'll go down into the pit below. Then you'll climb up and get into another car that is parked in the next bay.

"Switching cars, good idea."

"Look underneath the carpeted floor pad beneath your feet. You'll see an interesting surprise. It's something I came up with myself."

Jake lifted up the removable square of carpet and looked underneath. "Very nice, I'm impressed."

The driver nodded. "Works like a charm."

They traveled for a while, sticking to the posted speed limit and not attracting any attention. The driver said, "Don't worry about the police. The average cop in this city couldn't find his own dick in the dark."

At that moment, an armored car pulled out of an alley, got in front of the limousine and stopped. The limo driver had to slam on his brakes to avoid crashing into it.

Next, a black SUV pulled up behind the limo and pressed right up against the rear bumper. The armored car backed up a few feet until it was pressed against the limo's front bumper.

In just a few seconds, the limo had been pinned in between the two vehicles and trapped. Two gun ports on the back of the armored car opened, and two assault rifle barrels poked out, aimed at the limousine's windshield. There was a black GMC parked on the left of the limo; the roof opened, and a turret rose up that held a man and a mounted machine gun pointed at the limo driver.

Police in riot gear ran up and surrounded the limo, training their weapons on it. A voice spoke over a loudspeaker saying, "This is Sergeant Denton with the San Francisco police. We have you surrounded. Come out of the vehicle with your hands up."

Nobody exited the limousine. Denton approached the driver's window and rapped on it with the barrel of her pistol. The driver opened the window about a quarter of an inch.

Denton said, "You must be Dick. Wow, I found you and it's not even dark."

The driver must have realized they had eavesdropping lasers pointed at the car windows and could hear what was said inside, so he answered in Italian, *"Non parlano inglese,"* and raised his window.

Denton grabbed a sledgehammer out of a vehicle. She swung it hard against the window, but the big hammer just bounced off the bulletproof glass. The driver's hand appeared pressed against the darkened glass, giving Denton the middle finger.

Denton cursed and said, "Get the Jaws of Life and rip open the car door."

A policeman approached with the Jaws of Life device and proceeded to open the driver's door the way a can opener tears open a metal can. In moments, the door was torn off. The driver sat there calmly with his hands on the steering wheel. A lit cigarette dangled from the corner of his mouth.

Denton grabbed the driver by the scruff of his collar and pulled him roughly out of the car. She pushed him facedown onto the pavement, pressing her pistol against the back of his neck. The man had somehow managed to keep his cigarette in the corner of his mouth. With his cheek against the ground he let out a long plume of smoke and gave Denton a big smile. Denton stomped the cigarette out and nearly crushed the man's lips and nose along with it. He spat out the cigarette butt, smiled cheerfully and said, "Go screw yourself."

"Cover him," Denton said.

An officer pressed the barrel of an assault rifle against the driver's head. The driver winked at the cop and grinned. Denton pressed a button in the limo to unlock all the doors. She yanked open the back passenger door, holding her pistol up and ready to put a bullet into Jake Wolfe's face.

To her surprise, the backseat was empty. She pressed another button and popped the trunk, opened it with her gun drawn, but found it empty too. She was getting angry now as she pulled up the cover over the spare tire and looked underneath. Next, she returned to the backseat and pulled up the seat cushion. Somehow, someway, Wolfe and his dog had vanished. She ground her teeth and seethed with anger.

Everett, the Homicide Detail squad boss, walked over to the limousine and looked inside. "What have you got here, Denton?"

Denton stood up straight and said, "We have the limo that picked up the fugitive Jake Wolfe in an alley near Fisherman's Wharf."

"Do you have the fugitive or just the limo driver?"

"At the moment, we only have the driver, but—"

"Then you don't have a damned thing," Everett said.

"Wolfe was in this vehicle, but he escaped somehow. This isn't over yet."

Denton started ripping at the floor coverings. The carpet in the foot well came loose and exposed a trap door in the floor. She pulled it open and looked down to see an open manhole in the street below the car. "Get this limo backed up. He went out through the floor and into the sewer."

Everett looked at the trapdoor and raised his eyebrows, then looked at the driver lying on the ground.

The driver grinned at him and shrugged modestly as if he didn't want to brag, but that trapdoor he'd thought up had fooled them all.

Terrell Hayes arrived on the scene. He walked up to the limo and said, "What's the situation?"

Everett gestured at the backseat, and Terrell saw the open trapdoor. The vehicle behind the limo backed up, and a cop got into the limo and backed it up too, exposing the open manhole cover. Terrell looked at the hole in the street, turned to Everett and said only one word: "Wolfe?"

Everett nodded and tried not to laugh. Terrell did too. He looked down at the manhole and clamped his teeth closed to keep from laughing out loud and causing Everett to laugh along with him. If there was one sure thing about Jake Wolfe, the man was definitely entertaining. Terrell was glad that he and Jake had taken Everett fishing recently on Dylan's boat. They'd drunk beer, smoked cigars, caught fish, told funny stories and had a great time. But they'd never mentioned it to anyone. Everett had thoroughly enjoyed himself, and he'd made Jake promise that they'd go fishing again soon.

Denton saw Terrell and she got in his face. "You were talking to this fugitive on the phone not long ago. Did you help him escape from us?"

Terrell gave her his battle stare. He had a lot of female friends, but

Denton would never be one of them. "No, I was trying to talk him into coming into the station. But you found him—good work. Now follow him down into the sewer. Go get him, tiger."

Everett was apparently aware of the bad chemistry between these two and decided a team-building exercise was in order. "Both of you go down in the sewer," Everett said. "You'll each do a search in opposite directions. That way it will get done twice as fast."

Terrell looked at the squad boss for a long moment and said, "Down there, underground?"

Everett nodded. "Yeah, get going."

CHAPTER 80

Terrell motioned at the hole in the street and said to Denton, "Ladies first, this is your operation."

Denton scowled. "You go first, you're his friend."

Terrell walked toward the manhole. "Okay, if you're afraid, I'll lead the way."

Several cops laughed, and Terrell acted like he couldn't care less about climbing down the ladder into the dark and foul-smelling tunnel. The truth was, not many situations could rattle Terrell's nerves, but closed-in suffocating places with no fresh air were among his least favorite things. He wasn't quite claustrophobic but pretty close to it. Okay, very close to it.

The sewer's overhead lights weren't working, and it was so dark below the street that Terrell could hardly see anything. He pulled out his keys and pressed a tiny keychain flashlight. Nothing happened, the battery was dead. Cursing, he flicked his Zippo lighter which cast a wavering light. His eyes were big and round as he looked to his left and then to his right. Strangely, the walls of the ladder shaft seemed to be moving in a circular motion. Upon closer inspection, he realized with disgust that the walls were completely covered by a swarm of cockroaches, all running in a clockwise direction.

One very large cockroach ran across Terrell's hand that held onto the iron ladder rung. He cursed in surprise, jerked his hand away and dropped the remaining few feet to the tunnel floor. He accidentally dropped his lighter in the process. The lighter went out, leaving him in darkness again. In the still and quiet of the dark sewer, he could hear the rustling sound of the hundreds of multi-legged crawling insects scurrying across the dank cement walls that surrounded him.

His eyes adjusted to the dim light from the open manhole above and he was able to find his lighter on the filthy floor below his feet. He picked up the lighter, lit it again and stepped into the center of the main tunnel. There was a splash in a puddle near him as a rat ran across his right foot. He cursed again and tried to take a calming breath, but inhaling the thick stench of the sewer air did nothing to soothe his nerves.

Stepping back into the ladder shaft, he yelled up toward the street. "Drop me down a flashlight. The overhead lighting isn't working down here."

A moment later, a uniformed officer appeared over the rim, turned on a flashlight and dropped it to Terrell. The man grinned. "How does it smell down there, Lieutenant?"

"It smells like your breath," Terrell said. He stood still for a moment and listened. Did he hear the sound of a splash, down the tunnel to his right?

Denton climbed down the ladder and switched on her flashlight. She aimed it down the tunnel in each direction and then glared at Terrell.

"You go right and I'll go left," Terrell said.

"No way, that's what you want me to do. You go right, and I'll go left."

"Fine, have it your way," Terrell said, scowling. He'd known she would automatically be opposed to whatever he wanted.

Another rat ran past as the detectives set off in opposite directions into the tunnels. Terrell walked fast, wishing he was anywhere else but there. He'd always been in denial about his claustrophobia, but now he felt the irrational fear beginning to crawl up his back. The enclosed space was bad enough, but when you added the nonworking lights, the awful smell and the rats and cockroaches, it was a nightmare. He had to use all his willpower to make himself keep on walking farther away from the manhole and daylight and fresh air.

Terrell hurried down one branch of the tunnel, and soon he thought he heard another splash up ahead of him. It might be a rat, but he gave a low whistle-signal that Jake would remember from their combat days, and he started to jog toward the sound. The situation pulled him in two different directions—friendship versus duty.

He came around a curve in the tunnel and saw Jake and Cody about to escape through an access door.

Terrell pointed his flashlight at his face for a moment with his eyes closed and put a finger to his lips. Cody sniffed the air, but didn't growl at Terrell. Jake stood next to the door, waiting for his friend to catch up to him.

"You really got yourself into a mess this time," Terrell said in a low voice.

"Lots of the wrong people are mad at me, huh?" Jake said.

"Do you have any idea who impersonated you?"

"Agent McKay told me he's a wanted criminal. An assassin. Probably the same guy who shot those lawyers."

"Katherine Anderson used to be a prosecuting attorney. She fits the attorney pattern."

"But what's the motive behind the pattern?"

"Our guys found a tablet in your Jeep," Terrell said. "It had a lot of downloaded news stories on it about how Katherine once put an innocent man in prison. It makes you look like an angry vigilante seeking retribution."

"It wasn't my tablet; forensics will see that."

"I believe your story, but it will take time to prove."

"Wait, now that I think about it, the tablet might have been stolen from the *Far Niente* when somebody broke in and stole some vodka and cigars."

"You'd better get going. Denton is down here too. I sent her in the other direction, but she could be coming this way at any moment. I'm risking my job because I know you're innocent."

Jake frowned at the mention of Denton's name. "I already lost one dog to that sociopath and I'll fight her before I let her hurt this one."

"Never talk that way about cops, but I understand how you feel, and that's why you need to get going."

"I thought you were hell-bent on taking me into protective custody."

"It's not safe now that Denton is here, but once you get in the clear we can try again."

"Thanks, Grinds. I hope I'm not getting you into serious trouble here."

"You're always getting me into trouble. I'm used to it by now."

The two friends gave each other a grim smile. It was the same smile they'd used in worse situations far from home. In war battles when they weren't sure if they'd both make it out alive. They shook hands and Jake went through the door along with Cody, closing it behind them.

"Good luck, brother. Keep your head down," Terrell whispered, and he turned and walked back the way he'd come. He was half the distance back to the open manhole when he met Denton coming toward him from the other direction.

"Did you find any tracks?" Terrell said.

"No, did you?" Denton said.

"Nothing here either."

"I smell wet dog fur."

"You smell wet rats. I've seen several of them."

"You swear you didn't see Wolfe down here?"

"Cross my heart, all of that."

"I don't believe you."

"Feel free to search for yourself."

"You're damned right I will."

"Have fun. I'll see you topside. I'm out of here." Terrell walked away toward the ladder and the shaft of sunlight.

Denton jogged down the dark tunnel, with her flashlight in one hand and her pistol in the other.

Terrell hoped that Jake and Cody were moving fast. He worried that if Denton attempted to shoot Cody like she'd done to Jake's other dog, Gracie, Cody would defend himself the way he'd been trained as a war dog. Jake would also fight to protect Cody, and he might do something that everyone would regret.

CHAPTER 81

Terrell climbed up the ladder and back into the fresh air and daylight. He took a deep breath and said, "Remind me to never go into the sewer again."

One of the uniformed cops stood waiting for him with a small spray can of Ozium air freshener. He grinned as he sprayed it in Terrell's direction and said, "What is that *smell*? Oh, it's just you, Lieutenant, never mind."

"Nothing to smell here, move along," Terrell said.

Most of the police were gone, but a few remained, including Beth and Kirby.

"Let me guess, Wolfe gave you the slip," Kirby said.

"He gave all of us the slip," Terrell said. "But Denton is still searching the sewer. Why don't you go down there and help your partner?"

Kirby studied his fingernails. "Everett sent you two on that search, not me."

As Terrell walked away, he spat on the street and lit a cigarette to get the foul smell out of his nose and mouth. He inhaled smoke through his mouth and retro-exhaled through his nose, sending twin streams into the air.

Beth said, "Don't smoke too close to the personhole. You might ignite all the methane from the entire city's collective ass gas."

"Now I'm tempted to toss this cigarette in there just to see if it might torch Denton. She'd look funny with no hair or eyebrows, right?"

Beth shook her head. "Don't do it."

"I'm kidding. I already lit my lighter down there without any problem. And what exactly is a *personhole*?"

"It's a nonsexist name for a manhole."

"Feel free to call it a womanhole if you want. That has a catchy ring to it."

"I was just making a gender joke. Don't get your boxers in a bunch."

Terrell frowned and pretended to adjust his boxers. Beth laughed.

Down in the sewer tunnel, Denton was getting a full understanding of what it meant to be alone in the dark. A large rat ran across her path, and she almost yelled and fired her pistol. She gritted her teeth and told herself that it was better to be alone. That way, if she shot both fugitives, there would be no witnesses to contradict her police report.

She made her way along the tunnel until she found a metal door and two sets of wet footprints—a man and a dog. She tried the doorknob, but it was locked from the inside. The door was designed to open inward toward her.

Denton tried to call Kirby and tell him to bring a sledgehammer and crowbar, but her phone wasn't getting a signal. For a moment, she considered shooting her pistol at the doorknob, but she reconsidered because a ricochet bullet in a concrete tunnel could be deadly.

She took out her knife and wedged it in between the door and the doorjamb, moving the blade up and down and wiggling it. After some effort, the latch moved and came free of the strike plate. The door then flew open in Denton's face as if it had been pushed hard by someone on the other side. It hit her shoulder and knocked her backward, causing her to drop the knife and the flashlight.

Denton fell on her backside and saw a tall stack of large plastic five-gallon watercooler bottles rolling down through the door in her direction.

She tried to stand up and move out of the way, but the first rolling bottle crashed into her and knocked her back down. Another bounced up and hit the wall behind her, bursting open and spraying water on her. Several more bottles cascaded down the steps and into the sewer tunnel, knocking her around. She cursed Jake Wolfe.

Once the water bottle onslaught ended, Denton struggled to her feet. She was soaking wet, bruised, and filthy from rolling around on the sewer floor. The biggest bruise was on her ego. She put her knife in her pocket, grabbed her flashlight, and drew her pistol. She ran up the steps with her pistol up in front of her, ready to shoot the fugitives.

She found herself in a dark basement storage room filled with office furniture. There were desks, chairs, cabinets, more of the five-gallon water bottles, and endless shelves stacked with white cardboard file boxes.

Denton made her way to the other side of the room, went out the door and saw wet shoe prints and paw prints leading down the hallway. Her phone display was now showing a signal so she called Kirby.

"I'm inside an office building. I found their footprints and followed them in here."

"Which building is it?"

"I don't know yet, but get in the car and start the engine. I'll find the address and call you in a minute."

She ran down the hall and followed the two sets of footprints until she came to a service elevator. She pushed the call button, but the elevator didn't make a sound. There was a stairway next to the elevator and she went through the door and sprinted up the stairs past a door that said "Parking" and up to the next floor to a door marked "Lobby." She went through that door and came out into the lobby with her pistol in hand. Several people were milling about, and a woman saw the gun and screamed. Denton took her police badge off her belt, held it up and yelled at the people there.

"Police! Put your hands on top of your heads."

Everyone put their hands up, and Denton looked around but didn't see any sign of Wolfe or the dog.

"What address is this? Did you see a dog in here?"

The frightened people all just stood there, not saying anything.

They stared in surprise at the wild-eyed woman in her filthy clothes who was asking crazy questions.

Denton cursed and went back to the stairway. She ran down one flight and through the door to the parking area. In the garage, the service elevator had the door blocked open by a trash can. There were faint wet dog paw prints on the cement, leading toward the street. She ran in that direction, but the prints dried up and she couldn't tell if the fugitives had kept going straight or had changed direction.

When Denton reached the street, she looked at the signs on the corner and called Kirby to report her location. She holstered her pistol and ran up and down both sides of the street, asking people if they'd seen a man with a golden-haired dog. Nobody wanted to talk to the angry woman with the badge and the dark blue windbreaker that said POLICE. They just shook their heads and walked away as fast as they could.

Kirby drove up in the unmarked police car and parked illegally with his flashing lights on. He got out and met up with Denton.

"They came up an elevator in that parking garage," Denton said, pointing her finger. "Then they headed in this direction. Their footprints ended, so I don't know which way they went from here."

"Do you think they'd risk taking a taxi again?"

"I doubt it, but call it in just in case."

Kirby went to the car and used the radio.

Denton saw an older woman who was selling cheap t-shirts on a rickety folding table. The woman was watching her, and then she quickly looked away in fear. Denton ran over there and shoved her badge in the woman's face. "You saw something, didn't you?"

The gray-haired lady shook her head. "No, I not see," she said in halting English. She appeared to be an immigrant from an Eastern European country, frightened of police and government officials.

"If you don't tell me what you saw, you could go to prison for the rest of your life."

The woman started crying. "No, please, I have daughter. No prison. I tell you."

"I can send your daughter to prison too. Did you see a man with a dog? Answer me."

Denton put her hand on her pistol and glared at the woman.

With a trembling arthritic hand, the woman pointed at a bicycle taxicab on the corner. It was a three-wheeled bike with a rider on the front and a wide seat in the back that could carry two tourist passengers on a leisurely ride for several blocks.

"Man and dog, go on ... bicycle," the woman said.

"Which direction did the bicycle go?"

The woman pointed out the direction and nodded her head.

Denton took off running toward the bicycle cab. She called out to Kirby, "Bring the car."

Kirby was standing next to the vehicle, talking on the radio. He got in and did a quick illegal U-turn.

When the pedicab driver saw an angry woman running toward him, he got on his bike and started to pedal away as fast as the contraption would go. Denton ran up and tackled him and knocked him off the bike. She wrestled him to a facedown position on the pavement and pressed a knee onto his lower back while grabbing his arms and twisting them behind him.

"Stop resisting!" Denton said.

"I'm not resisting, you're crazy," the man said. "Somebody help me, call the police."

"I *am* the police. Shut up and stop resisting or I'll break your arm and put you in prison."

"I'm not resisting. You never identified yourself—you just attacked me. I have witnesses."

"I'm looking for a murder suspect, a man with a retriever dog who got into a pedicab a few minutes ago."

"It wasn't my cab; can't you see that for yourself?"

"What cab was it? Where did it go? *Tell me!*"

"A rider named Lennie. I saw them go that way." The man motioned with his head to his right. "That's all I know."

It was the same direction the old woman had told Denton that the man and dog had gone. Kirby stopped the car next to Denton and said, "Let's go, get in."

"I'll be watching you from now on, you scumbag," Denton said, and she ran to the car.

The man on the ground groaned in pain. "I think you dislocated my shoulder."

Denton got in the passenger seat, and Kirby hit the gas before she had the door all the way closed. He'd wanted to have more turns driving the car, and now he was going to be driving it in a chase. This was what he'd been waiting for. He turned right at the corner and took off down the street at high speed with the lights flashing.

CHAPTER 82

At the hospital, Daniel said, "The paintball shooting was because of me. A Secret Service agent in Washington named Shannon McKay said it probably has something to do with my work in Congress."

"You mean he was aiming at you and missed and hit me instead?" Katherine asked.

"No, McKay's theory is that the man attacked you in hopes of distracting me so I'd miss the next few days of work. No one has any idea why that would be so important, but the Secret Service is studying my schedule and looking for clues."

Katherine stared at Daniel, her eyes red from crying. "A news cameraman shot at my belly to keep you from doing your job?"

"McKay believes it wasn't really that cameraman. She said the person who did it was wearing a facial disguise designed to look like him. They believe it was an international assassin."

Katherine's face grew pale when she heard the word assassin. "I'm a former prosecuting attorney. Does this have anything to do with the recent attorney assassinations?"

"Yes, McKay believes it is the same person. This is a classic old-school Soviet-style disinformation strategy. Whoever hired this shooter wants people to believe he's a crazy attorney-hating serial killer. That's a technique conspirators use to hide their real agenda, which in this case is interfering with Congress and the US government in some way."

Daniel held up a tablet and showed Katherine a news story by a reporter named Dick Arnold. The story documented highlights of Katherine's law career, and it speculated that Jake Wolfe was angry about how Katherine had once sent an innocent man to prison. The man had spent eight years on death row waiting to be executed for something he didn't do. Recently he'd been exonerated by the Innocence Project using DNA evidence. While the innocent man had been locked in jail, the actual criminal had escaped justice and had gone on to commit several more assaults, rapes, and murders.

"I feel terrible about the mistake I made with that man. I can never make it up to him."

"That man has nothing to do with this. But these manipulated news stories draw attention away from the shooter's real agenda. When and if the truth ever comes to light, it will be too late. The conspirators' goals will have already been accomplished, and their trail covered and witnesses eliminated."

"Who is behind this? You can't let them intimidate you."

"Are you kidding? They've already intimidated me. You and our baby are a thousand times more important to me than my career or my run for the White House, or anything else in my life."

Katherine's eyes softened and she held out her hand to him. Daniel took her hand in his. They both had looks of remorse on their faces. Someone had to apologize first, and since Daniel's body wasn't flooded with hormones from pregnancy, he felt that it was his job to start. "I'm sorry for arguing with you when you're in a hospital bed."

"I'm sorry too. I've been an emotional wreck," Katherine said. "I apologize for the things I've said."

That was good enough for Daniel, and he put his arms around Katherine and kissed her. She smiled as she kissed him back and thought about how he was always so willing to forgive and forget.

Daniel's phone buzzed, and he answered it.

"Daniel, this is Agent McKay."

"Hello, Agent McKay."

"Is that the Secret Service agent in Washington?" Katherine said. "Please let me talk to her for a minute."

Daniel nodded and said to McKay, "I told Katherine about the situation, and she'd like to speak with you. Okay, here she is."

Daniel handed his phone to Katherine.

"Agent McKay, this is Katherine Anderson. I thought of a crazy idea I'd like to run by you. It's dangerous, but it might work."

CHAPTER 83

Night fell on the city, and a thick fog blanketed the streets of the North Beach area of San Francisco.

Outside the stone walls of a beautiful old church, a tall man and his golden-haired dog hesitated for a moment on the steps in front of the large wooden door.

Jake wore a pistol hung in a shoulder holster hidden under his black leather jacket, and it felt heavy against his heart. He looked around, his highly observant eyes flicking here and there. He didn't see any threats, he only *felt* them. His instincts told him something was wrong. One of the hunters was close by and was coming in this direction. Jake felt the danger with an almost animal instinct.

The sky was darkly overcast, and clouds obscured the setting sun. The only people out and about in North Beach were driving in their cars or getting out of taxis to go into restaurants for dinner.

Jake had not eaten since breakfast, and his stomach growled with hunger. He wished he was going into one of his favorite Italian restaurants instead of into this church. He had a craving for the North Beach Restaurant on Stockton Street. It was a local landmark that had served soul-satisfying Tuscan-style Italian food for decades. His mouth was watering for their famous calamari vinaigrette as an appetizer. For dinner he'd try to decide between the sea scallops, the spaghetti with vodka sauce or the gnocchi with gorgonzola. He was hungry enough right now to eat all three. To drink, he might add a humble but tasty bottle of Montepulciano d'Abruzzo, the red wine favored by the great painter and sculptor Michelangelo. Or perhaps he'd splurge on some perfectly aged treasure of a Barolo from the restaurant's famous underground wine cellar. Good food was one of the few reliable pleasures left in life for him, along with the proverbial wine, women, and song.

Out of the swirling fog, there appeared a wrinkled old Italian woman with a shawl over her head. She walked slowly, and in her gnarled hands she held rosary beads and a well-worn Bible. Jake pulled on the door's large iron handle, opened the door and held it for her.

The old woman stopped mumbling her nonstop Hail Mary rosary prayers for a moment to say, "*Grazie*." Then she shuffled inside the entryway.

"*Prego*," Jake said, and he followed her inside, with Cody walking along beside him.

~

Moments after the door closed, an unmarked police SUV pulled up in front of the church. The eager young uniformed policeman in the passenger seat studied a photograph on the dashboard computer screen.

The rookie cop looked at the driver. "That's the fugitive and his dog. It has to be them. Who else could it be?"

The more experienced plainclothes cop sitting in the driver's seat gave the rookie a skeptical look. "That could be anyone. There are seventeen thousand people per square mile in this city and a lot of them have pet dogs."

"Maybe he's the fugitive and he went into the church to ask for sanctuary."

"Churches can't provide legal sanctuary any longer. They haven't since the seventeenth century."

The rookie checked his pistol and opened the car door. "I want to go inside to look around. Can you watch the door in case he tries to get away?"

"No problem. Just don't do any shooting inside the church, or the chief will come down on you like a ton of bricks."

The uniformed officer got out of the car and climbed the steps of the church. He kept his right hand on the pistol in his belt holster. He planned to enter the doorway alcove, hide in the shadows and wait for his target to come out. This was his chance to be a hero.

Inside the church, Jake's eyes adjusted to the soft light. Candles flickered in the semidarkness and the air smelled faintly of beeswax candles and wood polish. He scanned the church pews. They were empty except for the little old Italian grandma in a front row seat, still mumbling the rosary. There was something reassuring about her, like an ancient tree in the forest that could bend in a storm but never break. The journalist inside him wanted to sit with her, drink espresso together and listen to her stories about life. He'd take pictures of her beautiful, wrinkled face—every line representing a joy or sorrow in her personal history.

Jake dipped his fingers in holy water and made the sign of the cross. Next, he slowly walked along the right wall toward a set of three polished oak doors. Cody walked along beside him wearing his service dog vest.

The gracefully aging Father Sean O'Leary sat behind the center door, waiting with practiced patience for someone to enter one of the booths on either side, and for another confession to begin. It had been a long day; there had been a mass this morning, then a baptism and a funeral, followed by taking confessions for several hours.

He looked at his watch. His confession time for the day was just about done. Few people had their mind on church now that it was getting close to dinnertime. He felt the same way, and was looking forward to eating a hearty meal of chicken and dumplings, and then sipping an Irish whiskey while he curled up with a good book for the rest of the evening.

Just as O'Leary closed his Bible and reached for the doorknob, the door to the confessional booth on his right creaked quietly on old hinges as it opened and closed.

"Ah well, no rest for the wicked," O'Leary whispered to himself. He smiled at his own humor.

Somebody entered the confessional and knelt on the padded ledge. When the light went off, Father O'Leary slid the small window panel open so the two could talk through an ornately carved wooden privacy screen.

Out of the darkness, a deep male voice spoke quietly. "Bless me, Father, for I have sinned. It has been ... *many years* since my last confession."

The man's voice sounded familiar to O'Leary, but he couldn't place it. He'd listened to so many confessions, knew so many people. O'Leary heard a dog panting, and he smelled its wet fur. He guessed it could be a service dog. The man might be blind or have some kind of disability or health problem. Now O'Leary was glad he'd stayed and had not left for dinner. These two souls needed someone to care about them. He would listen to the man's troubles and offer him guidance.

There was a pause as the confessor gathered his thoughts, or swallowed his pride. Father O'Leary was accustomed to this. He gently encouraged the man. "Yes, we all sin, but the good Lord died for our sins. Confess and God will forgive you. What troubles you, my son?"

Late in the afternoon on a stressful day like this, O'Leary felt like saying, "I've heard it all by now, so just spit it out." He smiled again at his irreverent thoughts. That Irish whiskey was sounding better by the minute.

In the stillness, Jake took a deep breath and exhaled slowly. "Father, I have broken the sixth commandment. And I'll have to do it again soon."

O'Leary sat up straight in his chair. He leaned closer to the small square screen between the booths. "The sixth commandment. *Thou shalt not kill.*"

"Yes, Father."

There was another pause. This time it was O'Leary who took a moment to gather his thoughts. He ran a leathery hand through his gray hair. "You have killed another human being?"

"Yes, I've killed evil people, so many I've lost count."

As Jake confessed to his killings, he instinctively touched the pistol in its holster. He felt he should leave the confessional soon. He had that bad feeling again that something might go wrong at any moment.

"Are you a soldier?"

"I recently served in the Marines, deployed overseas. I was injured in battle, and I spent some time recuperating in the hospital. A CIA agent paid me a bedside visit there, and recruited me to be a shooter … an assassin."

"Assassin," O'Leary said slowly, pronouncing each syllable. It had been many years since he'd said it himself, back in Ireland. "But you were an assassin for the government, not for organized crime."

"That's a matter of opinion. Some people think of governments as a type of organized crime."

"Feel free to talk about it, if you need to get it off your chest. You're anonymous here, and I'm bound to secrecy by my vows."

"I worked for a black ops team that waged war against high-value targets. We were like a well-oiled killing machine."

"It sounds like the CIA and their drone strikes."

"Good guess. It was similar to a branch of the CIA known as the JSOC. Whenever they tracked down a major terrorist who could not be hit with a drone strike, they would send in one lone assassin to infiltrate."

"Similar to what a military sniper does, but up close and personal?"

"Exactly. I was like a mafia hit man. Kick the door open and fight to the death."

"But you were doing your duty and serving your country when you killed enemies in the line of fire. The cold wars and the fights against terrorism and violent crime are still wars nonetheless. It wasn't personal, and now you are sorry and you seek forgiveness from God. Is that right?"

"I'm not sure what I feel. The faces of the dead haunt my dreams. But I believe that I was justified in exterminating a few two-legged animals to save scores of innocent people, including women and children."

"Did you? Save the lives of innocent people?"

"Yes, Father, I killed the killers. The same way a sheriff in the Old West would get into a shootout with criminals to protect the townsfolk."

Jake pressed the confessional door open just a crack so he could peek out and see the front door of the church. His feeling of danger was getting stronger. He wasn't sure, but he thought he could just make out the shadow of a man hiding in the alcove. Cody was showing his teeth and making a very stealthy but distinct growl in his throat. Jake thought of it as Cody's jungle growl.

O'Leary said, "So you were the modern-day marshal, and now you may be feeling your own mortality. Those Wild West lawmen saved many lives, but very few of the lawmen lived to a ripe old age themselves. Their power came with crushing responsibility, constant danger, and often an early grave."

"True enough, but the only way a sheriff could keep the people of his town safe from the attacks of murders was with swift and stern justice. It was not exactly what I dreamed of doing with my life, but at that time and place, someone had to do it."

"Yes, someone always has done it and someone always will. But ask God to forgive you for these killings and he will. Then try to forgive yourself."

Jake peered through the crack in the door and saw the old woman walking slowly toward the doorway. "I've said too much. I don't want to get you involved in my troubles."

"People from Ireland know all about *troubles*, but I'm far too old now to be the least bit afraid of anything. Tell me, where did you do your assassin work?"

"Overseas. I was a troubleshooter in the most literal sense. When they tracked down an extremely troublesome terrorist, I would find him and shoot him. No more trouble."

"So, it was your military duty to terrorize the terrorists."

"It was my duty to kill them, and when I did my duty, I was acting on orders from my government. But I came here because I want absolution. I want to be forgiven for my past killings. I'm carrying the weight of all those lives on my conscience. I see their faces in my sleep, and I have this recurring nightmare that I'm going to have to fight them again to protect my family and friends."

"Many people have nightmares, lad. I'd imagine it to be even more common for someone who has seen the terrible things you've seen."

"The first terrorist I executed was the coward who set up a roadside bomb that killed two of my closest friends. He also shot a young girl just for going to school, and he made a video of himself beheading a woman who had dared to drive a car."

"I believe God will forgive you for killing a beast like that."

Jake started taking deep, angry breaths. "He was a beast who killed men, raped women, and abused boys and girls. When I put a bullet in his head, I had no doubt that I'd made the world a better place."

"Are you feeling remorse now that some time has passed?"

"I'm not sure. The killing took a heavy toll on my heart and soul. And yet I'd do my duty again if it was the only way to protect the innocent."

"I understand, my son. I wasn't always a priest, you know."

"I hate to say this, but when I shot that man, it felt good. I was glad to see him die. Father, if I killed evil beasts like him, does that make me evil too?"

O'Leary paused a moment as he considered how to answer. "I've also wrestled with that question on many a sleepless night. Nietzsche said that whoever fights monsters should see to it that in the process he does not become a monster."

"And he said, if you gaze long enough into an abyss, the abyss will gaze back into you."

"That's why you need to stay away from your previous violent line of work. Find a peaceful profession and let your soul rest."

"I'm no longer working for the government, but there is a killer here in the city who is challenging me to a fight. He impersonated me, and now I've been falsely accused of a crime he committed."

Father O'Leary weighed this new information and wondered if the man was delusional. He patted his empty pocket, wishing for his Peterson pipe and Old Dublin tobacco so he could *think*. "Do you feel it's your job to stop this killer—or could you let the police handle it?"

"I may have no choice, Father. He seems to have a personal grudge against me."

"May angels protect you, then. Are you married? Do you have children?"

"No, but I worry about this criminal targeting my family and friends."

O'Leary was an old-timer who had seen that kind of violence long ago as a young child in Belfast, Northern Ireland. When he heard the concern for loved ones, he felt a familiar lump in his throat.

"Family and friends are what matter most in life. Can you ask your former government employers to help you with this problem?"

"I haven't spoken to them for quite a while. I've avoided any contact because I was trying to put that violent life behind me."

"As you should. You've done your duty in service to your country, and now you should leave the battles to others. It's not your fight any longer. You can walk away."

"Speaking of walking away, I have to be going now. But I'd like to hear you say that I'm forgiven. You still do that kind of thing here, right?"

"Yes, of course," O'Leary said, and he recited the prayers that he'd said so many times to so many anonymous people. He added, "And now forgive yourself."

Jake stood on the kneeling pad and reached up, unscrewing the lightbulb above his head so it would remain dark as he was leaving the booth. He didn't look forward to going on the run again, but he was very much opposed to being put into a cage for a crime he hadn't committed.

"Let me ask you a philosophical question, Padre," Jake said as he opened the door a crack and looked out. "It's in regard to a moral dilemma I grapple with. The question is this: if a man like me had been able to assassinate Hitler or Stalin or Mao, and it might have saved the lives of *tens of millions* of innocent men, women, and children ... would God approve of the premeditated and cold-blooded killing of that one man?"

"Well, now, you do bring up a difficult moral dilemma. It's one I've personally faced, years ago, in Ireland. In theory, keeping in mind that the Bible says God approved of the killing of his own beloved son on the cross to save millions of souls, how could I judge someone wrong if he or she saved millions of lives by killing one evil person such as Hitler?"

O'Leary's words went unanswered, and he heard the door click shut as the man and his dog left the confessional booth. Then the realization struck him of where he'd heard that deep voice before. It was a man who sometimes volunteered and helped feed the homeless at the soup kitchen dinners. "Oh, my goodness, it was that rascal Jake Wolfe," he whispered.

Jake stepped out of the confessional booth, and his intuition of danger flared up again. His sensitivity was unexplainable, but he'd learned to trust it. He felt that hunters were closing in on his location, and a violent confrontation was imminent. The elderly Italian woman was slowly pushing open one of the great doors. Jake looked past her through the partly open door and saw a black SUV parked out front. Jake's keen eyes noted the glow of someone drawing on a cigarette while standing behind the vehicle. He could just barely see the outline of a person leaning against the SUV in the dark.

"Cigarettes can be the death of you," Jake said.

CHAPTER 84

When the large door at the front of the church was closing, Jake looked closely at the alcove and caught a glimpse of a uniformed cop hiding there. The inexperienced man leaned in for a quick look at the last moment and then ducked his head back out of sight. There were two hunters, one outside by the vehicle and another inside by the church's door.

Cody let out a low growl. He was ready to fight, but Jake wanted to avoid any confrontation with the police. He turned in the opposite direction from the door, and they walked behind the altar and through the curtained alcove where the priests entered to say mass. Jake found the back exit he'd seen earlier when he'd done recon outside the building.

He and Cody went out into the alleyway behind the church, staying close to the wall in the shadows in case a third hunter was waiting there. A thick fog was drifting down the alley and climbing over building walls and roofs. Jake saw the silver-haired Italian woman crossing the street in front of the alley. The vehicle was still parked in front of the church.

Jake stepped back into the doorway alcove, out of sight, and he heard a sound in the room behind him. He swung around, raised his fists and prepared to deliver a quick knockout blow to the opponent's head. Cody stood still by his side, at attention with teeth bared but remaining quiet and ready to attack, obeying the hand signals Jake had given to him. The door opened slowly, and Father O'Leary appeared. Jake visibly relaxed, lowered his fists and gave Cody a command.

"I nearly broke your jaw, Padre," Jake said.

"And I almost gave you the shock of your life, young Mr. Wolfe," O'Leary said, lowering a Taser.

O'Leary watched Jake's face change in a sort of metamorphosis. For a moment, it had shown the look of a warrior. Next, that emotion had melted away as it showed amusement at the priest's Taser. Finally, it had changed back to the guarded and world-weary face of a man who had seen too much, a man who had often been stabbed in the back by life. O'Leary knew the feeling and he sometimes saw the same look on his own face when he gazed in the mirror. His housekeeper called it his resting bitch face. That always made O'Leary smile, in spite of himself. "Where is Mrs. Lombardi, the woman who was praying?"

"I saw her walking down that street. She's okay," Jake said, tilting his head in her direction.

"It's a good thing she's okay," O'Leary said, looking past Jake at the woman as she slowly walked away into the fog. "Her grandson is a mafia soldier, and he'd become very upset if anyone bothered her."

"I might know a cousin or someone in the family."

"For some reason that doesn't surprise me. Is that Stuart's dog, from the funeral?"

"Yes, Stuart's parents thought it would be best if Cody lived with me, so I'm adopting him."

O'Leary nodded in approval. "As for these men who are after you, I shocked one of them until smoke came out of his ears."

Jake grinned. "You tasered a police officer?"

"It was an accident, he surprised me."

"The police should not be coming after me, Father. I'm one of the good guys, and I'm on their side. We just have a temporary misunderstanding."

Father O'Leary nodded thoughtfully. He approached closer to Jake and held up a photograph. "The man I shocked had your photo in his shirt pocket. And look at this."

O'Leary held out his phone, and the display screen showed an internet news story by a reporter named Dick Arnold. It featured a photo of Jake's face along with the words, *Wanted by the FBI. The Bureau is offering a $50,000 reward for information leading to his arrest.*

That news scene cut to video of a woman telling Dick Arnold, "I was Jake's high school sweetheart. I never knew then that I was dating a boy who would grow up to become a killer."

Jake tried to remember the woman and decided she was nobody he'd ever known. She was just some attention-seeking whacko. Another sound bite followed, of a man standing in front of the building where Jake had lived with Gwen. "I guess you never really know your neighbors. Jake seemed like an ordinary guy although he was a loner who kept to himself."

Jake sighed and shook his head at the stupidity of the average adult.

"The talking heads are saying you tried to harm that good woman Katherine Anderson," O'Leary said. "But that doesn't make any sense after what you've told me."

"A criminal impersonated me. I wasn't anywhere near where it happened."

"I hope you have a good alibi. I thought that might be you in the booth when you called me *Padre,* but you didn't speak with a Spanish accent."

"In the Marines, we called any chaplain of any faith *Padre.*"

Jake leaned out and peeked around the corner of the doorway alcove. "There's another cop in front of the church, smoking a cigarette next to an SUV. He's just standing there, waiting for me or his partner to walk out the front door. Any moment now, he's probably going to enter the church to see what's taking so long. I've got to get going."

"You're an unusual man, Jake. However, I think you and I may become good friends. Visit me again when you can. Here's my private mobile phone number."

Father O'Leary handed Jake a card and then tilted his head toward a wooden fence down the alley and said, "Use the hidden gate in that fence to go through the yard to the next street and be on your way. I've been saving some special Irish whiskey for a grand conversation. I say we open it the next time you visit. Hopefully under less stressful circumstances."

Jake shook the priest's hand and looked him in the eye. "Thanks. I could use a friend like you. So, it's true—you weren't always a priest, were you?"

O'Leary got a sad look in his eyes, hooked a finger in his high collar and pulled it to the side, exposing a rope burn scar on his neck.

"I got this scar when I was a young child in Northern Ireland. On the night of Bloody Sunday, I was walking home in the dark—a drunken British soldier tried to hang me, and failed. A neighbor heard my cry for help and came to my assistance. The hangman ended up dead instead of me. The fortunes of war."

"That was a day of tragedy for everyone on all sides."

"I've never told anyone here about it until now. At first, I began this job as a kind of witness protection program. The job has grown on me over the years, and I try to help people here as best I can."

"You've helped a lot of people. You are forgiven," Jake said.

O'Leary gave a weary smile at Jake's pardon and said, "Go on with you now, before that other police officer comes looking for you. Meanwhile, I'll explain to the fine folks in law enforcement about this mysterious electric-shocking of a cop by some unseen assailant. The Taser hit the poor man right on the butt, too. He won't be able to sit down comfortably for a while."

O'Leary set the stun gun inside a hidden cabinet, closed it and locked it, then nodded at Jake and walked out the door and down the alley toward the front of the church.

Jake and Cody made their way in the other direction, went through the gate in the fence, and vanished into the fog and darkness of the night.

~

The plainclothes police inspector standing next to the SUV used his compact night vision zoom binoculars to watch Jake and Cody make their escape. He made no move to chase after them or call for backup. The cop took a puff on his cigarette as he thought up a good lie to tell about how Jake Wolfe had magically given him the slip.

Father O'Leary walked slowly toward the cop, and when he was a few feet away, the man spoke to him.

"Hello, Father. I'm Lieutenant Terrell Hayes with the San Francisco

Police Department. I don't suppose you've seen one of my men around here, have you? I seem to have misplaced a rookie officer I'm supposed to be training tonight."

O'Leary noticed the binoculars, but he didn't say anything about it. "Yes, Officer, I believe I can help you with that. Come this way, please."

"Thank you, Padre." Terrell tossed the binoculars on the driver's seat of the vehicle and closed the car door.

As the two men walked toward the church, O'Leary said, "I believe I saw you at Stuart's funeral, didn't I?"

"Yes, I was there, and that was a beautiful eulogy you gave. Stuart's parents were comforted by your kind words."

Father O'Leary nodded. "Such a tragic loss of a good lad."

The priest and the cop turned and looked at each other as they walked, and their eyes shared a secret between them without speaking of it. They'd both helped a wanted fugitive escape from the law. Technically that was a serious crime, but both of them felt that in some situations, the law was wrong, and the right thing to do was to question it and disobey it.

Terrell was taking a big risk here, but he was relieved that Jake had made his getaway. As long as his friend was out on the streets, he was capable of taking care of himself. Terrell would let his friend run free, and he'd hope for the best. He figured that if he got fired from the SFPD over this, he would just find some other career. He'd been looking for a job when this one had come along, and he could look again. He'd saved Jake's life once already, and now he felt responsible for the fool. Jobs might come and go, but some friendships were forever.

CHAPTER 85

Two blocks away from the hospital, Zhukov sat in a parked car and gazed at the building through a pair of binoculars. Looking for a way to enter without being seen, and take another shot at Katherine Anderson.

He saw serious-looking men and women guarding the outside. Each of them wore a dark suit and had an earbud in one ear. There was the subtle bulge of a shoulder holster under their suit jackets.

Zhukov silently cursed them for being so good at their jobs. He studied the entrance to the parking garage. Security looked tight at the entrance and exit. He gazed up at the edge of the roof and saw a man lean over and look down at the street. Lastly, he checked out the buildings across the street from the hospital, in the front and back and sides. There were government people everywhere.

He made a phone call. "Yes, Ivan," Elena said.

"Didn't you say you had a small, quiet drone the size of a toy remote-controlled plane, with a thermal camera attached for night work?" Zhukov said.

"Yes, it's powered by electric fans that are so quiet you can't hear them."

"That's the one. I want you to fly it around the hospital and the nearby buildings, look in windows, check the rooftops, and maybe even fly in and out of the parking garage."

"No problem. I can launch it within ten minutes."

"Launch it in five minutes and have a backup unit ready to fly as a replacement in case it gets shot down. Send the surveillance video to my phone."

"I'll send you a text when it's in the air."

Zhukov ended the call and said, "You've got to love technology. The Americans invent all this amazing stuff and then other countries steal it and use it against them."

Jake stayed on side streets and tried to stroll along casually as if he were simply out walking his dog after dinner. More fog rolled in as the temperature dropped, as so often happened in San Francisco, the City by the Bay. Jake was grateful to have the fog helping to obscure his movements. He was angry that he was still a wanted man. Hopefully by tomorrow this mistaken manhunt would be over. Right now, he needed a place to hide and avoid arrest.

Jake thought of a nearby park where he and Cody could hide out for a while in the dark among the trees and bushes, and he made his way in that direction. As they walked along, Jake kept watch all around him and made sure he wasn't being followed. Most of the neighborhood residents were inside their homes, having dinner or watching television. The drivers of the few cars that passed by on these back streets paid no attention to the man walking his dog.

A block up ahead, several people came out of a building, talking and laughing. Jake and Cody ducked into a dark alley to avoid being seen. Halfway down the alley, they passed by a dumpster. Cody alerted and made a vicious growl, showing his teeth. Jake drew his pistol, and at that moment, a homeless man stepped out of the shadows holding a rusty knife in his shaking hand.

"Give me your wallet and nobody gets hurt," the man said. When he saw the gun pointed at him, and what appeared to be an attack dog snarling at his crotch, his shoulders slumped and he shook his head.

Jake ordered Cody to hold and then spoke in a commanding voice to the man. "Drop the knife and put your hands behind your head with your fingers interlaced. Do it now."

The man followed the order in a calm manner and showed no fear. Jake studied him for a moment and saw that his long hair needed to be washed. So did his red-and-black checkered flannel shirt. His worn-out jeans looked ready to fall apart at the seams. He had the shakes, but he wasn't trembling from fear. He seemed to be in desperate need of liquor or a drug.

"Do you need a drink?" Jake said.

The man stared hard at Jake for a moment to see if he was playing with him, and then nodded.

"You can lower your hands, but don't move a muscle or my dog *will* hurt you," Jake said.

The man slowly lowered his hands. Jake holstered the pistol and opened his backpack, taking out two small bottles of Hennessy's cognac.

When the man saw the liquor, he licked his lips, and his Adam's apple bobbed up and down as he reflexively swallowed. Jake handed both bottles to him, and the man drank one down quickly in a long gulp. He let out a sigh of relief.

"Thank you, friend."

"Have booze, will travel—that's how I roll," Jake said.

The man didn't smile. He looked at Cody. "Is that a war dog? He has the look."

"Yes, he's a Marine. What branch of the service were you in?"

The man stared off into the distance as if seeing foreign lands far away. "Army. Seventy-Fifth Ranger Regiment out of Fort Lewis in Washington State."

"Army Rangers, that's impressive. You have my respect."

"Where did you serve?"

"In the Marine Corps infantry, and then I volunteered to be an IED detector dog handler."

"I wish a dog like that could have found the roadside bomb that got my leg."

The man slowly bent over and pulled up the cuff of his left pant leg, exposing an artificial plastic-and-metal prosthesis from the knee down.

"Be glad you lived through it. Some of my friends didn't."

"I do try to be thankful, but I've had post-traumatic stress ever since," the man said, and he drank down the other small bottle of liquor.

"I had a slight touch of PTSD for a while too. There is help available. You don't have to suffer through it alone. This too shall pass, but that's easy for me to say since I didn't lose a leg."

"I've found that liquor helps the most. I drink at nighttime to stay numb and get some sleep. Got any more alcohol in that backpack?"

"No, fresh out. Are you drinking on an empty stomach? That will kill you pretty quick."

"Nothing lives long, only the mountains and the rivers. Soon we all return to our Earth Mother."

Jake looked at the man's long, straight black hair, the shape of his face and how he had no beard.

"Are you Native American?"

"I'm one of the Zuni people, from New Mexico. The words I spoke are from a death song."

"Don't sing it yet. Listen, do you want a part-time job? All it pays is three meals a day and a place to sleep, but you'll be safe and you won't have to fight people every day just to live."

Jake looked at the way the man was favoring his right hand, as if he'd been injured recently.

The man saw the look, rubbed his sore wrist and said, "Three hots and a cot? What do I have to do? Don't mess with me."

Jake held his jacket open to remind the man of the pistol in its holster. "All you have to do is help serve dinner at a soup kitchen, listen to a sermon and then wash dishes afterward. I'm warning you, though. If you were to harm anyone there, I would find you and cause you a thousand times more pain and regret. Fair enough?"

"Yes, fair enough. I've already had enough pain and regret in life. I just want to live in peace."

"I know the feeling," Jake said, and he handed the man one of the throwaway phones, along with Father O'Leary's business card.

"Call that guy. Tell him that a man with a golden dog gave you this number and said to call the padre. He'll know it was me. Ask if you can work at the soup kitchen. Call him *before* you pawn that phone and drink any more alcohol. Is that a deal?"

The man finally smiled. "Deal," he said.

Jake handed him some twenty-dollar bills. "Get some food before you drink any more booze."

"Thank you, brother. It's been a while since I had a meal. I've been thinking about cheap cheeseburgers all day long."

"What's your name?"

"Paul. What's yours?"

'I'm Jake and this is Cody." Jake didn't shake the man's injured hand. He just gave a command to his dog and began walking down the alley. Jake looked over his shoulder and said, "This is your chance —don't blow it."

Paul stared at Jake and then at the phone in his hand. He nodded, took a deep breath and tapped in the phone number to call O'Leary.

Jake and Cody went down several more alleys. They were getting closer to the dog park that Jake had in mind as a hiding place. As they reached the end of another alley and were crossing the street, a car drove up out of an underground parking area and turned toward them. The car's headlights shone right on the pair as they were in the middle of the crosswalk.

The car stopped, and two men got out. One of them said, "That's him, the wanted guy on the news. We can get the reward."

Jake heard what was said, and he saw that the man had a pistol in his hand. "Run, Cody, run now," Jake said, and the two of them took off sprinting toward the corner of a building to the right.

The man with the pistol yelled, "Stop or I'll shoot. This is a citizen's arrest."

When the runners didn't stop, the man illegally fired off several rounds in their general direction. His unskilled shots hit a parked car, a family's living room window that shattered on impact, and … Cody.

Cody cried out in pain as he fell and skidded on the sidewalk. Jake went temporarily insane. He roared in anger like a wild animal, drew his pistol and began firing.

When the two men heard the furious battle cry and saw the pistol, they panicked and took off running. Jake was barely able to control his rage. He fired rounds into the man's car engine over and over again, destroying it beyond repair.

Jake yelled and cursed as he fired his pistol. "You shot an American war dog. You shot a sergeant in the Marine Corps. You'd better run for your lives, you traitors. If I ever see you again, I'll kill you!"

He then trained the pistol on the fleeing attackers. It would be justifiable self-defense. He gritted his teeth and then shook his head. His concern for Cody and his strict training overrode his anger. Jake returned his pistol to its holster and then carefully picked up Cody in his arms, holding the dog's wounded area tightly against his chest to try to slow down any flow of blood.

"I think it's only a flesh wound, but don't you die on me, Cody. That's an order!" Jake said.

Jake began to run, carrying his injured brother. Thoughts of previous battles flashed through his mind. The memories of similar horrific events were painful, but they also helped him to know what he had to do to save his friend. And he would save him, or die trying.

Cody growled in pain from the wound and from being held tightly and jostled as his alpha ran down the street.

Jake's quick assessment revealed that Cody'd only been winged along his shoulder with a skin-deep flesh wound and that the bullet had not entered his body. He kept up a pep talk as he ran, his leg muscles starting to burn with the exertion.

"You're going to be okay, Cody. Just hang on and I'll get you fixed up quick. Stay with me now. Just keep on breathing in and out. You can do it. Hold tight, we're almost there."

CHAPTER 86

Sarah Chance worked alone in her veterinary clinic, staying late and finishing up some paperwork. As she worked, she received a text message on her phone from Madison, her receptionist employee.

OMG, is this that guy you said you'd bumped into at the TV station?

The text had a link to an online news story by a reporter named Dick Arnold. Sarah gasped when she saw the suspect's photo with a caption that said, "Wanted Fugitive: Jacob Wolfe, Photojournalist."

"That's him, the guy who talked to me," Sarah said out loud. She felt a chill go down her spine. Maybe he'd been stalking her. He was accused of assaulting a pregnant woman and her unborn child, shooting the woman's belly with a paintball gun. What kind of sick person would do such a thing? Other photos showed that he'd been at all three crime scenes of the recent attacks on lawyers.

There was a sound bite from Mayor Burgess. He faced the news cameras with his blow-dried hair, brightly whitened teeth, and an obvious facelift. A man in his fifties trying to look thirty and not succeeding. Burgess said the city police would hunt down this man with every resource available. He promised swift justice.

Sarah had met SFPD Sergeant Beth Cushman when she'd brought her cat to the clinic. She looked up Beth's number in her client list and made the phone call on her mobile phone. The call went to voicemail, and Sarah left a message.

"Hello, Sergeant Cushman, this is Dr. Sarah Chance at the pet clinic. I just saw the news about this Jake Wolfe person and I wanted to tell you that he physically bumped into me recently and talked to me. I don't know if that's helpful, but I thought you should know."

Sarah ended the call and got up and walked through her clinic, making sure all of the doors and windows were locked up tight. She opened her purse and checked her small .380 pistol. It might not be a very big pistol, but if she fired it at close range, it could make a serious hole in an assailant. She had it loaded with hollow-point rounds. Every time she held the pistol, she remembered the rhyming advice that her instructor had repeated. "Two in the chest and one in the head; makes the enemy dead-dead-dead."

Now all she had to do was go outside all alone and walk in the dark and fog to her car that was parked three blocks away. Hopefully, the stalker wasn't hiding out there, watching and waiting. No problem —that kind of thing built character, right? It merely required bravery, good luck, and nerves of steel. What could go wrong?

Jake had never run a mile while carrying a large dog in his arms before, but there was a first time for everything. His leg muscles were on fire when he finally made it to the dog park. Cody needed medical care, and he needed it now. Jake believed he was going to be okay, but he would not rest for one second until he was absolutely sure. He was overprotective of dogs, and if anybody tried to stop him from saving Cody's life, he would take swift and violent action.

As soon as he and Cody were hidden behind some bushes at the new park, Jake studied the veterinary clinic across the street, the one he'd seen on the TV commercial. This would have to do. The all night pet hospital was too far away. He couldn't waste a single minute.

The clinic appeared to be closed. The front light was on but the inside rooms were dark.

"Time to fracture a few laws for the good of my dog," Jake said. He carried Cody across the street and went around the side of the clinic to the back. The sliding glass door was a welcome sight. Those were usually pretty easy to open. If anyone asked him how he knew which doors were easy to open, he'd just say he had no comment. The truth was, in his youth he might have bent a law now and then with his group of rebellious friends.

A picnic table sat next to the door, and Jake gently set down Cody on the tabletop.

"Cody, stay, don't move."

Cody looked at Jake with pain in his eyes, but obeyed the order.

Jake peered down through the glass door at the track it slid on and was glad to see there wasn't a wooden dowel there. He didn't see any burglar alarm sensors attached to the door either. Jake got a firm grip on the handle of the sliding door and began to move it up and down, working on the lock. Soon he could feel the latch loosening. A slight gap appeared between the door and the frame. He took out his KA-BAR knife, slid the blade into the gap and worked it against the latch. After a few moments, the latch clicked and came free. Jake slid the door open, picked up Cody and carried him inside, then slid the door closed behind him by pushing his elbow against the handle.

He used his arm to bump up a light switch to the on position and found himself in a dog-grooming area. There was a door at the other end of the room. He walked to the other door, and as he went through it, he used his elbow to turn off the light in the grooming area and then turn on the light in the hallway. Several doors in the hall stood open, and Jake went through one into a treatment room with a patient table. He turned off the hallway light and turned on the light in the treatment room, then set Cody down on a tabletop designed for medical procedures.

"Okay, Cody, I'm going to fix up that wound. This is going to hurt, but I'll find some Novocain and give you a shot."

Cody stayed still and made a brave sound in his throat. Jake opened cabinets and found the supplies he needed. He put some hemostatic powder onto Cody's cut to stop the bleeding, then hooked up an IV saline drip to get some intravenous fluid into Cody and help him overcome his blood loss. Next, he found some Novocain, loaded up a syringe and gently injected it in several places to act as a local anesthetic.

Jake rubbed the back of his neck, took a stressed breath and exhaled loudly. "Okay, what's next? Are we ready for sutures? I think I remembered everything. Let's do this."

While the medicine was taking effect, Jake put on surgical gloves. Cody's skin was numb around the wound, and Jake gently probed it with a clean scalpel to look for the bullet. He was relieved to see that it was only a flesh wound, just as he'd thought. The bullet had barely grazed Cody. It had torn open his skin like a knife blade as it passed by but had not lodged inside his body or caused serious trauma.

Jake let out one of the biggest sighs of relief of his entire life. He just couldn't lose another dog. He tried to hide his feelings from Cody, but for a moment he felt like he might vomit. He took some deep breaths and pressed his face against Cody's face until the feeling passed. Cody licked Jake's cheek and huffed at him.

Now it was time to close the wound. Jake used a sterile needle and some suture material to begin sewing up Cody's skin and creating stitches. It was slow going with such a long cut, and the stitches weren't very neat and tidy. But Jake was in a hurry, and the battlefield sutures would heal just fine. Cody's fur would hide the long scar.

Sarah jogged the three blocks to her car. Her left hand held her purse and her right-hand was inside it, holding the pistol. She quickly got into her car and locked the doors. Her clinic was on a street corner, directly across from the dog park but she always parked her car a few blocks down the side street, leaving those front parking spaces open for potential customers.

It had been stressful to run three blocks in the dark, but at least she'd avoided going near the darkened dog park with all its bushes and shadows. Once she started the car's engine, she felt relieved. However, a moment later, she thought she might have seen a light go on and off inside her clinic. She sat there in her car and wondered if she'd imagined it. She then caught another flash of light in one of the back windows. That was impossible. She'd made sure to turn off all of the lights. She released her parking brake and drove with her headlights off, then slowly pulled her car up next to the clinic and parked.

Her brain said it was a mistake to go inside and investigate, but her heart said nobody was going to mess with her life's work and get away with it. After all her long hours, the lawsuit, the collection agencies, and everything else ... a burglary by some drug junkie hoping to steal ketamine was just the last straw.

She turned off her car engine, quietly got out of her car and clipped the SOB "small-of-the-back" holster inside the back waistband of her pants. She kept the pistol in her right hand, and in her other she held her purse with her keys and phone inside. Walking slowly and approaching the back sliding glass door, Sarah looked inside and saw that the other door across the grooming room was open just a crack—even though she was sure she'd closed it all the way when she'd left. The hallway light didn't appear to be on, but now there seemed to be another source of light, maybe coming from one of the treatment rooms.

Sarah gently pushed on the sliding door handle, and the door slowly slid open. Now she was sure someone had broken in. She'd locked that door and checked it twice. She felt a cold chills run up and down her spine. Her heart pounded as she went inside and closed the door, then crossed the room and opened the other door. She leaned her head out into the hallway and quickly pulled it back.

There was a light coming from one of the treatment rooms down the hall. The door was closed, but the bright light came through the narrow vertical window above the doorknob. The smart thing to do would be to go back outside, get in her car and lock the doors, and then call the police. But Sarah was angry at this intruder for daring to break into her clinic. She wanted to practice her martial arts training on his face.

Her temper flared, and her anger overrode her fear. She left her purse on the counter but took out her phone and put it in her pocket. She then held her pistol out in front of her as she crept quietly down the hallway. When she got to the door with the light in the window, she took a quick peek inside. There was a man in the room with his head turned away from her to his right. He was doing something to a Labrador retriever dog that was lying on the treatment table. The dog had blood on its fur and appeared to be in pain.

She took a deep breath and then burst through the doorway and yelled, "Hands above your head! Don't move or I'll shoot!"

The man stood perfectly still and slowly raised his hands. The dog started barking and snarling, but the man said, "Out, Cody. Out, boy."

The dog quieted, but he watched Sarah with a pained look in his eyes.

"What do you think you're doing?" Sarah said. She held the pistol with both hands and pointed it at the man.

"I'm almost done here, sorry for the intrusion."

"Turn your head slowly so I can see your face. And keep your hands up or I swear I'll put a bullet in you."

Jake turned slowly and looked at Sarah. When Sarah saw his face, she gasped.

"It's you! Are you stalking me?"

"Now just calm down, Sarah, and let me explain."

"You know my name?"

"Relax; your name is on the front door, on your TV commercial, and on your name tag."

Sarah saw him glance at the name tag on her breast for a second, and her eyes narrowed in anger. "Don't move a muscle or you're a dead man."

"At the moment, I'm not moving any of them except for flapping my jaw. But while you hold me at gunpoint and threaten to kill me, I'd like to finish suturing my dog's wound if you don't mind."

Jake slowly lowered his hands and turned his attention back to his dog, ignoring Sarah.

"What did you do to that poor dog? Why is there blood all over the front of your shirt?"

"I saved his poor life. My shirt has his blood on it because I ran here while carrying him in my arms, after a citizen vigilante shot him. Oh, and my name is Jake, by the way."

"I know who you are. I saw a TV news story about you shooting a pregnant woman in the stomach."

Cody barked at the two of them, and Jake said, "Easy now, stay put, buddy."

Cody growled, but he held still.

Sarah noticed some cash money in a heap of bills near the sink. "I see you robbed my petty cash box."

"Actually, I left that money to pay for the medical supplies that I used."

Sarah glanced at the cash again and noticed it looked like a lot more money than had ever been in her petty cash box, but she remained unconvinced. "Save your lies for the new friends you're going to meet in prison."

As Jake continued to sew up Cody's wound, he said, "I'm curious, Sarah, are you part French?"

"I'm part French-Canadian, not that it's any of your damned business."

"I thought so. It was just a good guess because you have that cute mouth some girls get from speaking French words."

Sarah scowled at him. "How nice, a burglar that flirts. I should just shoot you now and get it over with."

"You won't shoot me."

"How can you be sure?"

"Because of that money I gave you. I'm a paying customer, and you need more of those. Did you do a mental count of how much cash is there?"

The question caused Sarah to reflexively turn her head for just a second to look at the money again. Jake lunged at her, grabbed the pistol out of her hand and stepped back out of reach.

It happened so fast that Sarah was stunned. Now Jake was holding her gun and pointing it at the floor in front of her. When she'd been caught by surprise, Sarah had moved her foot that had been holding the door open. The door swung closed behind her on automatic spring hinges and blocked her escape route with a resounding thud.

Jake saw her face get pale as the door closed. He aimed her pistol off to the side. "The real reason I knew you wouldn't shoot me is that you still had your pistol's safety on."

"Give me back that pistol, right now."

"Just FYI, when your weapon is taken away from you, you're not in a position to make demands. I'll just set it over here, along with the money I paid you."

Jake turned around and set the pistol on top of the money on the counter.

The moment Jake's back was turned, Sarah attacked him with a flurry of martial arts kicks and punches. She landed several blows on his back, but he turned around and began counterpunching and kicking. None of his blows landed on her face or body, but they blocked everything she had to throw at him. He slowly advanced toward her a step at a time, moving her backward, all the while keeping a bemused smile on his face.

As they fought each other, Jake said, "Have you been trained in *Jeet Kune Do*?"

Sarah threw more punches and kicks at him. "You *have* been stalking me."

Jake countered her moves and blocked the attack of her fists and feet. "No, I haven't been stalking you. It's obvious by the way you fight that you know Bruce Lee's fighting style. That's what I use myself."

Sarah was nearly backed up against the closed door. She attacked again with a desperate fury as if her life depended on it. Jake countered her every punch and kick with what are known in the art of Jeet Kune Do as intercepting fists, stop hits, stop kicks, and simultaneous parrying and punching. Try as she might, Sarah could not land a blow on Jake's face or body. That drove her to fight even harder.

"We need to stop this now," Jake said between kicks and punches. "I have to sew up my dog and be on my way."

"We'll stop when you drop," Sarah said, and she threw a powerful kick that Jake deflected.

"Have you noticed that I'm doing my best not to hit you? It's because I don't want to."

"You couldn't hit me if you tried."

With lightning speed, Jake's hand flew out and he gave a playful slap to the side of Sarah's shoulder.

Sarah didn't feel any pain from the slap, but it was clearly a huge blow to her ego, and now her eyes blazed in anger.

"You're going to be sorry for that," Sarah said, and she threw several punches at Jake's eyes.

Jake shrugged and countered the repeated punches. "I was just trying to get your attention and end this pointless fight. And, yes, I am sorry. I apologize for breaking into your clinic, but my dog was bleeding to death. You might've done the same thing to save a life."

"You think you can win because you're a man, but you're going down."

"My advantage isn't because I'm a man, it's because I have several more years of practice than you do. I'm also taller and I have longer arms and legs."

"The bigger they are, the harder they fall."

"By the way, you want to keep your left elbow up a little higher," Jake said.

Sarah stepped back from her attack to catch her breath for a second. "Why should I believe a criminal?"

She lifted her left elbow some and then moved in and threw a punch at Jake's face followed by a kick at his knees.

Jake blocked the blows. "See, keeping that elbow up helped a lot, right? Look, all I can say is, I've been falsely accused. I hope you might understand since you were also falsely accused of harming that young woman when you acted as a Good Samaritan."

Sarah gritted her teeth at the mention of her trial and the hell she'd been going through with the legal system. She was an emotional person, and her anger now flared to its peak. She made an animal sound and threw several fierce punches at Jake's throat.

Jake had to fight harder to block the attack now that Sarah had her left arm working better for her. He was impressed.

Cody noticed the increase in the danger level from Sarah and began barking again.

"Out, Cody, stay," Jake said.

"After I kick your ass, you're going to jail," Sarah said as she gasped for breath. "For breaking and entering, burglary, stealing medical supplies, criminal trespass, assault and battery, practicing medicine without a license and… being an asshole."

"Sorry for entering here without permission," Jake said. "But if it's against the law for me to save my dog's life, then I say screw that law and the fool who wrote it."

"That's exactly what a criminal would say."

Jake stepped back away from Sarah and lowered his hands to his sides. "No, it's what a free man who loves his dog would say. But I don't have time for this. So, go ahead and hit me, Doctor. Get it out of your system."

CHAPTER 87

The moment Jake lowered his hands, Sarah threw a hard kick to his chest. She followed up with several wicked punches to his stomach and face, drawing blood from his nose and mouth. He just took the punishment and calmly looked her in the eye the whole time. Sarah paused for a moment and stepped back in surprise that he was letting her use him as a human punching bag.

Jake bowed in acknowledgment of her fine effort. Then he spoke in the voice of an instructor. "Left elbow up—deflect this kick." He jumped up and seemed to float in the air in slow motion as he threw one expertly aimed kick at her chest, right between her breasts.

Sarah raised both hands in defense and caught Jake's foot in a solid grip. She tried to deflect the kick, but it raised her up off her feet and flung her backward. She slammed against the closed door, slid down it and landed on her butt.

Cody barked at the sight and smell of Jake's blood. Jake stayed back, giving Sarah some space. He calmly spoke to Cody. "Out, Cody, don't attack. She's a friend of ours, she just doesn't know it yet."

Cody obeyed and held still, but growled and showed his teeth.

Sarah struggled back to her feet and into a fighting stance, leaning her back against the door with her fists up in front of her. Her breathing was ragged, and her legs felt wobbly, but she would never back down from a fight and was ready to go another round.

"Please give it a rest, Sarah," Jake said. He stood there with his hands relaxed by his sides, and blood dripping from his nose. "Next time, allow the kick to come at you, and deflect it with your left fist, as you step into your opponent and throw a punch with your dominant right hand."

Sarah could see that Jake's body language was nonthreatening and patient, like when her Wushu master was teaching a promising student a new martial arts technique. She finally believed that he didn't want to fight her. She lowered her fists but was now concerned about the threat from the dog. Her training had taught her all about animal behavior. This dog had his hackles up and was baring his teeth. She had a way with dogs, but this one appeared ready to bite her. "What did you mean by ... attack?" Sarah gestured at Cody.

"Cody is a Marine war dog, highly trained and protective. I could give him the order, and wounded or not, he would leap from the table and fight to protect me. You'd never get out the door fast enough."

Sarah's face went pale, and she swallowed. When she'd been in veterinary college, she'd been trained on how to care for guard dogs, police dogs, and military dogs. It was a dangerous job, and so far, she'd avoided it. This retriever looked so huggable, like they all did. It was a little bit disturbing to learn that he was trained to bite on command. She realized that this man might be a military-trained killer too. Either one or both of them could have harmed her already. Why hadn't they? Was he telling the truth?

Jake saw the fear in Sarah's eyes and felt bad. He picked up Sarah's pistol off the counter. When she saw him do it, she inhaled sharply in fear.

"I also could have shot you with your own gun if I was the bad man that you think I am."

Sarah's body stiffened as Jake held her pistol by the barrel and handed it to her grip-first with the barrel pointing at himself. She snatched the pistol from his hand and pointed it at him, but kept the safety on. Her hands began shaking slightly from relief.

Jake noticed the tremble and said, "Please be careful with that pistol. I didn't give it back to you so you could shoot Cody or me by accident. Where did you get that thing, anyway? It's a complicated process to get ahold of one of those pocket rockets now that California is trying to ban them."

"First, you knock me on my butt and let me get up again. Next you stop your dog from attacking me. And now you give me back my pistol … why?"

"This is your clinic. I'm trespassing. Plus, I have this other gun I could have used if I'd really wanted to."

Before Sarah fully grasped what Jake had said, she saw him turn and calmly lift up his leather jacket. He reached underneath it and took out his own pistol, holding it up and showing it to her but not pointing it at her. Sarah felt weak in the knees when she saw the serious piece of hardware.

"Being shot up close with this is something we describe in military terminology as a non-survivable event," Jake said, and he smiled kindly at her.

Jake set his pistol down and turned back to Cody. He began the amateurish suturing of the dog's wound again, ignoring Sarah.

Sarah kept her pistol trained on Jake, but she didn't know what to say. He acted like some kind of stone-cold killer military type, but his eyes revealed a hidden gentleness when he looked at his dog. As she watched him working to save Cody's life with no concern for his own safety, it made her heart ache. He wasn't doing the job up to her high standards, and she had to fight the urge to push him aside and do it herself.

"Feel free to point your pistol at me while I work," Jake said. "But if you do fire that weapon, please aim high so you don't accidentally harm my dog."

Another drop of blood ran from Jake's nose down his lip and chin, but he ignored his own bleeding and focused on Cody. When Jake leaned in for a closer look at the stitches, Cody craned his neck and licked his master's bloody face. Jake gave a tight smile to Cody and patted him on the head.

"Hang in there, buddy. That was a close call, but you're going to be okay. As long as Sarah doesn't shoot us before she gets to know us."

Sarah felt a strange attraction to these two outlaws. Jake's actions had repeatedly demonstrated that he could have harmed her, but he'd purposely avoided it and was even risking his life now to avoid it.

Against her better judgment, Sarah lowered her pistol and pointed it at the floor. "Explain yourself. What's going on here?"

Jake didn't immediately comply with her request. He continued working quietly for a moment longer and then glanced at her briefly and went back to work. As Jake continued to sew up Cody's wound, he nodded his head. "I guess I do owe you an explanation. I was impersonated by someone wearing a mask that looked just like my stupid face. The impostor shot a paintball at Katherine Anderson—the former prosecutor and currently very pregnant wife of Congressman Daniel Anderson."

"Sounds like BS if you ask me."

"I didn't ask you, but I agree that it does sound like BS. Everyone thinks I did it, even though I have an alibi."

"Do you have any proof?"

"No, I don't, but a Secret Service agent believes me. I just need to hide out for a while until the police figure out I'm innocent."

"Who hurt this dog?"

Jake noticed that she said it in an angry, demanding, and protective way. He liked that about her. She was a badass veterinarian. He continued sewing up Cody's wound and talking as he worked. "A couple of vigilantes tried to capture me for the reward money. One of them shot at me and grazed Cody instead. It would've been legal for me to return fire at those men in self-defense, but I let them live."

"How much is the reward?" Sarah held her pistol in a tight grip.

"Never mind, I probably shouldn't have mentioned that. No offense, Sarah, but you need to be quiet now so I can concentrate on Cody."

Sarah glared at Jake when he told her to be quiet. Her mobile phone chimed in her pocket.

"Go ahead and answer that, and do whatever your conscience tells you to do. Call the police if you want to sell us out for the reward. All I really care about right now is making sure Cody is okay."

Sarah answered the call and heard the voice of SFPD Sergeant Beth Cushman. "Hi, Sarah, I hope I'm not calling too late."

"No not at all, Sergeant Cushman, thank you for returning my call."

Jake looked at Sarah. "I know Beth; let me talk to her for a minute."

Sarah shook her head. She held her phone in one hand, and her pistol in the other.

Beth said, "Sarah, you can call me Beth."

"Thanks, Beth. I was just calling you about that wanted fugitive I saw on the news, Jake Wolfe."

Jake shook his head and grumbled something about "Benedict Arnold."

"Yes, I heard that on your voicemail. Jake is actually a close friend of my police partner, Terrell Hayes."

"Is he dangerous? Did he really shoot a paintball at that woman? I heard a rumor that a Secret Service agent believes it was someone else wearing a mask disguised to look like him."

"I heard about the paintball, but not about anyone wearing a mask. How and where did you get this information?"

"Um, it was on one of those radio call-in talk shows. They always have a lot of conspiracy theories on there."

"Hmmm," Beth said. "Where are you right now, Sarah?"

"I'm still at my clinic, working late."

"I heard on the police radio that some vigilantes took a few shots at Jake. A witness stated that they may have hit his dog. I hope they're both okay."

"I hope so too. Thanks for the info. If I see Jake and Cody, I'll give you a call."

"Please do. Be sure to call me directly on this mobile number instead of calling police HQ, the FBI, or anyone else, okay?"

"Okay, thanks again, Beth. Goodbye."

Just as Sarah said goodbye and ended the call, Cody let out an impatient bark at Jake.

Beth heard the dog, just before the call ended. She smiled a rueful smile and wondered how Sarah could know that Jake's dog was named Cody. Beth hadn't mentioned the dog's name, and it wasn't on the news.

Beth remembered the video that Terrell had shown to her, where Jake's fiancée had threatened to file a false police complaint against him. Jake had ended his engagement to Gwen, and it looked like he wasn't wasting any time meeting someone new, namely Sarah Chance.

Terrell had once told Beth that Jake Wolfe was known to be a silver-tongued devil. He had a way with words and a way with women. Just some kind of gift. Beth thought it was true. Jake was a charming rogue—she had to give him credit for that. Right now, he was probably working his charm on the warm-hearted and emotional veterinarian. The question was, what should she do about it? It was her job to go and arrest Jake—but instead, she made a call to Terrell. While she waited for him to answer, she looked up the phone number of the Secret Service.

CHAPTER 88

Sarah put her phone in her pocket and tucked her pistol into the holster in the back waistband of her slacks. "Lucky for you, your story checks out, Mister Fugitive. Now step aside and let me see how badly you've botched this medical procedure."

"Thank you. I owe you a big favor," Jake said, and he stepped aside.

"Sure, that's what all the fugitives say."

Jake said to Cody, "Out, Cody; lay still. This is a Navy Corpsman. She's going to treat your wound."

Cody barked once and watched Sarah with his intelligent eyes.

Jake respected the Navy Corpsmen. They ran into combat alongside the Marines and could perform medical miracles in the middle of a firefight with bullets flying past them. They were warrior doctors who were as good with a rifle as they were with a medical kit.

Sarah bravely scratched the war dog behind his ears and under his chin, studied his wound and spoke comforting words to him. "You're going to be okay, Cody. You're such a brave dog, aren't you, boy?"

Cody's tail wagged and thumped on the metal table a couple of times. He appeared to instinctively understand that his alpha considered this person a friend and equal, and respected her skills. She'd fought hard with his alpha. Now they'd made peace with each other. There were a lot of male and female human pheromones swirling around in the room. Cody could sense their attraction to each other.

Sarah put on her black horn-rimmed glasses. She knew that many dogs have an ID number tattooed in their ear, and she always checked every dog she treated. She looked in Cody's ears and saw the military ID tattoo. It was different from any tattoo she'd seen before.

Jake saw her checking to see if he'd told the truth. He got his wallet out of his back pocket, removed a photo and showed it to her. Sarah glanced at the picture and saw a somewhat younger-looking Jake, wearing desert combat camo clothing and boots. He was standing in front of an armored military vehicle near some desolate sand dunes. A dog was standing next to him. On the other side of the dog was a rugged Marine with a cigarette in his mouth and a frown on his face. He was holding a dangerous-looking rifle.

"That's me and my buddy, Terrell Hayes, along with my Marine Corps war dog ... Duke."

Sarah nodded her head and made a point of not asking about Duke. The way Jake had said the dog's name seemed to expose some buried emotions. She focused her full attention on suturing up the part of Cody's wound that Jake had not worked on yet. It was a long cut on the surface of the skin. One inch closer and the bullet would have entered his body and killed him.

When Jake saw Sarah caring for his dog, looking like an angel of mercy and wearing those glasses, he felt a pressure in his chest. He was impressed with her deft hands, talent, and skills. It was obvious she loved animals. She was the best veterinarian he'd ever seen. His blood pressure started to rise, and he took a deep breath.

Sarah felt his eyes on her, and she glanced up at him over the top of her glasses. Jake was mesmerized.

"What?" Sarah said.

"I'm just ... impressed with your work. I have a lot of respect for you."

Sarah felt flustered by his gaze and compliments. It pleased her and bothered her for reasons she didn't clearly understand at the moment. Until now, no man had ever said that he respected her work. Why was that so hard to say? This man seemed to find it easy and natural.

Cody also watched Sarah, and his eyes twinkled with affection as he looked at her face. Cody seemed to breathe easier now. This woman had shown that she could take good care of him and keep him alive. She was better at this medical work than his alpha was.

"I like your tattoo," Jake said.

Sarah just nodded and remained focused on her work. The tattoo on her left arm was of a goddess carrying a bow and a quiver of arrows, accompanied by two hunting dogs. Many people commented on it. Few understood it.

"That looks like Artemis, the Greek goddess of the hunt, and protector of life."

She glanced up in surprise. "Yes, it's Artemis. She was also the protector of animals."

"Good archetype for a veterinary doctor."

"How do you know about Artemis?"

"I've studied some Greek mythology. She's one of my favorites."

"Where did you study—what college?"

"I self-studied in the Marines, reading books on my phone when I was in a hospital bed recovering from injuries. Nowadays when I can't sleep at night, I study law and Stoic philosophy."

Sarah was surprised, and she wondered why he couldn't sleep at night. After a few more stitches she finished treating Cody's wound. She tied off the suture and removed the IV needle, then stepped back and nodded her head, satisfied with her work.

Jake was impressed. "You did that incredibly fast, and the work is perfect."

The third of the stitches that Jake had worked on for so long were messy, and the two-thirds Sarah had completed in minutes were obviously done by a professional.

Sarah shrugged modestly. "Plenty of practice. By the way, where did you get your knowledge of medical procedures? Please tell me it wasn't on the internet."

"Part of my Marine training as an IED dog handler was in canine first aid."

"You were doing okay here. Cody would have been fine, but don't quit your day job."

"I owe you for your help. Did I leave enough money there?" Jake pointed at the pile of twenty-dollar bills he'd left for her.

"Don't worry about it," Sarah said. This time, she didn't turn her head or look in that direction.

Sarah gently applied some salve onto Cody's stitched-up wound and then taped clean bandages over it. "Once I get this taped up, you two should probably get out of here."

"Cody is pretty weak from the loss of blood. Could I pay you to keep him here in a kennel for a day or two? Until he heals up some?"

Cody growled at Jake and pawed the table.

"Cody, you've lost blood and you need to rest, not go running through alleys and parks," Jake said. "Your stitches could pull loose. I'll be back for you in the morning, I promise. Come on, be reasonable."

Sarah raised her eyebrows when Jake talked to the dog as if it was a human who could understand his words. Cody growled and whimpered and made a move to climb off the table. He was loyal down to the bone, and war dogs have never been known for being reasonable.

Sarah and Jake both reached out for Cody to make sure he didn't jump off the table and possibly rip open his fresh stitches. They were shoulder to shoulder, pressing against each other, and their hands were touching under the dog's belly as they both held Cody and lowered him to the floor.

Sarah thought that Jake let his hands linger against hers for a moment longer than necessary. His touch and body heat made her heart beat faster. He wasn't what she'd consider Hollywood handsome, but he was good looking in a rugged way, and had plenty of that powerful aphrodisiac known as self-confidence. She couldn't deny that Jake brought out a desire in her to be close to him.

This was what it could be like if she had a partner in life. Not that she was considering present company to be in the running for that. No way; this guy was nothing but trouble, although he was a six-foot-tall hunk of bad-boy trouble. But that was the last thing she needed in her life now, right?

~

Jake noticed that after they set Cody down safely, Sarah looked slightly flustered for some reason. But she took a deep breath and spoke in a businesslike tone. "I have a large walk-in kennel down the hall. When I rented this space, I noticed that it had a good-sized storage closet. We added a horizontally split door with a window in the top half and made it into a sleepover area for the large dogs. Let me show you."

"Okay, let me grab a clean shirt out of my pack," Jake said, "Once Cody is situated, I'm going to take a minute to get cleaned up in the bathroom." Jake reached into his backpack, took out a clean shirt and carried it with him as they all went out the door. Sarah took them down the hall to a kennel room with a thick dog bed on the floor, along with a bowl of water and a chew bone.

Cody walked slowly and carefully due to his wound. He sniffed around the den and then drank some of the water from the bowl.

Jake looked at Cody and felt a weight on his heart. "I don't suppose you have any dog food on hand, do you?"

"Yeah, I've got some right here." Sarah opened a cupboard and took out a plastic storage tub of dry kibble, along with a glass canning jar full of wet dog food.

Cody growled in hunger when he smelled the food.

"Say please, Cody," Jake said.

Cody made a growly sound in his throat and pressed his head against Sarah.

"Such good manners," Sarah said, and she placed the bowl of food on the floor by the water bowl.

Cody attacked the food and gobbled it quickly.

"Thank you. He was really hungry," Jake said.

"It goes against my better judgment, but I'm willing to keep Cody here for a few days while you get your problems straightened out. You have to sign a medical care consent and power of attorney form to give me legal authorization to be the caregiver for your pet and be in charge of him when you're not present."

Sarah took a paper out of a drawer. Jake scribbled his signature on the form. She folded the paper several times into a square and put it in her back pocket.

"After all the legal hell you've been through, I understand the paperwork formalities," Jake said. "And thank you. I can't tell you how much this means to me."

Sarah saw him look at Cody the way a parent looks at their child. "You really love that dog, don't you?"

"He's family to me. I'd do anything for him. I had a black Lab, but she died recently. So, when Cody was bleeding, I just ..." Jake went down on one knee and patted the dog bed. Cody stretched out on it and let out a tired sigh. Jake scratched Cody behind his ears and petted him, then kissed him on the top of his head.

Sarah got a warm feeling when she saw how much Jake loved his dog. "Why don't you hide out at your girlfriend's place? Weren't you on the news hugging someone who looked like Barbie?" After Sarah said that, she looked at Cody and avoided eye contact with Jake.

Jake noticed it and smiled. "I was engaged, but I broke up with my fiancée. I'm not dating anyone right now. The woman you saw me with on the news is just a friend. She was in trouble, and I was helping her out. She's looking for a wealthy trophy husband, and that's not me."

"Relationships are so superficial these days," Sarah said, almost as if she was talking to herself.

"What about your boyfriend? Isn't he worried about you right now?"

"I'm single, but I've been seeing a non-commitment kind of guy on and off. He's emotionally unavailable to me, and he spends every waking minute glued to his phone. The relationship is going nowhere."

The two of them looked at each other and Sarah saw a sexy animal magnetism in Jake's eyes that made her shiver in a good way.

Standing close to Sarah made Jake realize she wasn't just cute, she was beautiful in a wholesome, natural way. He'd failed to see it clearly before, simply because she didn't advertise it. She wasn't wearing a lot of makeup. Her hair was pulled into a simple ponytail. She didn't wear sky-high heels or tight clothes. And she only wore a few pieces of jewelry—gold earrings and a gold chain necklace with a green jade stone.

Jake had thought that Sarah was very cute and he'd felt attracted to her, but now he saw her as smoking hot and gorgeous. He felt a powerful urge to put his arms around her, pull her close, and kiss her. However, after the breaking and entering, pointing guns at each other and fighting with martial arts, it didn't exactly seem like the right moment to be romantic.

"Once this manhunt is over, you and I are going out to dinner at Amborgetti's Italian restaurant."

Sarah felt that Jake was a sexy, confident man who knew what he wanted and went after it. He seemed to look right into her heart, and he might be thinking about kissing her. She felt conflicted. Did she want him to kiss her or not? He was a total bad boy and currently in a lot of trouble. Spending time with him would be a walk on the wild side. But he did seem to have a genuinely good heart inside that muscled chest of his. Sarah's own heart was beating fast, and she felt warm all over. If she simply leaned in a little, tilted her head, and half-closed her eyes, Jake would probably …

The sound of vehicles screeching to a halt outside of Sarah's clinic broke the moment. Car doors slammed, and bright lights shone into the building's front windows. A commanding voice crackled over a vehicle loudspeaker. "This is the FBI. You are surrounded by armed agents. Come out with your hands over your heads or we will come in shooting."

CHAPTER 89

Jake saw Cody respond to the shouted threats. His dog began barking and tried to stand up. Loyal, faithful and protective.

Jake commanded Cody to be still and then he looked at Sarah as if he was going to command her too, but he paused a moment before speaking. "I'm sorry, Sarah, I stayed here too long."

"What are you going to do?"

"I'll wait in this room with Cody. You shut the door and lock it. Tell the FBI you captured me using your pistol. You held me at gunpoint, ordered me to go in here and then locked me inside."

"But what about ...?"

Jake took one of her hands in both of his and said, "Please just do it. Trust me, Sarah. There is no way Cody and I could escape from the FBI. They are hella good at capturing fugitives, and we could all get shot by accident."

Sarah didn't pull her hand away. "Okay, okay, but this is crazy. I need to take a deep breath."

"Focus. Use your martial arts training."

"My training didn't prepare me for armed federal agents storming my clinic!" Sarah said.

Jake continued holding Sarah's hand in one of his and leaned in, put his other hand on her waist, pulled her close, and kissed her on the lips. Sarah didn't seem as surprised by the kiss as Jake had thought she might be. She kissed him back and afterward neither of them wanted to let go. But Jake knew that the FBI's clock was ticking, so he held Sarah at arm's length and gave her a pep talk.

"You can do this. It's your clinic and you are in charge of it. Go out there and tell them what you want them to believe. Sell it to them."

There were more shouted demands from outside. Sarah nodded at Jake. "I can do it. I've got this."

She went out of the room, closed the door and turned the dog-proof deadbolt. Some well-trained dogs like Cody could open doors, but not this one.

Sarah marched toward the front door of the clinic, but before she could reach it, an FBI agent used a battering ram against the door. There was a loud crash and the door flew open. A group of FBI agents came running into the clinic. Several were wearing black body armor riot gear. They pointed automatic weapons with red laser sights at Sarah. She stood very still with her hands over her head.

An agent shone a spotlight on her face, blinding her. "Hands on top of your head, lace your fingers together!"

Her heart thumped in fear but she pretended to be calm. "My hands are already over my head. The person you want is locked in the room to my right. That closed door with a light in the window."

A female agent walked directly toward Sarah. She was wearing a pantsuit with an FBI windbreaker over it. The agent took Sarah by the arm, handcuffed her hands behind her back and then held her credentials up so Sarah could see them. "FBI Special Agent Reynolds. Who are you? Identify yourself."

"I'm Dr. Sarah Chance, I run this veterinary clinic. My picture is on the wall right there and my ID is in my purse. You broke down my door, but you don't know who I am? Do you even know what the hell you're doing?"

Agent Reynolds roughly frisked Sarah and found the small pistol in the back of her pants waistband. "Gun!"

Another agent cursed. He began turning on lights and checking the treatment rooms. He found Jake's pistol and his leather jacket, and he too called out, "Gun!"

FBI agents swarmed all through the clinic. Sarah said, "I was on my way to open the door for you. Why did you have to break it down?"

"That was standard operating procedure when you failed to open the door fast enough," Reynolds said.

"You didn't give me any time to open it."

"Shut up. Where is Jake Wolfe?"

"Make up your mind, do you want me to shut up or answer your question? I told you once already. Jake Wolfe is in that room right there."

Sarah inclined her head toward the kennel room door. Reynolds grabbed Sarah's arm in a vicelike grip and marched her over there. She looked at the door as if it was a snake coiled to bite her, and then moved her head over the window for a split second and quickly stepped back.

Sarah said, "He's unarmed; your other agent found his pistol."

"Keep your mouth shut unless I ask you a direct question," Reynolds said. Then she called out, "The suspect is in this room. His shirt has bloodstains on the front of it. He should be considered armed and dangerous."

Sarah glared at Reynolds. She didn't speak, but her eyes blazed in anger.

Reynolds saw the look, pointed at Sarah and said, "Somebody cuff her feet."

An agent put plasticuffs on Sarah's ankles, then a man who appeared to be in charge strutted in through the front door. He was wearing a suit with a blue FBI windbreaker over it that matched the one Reynolds had on.

He spoke to Reynolds. "Nice work, Special Agent Reynolds, you did good."

"Really?" Sarah said, biting down on her fear, but releasing her anger. "I'm the one who captured the fugitive and locked him in that room. All you did was break down my door and act all tough."

"And who might you be?" the man asked, appearing amused at this pint-sized female who presumed to question his official authority.

"I'm Dr. Sarah Chance, and this is my clinic. Who are you, why are you trespassing, and how soon can you repair my front door that you vandalized?"

"Brad Oxley, FBI Special Agent in Charge. You didn't call the police, so my guess is you're guilty of the crime of aiding and abetting the flight of a wanted fugitive."

Sarah shook her head. "No, your guess is wrong, *Brad.* And I'd like to see some ID. Otherwise you're trespassing, breaking and entering, and committing assault and battery while wearing a spiffy FBI jacket that you might have bought on eBay."

Oxley scowled and sucked in a big breath. "Now you listen to me."

"No, you listen," Sarah said. "Here's what happened. I worked late and then closed up shop. When I got into my car and drove past here on my way home, I saw a light on inside. I got my pistol out of my purse, which I have a legal permit to carry, and I went in through the back door. Once inside, I found that man performing first aid on a dog."

When Sarah said "that man," she looked over at the kennel door with the window in the top half. She saw that Jake was standing close to the door and listening to her story, probably memorizing it. He was smiling cheerfully like an innocent man who didn't give a damn about this situation. Several red laser dots from weapons were targeting Jake's chest through the glass window.

"That's it, that's your cute little story?" Oxley said.

"I yelled for him to put his hands up, and lie facedown on the floor," Sarah said. "When he did, I closed the door and turned the deadbolt."

"That's a nice, tidy explanation," Oxley said. "Do you want to enlighten us as to why you didn't call the police?"

A woman standing off to the side said, "She did call the police, she called me."

Both FBI agents turned and looked at a plainclothes police detective, who had short red hair and a badge on a lanyard around her neck. She was wearing a windbreaker that said POLICE, along with a baseball cap that said SFPD.

"Identify yourself," Oxley said. "What are you doing here? This is an FBI bust."

"As I told your team on my way in, I'm Sergeant Beth Cushman. SFPD Homicide Detail. Dr. Sarah Chance is a friend of mine. She takes care of my cat. Approximately fifteen minutes ago, Sarah called my mobile phone, and I called her back. Sarah said she had detained an intruder at her clinic, and she asked me to please come over right away. Here I am, but I didn't expect to see the FBI here too. Do you guys respond to break-ins at pet clinics now, or was it just a slow day at the Bureau?"

Oxley's neck turned red in anger. "That man is a major fugitive, wanted by the FBI."

"Really? Who do you have in there? Somebody who tried to steal a toenail trimmer for a terrier?"

"It's Jake Wolfe, you idiot. You're telling me you didn't know that?"

"Don't call me an idiot," Beth said. "That shows a lack of professional decorum. It's going into my report. And, no, I didn't know who you had there. Sarah only said a man broke in, and she had him locked in a dog kennel. I had a good laugh about that, then I drove over here to help her with the situation."

Sarah was surprised to see her friend, but she realized Beth must have guessed that Jake was here. Now Beth had overheard Sarah's story and she was lying to the FBI about the details, just as Sarah had lied. It was a crime to lie to a federal agent. She felt very grateful for Beth's friendship and loyalty.

"Your phone records had better back up your story, Cushman," Oxley said, and he gave her a contemptuous look, up and down, that made Beth grind her teeth.

"Obviously, both of our phone records will show her call to me and my call back, within the last quarter hour or so," Beth said. "That means, if I'm not mistaken, that this is my bust, and you should back off and give me jurisdiction."

Oxley shook his head. "Nice try, but no chance, Cushman. We've been working on this case nonstop, with people watching every dog park and veterinary clinic in the city."

"But Sarah called it in," Beth said.

"Wrong again," Oxley said. "One of our citizen snitches caught a glimpse of a man with a dog who might fit the description of the suspect, and who appeared to go to this clinic. That snitch is getting the reward, and there is nothing you can do about it."

Sarah spoke up and said, "It doesn't matter if some snitch called in a possible sighting. You've probably had hundreds of those calls. I was the one who captured the man, locked him in that room and called a police officer. All of this happened long before you arrived at the scene. I had no idea he was wanted by the FBI, but if anyone gets a reward, it's going to be me."

When Sarah mentioned the man in the room, she looked over toward the door again, and so did Agent Oxley and Beth Cushman. They all saw Jake calmly taking off his bloodstained shirt and getting ready to put on a clean one. As Jake stood there shirtless for a moment, Sarah noticed that he had a variety of scars on his broad chest and flat stomach. He'd obviously been through some battles.

Oxley turned to Sarah. "I think it would be best if you told your story under oath. You're going to the federal building."

"No, thanks, Brad, I have other plans for this evening."

Oxley snorted at her, turned to his crew and said, "Take both suspects down to HQ. Put Chance in the backseat of a Bureau car and put Wolfe in the Paddy wagon."

Sarah asked, "What could you possibly be charging me with?"

"Suspicion of aiding and abetting the flight of a wanted fugitive, obstruction of justice, and interfering with a federal investigation," Oxley said.

Two FBI agents picked Sarah up, one by each arm, and carried her away as if she weighed nothing.

CHAPTER 90

When Beth saw the agents grab Sarah, she said, "You're arresting the person who captured the fugitive for you? I guess you really don't want to pay that reward."

As Sarah was being carried toward the door, she turned her head and looked back at Jake. She saw him watching her through the kennel window, with a crooked smile on his face. His expression seemed to say that he was impressed by her spunk but was feeling apologetic about the inconvenience he'd caused.

Jake put one finger to the front of his lips to indicate that Sarah should be quiet and not say anything. Sarah nodded to Jake and then she was carried out the door.

~

The two FBI agents marched Sarah outside to an unmarked four-door sedan and put her in the backseat.

Sarah knew that if they took the cuffs off her hands and feet, she could use her martial arts skills to kick their asses. All she had to do was remember to keep her left elbow up, and nobody could stop her. Well, maybe nobody except for Jake Wolfe.

She was known for her hot temper, but she made a conscious effort to go along peaceably with what she considered a needless act of intimidation by Oxley. If she'd been more submissive, they might not have arrested her. But being submissive wasn't part of her personality, and she couldn't fake it.

~

Inside the clinic, Beth spoke to Oxley. "Can you give me one of your business cards? I need to fill out a report. Here's my card in case you have any questions for me about Sarah Chance."

They exchanged business cards, and Beth looked at Oxley's card and tapped her phone. "I don't suppose you'd believe me if I told you that a Secret Service agent is convinced Jake Wolfe is innocent, and a criminal impersonated him with a high-tech facial disguise."

Oxley shook his head. "No, that's the dumbest conspiracy theory I've heard in a long time."

"I called the San Francisco office of the Secret Service and spoke with an agent named Easton. He sent me a copy of a memo from Washington D.C. I just now forwarded it to your email."

Oxley's phone vibrated. He checked the display and saw Beth's email, but didn't read it. "Does this also explain who shot JFK, and that UFOs are real? Your absurd theory is duly noted. Now get out of the way, Cushman, unless you want to face charges of interfering with a federal investigation—the same as that smart-mouthed veterinarian."

Beth slowly stepped aside, but her eyes never left Oxley's. She wasn't the least bit intimidated by anyone, and she wanted this guy to be aware of that.

Off to Beth's left, Reynolds and another agent approached the kennel door and pointed their weapons at Jake.

Reynolds said, "Lie facedown on the floor with your feet toward us and your hands behind your head. If you move, you're dead."

Jake rolled his eyes. "Oh, great, I just put on a clean shirt." He complied with the request, and the agents could hear him giving commands to his dog. Reynolds put on nitrile gloves and opened the door partway. The other agent kept his pistol trained on the fugitive while Reynolds used a stun baton to give a brief shock to the dog. Cody howled and was stunned senseless for a moment.

Jake cursed at the agents when they shocked his injured dog. He started to climb to his feet, but Reynolds used the stun baton to shock him on the backs of his calves. Jake shook like a leaf in a storm and crumpled to the floor, temporarily immobilized.

The shock from the baton was less debilitating and less long-lasting than from a Taser. She had to move fast. She set down the stun baton and grabbed Jake's feet, slapped metal cuffs on his ankles and dragged his body out of the kennel room. "Cuff his hands."

An agent quickly handcuffed Jake's wrists behind his back, then stood with his pistol aimed at him. Reynolds used her gloved hand to grab Jake's bloody shirt out of the sink and drop it in a plastic evidence bag. With that done, she slammed the door shut before the dog could recover and attack her. Next, she frisked Jake and found a long KA-BAR knife at his lower back, held sideways by a belt sheath. There was also a small SIG P238 pocket pistol in an ankle holster. "Another pistol and a knife."

"Only cops and criminals wear ankle holsters," Oxley said. "Swab him for DNA and take him away."

Reynolds tore open a packet and used a cotton swab to take a DNA sample from the inside of Jake's mouth. She put the swab into a clean evidence container. Two other agents picked Jake up, each one holding him by a bicep and under his armpit, and dragged him toward the front door.

Beth watched this, glad they'd closed the kennel door. If Cody woke up and saw these people manhandling Jake, he'd tear one of the agents a new orifice. Beth had a feeling she should do something with the dog, to keep him safe from harm.

"Okay, Oxley, you win," Beth said. "The FBI gets the bust, and I get stuck with the sleeping dog."

Oxley laughed. "You can babysit Scooby-Doo there while we take public enemy number one downtown and interrogate him."

Beth shrugged and held up the palms of her hands in a false signal of defeat. "That's okay, you guys are at the top of the food chain. Just don't be surprised when that Secret Service agent calls your boss, and then your boss asks you to explain why you ignored the information. My conscience is clear; I tried to help you."

"Sure, Cushman, if you think you somehow know more about this situation than the FBI does, it's only in your dreams."

"Maybe or maybe not. I'm an investigator, and my investigation found that Congressman Anderson was under Secret Service protection at Moscone Center. Their agents were right there on the scene, so they obviously know more about this than you or I or anyone else could. Think about that on your drive back to FBI HQ."

"You're full of it," Oxley said, but a glimmer of doubt began to show in his eyes.

"Suit yourself, Oxley. Feel free to believe whatever you want. You go ahead and embarrass yourself by arresting those two innocent people. Meanwhile, I'll worry about the injured dog. I'll just leave him in the kennel for now. It's as good a containment area as any."

"Maybe your imaginary Secret Service agent friend can help you clean up after the dog takes a dump."

"If he does, I'll mail it to you for evidence, okay?"

Oxley dismissed Beth with a shake of his head. He walked away mumbling something about her pushy attitude.

Beth looked at her phone as she stood in front of the door, blocking Cody from view. She deleted the voicemail from Sarah. That voicemail was the only evidence that she'd lied to a federal official, unless Sarah broke down under FBI questioning. The FBI was notoriously efficient at getting people to talk.

Outside of the clinic, television news reporter Dick Arnold stood across the street taking video of the FBI agents as they dragged Jake Wolfe to their vehicle. Arnold zoomed in on Jake so the TV viewers could see him clearly. Jake was unconscious; he had blood on his face, and his hands and feet were locked in cuffs. Arnold grinned as he sent the video to his news station and it went live on the website and on television.

The rest of the FBI agents finished clearing the other rooms, bagging up Jake's two pistols and his knife and leather jacket, along with Sarah's pistol and her purse. Oxley gave an order and the group of agents got into their vehicles and left the scene just as fast as they'd arrived.

The broken front door of the clinic swung back and forth in the breeze as the vehicles drove away.

CHAPTER 91

Terrell Hayes had been standing off to the side of the clinic front door. He'd quietly observed the FBI agents while maintaining his distance and looking at his phone. He was wearing the same police jacket and hat that Beth Cushman had on. His ID hung on a lanyard around his neck. Now that the feds had left, Terrell walked over to his partner. "I headed right over here when you called me, but when I arrived there were FBI agents everywhere."

"Thanks for standing by. Oxley was angry about a cop being here. Two would've made him twice as mad."

"You looked like you had things well in hand. I'm known to be friends with Jake, so I just kept my mouth shut and avoided drawing attention to myself."

"I like that whole 'you keeping your mouth' shut thing. That works for me."

Terrell smiled at his sassy partner. They both looked through the window and saw Cody lying on the dog bed. He'd awakened from the shock of the stun baton, but was temporarily too weak to stand up. He watched them with his bright eyes.

"Is it just me, or is that the smartest-looking dog you've ever seen?" Terrell asked.

"He looks scary smart. Don't you, boy, huh?"

Cody barked once and nodded.

Terrell and Beth exchanged a look.

"What do we do with him?" Beth asked. "This isn't a bad place for him. Sarah's assistant will take care of him when she arrives in the morning. I had my cat boarded here for a weekend when she was sick."

"We should get the front door repaired, or somebody will steal everything in here that isn't nailed down." Terrell said. "They'll probably set up a meth lab and blow the place up by sunrise."

Beth took out her phone. "I'll call a married couple that runs a twenty-four-hour locksmith service."

"Sounds good. I think Jake would want me to take Cody to my house," Terrell said. "My dog Boo-Boo will be happy to have a visitor."

Beth tapped on her phone display. "I just sent you an email. On my drive over here, I spoke with a Secret Service agent named Easton who believes Jake was impersonated. He sent me a memo and I forwarded it to Agent Oxley."

"Maybe I'll go down to the FBI office and see if I can help straighten this out. What's the shortest route to get there from here, anyway?"

Beth shrugged. "Why are you asking me? Do you think my uterus has a built-in GPS?"

"It doesn't? Can you get a refund?"

Beth exhaled loudly in exasperation, but she was smiling at the joke and the look on her face indicated she was thinking of a way to even the score with Terrell. She walked over to the front door and made the call to the locksmiths, then took pictures of the door and the lock, and sent the pics to their phones.

Terrell was standing by the kennel door when he heard a sound coming from inside the room. He looked through the window until he located the source. There was a cheap throwaway phone on the counter. He could just see part of it peeking out from the other side of a plastic storage container full of what looked like dry dog food. He could barely hear a tinny sounding voice coming out of the phone. He cautiously opened the kennel door and stepped inside.

"Good dog, Cody. You remember me from when I used to visit Stuart's house. So, we're cool, right?"

Cody was still woozy, but he sniffed Terrell's familiar scent and looked up at him as if to say, "What are you talking about, fool?"

Terrell stepped inside the kennel and closed the door. He picked up the phone and heard a cultured voice saying, "Hello, Jake, are you still there? What is happening, young man?"

Terrell spoke into the phone and said, "Hello, who is this?"

"This is Gregory Bart Bartholomew, attorney at law. I received a call from my client, Jake Wolfe. He told me the FBI was about to take him into custody along with a friend named Sarah Chance."

"That's correct. They're both in custody and on their way to FBI HQ right now."

"Oh dear, that means I'll have to put on shiny shoes, leave home, and drive over to the city at this inconvenient evening hour."

Terrell smiled. "I was called away from home and had to put on my shiny shoes on account of Jake too. I know exactly how you feel."

"Jake does have a bad habit of getting into these kinds of situations, doesn't he? With whom do I have the pleasure of speaking?"

"Lieutenant Terrell Hayes, SFPD. A friend of Jake's."

"What is your take on the situation, Lieutenant?"

Terrell caught Bart up on what had happened.

"That's remarkable," Bart said. "I'm not sure why they'd arrest the veterinarian, but those federal cowboys do get carried away sometimes. Okay, I'll be on my way to the FBI in just a few minutes. Hopefully, the two 'dog clinic desperadoes' won't say anything until I arrive."

"I'll give you my mobile phone number. Call me anytime if I can help with Jake's case. He's one of my best friends." Terrell recited his mobile phone number.

"Thanks again, Lieutenant. I hope we can have lunch one day soon. Goodbye for now."

Terrell ended the call and thought that Bart Bartholomew seemed like an okay guy. Not all lawyers were bad people. That was just as prejudiced a concept as saying all people of a particular race were bad. Most lawyer jokes were actually old racist jokes where the word "lawyer" had been substituted for a racial slur.

Beth returned to the kennel door and looked through the window. When she saw Terrell in the room, she smiled.

Terrell heard the door's deadbolt lock turn and click. Beth was grinning at him through the glass window. Then she turned and walked away.

He scowled. "Beth, open that lock. Not funny, partner. Cushman, do you hear me? Dammit, Scooter!"

Cody panted Ha-Ha-Ha.

CHAPTER 92

At the federal building, FBI agents removed the ankle cuffs from Jake and Sarah and marched them separately toward two different interrogation rooms. The two groups passed by each other and Jake said, "My attorney is coming. Don't say a word until he gets here."

Sarah nodded, and the agents escorting Jake told him to shut his mouth. They pushed him into interrogation room number one, while Sarah was escorted down the hallway to another room.

Jake found himself in a cold, bare room with CCTV cameras in all four of the upper corners. The agents made him sit at a heavy table that was bolted to the floor, cuffing his feet to a metal ring set into the floor and his hands to another ring on the table. Jake took a deep breath and mindfully refrained from any resistance, whether verbal or physical. Part of his martial arts training had been on how to keep your cool and to remain detached and above it all. The training worked most of the time, but not always.

This was definitely not one of the "friendly" interrogation rooms where they tried to get you to relax and talk while having a cup of coffee. Jake hoped that Sarah was in one of the nicer rooms and he felt sorry for getting her involved in this. He'd simply had no choice but to break into her clinic. Cody's life had depended on it.

~

FBI Agent Knight was walking down a hallway toward an elevator, on his way home after a long day of hard work.

He saw an elevator open up at the other end of the hallway and a group of agents stepped out and escorted Jake Wolfe toward an interrogation room. Knight checked his phone and saw an update about Wolfe being apprehended by Oxley. He let out a tired sigh and sent a text message to his wife to let her know he'd be working late again. As he headed to the interrogation room, a sense of weariness came over him.

Knight felt that Jake would probably talk to him more readily than anyone else at the Bureau and there was no doubt he owed Jake a favor or two—or half a dozen. Meanwhile, his wife and kids were enjoying a nice dinner without him again. He ached to go home and hug his family and enjoy a home-cooked meal with them.

When Knight arrived at the interrogation room, he asked the agent outside the door to let him speak with one of the lead agents. Reynolds came out into the hallway and listened as Knight explained his reasoning to her.

Reynolds agreed that Knight could be in on the questioning as long as he understood that she and Oxley would be in charge. Knight would only assist. They could use the good guy/bad guy technique on Wolfe.

Knight wanted to say that the Jake Wolfe he knew was far too smart to fall for that old trick, but he just agreed and went along with Reynolds. She was ambitious and dedicated and had a habit of doing everything by the book. She'd probably been a straight-A student in school, her sock drawer was perfectly organized, she'd never had a traffic ticket in her entire life, and she wouldn't dare to fart without filling out a government form in triplicate.

The two agents went into the interrogation room and Knight raised his eyebrows at Jake. His friend nodded back in understanding and gave him a tired smile.

~

Reynolds whispered to Oxley about Knight joining them and he agreed to it. Oxley then dropped a thick file down on the table with a thud and stared at Jake like a predator looking at its prey. Jake smiled calmly at Oxley.

Knight sat down at the table toward the end as an observer. He kept a neutral expression on his face and placed a small notepad and a pen on the table in front of him.

Oxley began the questioning. "Anything you'd like to get off your chest, Wolfe?"

"Where is my dog?"

"I'll ask around. In the meantime, do you want to make a confession and save us all some time?"

"Go find out the current status and location of my dog. After that I might have something to say."

"You have it backwards. First you're going to confess and then we might tell you about your dog."

"Don't even think about using my dog as a bargaining chip."

"Admit that you shot Katherine Anderson and I'll try to help your precious pet. Otherwise I might have him sent to the animal shelter."

Jake's eyes darkened and he stared at Oxley. "I'd like to exercise my right to consult with an attorney and to have that attorney present during questioning. These rights are guaranteed by the Supreme Court's Miranda decision. I do not waive these rights or my Fifth Amendment Constitutional rights. At this time, I'd also like my phone call that is guaranteed by law."

"You must be guilty if you want to lawyer up so fast."

"The reason I want my attorney is so he can protect my dog from your threats."

"Do you have any idea how much trouble you're in with the FBI?"

"Sure, every time I watch a movie I see your warning at the beginning that says the FBI will put me in prison for five years if I make a copy."

"Are you an activist? Have you ever participated in any protests or movements?"

"I've actively participated in my daily bowel movements. Do those count?"

"You don't seem to be taking this seriously. We have you on video committing a crime and there are dozens of witnesses."

"I understand that it looks bad, but I was impersonated by a man wearing a disguise. Talk to Agent McKay at the US Secret Service if you don't believe me."

A strange look crossed Oxley's face as he once again heard about these supposed Secret Service agents.

Knight said, "Jake, we just have a few things we'd like to understand. Your answers can help with that. Why not help us so we can help you?"

"Thank you, Agent Knight. As you know, I have the utmost admiration for the good people of the FBI who serve with distinction and keep America safe, often at the risk of their own lives. But with all due respect to you fine folks, you have the wrong man here. Meanwhile you're letting the real criminal get away. He's laughing at you and me right now. Making fools of us while plotting his next crime."

Oxley opened a file folder and slid an eight-by-ten photo across the table in front of Jake. He tapped his finger on the photo. "That's you standing by the TV camera weapon at the scene. Do you deny it?"

"Yes, I deny it. I wasn't there. That's an impostor wearing a facial mask."

Reynolds said, "I know what I see in the photo evidence. I see you committing a crime."

"No offense, but you're both wrong. I know you think that's impossible, but nobody is infallible. Your investigation will soon find that my fingerprints are not on the camera weapon. My DNA is not anywhere at the scene. A US Secret Service agent will testify that it could not be me and was not me. I can also get a copy of a CCTV video from the Marina Green, along with some witnesses that will prove I was miles away from the Moscone Center when the crime occurred."

"You want to see yourself on video? Fine, here you go," Oxley said, and he picked up a remote control and turned on a TV monitor on the wall.

Jake saw a video of a man that looked almost exactly like him. That disguise might fool his own mother. Anger burned in his chest as he watched the impersonator standing behind a television news camera on a stand, with a weird grin on his face. The man left the room, and then the video went into slow motion as the TV news camera shot a projectile toward the stage. The camera angle changed, and Jake saw a streak moving in slow motion from the camera toward Katherine Anderson. A red bloom appeared on her stomach and she screamed and fell down. Her husband yelled her name, knelt down next to her, and called for a doctor.

The sight of a pregnant woman being shot caused Jake's heart rate to shoot up and his fighting instincts to kick into gear. He cursed and tried to get to his feet, but the cuffs held his hands immobile. He stood there bent at the waist.

Reynolds raised her fist, ready to punch Jake. "Did that get you all excited, you pervert?" She stared at Jake's crotch to see if he was becoming aroused.

Jake saw her do it, and he let out a sigh, shook his head and sat back down. "It made me angry that someone would shoot at a pregnant woman, and that he impersonated me while doing it."

Reynolds shook her head. "It's no use trying to lie your way out of this. You're guilty, and we're going to send you to prison."

Jake looked at the TV screen again. "What is the current status of Katherine and her baby?"

"Nice try, pretending you care," Oxley said. He showed Jake a tablet computer in a plastic bag. "Evidence found in your Jeep indicates you've been stalking former prosecutor Katherine Anderson because she put an innocent man in prison and you think she should pay for her mistake."

Jake shook his head. "That's just some planted evidence to lead you on a wild goose chase. It seems to be working well, too. You're taking the easiest, most obvious route. The path of least resistance."

Oxley worked the remote control. The TV monitor showed the news photos and video that Jake had taken at the golf course murder. "So, you just happened to be at the scene of the first attorney assassination crime, right at the moment Caxton was shot?"

"I was following Caxton while doing a news story for my employer. I have a dash-cam video to prove it."

The images on the TV changed to show a news photo of Jake with Kelli. Reynolds said, "There you are at the second attorney murder scene too. In the arms of a half-naked suspect. When we questioned your ex-fiancée, Gwen, she told us you and Miss Iverson had sex on the *Far Niente* boat a few hours after the murder. Did the killing of Max Vidallen get you aroused?"

"Reynolds, you seem to be sex-obsessed and to have a one-track mind," Jake said. "Let me guess, when you look at an inkblot test you don't see a butterfly. You see … butterfly sex?"

Reynolds pointed her finger at him. "Your ex-fiancée also had to file a restraining order against you for domestic violence. And you violated those laws by failing to turn in your pistols to the police for safekeeping."

"Gwen lied under oath and filed a false police report. If the police don't arrest her for those crimes, you're subjecting me to selective prosecution. That will help me beat this fabricated case. Thanks very much."

Oxley sneered at Jake. "There's no point in playing cute—your ass is going to prison."

Jake raised his eyebrows. "Are you saying I have a cute ass? Sorry, you're not my type."

Oxley's face turned red. He stood up with his hands balled into fists.

An agent knocked on the door and opened it, interrupting him. "The suspect's attorney is here."

CHAPTER 93

Oxley cursed under his breath about the arrival of the attorney. How could he get here so soon? Wolfe hadn't made a phone call yet.

Gregory "Bart" Bartholomew entered the room and smiled at everyone. "Good evening, ladies and gentlemen. It's always a pleasure to meet with agents of the FBI, whom I so admire."

Jake said, "Thanks for calling me a gentleman. Nobody else ever does that except at the gentlemen's club."

Reynolds said, "Shut your mouth, Wolfe."

"Could you put that in writing, Reynolds? A minute ago, you were trying to get me to talk. Now you want me to remain silent? I'm confused."

Bartholomew said, "Jake, did any of the agents inform you of your right to remain silent and to have your attorney present during questioning?"

"Yes, before the questioning began, Agent Reynolds read me my rights and asked me if I understood them."

"You look as if someone punched you in the nose. I hope it wasn't one of these fine people," Bart said.

"No, it was Sarah Chance. She captured me long before the FBI arrived. She should get the reward money, by the way. However, my face did get smacked again when the FBI agents Tasered me, and I fell facedown on the floor."

Reynolds said, "Wolfe was told to lie on the floor and put his hands behind his back. He obeyed at first, but then he shouted profanity and began to get back up on his feet. He acted in a threatening manner and had to be subdued."

"That's because you shocked my injured dog."

Bart said, "Jake, were you allowed to make a phone call?"

Jake shook his head. "No, I'm afraid not, counselor."

"Well, that mistake helps our case considerably."

Oxley snorted. "There was no mistake. We were getting around to it. The suspect was not denied his phone call."

Bart wrote something in a small notebook. "Jake, did you tell these agents that you wanted your attorney present during questioning?"

"Yes, but Oxley and Reynolds just kept asking me questions anyway. Oxley said I had a cute ass, or something like that."

Bart looked at the agents and raised his eyebrows. "Is that correct?"

Oxley glared at Jake. "He was informed that he had the right to remain silent, but he just kept shooting off his big mouth. Anything he said can and will be used against him in a court of law."

"Were these proceedings being recorded?"

Oxley shrugged. "That information is on a need-to-know basis."

"I'll assume audio and video were being recorded, and I'll get a subpoena for a copy of that recording. It probably won't be admissible in court anyway. Nobody allowed my client to call his attorney or have me present during this questioning."

"Wrong again," Oxley said with suppressed anger in his voice. "I already told you that we were getting around to it. He could have shut his big mouth at any time."

"My client won't be saying anything further, nothing whatsoever."

"No problem. Maybe he'll change his mind after spending the night in custody, and probably longer, much longer."

Bart wrote down another note. "I'll be having a word with the judge who sets the bail."

Jake said, "It's okay about the phone call. I don't have my phone with me, and it has all my numbers stored in it. The only phone number I can remember right now is the one from that carpet commercial jingle on television." He started singing the jingle, "Eighhhht-hunnn-dredddd..."

Bart shook his head at Jake, then said to Oxley, "Your weak case is further weakened by the tainted fruit of the poisoned tree."

"I have no idea why you are rambling on about fruit trees," Oxley said, obviously bluffing.

"Yes, that's obvious, and it just makes my job easier. I thought most FBI agents were former lawyers."

Jake said, "Lawyers with guns? What could be better?"

Reynolds spoke up. "We have plenty of former lawyers. You'll get to meet some of them soon, when they file formal charges against pretty boy for domestic terrorism."

Bart sighed. "Acts of *paintball* terrorism? Is that what you'll say in front of the TV cameras, Agent Reynolds?"

Reynolds held out her hand and counted on her fingers. "Assault on a prosecutor, carrying a concealed weapon, violation of a restraining order, breaking and entering, burglary, carrying an illegal knife, resisting arrest, lying to a federal agent—"

Bart interrupted Reynolds and said to Jake, "Other than being punched in the face, are you doing okay?"

Jake shrugged. "I'm kind of hungry."

Knight said, "Bart, as much as we appreciate your law debate, we have work to do. Are you finished here or did you have any further questions?"

"Yes, I wish to speak privately with my client now. Per attorney-client privilege."

Knight stood up. "You've got five minutes."

"Thank you, and as a polite reminder to everyone, if you record my conversation you will be violating the laws of attorney-client privacy and your case will be thrown out of court."

Knight motioned to Oxley and Reynolds by inclining his head toward the door. Oxley exhaled loudly, then got up and walked out. Reynolds glared at Jake and then followed Oxley. Knight nodded thoughtfully at Jake, left the room and closed the door behind him.

In the hallway, Knight said, "I'm going to make a quick phone call to my family. I'll be right back."

"Sure, go ahead," Oxley said in a dismissive tone. "Take your time. You weren't helping us anyway."

Knight walked down the hallway toward a break room that offered some privacy.

Oxley glared at Knight's back as he walked away. He turned to Reynolds and gestured toward the one-way mirror. "Keep an eye on those two. I'm going to use the restroom."

Reynolds sat at a desk in front of the one-way mirror glass, unseen by the two people in the room as she watched them talk. Her eyes followed the movements of their mouths as their lips formed the words. Unknown to everyone else, Reynolds was able to read lips. That talent had given her a secret advantage in life. She'd kept the secret to herself so that unsuspecting people wouldn't know about her ability and try to circumvent it.

Reynolds was pretty sure that lip reading would be considered a violation of the laws regarding attorney-client privilege and confidentiality. She told herself that right now she was using it to find the truth, although possibly doing so illegally. She was confident that she could follow the real truth, and not just look for selective info that confirmed her biased personal opinions.

The computer monitor on the desk in front of Reynolds showed a video feed from the four cameras in the interrogation room. The images were split into four squares on the screen. She zoomed in one camera on Jake's face and another on Bart's, to get a close-up look at their mouths as they spoke.

Inside the interrogation room, Jake said, "A woman named Sarah Chance was arrested at the same time I was. She's innocent, and there was no reason to charge her with anything. Can you please represent her and get her out of here?"

"Yes, I'm aware of that. I'll get Sarah out of here and on her way home ASAP," Bart said.

"I'm worried about my dog, Cody. I need Sarah to take care of him until I can get out of here."

"Understood. I'll fight for Cody just as I would any other member of your family."

Jake looked around at the many cameras and then at the big mirror on the wall. "You don't really believe they're going to let us speak privately here, do you?"

"The law says they're required to, but I never count on having privacy in any government building. However, if they overhear us, maybe they'll learn something. All I wanted to tell you was to be polite to the FBI, even if they are not polite to you."

"I thought I was very polite and cheerful and understanding about my false arrest."

"But you were also sarcastic. The last thing you want is to get an FBI agent gunning for you with a personal grudge because you made a joke."

"I guess I can see how that might not be a good thing."

"You can't even imagine. You have no idea. Anybody in law enforcement with a personal grudge can make your life a living hell. Hardly anyone can stop them. Trust me—there are plenty of ex-lovers who could testify about this."

Jake looked at the mirror, as if speaking to whoever was secretly watching. "Ever since I was a kid I've always admired the FBI agents. They were the very best, the untouchables, the G-men. The current director of the FBI is the best of the best, an excellent person to run that powerful organization."

Bart nodded. "I agree. The current director is a real genius, and the majority of the agents live up to their reputation of being the very best. That's another reason to be polite. FBI agents work very hard and serve honorably with pride and dedication. They see horrific crimes, and they risk life and limb for their fellow Americans. Yet they hardly ever get any thanks from anyone."

"That's true. My friend Agent Knight is one of the finest people I've ever known. I sleep better at night because people like him are on the job."

"Oxley and Reynolds are good agents like Knight, they just don't know you as well as Knight does. You want to be friends with them, not get on their bad side with sarcastic remarks."

"I'll try my best, but I've never been known to play well with uptight starched-shirt authority types who are on a power trip."

Bart looked at his phone. "My researcher also found that Reynolds served in Afghanistan. She did site exploitation work after Navy SEALs raided and secured terrorist camps. She was part of an FBI team that went to battle zones and sifted through evidence. She might even have found clues that helped provide intel for Marine infantry platoons."

"Really? I had no idea. I admire Reynolds for putting herself in the danger zone like that."

"She's a highly capable agent, and she thinks you're a criminal who shot at a congressman's pregnant wife. You're innocent, but she doesn't know that yet. It's perfectly reasonable for her to want to put you in a cage. The bottom line is … always be polite to the FBI. Never challenge them or get them angry at you. Is that understood?"

"Yes, it's just my habit to joke around with everybody. I make a lot of stupid remarks that don't mean anything. But I promise I'll try to be more serious and less irreverent with Oxley and Reynolds from now on. They obviously can't take a joke, and they act like the religious police."

"Maybe you bring it out in them. You always challenge people in authority, and then you're surprised when they act in an overly authoritarian way toward you."

Bartholomew stood up and knocked on the door. When Reynolds opened it, he said, "All finished here. Thank you, Agent Reynolds. Where may I find Sarah Chance? She's my client too. I'd like to see her now."

Reynolds thought about what Jake had said. She didn't believe him. He was lying and hoping at least one agent in the FBI was dishonest enough to violate their oath to support the Constitution. It dawned on her that he'd been right … about her. She spoke in anger to an agent in the hallway. "Take this attorney to see Sarah Chance. She hasn't said a word anyway."

While the door was open for a moment, Jake overheard the conversation about Sarah. He smiled at this bit of good news. Sarah was a tough and resourceful woman. She hadn't started up her own business from scratch by being weak or easily pushed around.

Before Bartholomew closed the door, he looked back at Jake. "Hang in there. Patience is a virtue. Smile and be polite."

Jake nodded. "Okay, but I'm still kind of hungry."

CHAPTER 94

Jake sat patiently in the interrogation room, remaining seated with his hands cuffed to the table.

The door opened and Agent Knight returned along with Oxley and Reynolds.

Reynolds said, "So, you're hungry? Good, maybe if you get hungry enough you might remember something you wanted to tell us."

Jake nodded. "I do want to say one thing. I want to apologize to all of you for joking around. I'm sorry. It was nothing personal. The problem is, I don't know anything that could help you. If I did, I'd tell you. In the past, whenever I've had any helpful information, I've always called Agent Knight and passed it along to him. He can confirm this. It's also on record in your very own Bureau files, which can be subpoenaed in any court case I might be involved with."

Knight looked at Oxley and Reynolds. "That's true. Jake has provided useful tips to the Bureau. Some of his tips resulted in arrests that made the Bureau look good. I even got a call once from the director telling me to continue my work with Jake, and that he was considered a valued media source."

Oxley scowled at Knight. "The director called you? I don't think so."

Jake said, "Reynolds, it looks like you and I have something in common. I understand you served your country overseas in the

Middle East. The work of the FBI there was important, although hardly anyone knows about it. I'd just like to say thank you, ma'am, for your service."

Reynolds looked at Jake and didn't say anything, but there seemed to be a more thoughtful look in her eyes for a moment.

Knight's phone vibrated, and he answered it. "What? That doesn't make any sense. Fine, go ahead and show him in."

"Show him in? Who are you talking about?" Oxley said.

"Apparently, a special agent from the US Secret Service is here to see Jake Wolfe."

Jake smiled. "I sure hope he or she is bringing me something to eat."

"Why did they call you instead of me?" Oxley said. "I'm the agent in charge. This is my case."

"I don't know. The FBI operator said a Secret Service agent named Easton from their San Francisco Field Office was here, asking for me by name. I have no idea who he is. Maybe the Secret Service found my phone number in Wolfe's call records."

A few moments later, Special Agent Easton was escorted into the room. He was dressed in a tailored dark suit, a crisp white shirt with a gray tie, and black calfskin shoes. He had a commanding presence about him and was a man of few words who did not say hello or introduce himself.

Easton held up a strange looking phone and compared Knight's face to the photo on his phone, then presented his credentials to Knight. He glanced at Jake and looked around the room, quickly taking in the details with a trained professional's eyes.

Knight looked at the ID and slid the cred pack over to Reynolds. She studied it and handed it to Oxley who glanced at it in disbelief, then grunted and flicked the cred pack so it skidded across the table back to Knight.

"Agent Easton, please have a seat," Knight said, handing the ID back to him. "What can we do for our fine colleagues at the US Secret Service?"

Easton remained standing and placed his ID back into his pocket. "I'm here to take Jake Wolfe into Secret Service custody at this time."

Jake looked somewhat bemused at this turn of events, but he just returned Easton's appraising gaze and said, "Sure, why not? This kind of thing happens to me every day. Do you guys have any food at the Secret Service office?"

Oxley laughed. "No way, Easton. This is our case and our jurisdiction. Nice try, though. Now get out of here."

Easton did not react to the challenge except to reach into the inside left breast pocket of his suit coat and remove a business envelope. It had the US presidential seal on the upper left corner. He opened the envelope, unfolded a letter on White House letterhead and handed it to Knight. "By order of the president of the United States, I hereby request that you immediately relinquish Jacob T. Wolfe to the custody of the US Secret Service."

Knight held the letter gently like it might burn his fingers. It was definitely from the White House. It had the presidential seal, and was signed by the president. The letter said Jake Wolfe was not to be detained by any city, county, state, or federal law enforcement agencies. It was a top-secret matter of national security. All intel was on a need-to-know basis. Failure to obey the presidential emergency order could result in serious fines and imprisonment.

Knight silently handed the letter to Reynolds. She read it and gave it to Oxley.

"This letter is obviously a fake," Oxley said. "You guys from Washington can fabricate any kind of documents you want. I'm not buying this letter or your story."

"I'm from the San Francisco Field Office, not from Washington," Easton said. "But there are people in D.C. who are expecting your full cooperation."

Easton tapped on his phone display and sent a text message, then stared hard at Knight again as if waiting for him to do something.

Knight's phone buzzed with an incoming call. When he answered it his eyes opened wide in surprise. "Yessir, Director Walker, one moment, please." He turned on his phone's speaker, increased the volume and set the device down on the table.

When Oxley and Reynolds heard the name of the FBI director, they stared at the phone in surprise.

An authoritative voice on the phone's speaker said, "This is FBI

Director Thomas Walker in Washington. D.C. Can everyone hear me clearly?"

"Yes, sir," all three FBI agents said in unison.

"Oxley, I'm ordering you to release Jake Wolfe to the Secret Service, and you'll follow my orders immediately if you want to continue working for the Bureau. You will also drop any charges against the veterinarian, Sarah Chance, and release her from custody. Understood?"

"Yes, sir."

"Goodnight." Walker ended the call.

The three FBI agents sat there with surprised looks on their faces.

Easton held out his hand. "The keys to the handcuffs, please."

Oxley reluctantly handed over the keys to Easton, and he glared at Knight while he did it.

Easton unlocked Jake's hands and feet. "You're going to behave yourself, Wolfe." It wasn't a question.

Jake rubbed the indentations made on his wrists by the handcuffs. "When have I ever misbehaved? That's just a rumor."

CHAPTER 95

Jake rode the elevator down with Easton and Knight. They arrived at the ground floor and walked toward the front door. Jake knew that the Secret Service must want something important from him, so he decided to milk it for all it was worth. He turned to Easton. "Is this about me serving my country again, in ways that I can never talk about?"

Easton just nodded.

"Well, there are a few things I need help with first. Quid pro quo. Otherwise, you can tell McKay I'm not going to give her a damned thing."

"Such as?"

"First of all, where's my dog? Is Cody okay?"

"Lieutenant Terrell Hayes took Cody home with him."

Jake let out a sigh of relief. "How soon can you get Sarah Chance out of here?"

"She's already free. Your lawyer is driving her home."

"The door to Sarah's clinic was left broken open."

"Officers Hayes and Cushman had it repaired by a locksmith. You owe them some money."

"Two friends of mine own a taco truck. They helped me find the assassin. SFPD Sergeant Denton arrested them because she has a personal grudge against me. Can you bail them out and get the charges dropped?"

"I'll make some phone calls."

"A limousine driver was also arrested by Denton. It was my fault. I want him released, and the charges dropped."

"My intel is that he was bailed out by a big man named Mo. We can work on getting the charges dropped."

"Thanks. You want to be on the good side of Big Mo."

"I know everything there is to know about the Amborgetti family. Including your past employment at their restaurant, and your recent fugitive recovery work as a bounty hunter for their bail bonds agency."

"My Jeep was blown full of holes, and then impounded by the police. Any idea of the current status?"

Easton checked his phone as he walked along. "Your Jeep is out of impound. We have a mechanic working on it."

"The FBI agents took my leather jacket, two of my pistols, my KA-BAR knife and my phone."

"Those are at the front desk."

"Thanks for doing all of this, and for getting me out of here," Jake said. "Even though I'll probably regret this later, right?"

Easton nodded wisely.

"How do you Secret Service guys know every detail of what's going on everywhere?"

Easton didn't answer. The look on his face said he'd done enough talking for now—far more than usual.

When the trio reached the front desk, Easton retrieved a hard black plastic case and a black leather jacket. Easton handed the jacket to Jake, but not the case that held Jake's weapons.

Jake put on his jacket and shrugged. He knew there was no use arguing about it.

Easton and Jake walked to the front door of the building with Knight following close behind them.

Jake stopped at the front door. "Easton, in the interrogation room, you seemed to be aware that Agent Knight is a friend of mine."

"Correct."

"Then you must know that Knight is a hell of a good man. I was thinking that you two should keep in touch. Stay in the loop and compare notes. Maybe talk on the phone once in a while if an important case overlaps the two agencies."

Easton looked Knight in the eye for a moment, appeared to make some kind of decision and then handed him a business card. Knight seemed surprised by this turn of events, but he gave his card to Easton.

Jake shook Knight's hand. "Thank you, Agent Knight, you're a good friend. We'll have to go fishing sometime. Take the boat out on the ocean and have a few beers."

Knight nodded. Appearing as if he had a lot of questions, but few answers.

Jake walked out the door and climbed into a black Chevy Suburban with darkened windows.

Two blocks away from the federal building, Ivan Zhukov was sitting in a car watching the front doors through a pair of night vision binoculars. He smiled when he saw his prey coming out of the building. "Ah, Mr. Wolfe, my old friend. I'm looking forward to pissing on your grave."

CHAPTER 96

Easton got into the driver's seat of the Suburban while Jake climbed into the front passenger seat. The vehicle started moving, and Jake felt the business end of a pistol barrel pressed against the back of his head.

Jake sat very still as he heard a voice from his past say, "Alfa Delta Five. Echo Bravo Niner. Zulu Lima Two. Whiskey Tango Seven."

It was the voice of CIA case officer Chet Brinkter. The man who'd recruited Jake to volunteer for several black ops missions in unnamed war zones.

Jake responded with his own code. He made no move to turn and look behind him. He knew who was sitting there. Brinkter was the absolute most sneaky, deceptive, conniving, and dangerous covert spy he'd ever met. Jake respected the man's skills, but he felt that the two of them had unfinished business. There was bad blood between them, a grudge to be settled, with their fists if necessary. He was glad that Brinkter was here. Now he could punch him in the face.

"Hello, Brinkter, how's your sphincter?"

Brinkter lowered his pistol. "Don't worry, Wolfe, that bit of fun was just for old times' sake. I mean no harm to my former field operations officer."

"Did you mean no harm that time you abandoned me in the desert and left me there to die? Marines never leave anyone behind. I guess you missed that briefing."

"I'm not a Marine, and that was simply an unfortunate mix-up in communications."

"Why are you here? Where are we going?"

"I'm only here in an advisory capacity because you know me from the past. Easton has been ordered to bring you to a local safe house for a meeting."

"I already told Easton I'd go along peaceably. You can tell the woman next to you to take her finger off the trigger of that pistol."

Brinkter looked to his left and saw the Secret Service agent in the seat next to him remove her finger from the trigger and hold it straight alongside.

"I see you're still able to charm the ladies," Brinkter said.

Jake shrugged. "No charm involved. She's just acting like a professional. Maybe you should try it sometime."

The woman said, "You never looked at me. Your eyes were facing forward as you talked. How did you see the pistol?"

Jake continued facing the windshield. "When I opened and closed the car door, I saw your reflection for a moment on the inside of the door's window glass."

"The interior of the vehicle was dark. The overhead light was off."

"Even though your pistol is black, I saw it clearly while you held it in front of your white blouse."

"Not bad for a civilian. Or should I say, not bad for the *Trouble Shooter*."

Jake slowly turned and looked directly at her for the first time. "Who told you that name?"

"A little birdie told me."

"And what's your name?"

"Agent Greene."

"Nice to meet you, Greene. You and your little birdie must have high security clearances."

"Higher than yours."

"Are you sure about that?"

A look of doubt crossed Greene's face.

Jake turned and faced forward again.

CHAPTER 97

Ivan Zhukov sat in his car and watched the building through binoculars. He'd been hoping that Wolfe and his lawyer would leave together. It would've made it easy for him to follow the lawyer's car and put a bullet into Wolfe's brain. He might have to shoot Bartholomew too, but that would just be one more dead lawyer.

However, Bartholomew had left the building with Sarah Chance instead of Wolfe. She was the veterinarian he'd heard about as he listened to the SFPD frequency on his phone's police scanner app.

Soon after Bartholomew left, Wolfe appeared with a serious-looking man in a well-cut suit. They both got into a black SUV. Zhukov felt tempted to take a shot at Wolfe as he got into the vehicle, but there wasn't a clear line of fire. And he'd never be able to escape afterward. Not if he fired a weapon anywhere near the federal building.

The Suburban drove away, and Zhukov followed from a discreet distance. The man driving the vehicle ahead of him gave no indication that he knew he was being tailed. The SUV cruised along at the designated speed limit and didn't make very many turns. At one point, the Suburban stopped at a light, with a few cars separating it from Zhukov's. Just as a garbage truck began slowly entering the intersection, the SUV jumped the red light and shot forward, passing in front of the truck. Once the SUV was across the street, the garbage truck rolled forward and came to a stop, blocking the intersection. The driver got out and popped the hood, as if he had engine trouble.

Zhukov was stuck between two cars and he couldn't see past the large garbage truck. He had no idea where the SUV was going. He cursed and thought that he had to hand it to the guy driving the SUV. That man knew how to take precautions.

Zhukov got out of his car and ran up to the intersection. He got there just in time to see the SUV make a right turn at the end of the block. He ran back to his car and told the driver in the car behind him to back up. The man just shook his head behind his car window and went back to talking on his phone. Zhukov pointed his pistol at the man's face and said to back up or die. The man panicked and moved his car in a hurry. Zhukov got into his vehicle, backed up and then drove up onto the sidewalk. He bypassed the cars in front of him and turned right on the cross street.

As he headed in the direction the SUV had been going, he drove in a search pattern, but the vehicle was nowhere in sight. The driver of the SUV was a professional; Wolfe had escaped. Zhukov now had to consider other options. He should just let Jake go and move on, but his pride wouldn't allow it.

Perhaps he'd have a word with the veterinarian. She'd left the building with Wolfe's lawyer and might have some idea of where that SUV was going. Or maybe he could use her as bait to get Wolfe to come to him. It was time to call his computer hacker and find out where Sarah Chance lived. He would pay her a surprise nighttime visit. He hoped Sarah had some vodka in her liquor cabinet. Interrogating people was such thirsty work.

CHAPTER 98

Jake looked around in curiosity when Easton drove up to a home on a large property and parked inside the three-car garage. The automatic garage door closed and the passengers exited the vehicle. Easton led the way through a door that opened into the safe house.

Jake stopped and said to Greene, "Ladies first."

Greene motioned for him to go ahead and said, "Yes, by all means."

Jake smiled and stepped through the door. "Age before beauty."

Greene ignored his flattery.

As the group walked through the house, Jake studied the layout for potential escape routes. He noted that the large living room had been turned into a meeting area. There were several folding tables with chairs around them. One wall held three large flat-screen televisions. Jake figured that the bad news would be seen on those screens.

They sat down at one of the tables and a woman wearing a phone headset walked over and set down an urn of coffee and a platter with dinner rolls and pats of butter. Each table held supplies of generic government-issue coffee cups, silverware, napkins, creamer and sugar, ballpoint pens and lined notepads. The woman with the headset told Easton, "Three minutes. And remember, these are two-way televisions. They can see and hear you at any time."

Easton nodded and pointed a remote control at the center television display. It came on, and the screen showed a blue background.

Jake poured a cup of coffee. "Do you have any Bailey's Irish Cream in this disreputable establishment?"

Green shook her head. "No alcoholic beverages."

"I figured as much. That's why I knew this place was disreputable."

Brinkter tapped a pen on a notepad. "Wolfe, do you have any questions before the meeting?"

"Yes, who was the first man on Uranus?"

"Still the funny guy, aren't you?"

"You should appreciate my sense of humor, Brinkter. It's the only thing that keeps me from killing you."

Greene asked, "Jake, are the stories about you true—what you did overseas?"

Jake ignored the question.

"She's seen part of your file and knows some of your history," Brinkter said.

"I'd like to forget that part of my history. It was like … temporary insanity."

Greene nodded. "I understand. I was just curious about whether you really volunteered to get a deep tan, grow a beard, dress in the local clothing and walk barefoot for miles through the desert. Then go into a village marketplace, pull out a folding-stock AK-47 from under your robe and shoot a wanted terrorist at point-blank range and … just vanish into the surrounding area and hope you survived."

"I don't want to talk about it."

"He was fighting a secret war that the public never hears about," Brinkter said. "The targets were the worst of the worst terrorists."

"I read in your file that when you'd come face-to-face with the terrorist, you'd recite a biblical quote as you shot him," Greene said.

"Numbers 35:19," Brinkter said. "The avenger of blood shall put the murderer to death."

Jake let out a loud breath. "FYI, Greene, I didn't volunteer. I was serving in the Marines, got injured and almost died. I was medically evacuated to a hospital, and while I was healing up, Brinkter visited me and made me an offer I couldn't refuse."

"What kind of offer, money?"

A flash of anger rose up in Jake for a moment, but he kept his emotions under control. "No, it was more like a hostage negotiation.

My good friend Dylan was sent to prison simply for getting a ride home from a party. The car was pulled over by the police, they found some crack cocaine on the driver, and Dylan was in the wrong place at the wrong time. Brinkter proposed my 'volunteer' work in exchange for getting my innocent friend released. Plus, Brinkter told me some terrible facts he'd gathered about the target."

Brinkter said, "Your record says you volunteered. All brave and noble of you, so get used to the idea."

"What kind of facts?" Greene said.

"That man was responsible for a roadside bomb that killed one of my friends. He shot a girl for going to school, and he ordered the beheading of over two hundred young women who refused to be sex slaves for his terrorist group. The Joint Special Operations Command had found his location. But JSOC couldn't hit him with a drone strike because the coward always used a group of children as his bulletproof shield."

Brinkter said, "Command didn't want any civilian casualties, of course, so their hands were tied. However, a lesser-known agency planned two other ways to get this particular terrorist. They would either use a sniper from a very long range, or use a black ops assassin up close and personal."

"And Jake became one of the assassins?" Greene said.

"Yes, we 'borrowed' him from the Marines and I have to admit he was damned good at it. He was fearless, reckless, and full of surprises. He soon had a price on his head. Wanted dead or alive by the terrorists."

Jake didn't say anything. He just stared at Brinkter, thinking about the time the man had abandoned him behind enemy lines while bounty hunter terrorists were hot on his trail. If they'd caught him, he would've been tortured for days, and then beheaded in a video on YouTube.

~

In another part of the city, Ivan Zhukov received a call from Elena. "I have that information you wanted about Sarah Chance. She was released to Wolfe's attorney, and he gave her a ride home. She's there now."

Zhukov smiled. "I need her address."

"I'll send it to your phone," Elena said. She ended the call and sent a text.

Zhukov wondered what kind of sleepwear Sarah Chance wore to bed at night, or if she slept in the nude. He would soon find out.

CHAPTER 99

The woman with the headset walked past the table again. "Stand by. They'll be on-screen any moment now."

Brinkter said, "What would you like to hear first, Jake, the bad news or the worse news?"

"My guess is you want me to risk my life to do some impossible thing for you. And all I'll get for my trouble is a form letter of thanks, rubber-stamped and placed in my secret file."

"We want you to exterminate a Russian assassin. If you survive, we'll help you take care of this FBI fugitive situation."

Jake shook his head. "No, thanks. I'm done being your expendable weapon."

"If you refuse, I can have you arrested for breaking and entering at the veterinary clinic, carrying a concealed weapon, resisting arrest, and possession of stolen government property."

"Sarah won't press charges for breaking and entering. I have a permit for concealed carry. And what stolen property are you talking about?"

"The dog. You didn't complete the paperwork yet. That dog was the property of the United States government. Cody was assigned to Stuart. You don't have proper legal title to him yet. If you don't cooperate, we might have to repossess him."

"You stay the hell away from Cody or my lawyer will squeeze your nuts in a vise. But you'd probably enjoy that, huh, Brinkter?"

Brinkter glared at him. "You also violated the terms of a restraining order by failing to turn in your weapons to the police. You and Terrell Hayes could both be arrested on illegal weapons charges. You're in deep trouble, Wolfe. I've got you exactly where I want you."

Jake didn't reply, but the look of controlled anger on his face spoke volumes.

Brinkter used a dinner knife to spread butter on a bread roll, then gestured toward Jake with the knife as he talked. "My friends in law enforcement could also do an entrapment on your mother at the winery. Send in a girl who is underage but looks twenty-one. Have her buy wine with a fake ID. Then arrest your mother and use the asset forfeiture laws to take away her winery and vineyards, her home and business, bank account, and cars. How would that be, huh, tough guy?"

Jake leapt to his feet and lunged at Brinkter, flying over the tabletop and scattering the coffee cups and silverware. He knocked Brinkter off his chair and onto his back, grabbed a handful of his hair with his left hand and pressed a ballpoint pen against his face right below his eye. Brinkter froze, looking at the pen, feeling how its point touched his skin. He'd dropped the butter knife in surprise and was now empty-handed.

"Now I've got *you* exactly where I want you, Brinkter," Jake said.

"Drop that pen and get off me immediately," Brinkter said, fear in his voice.

"Threaten my dog and my mother again. Go ahead, I want you to. And then I'll shove this pen through your eye and into your brain, exactly the way your people taught me to do it."

Easton stood next to them and pressed the barrel of his pistol against Jake's temple. "Back off, Wolfe. And, Brinkter, you might want to stop antagonizing the human weapon you created."

Brinkter started to say something but thought better of it and kept his mouth shut.

Jake said, "Easton, if you fire your weapon, my death reflex will cause my arm to jerk and either kill Brinkter or turn him into a vegetable."

"Is it worth dying for?"

"I'm thinking it over," Jake said, and he looked into Brinkter's eyes without any mercy.

Brinkter appeared as if he might be making an effort to control his bladder.

Jake heard rapid footsteps behind him. He saw two red laser sight dots appear on the wall in front of him and then move down and vanish when they were trained on his back. He knew that his angry reaction had been a mistake. But he'd wanted to grab Brinkter by the throat for a long time, and something had finally snapped inside him.

"I've got this, hold your fire," Easton said.

The center TV screen flickered and then displayed the round seal of the President of the United States. That dissolved and the image of a woman appeared on the screen. She was sitting on a couch, wearing a charcoal-gray suit jacket over a white blouse. There was the slight telltale bulge of a pistol under her left arm where a shoulder holster would be located. She stared directly at the camera with a no-nonsense gaze and projected the image of a powerful, capable and dangerous person—someone who could give an order and you'd be dead or soon wish you were.

"Jake Wolfe, this is Agent Shannon McKay of the United States Secret Service. I'm pleased to see that you are alive and well and free of incarceration."

Jake recognized her voice from the recent phone calls. He glanced at the screen for a second and then returned his gaze to where he held the pen near Brinkter's eye. "Agent McKay, it's a pleasure to put a face to your voice. Thank you for calling me when I was impersonated, and thanks for being my alibi."

"I was observing all of you just now," McKay said. "Brinkter, I suggest that you apologize to Wolfe so we can move on and get down to business."

Brinkter spoke in a fake polite voice and acted as if this was all nonsense, but he couldn't hide the fear in his eyes. "Okay, sure. I'm sorry, Jake. I apologize to you and to your mother, and to your … dog. Do you feel better now?"

"No, but I'm glad we had this little talk." Jake removed the ballpoint pen from below Brinkter's eye and dropped it on the floor.

Easton withdrew the pistol from Jake's head but kept it trained on him. Jake stood up and slowly went around the end of the table and back to his chair. The two men on the response team kept their weapons trained on Jake. He just nodded at them in respect, turned his back on them and sat down.

Easton holstered his pistol. "You men can stand down."

The two men pointed their rifles at the floor but stayed where they were and kept their eyes on Jake.

"Wolfe, you might want to work on your people skills," Easton said.

"You made a joke, Easton, way to go," Jake said.

Brinkter got up off the floor and sat in his chair. "Wolfe, I could send you to prison right now for assaulting a federal official."

"No, I was simply acting in self-defense after you waved that knife at me in a threatening way."

"I was just buttering a roll with a dull piece of silverware. Who would believe that you felt threatened?"

Jake grabbed a dinner knife from the table next to his and threw it forcefully at the wall behind Brinkter. The knife flew in a silver blur, and its blade stuck deep into the sheetrock. "Any questions?"

McKay said, "Jake, you're in this meeting because the Secret Service is trying to apprehend the man who impersonated you at the Moscone Center. I'd appreciate your help, working with Easton and Greene on a manhunt."

Jake stared at her. "I'd gladly help your team hunt that man down. I have a grudge to settle with him. But why is Brinkter here?"

"He's here as someone you and I both know in common. I brought him into this meeting because I'd hoped he'd be a positive influence. Apparently, he was doing the opposite."

"I have several good friends in the CIA, but Brinkter isn't one of them," Jake said. "How can I help you with your mission, McKay?"

"Before I tell you any more, I have to inform you that this information bears the classification of Above Top Secret. The highest level of classified information under Executive Order 13526."

"Understood. Are my clearances still in effect?"

"Yes, you still hold an active Department of Defense collateral clearance and a blanket Top Secret/Sensitive Compartmented Information clearance. Please reaffirm your responsibilities now."

The woman with the headset placed a Bible on the table. Jake put his left hand on the Bible and raised his right hand. "I understand my responsibilities regarding these top secret clearances, and I hereby swear an oath to uphold them, so help me God."

McKay made a notation as Jake recited the memorized response. "Reaffirmation oath accepted and recorded. It is my duty to remind you that if you violate any top secret clearances, you could be charged with high treason and face life in prison or the death penalty."

"Noted and agreed."

"We're holding a late-night meeting that concerns you. There are people here who want to have a personal word with you."

The camera zoomed out and showed Congressman Daniel Anderson, seated next to McKay. He looked like he'd aged several years overnight, but his jaw had a determined set to it and his eyes still had fight in them. He reminded Jake of a boxer who'd taken a hard punch but had gotten back on his feet for another round.

"Congressman Anderson, I hope Katherine and the baby are doing well," Jake said.

"Yes, there are complications, but they're both getting the best of care. I've been informed that the person who shot a paintball at Katherine was wearing a mask to impersonate you, Jake."

"That's true. I was nowhere near the scene. The shooter called my phone to gloat about it."

"You must be almost as angry as I am right now."

"If that means you want to beat the man half to death with your fists, then, yes, we both have that in common."

"I'd prefer to be with my wife right now. But Katherine argued that it was my duty to fly back to Washington, because that seems to be what the shooter wanted to stop me from doing."

"Why? What was the shooter's motive?"

"The NSA picked up some phone chatter that indicates there are people who will make massive profits if they can keep me out of D.C. for a few days. We don't know how or why yet, only that there may be innocent lives at stake."

"The FBI can hunt down the people who are responsible and make sure they never do anything like this again."

"I'm in this meeting because my hope is that we can talk you into helping to do that, and do it with what you call *extreme prejudice*."

Jake's eyes narrowed. "You picked the wrong guy. I've had enough fighting. I've done my duty and now I just want to live my life in peace."

"A taxi driver overheard you saying you wanted to help with the manhunt to capture the impostor."

"I said I wanted to help investigate—not assassinate."

Agent McKay held Jake's gaze as if she'd been expecting this and knew he was weary of war. "Jake, there are two other people here in the Oval Office who want to have a word with you."

At the words *Oval Office*, Jake sat up straighter and watched in surprise as a second TV display came on and showed another area of the room.

The president of the United States appeared, sitting at his famous desk. And seated across from President Kaufman was four-star General Lloyd Clemens of the US Marine Corps, his uniform ablaze with ribbons, badges, and insignia.

CHAPTER 100

"General Clemens, sir," Jake said, getting to his feet and standing at attention.

"Have a seat, Jake," President Kaufman said.

Jake ignored President Kaufman, remained standing and looked at General Clemens for orders.

"As you were, Marine, be seated," Clemens said.

Jake sat down and folded his hands in front of him on the table. He noted that President Kaufman didn't appear offended when he looked to General Clemens instead of him. His guess was, the president had learned a lot about Marines, because they flew his Marine One helicopters and guarded Camp David. They worked closely with the Secret Service to help protect the president and his family.

"Jake, I have three questions for you," General Clemens said.

"Yes, sir."

"Do you believe it is true that *once a Marine, always a Marine*?"

"Yes, sir, I know that's true."

"If you were in this office, and a terrorist tried to harm the people here, would you fight like a patriotic American to protect them from harm?"

"Affirmative. You know I would, and I know you would too, sir."

General Clemens nodded in agreement and looked thoughtfully at Jake for a moment. "Right now, a known terrorist is threatening

Congressman Anderson and his wife, Katherine. The killer is right there in San Francisco where you are. We need a patriot who can put him out of business."

"Understood, General. What is your third question, sir?"

"Will you listen to what the president has to say and give it your full consideration as a civilian who agrees that *once a Marine, always a Marine*?"

"Yes, sir."

President Kaufman said, "Jake, we have a situation. One that requires a particular set of skills and someone who is willing and able to use those skills in the defense of his nation. I've been told that you're the right man for the job."

"With all due respect, Mister President, there are other people who are far more qualified than me to perform this mission."

"That's true, but you might change your mind when you hear the details. This is a highly covert op, and it concerns you personally. The assassin who shot the paintball at Katherine Anderson is a former FSB agent and Russian mafia hit man named Ivan Zhukov. The KGB may have changed their name to the FSB, but it's still the same old business as usual."

"Understood."

"Zhukov did wet work for the FSB, but he left the service due to severe injuries. After he recuperated, he went to work for the Russian mafia oligarchs for a time. Now he's gone out on his own as a freelance killer. He's been leaving a trail of dead bodies all across the world."

"Zhukov sounds like a dangerous snake."

"Exactly, and we need someone to cut off the head of that snake."

"The US Marshals hunt down and capture thousands of dangerous fugitives every year. They'd be your best choice to capture Zhukov."

General Clemens spoke up. "No one said we wanted Zhukov *captured*. If you accept this mission, your orders will be to kill the enemy the way you were trained to do on overseas missions."

Jake stared at Clemens for a moment. "How can that be legal here in the United States?"

Kaufman answered Jake. "I've issued an executive order for Ivan Zhukov to be killed as an enemy combatant, under the same legal precedent that guided our Navy SEALs on the raid that killed Osama bin Laden."

"There must be a specific reason why you want me for this mission."

"You are correct, there are two reasons. First, McKay feels you've made Zhukov angry at you by taking his photo and showing his face on TV. My hope is you can draw his attention and act as a lightning rod."

"Draw his fire, you mean. So basically, I'm acting as bait for a trap."

"More like a challenge to a fight that his ego cannot ignore. I'm hoping you can make him so angry that he drops what he's doing and comes at you instead."

Brinkter said, "Making people angry is Wolfe's specialty."

President Kaufman ignored Brinkter. "Second, the NSA picked up Zhukov's voice on a mobile phone threatening to kill Congressman Anderson. He also mentioned your name, Jake."

A grainy surveillance photo of Zhukov appeared on the third TV monitor. Underneath the photo was a written quote of something Zhukov had said. As Jake read the words, a recording played the familiar accented voice that had taunted him on his phone.

"If Congressman Anderson tries to get on a flight to Washington, I will kill him, no matter what. I guarantee that."

"What about the photojournalist Jake Wolfe who is causing problems?"

"Stalin said that death solves all problems; no man, no problem. If Jake Wolfe gets in my way again, I will start killing his family and friends, one by one, until nobody is left alive. I already know where his parents and his sister live. I know the school where his friend Alicia is a teacher. And I know where Sergeant Beth Cushman lives with her young son. There are many ways to get to Wolfe."

Jake felt like he'd been punched in the stomach. His gun hand twitched. He placed the fingertips of both hands together in front of him. His eyes narrowed, and his anger started to hum in the background of his nervous system like a battle hymn.

President Kaufman observed the look of cold fury on Jake's face. "The Secret Service had to smuggle Congressman Anderson out of the hospital by having him lie down on a gurney, covering him with a sheet and then putting him aboard a medical helicopter. They took him to a private airstrip so he could board Air Force Two and fly straight to Washington. He had to go through all that just so he could do his job in Congress."

"I'd say that is an unacceptable situation for a congressman to be in."

General Clemens nodded at Jake in agreement. "This assassin is a clear and present danger to the government and the citizens of the United States. Maybe you're familiar with the George Orwell quote that says people sleep peacefully in their beds at night only because rough men stand ready to do violence on their behalf."

"Yes, sir, my boot camp drill instructor said that."

"That's what the president and I are asking from you right now. To be perfectly clear here, we're asking you to kill Ivan Zhukov."

There was a pause while everyone thought about what Clemens had said.

"If the assassin walked into this room right now, armed and dangerous, I'd put a bullet in him," Jake said. "But I thought it wasn't legal for CIA case officers to operate on American soil."

President Kaufman said, "You will not be working as a temporary CIA case officer this time. You'll be deputized into the U.S. Marshals Service, to make sure you have nationwide federal jurisdiction to hunt down Zhukov."

"Similar to the way Wyatt Earp and Doc Holliday were deputized for the shootout at the OK Corral in Tombstone?"

Kaufman nodded. "Exactly. The U.S. Marshals Service is responsible for apprehending wanted fugitives. Marshals are also called upon to protect government officials in the judiciary. Most of this assignment falls within the established parameters. The director is authorized to deputize you by US Code Title 28, Section 561. However, U.S. Marshals don't assassinate enemy combatants. You will claim that you had to kill Zhukov in self-defense when you attempted to arrest him. My executive order to kill Zhukov is classified as top secret, and you're bound by your clearances to keep it a secret."

McKay spoke up and said, "Jake, we don't have time to give you every detail right now. Briefly, Congress has secretly granted a blanket letter of marque and reprisal for one specific small team of the Secret Service. The letter legally converts your private vessel, the *Far Niente,* into a naval auxiliary. You become a commissioned privateer with jurisdiction to conduct reprisal operations worldwide, and you are covered by the protection of the laws of war. In addition, you'll be operating under admiralty and maritime law, which gives you broad legal powers on the water similar to what the Coast Guard has."

General Clemens said, "Hardly anybody understands these legalities. That's why you'll be deputized and carry a U.S. Marshals badge. People do understand a badge and a gun. Right now, though, the most important thing is that your country needs you, Jake. I'm asking you as a Marine and a man of honor to step up and fight for what's right."

To Jake, it was personal. He thought of the friends and family he wanted to protect from Zhukov. The man had to be stopped. This plan was Jake's best chance of doing that.

Jake stared at General Clemens. He knew that the odds of him living through this were fifty-fifty at best. It was almost a suicide mission. He was the latest sacrificial pawn in a game of chess that had gone on for centuries. He paused and thought it over for a moment before agreeing to risk his life. His instincts told him he was being manipulated here, in a similar way to how Brinkter had done it in the past. They needed him, but his reward would be nothing more than a pat on the back. He'd already been there and done that. The old military saying, "never volunteer," had proven in the past to be something he should have heeded. This time, he decided to make them pay for his commitment and sacrifice, and to make sure that Brinkter could never threaten his family again.

"General Clemens and Mister President, I will accept your request to hunt down Ivan Zhukov and fight him to the death, but under two conditions."

CHAPTER 101

There was a pause as General Clemens squinted at Jake. President Kaufman took in a long breath and exhaled.

"Let's hear your conditions, then," Kaufman said.

"First, I want my own copy of that presidential 'get-out-of-jail-free' letter that Easton used at FBI HQ," Jake said. "And it has to apply to my family and friends too. Brinkter has to stop threatening to have my loved ones arrested in entrapment schemes. Today, he threatened to have my mother set up in a sting operation and sent to prison. Sir, if my own mother and family and friends don't have any real freedom here in the land of the free, then what am I fighting for?"

In the image on the TV screen, President Kaufman frowned and he glared at Brinkter. "Brinkter, as of tonight, you cannot fabricate false evidence or do entrapments or sting operations of any kind on Jake or his family or friends. Is that clear, or should I have you reassigned with a one-way ticket to the middle of a danger zone on the other side of the world?"

"Crystal clear and agreed to, sir," Brinkter said, looking at Jake as if he wanted to choke him.

"Thank you, Mister President," Jake said. "The second request is that I want Brinkter and the CIA to wire one million tax-free dollars to the trust bank account of my attorney, Bart Bartholomew. To be distributed to me upon completion of the mission, or given to my parents if I'm killed in the attempt."

There was a long silence as everyone wondered if they'd heard Jake correctly.

"You can't be serious," Brinkter said.

Jake turned and looked at Brinkter. "Why not? The USA paid out fifteen million dollars each for information that lead to the capture of Saddam Hussein's two sons. You can pay a total of thirty million dollars to one man who made a few phone calls to tip you off about two faraway arrests, but you can't afford to pay me one million to fight a terrorist to the death, right here on our home soil? If that's the case, you can fight him yourself, Brinkter. Good luck with that. I'll be betting against you."

Brinkter folded his arms. "You are not getting one million dollars from the CIA. It's too much money."

"You pay peanuts, you get monkeys," Jake said.

"Forget it, Wolfe, you can go back to FBI custody right now for all I care."

Jake stood up. "Okay, then, let's go." He looked at the TV screen. "General Clemens, President Kaufman, I'm sorry I can't help you. But I'm sure Brinkter here can do the job for you instead. Good evening, sirs, it was an honor to speak with you both. If you want to talk again, I'll be at the FBI headquarters, being held on false charges by the well-meaning people there."

Jake turned and started walking toward the door. Easton blocked his path, staring Jake down. Jake stared right back and continued moving directly toward him. Easton didn't draw his weapon. Both men flexed their muscles, preparing for a fistfight they didn't want, but neither would back down from.

"Wait a minute, Jake," President Kaufman said.

Jake stopped a few feet away from Easton. He nodded in respect and then turned his back, trusting him. He faced the TV screen. "Yes, Mister President?"

"I'm not an unreasonable man, but you're asking for an almost impossible condition on short notice."

"That's true, but you're asking me to perform an almost impossible life-or-death mission on short notice. What is your plan B if I decline to fight and kill Zhukov?"

"Point taken, but we simply can't pay you a million dollars right now. However, I can and will authorize a reward of one hundred thousand dollars, as a bounty on Zhukov. The funds will be paid to you in the form of a reward upon successful completion of your mission."

"Thank you, sir. I guess that will have to do for now, but let the record show that you owe me another nine hundred thousand."

"Understood."

"I want Brinkter's office to make the payment of the one hundred thousand to my attorney. And I want it paid up front, tonight. I don't trust Brinkter any farther than I can throw him."

"What difference does it make who pays you?"

"Brinkter has lied to me, he's used me, he owes me, and he needs to pay me. He left me to die in the desert. It's the principle of the thing. As a man of principle, I'm sure you understand."

The president looked at Brinkter a long moment. "Well, Brinkter, what's it going to be? I want your team to pay this man. Or else I want you to personally go after Zhukov on your own as a civilian vigilante. Your orders will be to fight him to the death. Take your pick and make it quick."

Brinkter looked afraid, but he shrugged as if it was no big deal. "If you sign an order for me to give this loose cannon a hundred grand, then of course I'll carry out your orders. However, I want to go on record as advising against it. Wolfe's problem is that you never know what crazy thing he might do next. He has no respect for authority and he strays too far off the beaten path."

Jake said, "Maybe the beaten paths are for beaten men, and I prefer to be a trailblazer."

"Consider it done and ordered, Brinkter," Kaufman said. "Get to work on it immediately, and send me a memo when you wire the funds. I'll expect to receive that memo within the hour. You'll be keeping me awake tonight while I wait to hear from you. Is that understood?"

"Yes, sir, understood."

"Are you satisfied now, Jake?" Kaufman said.

Jake came back to the table and sat down. "Yes, Mister President."

Brinkter glared at Jake but kept his mouth shut.

Jake looked at him. "You mad, bro?"

Jake smiled, knowing Brinkter was going to have to pay him money, and finally pay him some respect. But Jake wondered if he'd live to spend any of it.

"Now, as your commander in chief," President Kaufman said, "I hereby order you, Jacob T. Wolfe, to kill the enemy combatant Ivan Zhukov, while acting under the federal law enforcement authority of the U.S. Marshals Service, and also secretly doing your duty under my presidential executive order. Time is of the essence. I hereby order all law enforcement personnel to give you their full support and cooperation during your mission, or face charges for the crime of interfering with a federal investigation."

Kaufman looked pointedly at Brinkter, Greene, and Easton. Brinkter sat still, but Greene and Easton both nodded at the president in agreement and said, "Yes, sir."

"We'll begin to carry out your orders immediately," Jake said. "Brinkter won't be coming with us."

General Clemens spoke up. "Jake, do your duty and make the Marine Corps proud, son. We're asking you to give your all. Whether it includes sacrifice, suffering, or pain—you just get it done."

"Yes, sir."

President Kaufman said, "Jake, I'm looking forward to having a meeting with you here at the White House after the successful completion of your mission. But for now, on behalf of all Americans, I offer our nation's thanks to you. Good luck."

The flat-screen televisions flickered and changed to a blue background with the presidential seal. Easton pressed a button on the remote and turned them all off.

The woman with the headset came into the room along with a dangerous-looking man from the U.S. Marshals Service. He wore a Glock in a holster on his belt. Introductions were made and the marshal began the process of deputizing Jake.

When it was done, Jake held a Marshals badge in his hand and felt the weight of responsibility that came with it. "It's a great honor to be deputized as a U.S. Marshal."

The marshal looked Jake in the eye. "You're damned right it's an honor, and you'd better be as good as they say you are. Treat that badge with respect, and stay true to the high standards of the U.S. Marshals Service or there will be hell to pay."

"I'll do my very best, sir, I give you my word," Jake said.

The marshal nodded, and he shook Jake's hand with a grip like a steel vise.

CHAPTER 102

Banks called Zhukov on the phone and said, "We have a new problem. Congressman Anderson was secretly transported to Washington. As you know, enormous sums of money will be won or lost depending on his actions. And of course, if things go against us, you'll be killed by my associates for your failure. That would be rather unfortunate as I so enjoy our conversations."

Zhukov cursed in Russian. "It's too late for me to follow Anderson to D.C. They'll be watching airports and flights, even private jets."

"None of that matters to the Council members. They want to know when you will neutralize the congressman as you promised to do and were paid to do."

"You ought to remind your Council that the final step of their plan has not yet occurred, so I have not yet failed. I'd like to know what you are doing to neutralize the other politicians who could block your plans."

"Our lobbyists are very busy. Some politicians are being bribed, while others are blackmailed or threatened. Anderson is the most significant problem. The one you're being paid vast sums to neutralize."

"I should have just killed Anderson in the first place, but you were against the idea."

"We didn't want to create a martyr. That could have caused our worst-case scenario."

"Did your Council have any backup plans, if the congressman failed to stay in San Francisco?"

"No, because you were supposed to be the very best at your job. Now that we have an emergency on our hands, perhaps you could kidnap Katherine and use her as a bargaining chip."

"Did Katherine travel to Washington with Daniel, or is she still in San Francisco?"

"According to our sources, she is still in the same San Francisco hospital. However, she's well protected by the Secret Service and the police."

"Maybe I'll actually shoot her with a real bullet like you originally wanted."

"If you had done that as we asked you to, we wouldn't be having this conversation right now."

"At the time, I had a problem with killing a pregnant woman. But if it comes down to her life or mine, that changes my outlook. I'm a practical man. There is always a way to get to someone like her. A sniper shot through a window, poison delivered in a flower bouquet or food item, exploding teddy bears."

"If she dies now, the congressman will become infuriated and even more determined to solve this mystery and thwart our plans. He's getting closer to figuring out the reason behind all of this. The best course of action may be for you to kidnap Katherine and hold her for leverage. That way, even if Anderson discovers our plans, he won't want to risk the lives of his wife and baby by trying to interfere with us."

"That kidnapping idea was previously rejected as being nearly impossible to implement. Recent circumstances make the odds even worse."

"You've often bragged about how you enjoy a challenge. Here's a real challenge for you. It would be nearly impossible for anybody else. But you are the true master, the legend, The Artist who does what no one else can."

"Flattery now, Chairman? You sound desperate, but I can't argue with your logic. I'll attempt to kidnap or frighten Katherine. The attempt alone, if sufficiently violent and horrific, should send a message to Daniel. He'll learn that missing a few days of work doesn't matter in the grand scheme of things, but my anger does. He and his wife and child would never be safe from me for the rest of their lives."

CHAPTER 103

Sarah Chance arrived home to her studio apartment, poured herself a glass of wine and looked in the refrigerator but didn't have an appetite. After the surreal experience of being arrested and held in FBI custody, her nerves were raw and her stomach was in a knot.

Sarah kept glancing at her phone, wondering if Jake would call. She'd be better off without Jake in her life, but she felt a strange connection to him.

There were plenty of texts and missed calls from Leonard, but her path in life was different than his. The man who captured her heart would treat her as an equal, but still be an alpha male who provided strong leadership and swept her off her feet. Was that too much to expect, and was there any reason a man owed that to her nowadays?

Sarah knew that Jake would be worried about Cody. She remembered that he worked at the television studio and used her phone to go online and find the website. Jake's photojournalist contact info was listed there, and her fingers seemed to have a mind of their own as they added Jake's number to her phone under the name "Bad Boy." As Sarah stared at the phone screen and drummed her fingernails on the tabletop, she decided to just do it. She sent Jake a text message and worded it carefully in case the FBI read it.

Hello, Mr. Wolfe. As your veterinarian, I wanted to let you know your dog Cody is okay and he's sleeping at Terrell's house.

Sarah then sat and sipped some wine and watched the phone like it was a magician about to do a magic trick.

~

SFPD Sergeant Cori Denton was at home drinking a gin and tonic and smoking a cigarette when she heard a phone vibrating from inside the file box of evidence for the Jake Wolfe investigation. She'd taken it home in violation of police procedures.

Denton jumped up off the couch, ran to the file box, and retrieved a clone of Wolfe's phone. It was an exact copy of the one found on the airport shuttle. The police tech named Roxanne had downloaded all the data from Wolfe's phone before the FBI had taken it away.

Wolfe's actual phone was probably still in an evidence locker at FBI headquarters. Denton hoped that either the battery was dead, or nobody would hear it ring or vibrate at this time of night. She saw that the clone phone had received a text from Sarah Chance. That raised her suspicions. She texted back. *Call me.*

The phone vibrated with a call. Denton answered it but didn't say anything.

She heard a female voice. "Hello, Jake? Are you there? It's Sarah."

Denton said, "This is Sergeant Denton with the San Francisco Police Department. You've called the phone of a suspected criminal and wanted fugitive. Identify yourself or I'll send a police car to find you and arrest you."

Sarah's heart sank. "My name is Sarah Chance. I already went through all this with the FBI. If you have any questions, you can talk to them, or to your fellow police officer, Beth Cushman."

"I remember you, Chance. I consider you a suspect in the murder of Max Vidallen. I have a lot of questions, and you're going to answer them right now."

"I'm sorry, but I only answer questions in the presence of my attorney. His name is Bart Bartholomew. If you wish to speak with me further, you'll have to call him first. Good night."

The call ended and Denton cursed. She accessed the police department computer records of the investigation of Wolfe. Sure enough, there was an entry for this evening. The FBI had found Wolfe at Chance's veterinary clinic and taken him into custody. Denton was furious that nobody had bothered to inform her. She was the lead SFPD investigator on Wolfe's case. This was an outrage, and so typical of the jerks she had to work with. It didn't matter to her if it was late at night and the case had been taken over by the FBI. Cushman had written a brief report and hadn't bothered to give Denton a courtesy call at home to update her on the status of the case. What was Cushman doing at the scene of an FBI raid anyway? And why was Wolfe captured at the clinic of that Sarah Chance woman? Sarah was looking guiltier by the minute.

Denton paced back and forth in agitation and sent a text to her partner. Kirby didn't reply. She then tried calling him but only got his voicemail. This was not right … she was not going to stand for it. She put on her jacket and grabbed her car keys.

Before she went out the door, she grabbed a bottle of pills and swallowed one with the last of her gin and tonic. Then she walked to her vehicle and sat down in the driver's seat. She fumbled for the keys and dropped them on the floor, and when she reached down to pick them up, she banged her forehead on the steering wheel. She cursed and started the car, excusing her drinking and driving by telling herself that she was above the law. She was on the side of the angels. She could do whatever she wanted and nobody could stop her.

Denton drove off, leaving the forgotten clone phone sitting on her table at home.

The phone vibrated again with a series of texts from Jake's former fiancée, Gwen.

Jake, we need to talk!
ANSWER ME!!
Jake?
Jake!!!
I'M PREGNANT!!!!
Hello?

No comment?

YOU JERK!!!!!

The phone then vibrated with repeated calls from Gwen that went unanswered.

CHAPTER 104

Zhukov drove slowly past Sarah Chance's home. It was a Victorian house converted into individual studio apartments and her unit was on the second floor. There was a light on inside her apartment and somebody was walking around.

He found a parking space two blocks away, lit up a Cohiba cigar he'd stolen from the *Far Niente,* and walked back so that he had eyes on Sarah's apartment, stopping one building down and across the street. He stood in a dark recessed doorway while he smoked the cigar and watched Sarah's building with night vision binoculars. The front door and the ground-floor windows didn't appear to have an alarm system installed. He'd never found a residential building anywhere in the world that he couldn't break into within a few minutes; this one would be no different.

Car headlights approached and Zhukov stepped back into the alcove, staying out of sight in the shadows. The car slowed down and stopped in front of Sarah's building and a spotlight shone from the driver's side of the vehicle and swept over both sides of the street. Zhukov flattened his back against the wall as the light passed over his location. That was close, and if the car moved forward a few feet, the light would shine directly into the doorway and expose him.

Zhukov held the cigar with his left hand, down by his side that was away from the light. His right hand reached into his coat and gripped his pistol. He was prepared to fire at the driver's window of the vehicle if it drove forward. The spotlight went off, however, and the car drove slowly away and down a side street.

Perhaps this was a trap and Sarah wasn't even home. A plainclothes policewoman could be waiting inside Sarah's apartment right now, walking in front of the window to draw Zhukov closer. And a sharpshooter could be watching her building from a window across the street, hoping to take a shot at him. His instincts told him Sarah wasn't worth the risk and he should focus on the higher-value target, even though that would be far more challenging. Now was the time to go see if he could kidnap, kill, or terrorize Katherine Anderson. He tossed the cigar in the gutter and quickly made his way back to his car.

Sarah peeked out her window and saw the dark figure leaving the scene. She called Beth Cushman on the phone. "I see him again. He's leaving now. Walking uphill on the other side of my street."

"Okay, I'll swing by again." Beth said. She turned her car around and headed back toward Sarah's home.

Beth didn't mind doing another drive-by to calm her friend's fears. It was normal for her to be paranoid and afraid right now. And who knew? If the attorney assassin really was here, Beth might capture him. When she pulled her car up in front of Sarah's apartment building, she saw another car driving slowly past on the cross street a block away. The car didn't have its headlights on and was creeping along. Beth aimed her spotlight at the other driver and turned it on. The man's surprised face was illuminated by the bright light and he sped away.

Beth recognized the face of the attorney assassin from the photo taken by the Golden Gate Bridge camera. She took off in pursuit and roared down the street, taking the turn so fast her tires burned rubber as she drifted sideways around the corner.

In the car ahead, Zhukov cursed at his own bold recklessness. He raced the engine to put some distance between himself and the pursuing car. He opened his black bag and took out a nearly full bottle of vodka.

Beth made a three-way call on her phone, to police headquarters and Terrell Hayes simultaneously. She turned on her phone's speaker and set the device on the passenger seat. The police operator answered, but Terrell didn't. "Officer Cushman in pursuit of the attorney assassin suspect's vehicle. Requesting backup, code eight." Beth described the vehicle and gave the location.

She saw the car ahead of her turn left and come to a screeching stop. The driver opened his door, stepped out onto the street and threw a flaming object directly at her car. He then began firing a pistol at her. For a split second, Beth watched in disbelief as a clear glass bottle with a burning rag in the top flew through the air toward her. At the same moment, bullets began to punch holes in her windshield.

Everything seemed to move in slow motion for her as she instinctively ducked her head to the right, below the level of the dashboard. A rain of bullets took out the windshield as the Molotov cocktail hit the hood of her car, exploded, and sent flaming liquid splattering into her vehicle through the open windshield. The car careened out of control with no one at the wheel and crashed into a parked vehicle, causing the two front airbags to deploy above Beth's prone body, pinning her down to the seat.

Flames began to roar inside her car as the ceiling cloth and the backseat caught on fire. Beth grabbed a ballpoint pen from her pocket and used it to puncture the airbags above her torso several times. As the airbags deflated, she crawled across the seat, out the passenger door, and onto the pavement. The back of her jacket was on fire, and she rolled on the ground as she'd been trained to do. She then tore off her smoldering jacket and patted down her legs, which still had some flaming spots of the burning liquid on them.

She moved away from her car as it became engulfed in flames but kept it between her and the shooter. Her stomach lurched as she realized that if she hadn't ducked, the burning liquid would have sprayed onto her face, hair, and chest. The smell of burning plastic and upholstery hit her nostrils and she vomited in the gutter, relieved it wasn't her flesh that was on fire. That had been as close to dying as she'd ever come. The thought of her child growing up without his mother hit her hard like a fist to her heart, and she felt dizzy.

A metallic voice was shouting questions from the radio inside her burning car. The front passenger door was open and she saw her phone on the floor, but flames were pouring out of the car and she couldn't get closer. "This is Cushman. If you can hear me, my car is on fire. It's burning up. I'm not injured, but officer needs assistance. Code twenty."

The radio gave a screech of static and died.

The light on her phone went out and then the screen cracked open as plastic parts inside began to sizzle and burn. She looked for her attacker's vehicle, but it was gone.

Doors of nearby apartments opened and people looked out at the flaming car and the woman wearing a pistol in a hip holster. After one look, several of them closed their doors and locked them. One young woman, who was wearing a tight t-shirt showing off some toned muscular arms, walked straight over to Beth. "I've called the police. What's the situation?"

Beth flashed her badge. "I *am* the police."

The young woman nodded her head. "I'm in the Navy Reserve, stationed at the NOSC in Alameda. What can I do to help you, Officer?"

"You can let me make a call on your phone."

"Roger that. Here's my phone."

"Thank you," Beth said, grateful that someone was willing to help. She entered Terrell's phone number as she heard the sirens of police cars and fire engines that were racing toward her location.

CHAPTER 105

At the safe house, Jake looked at Easton and said, "I need a ride to the hospital. I can take one of your vehicles, but I'd prefer if you'd drive and give me a hand with the mission."

Easton said, "I'll drive and we'll take that same Suburban. My orders are to assist you, so let me know what you need."

"I need weapons and backup shooters."

"Greene can get more weapons out of the locker. We can both provide backup for you."

"Let's roll."

They went out the door into the garage and Greene opened a cabinet. Everybody grabbed weapons and duffel bags, then got into the vehicle.

"Where are my pistols and my knife?" Jake said.

Greene handed him a black case. "I suggest you carry the same weapons we do. That way you have matching ammo and plenty of extra mags."

Jake looked in the case and found his pistols and knife, but not his phone. He took his KA-BAR knife out of the case and strapped the sheath and web belt around his waist so it rode horizontally along the small of his back. "Thanks, that's good advice about the weapons. I think the Secret Service is equipped with SIG pistols these days, right?"

Greene nodded and opened a duffel bag. She handed Jake a SIG Sauer pistol and a shoulder holster, along with several extra mags full of ammo. She held up an assault rifle. "I also brought along some suppressed MP5SD submachine guns loaded with frangible bullets. Those are good for indoor, close-quarters battle."

"Good plan for CQB in a hospital building."

Easton pushed the remote control device to open the garage door, and backed the vehicle out. He did a quick U-turn and then drove off, pressing a remote to close the garage door behind them.

"The FBI didn't put my phone in this case," Jake said. "I need a clean phone—two if you have them."

Greene dug in the duffel bag and gave Jake two throwaway phones.

Jake handed back one of the phones. "Put both of your phone numbers into this one."

While Greene entered the numbers, Jake used the other phone to call Sarah Chance.

"Hello?" Sarah said, uncertain of the number on her phone.

"Sarah, it's Jake. Are you at home?"

"Jake, where are you? Did you get out of FBI custody?"

"Yes, I did, but listen to me. It's not safe at your place right now. You have to hide out tonight. Stay with family or friends. Maybe go to a hotel."

"Why? What's going on?"

"They overheard the attorney assassin threaten my friends and family. He didn't mention you by name, but I want you to go to a hotel anyway."

"Will you be there too?"

"No, I'm going to be the bait to draw this guy into a trap."

"I can be bait too. I've already been to jail today, so maybe I'll be jailbait."

"This is not a joke, Sarah. It's a dangerous situation."

"Sorry, but I'm not going to hide. I have a pistol and I'm a good shot."

"I don't like this, but if you're going to use your pistol, be sure to click off the safety this time."

"I will, and you take good care of Cody. Don't let him get injured again like you did once already."

"Touché. Cody is with Terrell. If you get in a fist fight, keep that left elbow up."

"Okay, and if I see the attorney assassin, I'll thank him for shooting Max Vidallen."

"Why are you so stubborn?"

"It comes naturally to me," Sarah said. "I don't like being told what to do, and besides, I have Beth patrolling the street outside."

"Why is Beth there?"

"Somebody drove past my place several times going really slow, and after that I saw a man loitering in a nearby doorway."

"Dammit, Sarah, that's exactly what I'm talking about. I'm going to ask if Secret Service agents can go to your home and protect you."

"Secret what? Hold on. I see a car on fire, several blocks away."

"Is it Beth's car? Do you have binoculars?"

"I'm looking at it through my camera with the zoom lens. It might be Beth's car, but it's hard to tell. I'm going to jog over there."

"No, Sarah, call 911. If something happens to you … who am I going to spar with in Jeet Kune Do practice?"

"That's very touching, Jake, but I have to go."

"Wait, Sarah, listen to me."

Sarah ended the call.

Jake called Terrell next. "I think Beth might need backup."

"She just called me a minute ago, but the call dropped and now all I get is voicemail. Then I heard her call for backup on the radio. I'm going to drive there now."

"Bring Cody with you."

"Are you going to meet me there?"

"I can't. I'm on my way to the hospital to help the Secret Service capture the attorney assassin."

"The last I heard, you were in FBI custody. When did you make friends with the Secret Service?"

"There's no time to explain, and some of it is OPSEC."

"Operations security? More secrets and lies? I thought you'd left all that behind."

"Look, I can't talk about it. Once you know that Beth and Sarah are all right, bring Cody to the hospital. We'll need his nose to find the target."

"Roger that. Make sure you let the feds know to be expecting us."

"The feds know, and some of them are on their way to your house."

"What? Why are they coming to my house?"

"That's the other bad news. This guy threatened you, Alicia and her school, Beth and her kid, my parents and my sister. After the threat to Sarah, the Secret Service is sending agents to protect all of you.

Terrell cursed. "If the killer threatened Alicia and her school, I'll slit his throat."

"And I'll help you do it. I'm sure he's the one who tried to get to Sarah. It sounds like he might have torched Beth's car. We need to make sure she's alive, and then make sure this guy is … arrested."

"Got to go. I see black SUVs pulling up outside my place."

Jake ended the call and texted a news story to a friend at the TV station. His text said there was a gas leak near Alicia's school and classes were canceled for tomorrow. When that story ran, the kids could stay home and enjoy a day off. It would be inconvenient for the parents, but they'd have to deal with it. The woman at the TV station would definitely run the story—she owed Jake a favor. She'd recently been hounded by online stalkers and trolls, threatening her with awful things. It happened to women all the time on the internet. Jake had tracked down the worst troll via his IP address, paid him a late-night visit and made him sorry for his misdeeds. Jake had never talked about what he'd done to the troll, but the man had moved out of the state and never bothered any woman ever again.

Someone pounded on Terrell's door. As he went to answer it, he briefly told Alicia what was happening. She watched in disbelief as serious-looking men and women in dark suits entered her house and spread out to check all the rooms and windows. A helicopter was flying over the neighborhood.

The dogs weren't happy about having intruders in the house. Boo-Boo started barking and running all around the house. Cody stood still, watching the armed agents and letting out a low growl.

Terrell put Boo-Boo in the garage and closed the doggie door, then tried to give some commands to Cody. "Out, Cody, be friends."

Cody barked twice and appeared to shake his head. He continued watching the agents and sniffing the air for the scents of weapons, gunpowder, gun oil, testosterone, and estrogen. He did not know these dangerous people.

"Cody, you need to stand down," Terrell said. "We have to go find Jake. These people are Jake's friends. They're here to protect Alicia."

Cody gazed at Terrell for a moment with his bright eyes, then barked once and went over and stood by the door, waiting to go. Terrell was again reminded of how smart the dog was. It almost seemed as if Cody understood most of the words you said to him.

Terrell went over to Alicia. "I want you to wear your pistol in the belt holster."

"You know I don't like that thing."

"Like it or not, please carry it on your hip, the way I showed you. This is exactly the kind of situation we talked about. You promised me you'd do it if the day ever came when things got real."

"What's the world coming to when a schoolteacher has to wear a sidearm in her own house?"

Terrell didn't answer; he just put the black web belt with the holster and pistol around Alicia's waist and tightened it up.

The Secret Service agent in charge noted Alicia's pistol and nodded at Terrell in agreement. Next, Terrell held up a bulletproof Kevlar vest for Alicia to put on.

"Is this really necessary?"

"Kevlar was invented by a woman. Come on and show your support for female inventors."

Alicia rolled her eyes at his sales pitch, but she put on the vest as requested.

Terrell hugged and kissed her goodbye and then attempted to put a leash on Cody's collar. Cody snapped at Terrell's hand and moved away, out of reach.

"Let's roll, Cody. Jake needs your help, and I don't have time for your attitude."

Cody barked once and ran alongside Terrell to the police vehicle.

Terrell opened the door to the backseat of the police SUV. Cody just stood there and looked at him.

"Jake is counting on you, but if you can't follow orders I'll leave you behind. Are you good to go?"

Cody barked once.

"Then act like a war dog, not a temperamental pussy. Are you a Marine who understands the chain of command or not?"

Cody growled at Terrell, but he jumped into the vehicle's backseat and sat up straight, the way a military dog should.

"That's more like it." Terrell got into the driver's seat, turned on the police lights and siren, and roared off down the street. He used a small handheld device to turn all of the traffic lights green as he drove along.

At Beth Cushman's home, there was a loud knock at the front door. Her roommate, Zoey, was surprised to find several stone-faced government agents on the front step. Two agents came inside without asking permission. Two others stood guard outside. One in front and one in back. After the agent in charge explained the situation, Beth's son, Kyle, asked endless questions while Zoey sat wringing her hands. One agent handed a tablet to Zoey, and Alicia Hayes was on the screen. The tablet was using a program similar to Skype or FaceTime, but it was encrypted and private.

"Zoey, how are you and Kyle doing?" Alicia asked.

"We're okay. There are agents all over the place to protect us, but I'm still really nervous."

"Don't worry; these folks are the best at what they do. You're in safe hands. In fact, you've never been this safe in your entire life. Believe me."

Kyle came over next to Zoey and looked at the tablet. He saw the image of Alicia Hayes wearing a bulletproof vest and a handgun on her hip.

"Wow, Mrs. Hayes," Kyle said. "You are the most badass teacher ever. I can't wait to tell all the kids at school."

"Oh dear," Alicia said.

CHAPTER 106

Zhukov drove fast toward the hospital where Katherine Anderson was staying. Going there was ill-advised, but his pride was on the line. The manic aspect of his mental health condition was in full bloom, causing him to do reckless things that all seemed perfectly logical to him.

He parked several blocks away from the hospital, then walked in the shadows toward his objective. On the way, he dodged two Secret Service foot patrols. When he reached the back alley of a building across the street, he quietly climbed the fire escape to a parking area. He walked past rows of cars to the other side and studied the hospital across from him through a pair of night vision binoculars.

There were Secret Service agents stationed in front of the building, and others looked out various windows on several floors. No doubt many more were patrolling the halls and stairwells inside. They were formidable opponents, he had to admit. He wondered if they had an agent on the roof. Surely, they would, but that might be the least protected area of the building. He'd climb higher and take a look.

The lock on the stairwell was no match for his lock-picking skills, and he was soon leaping up the stairs two at a time. The door at the roof level was also locked, but he opened it just as quickly as the previous one. On the rooftop, he was nearly level with the roof of the hospital across the street, just a floor or two above. The buildings had been built during the same time period and were of similar height and construction.

Zhukov saw one person on the hospital roof across the street, looking around with binoculars. He or she was mostly studying the street below, with occasional glances at the windows across from the floor where Katherine was staying. Zhukov stood perfectly still and studied the person through his night vision binoculars. He saw that it was a man wearing a suit and an earbud communication device. He watched the agent and noticed that not once did the man look at the roof across from and above him. That supported his theory someone was patrolling this roof too.

Zhukov slowly crept along, staying in shadows and searching the area around him with his night vision gear. Yes, he saw movement at the southeast corner. Someone was walking in his direction. He hid behind a large heating and air conditioning vent and waited for the person to pass.

When the agent appeared next to the vent, Zhukov threw an expert punch to the throat and then a blow to the head that knocked the agent to the ground. The woman never knew what had hit her. She lay there unconscious, gasping for breath through her bruised windpipe. She'd survive but would only be able to eat soft foods through a straw for a week or two. Seeing no reason to kill the agent, Zhukov used plastic zip ties to bind her hands and feet, then put a piece of duct tape across her mouth.

He took off her earpiece and wrist microphone and placed the earpiece in his own ear. Listening to the talk on the earpiece didn't give him any indication his presence had been discovered as of yet. He looked through the binoculars and studied the windows of the room where Katherine was supposed to be staying, but he suspected that she might have been moved and the room was now a trap. There was no way the woman was going to stand in front of a window and present herself to be shot. He considered shooting the window anyway, just to send a message to Congressman Anderson. However, that might not be enough of a message. No, this situation called for a "boots on the ground" visit to the hospital building.

He opened his backpack and took out a crossbow that was broken down into pieces. He put it back together, loaded a bolt into the weapon and aimed it at the Secret Service agent on the roof across the street. The man was standing in front of a large air conditioning unit and holding his microphone up to his mouth as he looked through binoculars toward Zhukov's location.

Zhukov heard the man's voice on the earpiece, trying to contact the other agent who was unconscious. He took careful aim with the crossbow, and just as the man spotted him, he fired. The man tried to move out of the way, but it was too late, and the bolt flew too fast. The small, slender bolt pierced the agent's shoulder and slammed him into the housing of the air conditioning unit. It stuck into the sheet metal cover and held there, pinning the man like a butterfly in an insect collection. The drug on the arrowhead sent the man into shock … he could no longer talk or move his arms or draw his pistol. Seconds later he was rendered unconscious, and he would stay asleep for hours.

Zhukov fitted another bolt into the crossbow. This one had a grappling hook on the end instead of an arrowhead, and it was connected to a lightweight but incredibly strong, synthetic wire. He fired the bolt across to the other building's roof and it caught on a metal joist. He secured his end of the wire to a steel pipe. With that done, he attached a wheel device to the wire and stood on the edge of the roof in the shadows of the air vent. He looked down and didn't see anyone looking up at him; the crossbow was so quiet it hadn't attracted any attention.

It was now or never, time to go for a thrill ride. Stepping off the roof into midair, Zhukov held tight to the grips of the wheel device and flew across the street hanging from the wire, the way the Soviet Spetsnaz Special Forces had taught him. When he landed on the roof of the other building, he dropped the wheel device and walked over to the agent who was pinned to the air conditioning unit. He took the man's radio and earbud, and his badge and credentials. Even though he and the agent didn't look much alike, the ID might help him bluff or distract someone. Now it was time to go hunting for Katherine Anderson.

"I'm coming for you, my darling," Zhukov said. He went through a door into a stairwell leading down into the hospital.

CHAPTER 107

Dr. Brook entered Katherine's room. "It's time for the biopsy."

Katherine appeared worried as Dr. Brook applied a local anesthetic to her left breast.

Before bringing out the long needle, Dr. Brook opened the wrapper of a sleeping mask for Katherine to wear. "Please wear this mask and keep your eyes closed. This will go much easier for you if you don't look."

"All right, you're the doctor." Katherine put on the soft mask.

A nurse held an ultrasound wand over Katherine's breast to help guide Dr. Brook when her needle would puncture Katherine's skin and enter the lump or "mass" as they observed it on the monitor.

Dr. Brook opened the sterile covering and removed the needle. She took a deep breath and let it out, then carefully inserted the sharp point of the needle through Katherine's skin. She watched the image of the needle on the ultrasound display as she carefully pressed it onward through the breast, found the mass and slowly extracted a sample of tissue. Withdrawing the needle, she handed the syringe to the nurse. "Rush this to the lab, stat. Ask them to make it a top priority."

"Yes, doctor." The nurse hurried out of the room.

Dr. Brook placed a bandage over the site of injection. "You can open your eyes now, Kat."

Katherine removed the sleep mask and looked around. "That hurt."

"Sorry for that. The procedure went well. Now we just wait for the lab results and hope that everything turns out fine."

Katherine looked at the ultrasound display. "While you have that thing on, can we use it to see my baby?"

"Of course." Dr. Brook gently placed the ultrasound wand on Katherine's stomach. "Your baby has come through all of this in good shape. She's doing quite well."

"She? You can tell it's a girl?"

Dr. Brook's face reddened for a moment in embarrassment. "Yes, it's a girl. I'm supposed to ask your permission before I tell you that."

"It's okay. At first we wanted it to be a surprise, but our curiosity just kept growing along with the baby." Katherine smiled as she looked at the ultrasound image. "Hello, Baby Rachel. Mommy loves you, sweetie."

Dr. Rachel Brook felt a lump in her throat, but made an effort to keep her composure. She knew there was a chance the baby might have to go through cancer treatments along with her mother. It felt like her heart was being squeezed under a weight.

Katherine gazed with love at the ultrasound image. After all these years of trying, she was finally going to have a child. She had tears in her eyes, but she was smiling as she took a picture of the ultrasound with her phone and sent it to her husband, along with a text: *It's a girl! We're going to have a daughter!*

Dr. Brook removed the ultrasound device from Katherine's belly. The imaging had been recorded as a video and she set it to replay again and again so Katherine could watch it. She patted Katherine's arm and went out into the hallway to check on other patients. She was thankful that the test had gone well, but they still had to wait for the lab results; that news might be good, or it might be devastating.

In a stairwell near the roof of the hospital, Zhukov's phone vibrated with a text message from Elena.

Target located. She sent a text to her husband. I traced her phone GPS to the hospital's 7th floor. Room 710.

Zhukov smiled. "I've found you, Katherine."

CHAPTER 108

Jake didn't say anything as Easton raced toward the hospital with the lights flashing from under the front grill. His mind was focused on killing Ivan Zhukov. They arrived at their destination and turned onto the street where the hospital was located.

Greene asked Jake, "Now that we're here, what's your plan?"

"To improvise."

"That's it?"

"Pretty much."

"Great plan."

"The plan is we go into the hospital, search for Zhukov, and if we find him we kill him," Jake said.

"We don't try to capture him?"

"No."

The SUV pulled up in front of the hospital and was quickly surrounded by armed Secret Service agents. Easton showed his credentials. "Agent McKay was going to call and inform you about our arrival."

"Yes, we're expecting you," one of the agents said.

Their IDs were verified, and a mirror on a pole was passed under the SUV to check for any kind of explosive device. Easton was cleared to drive into the garage, but before he did, Jake and Greene got out of the vehicle, wearing black windbreakers that said "Federal Agent" on the back. Jake showed the letter from the president to the Secret Service agent in charge.

The agent read the letter and then stared at Jake in surprise. They'd all been trying to capture him just a short while ago; now here he was with this rare document from the president. The man used his phone to take a picture of the letter and of Jake, and he sent the pics to all the other agents in and around the hospital.

Jake borrowed an agent's night vision binoculars and studied the top of the hospital building near the roof. "Who do you have manning the rooftops?"

"We have agents on five different rooftops. One on the hospital roof, and one on each of the four buildings closest to the hospital."

"Check in with them by radio and send backup to the hospital roof and stairwells," Jake said.

Greene stared at the top of the hospital building. "What's going on?"

Jake handed her the binoculars. "Take a close look at the rooftop."

Greene studied the building for a moment. "What am I looking for?"

"There's a long, thin shadow on the wall, near the top."

"Okay, I see it. Why is that important?"

"I think the shadow is from a wire or cable that's running from this building to the one across the street."

Greene lowered the binoculars and stared at Jake. "A wire, from roof to roof?"

Jake nodded. "If my guess is correct, the perimeter has already been breached by the enemy."

"How did you know to look for that?"

"Because after a quick look around, that's the way I'd go in. You have to think like a killer if you want to stop one."

The agent said, "There's no answer from our agent on the hospital roof, or the one on that building across the street."

"I suggest you double the guard on Katherine Anderson's floor."

The agent barked orders into his fist microphone. Jake turned and started running toward the parking garage and Greene ran after him.

They found Easton and the SUV in the garage and Jake explained the situation as they strapped on flak vests, shoulder holsters, and belt holsters. Lastly, they grabbed MP5 assault weapons and extra ammo.

Jake said, "There are two stairwells, so we need four people. Two of us will take an elevator to the top and then work our way down. Two will start at the bottom and work our way up."

"You two take the elevators, I'll call another agent and we'll work our way up," Greene said. She tapped her phone and made a call.

"Let's do this." Jake stepped into the nearest elevator as Easton ran to another elevator at the other end of the garage.

~

Greene called the Secret Service contact on her radio and briefly relayed the plan. An agent appeared almost immediately, running toward her. They both headed for the chosen stairwells. Greene double-checked her weapon and went through the door.

It was cold in the concrete stairwell, but Greene felt a nervous sweat begin to form on her skin as she climbed the steps. She kept her eyes trained upward and held the barrel of her assault rifle pointed there. The only sound she could hear was that of her footsteps on the stairs. The noise seemed incredibly loud to her as it echoed up the hollow chamber. This was going to be a long and stressful climb.

On one hand, Greene hoped she would meet up with the killer and take him out. That would make her the hero and show the city what a woman could do. On the other hand, she hoped that he was in another area of the building so somebody else would have to deal with him. She'd never shot or killed anybody and she certainly didn't want to die tonight. Her heart was pounding as she continued climbing, step-by-step.

~

Jake's elevator reached the roof. When the door opened, he crouched on one knee in the corner with his pistol aimed high. A Secret Service agent stood there waiting for the elevator. His eyebrows shot up when he saw Jake aiming his pistol at him. He recognized his face from the photo sent to his phone, and he nodded at him in a cool and professional manner.

The agent was carrying an unconscious man over his shoulder in a fireman's carry. The man had something sticking out of him that looked like a crossbow bolt.

"You were right," the agent said. "Someone came over from the roof across the street, using a wheel-and-cable setup. I searched the rooftop, but I didn't find anyone."

"Can you give me this man's radio?" Jake said.

"His radio is missing, but take mine. I'll get another one when I'm downstairs."

"If his radio is missing, that means Zhukov has it."

"Yeah, and I called in a situation report before I realized that. I'm sure Zhukov heard me too."

The agent stepped into the elevator and pressed the button for the floor where the ER was located. His eyes met Jake's and he nodded, then the doors closed and he was gone.

Jake hoped Terrell got there soon; he needed Cody if they hoped to have any chance of catching this guy.

Jake thought about his orders to draw Zhukov's fire and spoke into the radio, taunting him. "Ivan Zhukov, if you can hear me, this is Jake Wolfe. I'm here in the hospital, and I challenge you to a fight. Man-to-man. Come out of hiding—unless you're afraid to face me, you coward."

CHAPTER 109

One minute Sarah had been looking out her apartment window, watching Beth's car go on a high-speed chase. The next minute she'd seen a car burst into flames. Was it Beth's car?

Sarah called Beth on the phone, but her call went to voicemail. She sent a text and got no reply. She grabbed a camera and looked at the burning car through the zoom lens. It was hard to be sure, but she had a terrible feeling that was her friend's vehicle.

Sarah's medical training, good heart, and loyalty to friends kicked in and she knew what she had to do. She grabbed her doctor's bag and added her pistol to it. She put on a windbreaker, went outside and took off running. As Sarah ran, she called 911. "Officer needs assistance. There's a vehicle on fire and I believe it's the personal car of SFPD Sergeant Beth Cushman."

Sarah gave her best guess of the cross streets at the location of the burning vehicle. The operator told her to stay away from the scene but she ended the call and continued to run. These streets were familiar to her, even in the dark. She was a weekend runner and knew every block of her neighborhood. She made good time and arrived at the scene breathing hard. The burning car was definitely Beth's Subaru.

Sarah yelled at the crowd, "I'm a friend of the police officer who was driving this car. Where is she? Is she hurt? I need to see her right now!"

A woman said, "She's not injured. I let her borrow my phone—she's over there making a call."

Sarah turned and looked to where the woman was pointing. She saw Beth and walked over to her. "When I saw your car, I was afraid that—"

"Yes, it looks awful, doesn't it?" Beth said.

"What happened? Did that prowler shoot your gas tank?"

"He shot at my car, but the fire was caused by a Molotov cocktail."

Sarah just shook her head in amazement.

Beth looked at Sarah's doctor bag. "Didn't you learn your lesson about being a Good Samaritan?"

"I guess not, at least not when it comes to my friends."

Beth smiled and gave Sarah a quick hug. "I'm glad to have you for a friend, Sarah."

"Same here, and thanks for protecting me from the guy who did this."

They looked at the burning car and Sarah knew it could be her apartment on fire instead. They'd both had a close brush with death tonight. It was something they now had in common—a bond they would always share—like sisters who had stuck together through hard times and had proven they could rely on each other.

Police cars and fire engines arrived on the scene. The firefighters began spraying water on the flames. A man who was standing near Beth and Sarah said, "You two are on the news." He held up his phone.

They looked at the display and saw footage of the burning car. A reporter named Dick Arnold sat behind a desk at his news station and described the scene in a breathless voice. He said that someone in the crowd had used their phone to take a video and upload it to the internet. Sarah's image appeared in the video as she ran up to the car with her doctor's bag in her hand. Dick Arnold said, "It appears to be Sarah Chance, from the Good Samaritan lawsuit. Coming to the rescue at yet another car wreck."

The female cohost said, "After the lawyer that sued her got shot by a poisoned arrow, I doubt if any other lawyers will want to try suing Sarah Chance again."

Sarah didn't smile at that news, but she felt a grim sense of satisfaction in knowing that most of the lawyers in San Francisco might be afraid of her now. Deathly afraid.

A nearby police car radio crackled and the dispatcher said, "All units, be advised ..." The dispatcher went on to say that the suspect from the Moscone Center shooting was believed to be at the hospital.

Sarah said, "Was she talking about the same guy who torched your car?"

"Yes, the shooter might be at the hospital where Katherine Anderson is undergoing some tests. I'd just heard about it from Terrell on the phone."

"Jake tried to warn me about a man who was threatening his family and friends. Is that who was prowling outside of my apartment?"

"That's my guess. He must have thought you were important to Jake. He was probably hoping to take you hostage or injure you in hopes of making Jake stand down and stop interfering with his plans."

Sarah's face went pale. "Jake called me and said I should go to a hotel."

"A hotel is a good idea."

"Where is Jake right now?"

"He's at the hospital, working with the Secret Service agents that got him out of FBI custody."

While Sarah tried to understand what Beth had said about the Secret Service, a black SUV pulled up with police lights flashing from under the front grill. The windows went down and revealed Terrell Hayes in the driver's seat and Cody in the backseat.

"Hop in, Scooter, we're needed at the hospital," Terrell said.

Beth returned the phone she'd borrowed, and then opened the front passenger door of the SUV.

Cody stuck his head out the back seat window and barked at Sarah. She patted him on the head and noted his bandage needed to be changed. Her heart ached to see the loyal dog working when he should be resting at home. "You're not taking Cody into danger, are you? He needs to rest and recuperate."

As Beth was getting into the car, she said, "Go to a hotel, Sarah. Pay cash. Lock the door and stay inside."

Before Beth could close her door, Sarah quickly opened the rear passenger door and got in next to Cody. Terrell turned his head and glared at Sarah. "What are you doing?"

"I'm going with you. Cody's wound needs medical attention and I'm his doctor." Sarah closed the door, and Cody barked once and rubbed his head against her arm.

"You are *not* going, Sarah," Terrell said. "Get out of the car."

"I'm going to change his bandage on the way to the hospital, whether you like it or not."

"I'm sure someone at the hospital can treat his wound. It's a friggin' hospital, right?"

"They don't have veterinary supplies," Sarah said, and she held up her doctor bag for him to see. "It will be more efficient to treat Cody in the car."

"His bandage looks fine to me. I think he'll survive."

"You're not a veterinarian. I am. Besides, Cody obeys me because he thinks I'm a Navy Corpsman who saved his life. Does he obey you, Terrell?"

"No, he doesn't, but you're a civilian, not a cop—you don't belong here."

"Cody is a civilian too. He's not a police dog, and he doesn't belong here either. I have a legally binding power of attorney to be in charge of Cody if Jake isn't available. How about if I just get out of the car right now and take Cody with me to protect his health and well-being?"

"Jake asked me to bring Cody to the hospital, and I don't believe you have any power of attorney."

Sarah reached in the back pocket of her pants and produced the form that Jake had signed, giving her legal rights in the custody, care, and treatment of Cody. "Read it and weep. If you won't let me change his bandages, I'll bring him to the hospital myself, in a taxicab. Let's go, Cody."

Sarah opened the car door and stepped out. Cody followed her and stood on the sidewalk. Terrell glanced at the form and then cursed and muttered something about hard-headed women, and paperwork, and unruly animals, and his career choices. "All right! Get back in the vehicle, both of you."

Sarah and Cody climbed into the car and Terrell floored the gas pedal, making the SUV's engine roar as they raced down the city streets.

Beth smiled at her partner's frustration with female stubbornness. She'd often brought it out in him. He would get over it in due time. She knew that from experience.

"You've got one thing right," Terrell said as he drove the vehicle fast and took corners with tires squealing. "That dog won't listen to a word I say, or do anything I ask him to do. And to think I used to carry extra water on combat patrols so Jake's dog Duke would have plenty to drink. Some gratitude I get from the canine community."

Cody panted Ha-Ha-Ha.

Sarah opened her doctor's bag, removed Cody's dressings, put some salve on the stitched-up wound, and covered it with a fresh bandage.

Beth said, "Why did the Secret Service help Jake get released from FBI custody? I'm guessing Agent McKay had a lot to do with that."

Terrell frowned. "I can't tell you why. The intel is on a need-to-know basis. But I can tell you something about Jake, and you can never repeat it. Understood?"

"Understood," Beth said.

Terrell looked in the rearview mirror at Sarah. "Understood?"

"Understood. I won't repeat what you say, I promise."

As Terrell drove he told Beth and Sarah a few facts about Jake's past. Only the parts he was allowed to tell. He was angry about the current situation his friend was involved in and he made it clear that he felt Jake had done enough, had given enough, and had suffered enough.

Sarah listened in disbelief as Terrell explained that, in a past life Jake had done some very dangerous work for the government. Terrell couldn't elaborate on it, but it was frightening stuff you never saw on the news. Right now, Jake needed his war dog by his side. Cody's nose could find anybody; there was almost no way to hide from him.

Sarah couldn't believe what she was hearing. Her heart was beating fast. She realized that although she'd been wishing for a more interesting and exciting man in her life, it was true what they said—you should be careful what you wish for.

CHAPTER 110

Police Chief Keith Pierce was at home having dinner with his wife Joyce and their two children. His meal was interrupted by a call on his mobile phone from Dr. Lang, the police psychologist. He frowned and let it go to voicemail. Lang called him again before he could even check to see if she'd left a message. Pierce shrugged an apology to Joyce and answered the call.

"Pierce."

"Chief, this is Dr. Lang. I'm sorry to call you at home at this hour, but we may have an emergency on our hands."

"What's the problem ... why is it urgent?"

"It's about Sergeant Denton. I'm afraid she might try to kill someone tonight."

"That's a serious allegation. What in the world would make you say that?" Pierce got up from the dinner table and went into the bedroom, closing the door so his children wouldn't hear the conversation.

"This is confidential doctor-patient information, but I was already preparing a psychological profile of Denton for your review. I'm allowed to share private details with you in a life-or-death situation."

"Get to it, then."

"For some time now, Denton has been in therapy for depression and anxiety. She was showing improvement until recently, when something changed for the worse."

"What changed?"

"Today she admitted that she went to another doctor without telling me she was doing it. She paid for it out of her own pocket so it wouldn't appear on insurance records. When we talked, she scoffed at and criticized the other doctor. He'd told Denton she might have an uncommon mental health issue known as delusional disorder. Including symptoms of both grandiose delusions and persecutory delusions."

"How does that impact her job performance?"

"If the diagnosis is correct, it would mean that Denton is suffering from grandiose delusions of immense self-importance. Along with the paranoid delusions that she's being persecuted as the victim of a conspiracy. If that were the case, I'd have to find her unfit for duty."

"What's the specific emergency tonight?"

"It's related to something else she told me, that she'd been holding back. When Denton was in the Army, she had to constantly deflect the advances of an officer who wanted to sleep with her. He wouldn't take no for an answer and she eventually filed a sexual harassment complaint against him. He retaliated by assigning her to mortuary affairs duty."

"Mortuary duty, as in preparing the deceased to be sent home for burial?"

"Yes, it was a heartbreakingly difficult duty to perform," Dr. Lang said. "One day she went to prepare a body and it was her boyfriend. Denton held him in her arms and saw his lifeless face. His blank eyes staring back at her but not seeing her."

"That's a terrible thing for anyone to go through. I'm sorry for Denton's loss, but how does that relate to the current situation?"

"There's a man here in San Francisco who looks so much like Denton's deceased boyfriend that they could have been brothers. When Denton moved here to the city and saw this similar-looking man, it was hate at first sight. She was furious that he was alive and her boyfriend was dead. She can't stand the sight of his face."

"Furious enough to want to kill him?"

"I didn't think so at first. Denton only told me that she wanted to arrest Jake Wolfe and put him in prison or run him out of town. Just to get him out of her sight. But a few minutes ago, she called me and left a ranting and almost incoherent message on my voicemail. I want you to listen to it."

Lang played the recording with Denton yelling something about how Jake Wolfe had to die or she would never have peace of mind.

Pierce was well aware of Denton's hatred of Wolfe. She went after him like a religious zealot persecuting a heretic. "The way she slurred her words makes me think she might have been drinking tonight," Pierce said.

"I think so too. I warned her not to drink if she was feeling angry, but she just cursed at me and ended the call."

"I'll try to get her on the phone right now."

"I tried calling her back several times before I called you, but she didn't answer."

"You did the right thing telling me about this. I'll try Denton's phone and also try the police radio. If she refuses to answer calls from the chief of police, I may have to put out an all-points bulletin to find her and detain her."

"I tried to warn you about this, Chief. People with delusional disorder are not usually violent, but Denton also has anger management challenges. She's a rare case with unusual circumstances. You should have listened to me. At the moment, I consider her a threat to herself, to her fellow officers, to Jake Wolfe, and to public safety."

"I'll get her partner and several more of our people out there looking for her immediately."

"Please let me know when you find her. She'll need to talk to me. I can help calm her down and prevent her from possibly becoming violent."

"I'll touch base with you in ten minutes," Pierce said. He ended the call with Lang and then tapped his phone to call Denton. His call went to voicemail and he left a message.

"Sergeant Denton, this is Chief of Police Keith Pierce. You are to drop whatever you are doing and report to my office, in person, immediately. Call me and verify that you are on your way. That is an order. If you want to have a job when you wake up in the morning, you need to report to me right now. No excuses will be accepted. Call me the minute you get this message."

Next, he sent a text message to Denton's phone and ordered her to check her voicemail and call him. He then called the police dispatcher. "This is Chief Pierce. Get Sergeant Denton on the radio, right now."

"Yes, sir."

Pierce could hear the woman making the radio call to Denton. There was no reply.

"Sergeant Denton is not answering the radio, sir. Shall I keep trying?"

"Yes, stay on it. I want Denton to stop whatever she's doing and report to me immediately."

"Understood."

"What is the current location of Denton's police vehicle?"

"Tracking data shows that her department vehicle is here in the parking area."

Pierce hung up and called Kirby.

Several miles away, Denton was driving in her personal car. There was a police radio walkie-talkie on the seat beside her. She had one hand on the steering wheel, and held a pistol in the other. "Where are you, Wolfe?" Denton said, waving her pistol at the passing buildings.

Sweat dripped from her feverish forehead. The fresh cuts on her left bicep stung and bled onto her shirtsleeve. Denton's phone repeatedly buzzed with calls, and the walkie-talkie crackled with requests that she should report to the chief of police. She didn't reply. She also heard a report that Sergeant Beth Cushman's car had been torched, and police units were on the way to the hospital in pursuit of the attorney assassin suspect.

"I'll bet Wolfe is there too. He always shows up wherever the assassin does. They must be working together. It's time to remove his face from my life."

Denton pulled over, reached under her seat and took out a portable police light. She set it on the dashboard, pressed the suction cups onto the windshield, and plugged the cord into the power outlet. She sat there for a moment as she took a prescription pill and swallowed it down with a drink from a bottle of gin. She then drove toward the hospital, with the police light flashing, running stoplights on the way.

CHAPTER 111

Jake made a quick search of the hospital's rooftop area, but Zhukov was nowhere to be seen. He headed into one of the stairwells and he heard the sound of footsteps approaching from below. That was probably Easton, but Jake sent him a text to make sure. *I'm above you at the top of the stairs.*

The footsteps stopped, and Jake received a text reply from Easton. *Approaching you now. Hold your fire.*

Easton approached carefully, just in case Jake had been captured and the text was actually from Zhukov, leading him into an ambush.

Jake leaned over the railing for a second to take a peek, and he saw Easton looking up and pointing his MP5 at him. Easton was alone, so Jake stood where he could be seen, making it easier for Easton to approach.

"See anything on the roof?" Easton said.

"Just the wire and the flywheel that Zhukov used to gain entrance to the hospital. I need my dog with me to find his trail. Can the Secret Service send their K9 units to help with the search?"

"Yes, our uniformed division is on the way with two K9 handlers and their dogs."

Jake's phone vibrated, and he answered the call.

"We're here with Cody," Terrell said.

"Take him to the roof. I'll meet you there."

Agent Greene had worked her way up several flights of stairs and was getting closer to the rooftop level. She passed by an oval metal door panel about two feet wide and five feet high marked "Maintenance Access" and stopped to take a look. When she pulled on the handle, the door didn't budge so she took out her key ring and tried a universal passkey. No luck, it didn't fit. As she wondered what to do next, she saw a thread hanging from the bottom of the panel door.

The thread might have been there for a long time. Torn from the clothing of the last maintenance person to enter the panel. But it was her only lead so far, and she reported it on the radio. "I found an access door in the stairwell. It looks like it might have been used recently and . . ."

Greene didn't get a chance to finish what she was saying because the door flew open and hit her forehead, then slammed the side of her head against the concrete wall next to the door, knocking her unconscious.

Zhukov climbed through the panel door and searched Greene to find her radio unit and turn it off, then picked her up and carried her through the panel opening into the access area, closed the door behind him, and turned the lock bar into place.

Jake listened to the intel from Greene, and then she was cut off. There was only a quiet static in his earpiece. He tried calling her phone, but there was no answer.

Jake asked Easton, "Can you access the plans of the hospital building and find out which floor that access panel is on?"

"Affirmative. On my way to Greene's stairwell now."

Easton went down the stairs. A moment later an elevator door opened and Terrell stepped out, followed by Cody and Sarah. Cody ran toward Jake, and when he reached his alpha, he stood on his hind legs, put his paws on Jake's shoulders and licked his face.

"Okay, down boy, good dog. Now get to work. Search, Cody. Search the area."

Cody began sniffing around the rooftop.

Terrell said, "Sarah changed Cody's bandage on the drive. She had a power of attorney form you'd signed."

"Yeah, I signed it."

"Once we arrived, I put a leash on Cody, but he refused to obey me —so I let Sarah bring him to you."

Sarah said, "Long time no see, Jake."

"Thank you for changing Cody's bandage, but it's highly irregular for you to be here. Stay out of the way and do whatever the Secret Service tells you to do."

Before Sarah could reply, Jake walked a short distance away to see where Cody was searching.

Terrell approached Jake and spoke to him in a low voice. "I brought Sarah along against my better judgment. Cody obeys her for some reason."

"It's all good. She's the best at what she does. Gifted, in fact. I'm sure Cody needed a fresh bandage, and he seems to have bonded with her. She can take care of herself in a fight too. She knows martial arts and isn't too bad handling a pistol. But she should probably leave now and go wait in your car."

"You can try telling her that. She's a hard-headed woman. Want me to handcuff her and have the Secret Service take her into protective custody?"

Jake shook his head. "If you or I get injured, we've got a hospital full of doctors to help us, but what if Cody gets hurt? Who will help him?"

"You've got a point there, but Sarah is not a LEO."

Jake pulled out his phone and tapped the display. "Let me get the okay from Easton."

~

Sarah overheard their quiet words. It was nice to feel appreciated by Jake regarding her work with animals. Few people ever seemed to notice or care, but apparently, he thought she was talented and gifted. He believed in her and that meant a lot.

She saw Jake put his phone away and walk toward the next area of the roof where Cody was searching. Jake was carrying some kind of scary-looking assault rifle. Their eyes met as he was passing by her, and she got the impression that he could understand her deepest feelings.

Jake stopped in front of her. "I requested permission for you to be at the hospital in case Cody needs your care. I got a tentative okay, but you're required to stay back at a safe distance."

"Okay, I will. Thank you.

Sarah looked into Jake's eyes and saw something she'd never seen before. She thought it might be the ancient dark look of the warrior, passed down through history and generations of fighters. Those eyes sought justice, battle, and blood—and they would not be denied. She got the feeling that this man had probably done bad things, maybe incredibly violent things, but only for the greater good and to protect the innocent from the predators.

Sarah felt torn—her head told her to go downstairs to the safety of the police vehicle. But her heart ached when she saw Cody working when he was injured.

"Jake, I've taken the veterinarian's oath: *I solemnly swear to use my skills for the protection of animal health and welfare, and the prevention and relief of animal suffering*. If Cody were to suffer a life-threatening medical emergency while I was sitting around in a car, I'd never forgive myself."

"I understand. Just be sure to stay back at a safe distance. There could be gunfire at any moment." Jake turned and called out a command to Cody. They both walked toward the edge of the roof.

Sarah watched Jake walk purposefully while carrying the automatic weapon. He was wearing a black Kevlar vest and a gun belt that held a pistol in a holster and several extra mag pouches. There was some kind of large sheath knife strapped horizontally across the back of his waist. He moved with the deliberate grace and stealth of an animal on the hunt.

This was a different and far more dangerous side of Jake's personality than what Sarah had seen so far. It was frightening. She was glad Jake was on the right side of the law.

CHAPTER 112

Jake and Cody stopped in front of the wheel and cable that Zhukov had used to fly between buildings. Jake gave Cody a command. Cody sniffed the handle grips on the flywheel again, then growled and showed his teeth.

"Where's the target, Cody?" Jake said. He spoke in a low voice he'd used many times in bloody battlefields far from home. "Seek, Cody. Seek, seek, seek."

Cody sniffed the scent trail and followed it to a stairwell. Jake opened the door, and Cody took off down the stairs. Jake and Terrell were right behind him. Sarah waited behind, thought about Cody and his wound, and then quietly followed.

Cody went down several flights of stairs and stopped. Jake opened a door and Cody began to sniff along a hallway. Two Secret Service agents stood in the hall; they had photos of Jake on their phones and were expecting him.

A female agent spoke up. "Mr. Wolfe, pardon the intrusion but I want to check to make sure you aren't the assassin wearing a facial disguise."

Jake nodded. "Understood. Make it quick."

She felt along the underside of his chin, pinched his cheeks and pulled his hair. "Sorry about that."

"No problem. It was an intelligent move on your part, but tell your fellow agents my dog would never follow and obey the killer. He knows my scent and my voice. If you see me with Cody, you can rest assured I'm the real Jake Wolfe." He turned and opened the door to another stairwell and went down the steps.

Cody raised his head high, sniffing a scent cone, and then down low.

Jake tapped his phone and called Easton. "We're heading down the stairwell that Greene was searching. My dog is following the target's scent trail."

"I'm in the same stairwell right now, climbing up toward you," Easton said. "Greene isn't answering her phone."

Cody arrived at the ninth floor and stopped in front of an oval metal panel door in the wall. A sign on the door said "Maintenance Access." Jake stood off to the side and tried the handle, but it was locked.

Jake held his assault rifle with both hands, raised it up above his head and then slammed the butt end down against the door handle.

A shot rang out from the other side of the door, and a hole appeared in the metal. A bullet ricocheted down the stairwell, pinging off several concrete walls.

Jake spoke into his wrist microphone. "This is Jake Wolfe reporting shots fired. Ninth-floor East stairwell. The target is in the maintenance access area." He wanted Zhukov to hear him on the radio, to make the man sweat. He hit the door handle with his rifle again, and this time the thin metal door banged open. He stood out of the way and waited for a bullet that never came.

They heard quiet footsteps; someone was approaching them on the stairs. Terrell held his weapon up and ready to fire. Then he lowered it, relaxed his stance and said, "Sarah, you're pushing your luck."

"I was keeping my distance, just as you told me to. I didn't know you were going to stop here."

Jake shook his head when he saw that Sarah had followed them. He didn't approve, but it gave him an idea. "Do you have a compact or a mirror of some kind?"

"Yes, I've got one here in my bag," Sarah said. She dug into the bag and tossed him a medical mirror on an aluminum stick. It was similar to the kind that dentists used but slightly larger.

Terrell stood off to the side and pointed his pistol at the open panel door. Jake turned to say "Cover me," but Terrell was already doing it. Jake pulled on the telescoping handle to lengthen it, held it out away from him in his left hand and used it to look through the open doorway. There were machines and ducts that went off in all directions. The ducts looked like large, square aluminum, sheet-metal pipes. There was also a scaffolding walkway leading away from the panel, with wooden planks about two feet wide.

Greene was lying unconscious on the walkway and Zhukov was right there, about to go around a corner behind a metal duct. As Zhukov turned, he fired an expert shot that blew the small mirror out of Jake's hand. The bullet ricocheted down the stairwell like the one before.

"Nice shot. At least it wasn't a hand grenade," Jake said. "Hopefully, that ricochet won't hit Easton. I'm going in after this guy. Greene is lying down on the other side of this door. She appears to be unconscious but alive. We need a nurse to take her to the ER."

"I'll carry Greene to the next floor and hand her off to a nurse," Terrell said.

"Roger that. Find out where this access area leads to. You can try to catch the target by surprise wherever he comes out."

"Affirmative."

"Sarah, you're in charge of Cody. Go meet up with Beth on Katherine Anderson's floor so Cody can patrol the hallways. Cody's nose can pick up Zhukov's scent before anybody else sees him coming."

Cody barked twice in protest and used his teeth to pull on the bottom of Jake's pant leg near his ankle.

Sarah crossed her arms. "You're just sending me to Anderson's floor because it's the most protected area of the building."

"It's also the most dangerous area, because that's where the killer is going," Jake said. "This isn't a debate. Terrell, can you let Easton know my orders concerning Sarah and Cody? If she doesn't follow orders, she's to be detained in Secret Service custody."

"Good to go … and if she's detained, how am I going to get Cody to obey me?" Terrell said.

Jake nodded and turned to his dog. "Cody, you are to follow

Terrell's commands, just like you would mine. That's an order. Do you understand?"

Cody barked once. Jake turned and went through the panel door.

Terrell immediately tested Cody's obedience to his commands. "Cody, come here. Heel."

Cody went to Terrell and stood right next to him.

"Sit," Terrell said.

Cody sat.

"Good dog."

Sarah asked Terrell, "Has Jake lost his mind, or overdosed on testosterone?"

Terrell noted the interplay of emotions between Jake and Sarah. He shook his head at Jake's ever-changing love life. "That's our boy Jake. He does this kind of thing. Nobody understands why. Not even him."

Terrell took out his phone and called Beth.

"Cushman."

"It's Terrell. The shooter might be planning to approach your location via an access panel or large air vent. Do you see either of those in the hallway near Katherine's room?"

"Let me look."

Terrell stood and listened to the sound of footsteps on linoleum.

Moments later, Beth said, "Yes, there's some kind of vent in the ceiling of the hallway. I'd say it measures about two feet by two feet square."

"Zhukov is making his way through the maintenance access areas. He could try to drop in on you through the ceiling."

"Understood. I'll talk to the agents."

Easton reached Terrell's position then. He was breathing deeply from jogging up and down various flights of stairs, but looked like he could climb many more. He held up his phone and projected a blueprint of the hospital building onto the wall. Moving his finger over the phone's screen, he zoomed in and moved the image around. A section marked "Access Areas" showed the layout of various areas, panels, machines, and the ducting system.

"It's a maze, but we know where he wants to end up. We could go to Anderson's floor and send one person up into the access area that runs above the ceiling. The Secret Service will also move Katherine to a different room."

Terrell nodded. "Good idea. Jake ordered Sarah to take Cody down to Katherine Anderson's floor so the dog can offer added protection."

Easton sent a quick text message to Agent McKay. "McKay said she'll allow it."

Terrell pointed at the access door. "Greene is on the other side of that panel. She's unconscious and needs medical attention. I'll take care of her."

"Roger that." Easton tapped his phone and held the display toward Sarah.

Sarah gazed at the video link of a woman in a dark business suit, sitting at a desk. On the wall behind her was the blue presidential seal. Next to the seal was an American flag. The woman spoke in a commanding tone of voice.

"Sarah Chance, this is Secret Service Agent Shannon McKay. You have no business being there, but it's an unusual situation and you've been ordered by Jake Wolfe to escort his military dog to Katherine Anderson's room. Are you willing and able to carry out these orders, or should Agent Easton handcuff you now and have you detained for your own safety? You have five seconds to make your decision or Easton will make it for you."

Easton took out a pair of metal handcuffs and stared at Sarah.

She looked at the handcuffs and accepted the facts of the situation. "Yes, I'll follow orders and help in any way I can."

Easton nodded, turned on his heel and took off down the stairs while talking to Agent McKay on his phone. Terrell climbed through the access panel and went down on one knee next to Greene. He saw her federal agent ball cap on the floorboards, put it in his back pocket, then picked her up in a fireman's carry and carefully squeezed himself back through the access panel into the stairwell.

Terrell carried Greene to the nearest floor and Sarah opened the door and held it open for him. A nurse saw Terrell carrying Greene down the hallway, and she grabbed a gurney and pushed it toward him. Two Secret Service agents made sure his face matched up with the copy of his ID they had on their phones.

"Put her down on this gurney," the nurse said. "Gently, now, that's good. Briefly tell me what happened. I see the injury on her forehead. What else do you know about her condition?"

"She's a federal agent who was struck on the head by a criminal," Terrell said.

The nurse frowned and checked Greene's eyes, shining a small penlight at her and studying her pupils. "I'll take her to the ER. Hopefully, she's only been knocked unconscious and there's no permanent damage."

"She has ID on her. Is there anything more we can do?" Terrell said.

"No, we'll take it from here." The nurse began to call out instructions to her team.

One of the Secret Service agents took a picture of Greene and sent it to Agent McKay. Terrell spoke to him. "We're taking the dog to search Katherine Anderson's floor. Can you take pictures of these two and distribute them?"

The agent nodded and took a phone pic of Sarah and Cody.

Terrell pulled out Greene's ball cap from his back pocket and held it up in front of Sarah so she could see the words "Federal Agent." He put the cap on her head. "Keep that hat on so you don't get arrested or shot by accident. If anybody has questions for you, just tell them to talk to Agent McKay. Now follow along with Cody as he does the search."

"We're ready. Let's go, Cody," Sarah said. She followed Terrell with Cody trotting by her side.

CHAPTER 113

Jake went through the access panel door and ran along the wooden plank in the direction he'd seen Zhukov go. When Jake reached the end of the walkway, he took a quick look around the corner of a large metal vent duct and saw Zhukov raise his weapon. He immediately jerked his head back a moment before a bullet hit the duct.

Jake got down on his stomach and peeked around the corner again with his MP5 pointed down the corridor. Zhukov saw him and fired off a wild shot as he ran, but the shot went high. Jake fired a burst of rounds that landed near Zhukov … one round hit him on the back of his right shoulder.

Zhukov was wearing a bulletproof vest, but the impact spun him around and knocked him down. Jake fired several more rounds in the direction of the prone man, but Zhukov had rolled out of sight and taken shelter behind a horizontal support beam.

There was a quiet pause and Jake ducked back around the corner in case Zhukov was taking aim at him. After Jake moved, several bullets struck the wood plank floor where his head and arms had been moments before. Jake stood up and held the MP5 high up near his head, then stuck the weapon around the corner and fired a quick burst blindly in the general direction of his target.

Zhukov was waiting in ambush, and he fired a well-aimed round from his weapon that hit Jake's MP5 and knocked it out of his hands, sending it flying over the scaffolding and down into the open shaft below. Jake cursed and shook his fingers from the sting of the shock. He felt his heartbeat rising as he drew his SIG pistol and checked that it was loaded.

Zhukov called out, "Wolfe, you're going to die tonight, and it's such a pity. I think you and I may be alike in many ways. We might have been friends under different circumstances."

"We're nothing alike."

"Don't fool yourself. You want to kill me, and you would enjoy doing it."

"Why don't you come at me right now and find out? Unless you're afraid. That's it, isn't it? You're a coward who only shoots unsuspecting civilians."

"Your crude attempts at making me angry are not working," Zhukov said. And yet the man fired a bullet in anger and hit the duct near Jake. After that there was silence, and Jake wondered if Zhukov was coming toward him right now in a sneak attack, or moving toward Katherine, or waiting in ambush for Jake to show himself.

Jake glanced around and saw a long chain hanging from a beam above him, one of many chains holding up the scaffold he was standing on. A crazy idea occurred to him, and he had enough adrenaline coursing through his veins to try it. Hopefully, if only one chain was removed, it wouldn't cause the scaffold to fall and take him down with it. He got a chain unlatched and he tested his weight on it. It seemed to be anchored with plenty of strength to hold his weight and more.

He stuck the pistol in his holster, grabbed the chain with both hands, and moved back a ways on the plank walkway, pulling the chain with him until it was played out. He looked down at the long fall into the empty shaft below him and then quickly looked away as he climbed over the railing of the scaffold. He wrapped the chain around his left leg, gripped it in both hands, and jumped out into the void.

The chain anchor on the beam far above Jake groaned as he flew through the air in a wide arc toward a far-off scaffold. His estimate of the distance was only a guess. If he fell short, he'd be left hanging in the air, at the mercy of his enemy. While Jake was airborne, he kept a grip on the chain with his left hand and both legs and used his right hand to draw his pistol and hold it out in front of him. He got a brief glimpse of Zhukov as he swung past a space between air ducts.

"Hey, cupcake!" Jake said. He fired rounds at Zhukov, striking metal ducts near him as he tried for a headshot.

The surprised look on Zhukov's face was amusing, and Jake laughed out loud, taunting Zhukov as he emptied the entire magazine from his pistol.

Zhukov took cover and fired off bursts from his automatic weapon but he was too late. Jake had flown past the opening and out of sight.

The momentum of Jake's swing took him to the far end of the scaffold and over the railing. He almost kept on going past it, but he used his foot to hook the metal railing's top bar as he passed. The impact on his foot felt as if someone had clubbed him with a metal pipe. It stopped his forward progress, and he was able to drop to the wooden plank below him. He stumbled, let go of the chain, and grabbed onto the railing to keep from falling. The chain rattled against the rail and flew back to where it had come from before he could grab ahold of it and tie it off.

A long horizontal duct stood between the two wooden plank walkways, blocking Jake's view of Zhukov. Jake reloaded his pistol with a full mag and ran down the plank, parallel to his enemy. His foot throbbed with pain as he ran, and he cursed at himself. "You just had to laugh it up and miss the shot, didn't you?"

Jake reached the end of the walkway and the duct and came around the corner with his pistol up, intending to go for the kill shot. Instead, he saw another panel door that was hanging open, and there was a smear of blood on the wall. "Got you," Jake said, and he ran toward the door.

As Jake ran, he felt a weird sense of danger to his left. He stopped and ducked, reversing direction as fast as he could. At that moment, an automatic weapon fired several bursts, and the panel door was shot full of holes.

Jake took cover and heard a clanging sound. He risked a quick look and saw Zhukov crawling through an access opening, into a large duct that went downward at an angle like a giant-sized playground slide. Zhukov fired his weapon in Jake's direction, and Jake stepped back behind cover.

The angled duct creaked and swayed, and Jake knew that Zhukov was going for a slide down the tube. He ran to the duct hoping to fire a shot at the escaping killer, but he was too late. Zhukov was out of sight, and only a smear of blood remained. Jake stepped back and methodically fired rounds into the lower part of the shaft. He started at the far end and worked his way backward.

After a moment, there was no movement from the shaft at all. Jake considered following Zhukov down the slide, but when he reached the bottom he'd be a sitting duck to be picked off with a head shot. Jake ran down the wooden plank walkway back to the panel door, stepped into the stairwell and called Terrell on his phone. "The shooter slid down a large duct. He may go into a crawlspace and try to drop out of the ceiling into Katherine's floor. I'm on my way down the stairs now."

"Roger that, I'll tell the agents," Terrell said.

Jake holstered his pistol and ran down the stairs, but was stopped by a Secret Service agent guarding the door to the seventh floor. "Hands above your head, don't move."

Jake raised his hands. "Listen to me. My name is Jake Wolfe. I'm working with you guys. See my spiffy jacket? The shooter is here on this floor, right now."

The agent's phone buzzed and he answered it. "Yes, Agent McKay. Yes, he's here. One moment."

The agent handed his phone to Jake. His body language indicated that he was not pleased about it.

Jake put the phone to his ear and said, "McKay, the target slid down a duct to the seventh floor. He might be in a crawlspace right now. If so, he could drop out of the ceiling."

"Officer Hayes brought it to our attention. I'm going to make an announcement on the radio, designed to confuse the shooter."

Jake touched a hand to his borrowed Secret Service earpiece and heard McKay's announcement. "This is Agent McKay. The target is in a duct or crawlspace above the seventh floor. We've moved our protectee away from the area and have cleared the eighth floor. Fire at will into the ceiling at any sound or movement detected."

Jake handed the agent's phone back to him. A moment later, Jake's throwaway phone vibrated. He answered it and Terrell said, "Someone is stealing my SUV. My car alarm is set up to call me when it goes off. I keep turning the car engine off remotely with my phone, but someone keeps turning it back on again."

"It has to be Zhukov," Jake said. "Who else would steal a police car in a building that's surrounded by police? I'm heading to the garage."

Jake got into an elevator and rode it downwards while calling Easton on his phone to let him know about the situation. Jake arrived at the basement parking level, exited the elevator and heard the police SUV's car alarm going on and off. He held his pistol up in front of him and ran toward the vehicle.

Moments later, Zhukov was finally able to override the alarm system in the SUV and keep the engine running. He drove fast toward the garage exit with the police lights flashing.

Jake saw Zhukov escaping and fired several rounds at the police vehicle as it roared away. Bullet holes appeared in the driver's door, and two starbursts appeared on the driver's window, but the car kept on going. Jake cursed as he remembered that Terrell's SUV had the armored upgrade to make it bulletproof.

Easton came running toward the armored black Chevy Suburban that they'd arrived in. Jake ran up to the vehicle at the same time. Easton got into the driver's seat as Jake jumped into the passenger side. The Suburban took off with a squeal of tires in pursuit of the fleeing Ford police interceptor. Jake put his window down so he could lean out and fire his pistol at Zhukov.

When Zhukov reached the exit, he didn't slow down. He held his hand out the window and flashed the badge he'd taken from the Secret Service agent on the roof. The badge and the police car made the cops and agents at the exit hesitate a moment. That was all Zhukov needed to maintain the element of surprise. He turned on the siren and then yelled orders over the vehicle's loudspeaker.

"I'm acting on orders from Agent McKay. Get out of the way. It's an emergency."

Zhukov glanced in his rearview mirror and saw a black Suburban approaching behind him. He punched the gas and drove straight toward the officers that were standing in front of the red-and-white-striped barrier arm.

Agent Greene came out of an elevator into the garage. She had a bruised bump on her forehead and fury in her eyes. Easton pulled up and stopped the SUV next to Greene for five seconds, and she jumped into the backseat. Easton drove off again with a roar of the engine before Greene even had a chance to close the door. He pressed a button and spoke over a loudspeaker. "This is Agent Easton. Stop that stolen police vehicle. Ivan Zhukov is driving it."

The two police officers who were standing in front of the exit had to jump out of the way to avoid being run over by Zhukov's vehicle. The stolen police car crashed through the barrier arm and then drove into the street. A rookie officer tried to pull his police car in front of Zhukov's SUV but missed by a few seconds. He blocked the following Suburban instead. Easton rammed the rookie's car hard, and the Suburban's reinforced bumpers pushed the car aside. Easton gunned the engine and roared down the street in pursuit of Zhukov.

Above them on the rooftop of the hospital, an FBI helicopter was coming in for a landing on the emergency medical helipad. The FBI pilot saw the two cars racing from the scene. He turned up the volume on the police scanner and heard what was going on. "The fugitive is in one of those vehicles," the pilot said.

FBI Special Agent Reynolds grabbed her assault rifle and said, "Let's get him."

The pilot took off after the two fleeing SUVs and shined a spotlight down on the street behind the vehicles as he flew the helicopter between tall buildings.

Reynolds put on a harness with a safety strap, opened the side door of the helicopter, and leaned out. She took aim at the closest vehicle, not knowing that Agent Easton was behind the wheel.

CHAPTER 114

Terrell decided that since Jake was heading to the garage, he'd go down an elevator to the hospital's front door and cut off Zhukov's escape route from outside of the garage exit. He saw Beth going out the door with Sarah and Cody following behind her. He then saw his own police vehicle drive past on the street, with a black Suburban in pursuit. A helicopter flew overhead and followed after the two cars.

Terrell pressed his key fob and attempted to turn off the engine of his vehicle, but the car raced away. He cursed and then spoke to Beth. "We need a vehicle. That was my car that just went by."

Beth nodded. "We're going to have to borrow one."

They headed toward a long row of police vehicles that were parked all along the sidewalk. At that moment, a black-and-white police car pulled to the curb and stopped. The uniformed cop in the driver's seat had his window down and Beth recognized him. "Wilson, where have you been? Everybody is going into the garage, and they're asking where you are."

Wilson looked at Beth in surprise. "They treat me like a mushroom. Just keep me in the dark and feed me BS." He got out of the car and took off running for the garage.

Beth smiled when she saw that Wilson had left the keys in the ignition after she'd distracted him. She got into the driver's seat. "Get in, let's move."

Terrell got into the front passenger seat, and Sarah opened a back door so Cody could jump in. She got in beside him and hoped Terrell wouldn't object. Beth hit the gas and drove fast in pursuit of the two other vehicles. Terrell reached over and turned on the lights and siren. He then looked at his phone display and called the throwaway phone Jake had used earlier.

Jake answered the call. "Grinds, we're in pursuit of your stolen vehicle. Zhukov is driving it."

"Yeah, time for plan B. We're coming up fast on your six in a black-and-white, and we're bringing Cody with us. Now I'm going to call it in to HQ."

"Roger that."

Easton drove aggressively as cars on the street ahead pulled over and out of the way of the two police vehicles. He brought the Suburban closer to the fleeing car and rammed into the vehicle's back bumper. The stolen police car took a sudden hard right turn, drove one block, and then took a left. Jake fired off a shot and hit the right rear tire of the car, but the vehicle had run-flat tires, and it didn't even slow down.

Easton wrestled with the steering wheel of the Suburban as Zhukov drove around the block and back onto the same street he'd been on before. Easton was able to keep Zhukov in sight, but he lost some ground and now trailed behind the lead vehicle. When he turned back onto the road they'd originally been on, Zhukov fired several rounds at his windshield, but they ricocheted off the bulletproof glass.

Jake wanted to take another shot at Zhukov, but there were just too many people in cars, and on the sidewalks, that could get hit by a ricochet.

The helicopter appeared overhead and shone a spotlight down at the rear vehicle, then switched to the front vehicle. When the light was not shining at Jake, he leaned out the car window and looked up and saw the large markings on the bottom of the helicopter. "That's an FBI bird above us."

"They probably don't know which car Zhukov is driving," Greene said.

"Easton, give me your phone," Jake said.

Easton handed it over.

Jake called Agent Knight, knowing he was probably at home watching TV with his family.

"Knight."

"This is Jake Wolfe. I'm with Agent Easton and we have an emergency situation. We're in a car chasing after the attorney assassin. Your FBI helicopter is flying overhead in pursuit. Can you get in touch with your crew and have one of the agents call Easton's phone? I have information they need, and they might try to shoot our vehicle by mistake."

"Copy." Knight ended the call.

Moments later, Easton's phone buzzed. Jake put the phone on speaker and thumbed the icon to answer the call. Easton said, "Agent Easton here."

A female voice said, "This is Reynolds. What's going on, Easton?" The noise of the helicopter rotor blades could be heard in the background of her call.

Jake said, "We're below you in the black Suburban, in pursuit of the stolen Ford police interceptor. The attorney assassin is alone in the lead vehicle. Take a shot at him when you feel it's safe from the risk of collateral damage."

"I can't fire at a police vehicle. Are you crazy?" Reynolds said. "Your voice sounds familiar. Is this Jake Wolfe I'm talking to? What the hell!"

"Yes, this is Jake. Think about it, Reynolds. I'm with Easton. You saw him gain my release from the FBI. Shoot the driver of the lead vehicle as soon as you can take a clean shot. The car has been armored, so you'll want to aim for the pillar between the driver's window and the passenger window behind him."

Reynolds cursed. "Wolfe, if you've lied to me about this, I'll put you in prison and throw away the key."

Jake looked at the car's GPS. "Easton, I think Zhukov may be heading for Pier 39. They have a three-hundred-slip marina. He could steal a boat and escape on the water."

Easton tapped the screen on the dashboard. It displayed an image of Agent McKay.

"McKay, Wolfe believes the target is heading toward Pier 39. Possibly to escape on a boat."

"Understood. I'll inform the SFPD Marine patrol to intercept on the water if necessary."

"The FBI has a helicopter overhead right now with Agent Reynolds on board. She can try to take out Zhukov."

"Good work. We definitely appreciate an assist from an FBI sharpshooter."

"Did you hear that, Reynolds?" Jake said.

"I heard it, we're on it," Reynolds said. "This helicopter has heat-seeking technology. It shows one human form heat signature in the driver's seat of the police SUV."

Reynolds lined up a shot at the driver of the police SUV and began firing her weapon.

Her first shot hit the driver's door window and ricocheted off the bulletproof glass. Her second shot hit the roof and failed to penetrate the armor. Her third shot hit the left front tire, but the run-flat tire kept on rolling. She took careful aim and lined up a shot at the pillar next to the driver's window.

Beth Cushman drove the borrowed police car as fast as she could push it as she tried to catch up to the two fleeing SUVs. Terrell's phone buzzed with a call from Jake.

"We think Zhukov is heading toward Pier 39."

"I'll call it in to HQ," Terrell said.

Terrell picked up the police car's radio mic and asked dispatch to send units to Pier 39 and get the police boats on the way there as well.

Beth took a shortcut that she hoped might get her to the pier faster. With her siren wailing and her lights flashing, she roared down a side street and expertly handled the vehicle as she drifted through intersections. Terrell used his remote to turn all of the stoplights green along the way.

Up ahead of them, Beth saw some people who appeared to be inebriated and loitering in the middle of the street, having an impromptu party. Beth got on her loudspeakers and yelled, "I can't stop. No brakes. Run for your lives."

The drunken people scattered in all directions, and Beth drove through the intersection while laughing over the loudspeaker.

Terrell said, "What if someone calls that in?"

"This isn't my car, what do I care?" Beth said.

"That's just wrong," Terrell said, but he laughed.

When Beth got closer to the pier, she saw a civilian vehicle ahead of her with a front-facing police light flashing on its dashboard. Beth stepped on the gas pedal to catch up. "Do you recognize that car up ahead? It looks similar to Denton's car."

Terrell got on the radio to dispatch again. "What kind of personal car is Sergeant Denton driving lately? Didn't she get a new one?"

"Denton recently bought a dark blue Mustang," the dispatcher said, and she recited the license plate.

"Tell the chief I think I see Denton's vehicle heading toward Pier 39."

"I'll report that to the chief right now."

A large truck pulled across the road and began slowly backing up to a loading dock, blocking Beth's progress for a moment. She lost sight of the Mustang and turned on the siren while Terrell yelled at the truck driver on the car speakers. The driver stopped backing up and instead drove across the street into a different loading area, clearing the road. Beth waved her thanks to the driver and roared off to catch up with the Mustang.

Zhukov heard several rounds ricochet off his vehicle. Next, a front wheel suddenly pulled to the left, and he almost crashed. He wrestled with the wheel and got the car driving straight again. Then a round hit the pillar behind his left shoulder. The bullet got through and went past his ear and into the dashboard. He cursed and started weaving to avoid another pillar shot.

He was almost to Pier 39 when the helicopter showed up in front of his vehicle. It hovered and turned sideways so the open door was facing his vehicle. A woman aimed a rifle at him and sprayed his windshield with a barrage of automatic weapons fire. The polycarbonate/glass windshield was soon covered with cracks, pockmarks, and white starbursts that blocked his view. He could just barely see out of an undamaged spot in the upper left corner of the windshield and was almost driving blind when he arrived at Pier 39 and drove up over the sidewalk and onto the lawn in front of the boat slips. He exited the car, put on his backpack, and ran toward the boats.

The helicopter appeared above him and a commanding voice spoke on the loudspeaker. "This is the FBI. Stop and put your hands over your head or we'll shoot to kill."

Zhukov drew his pistol, fired at the helicopter and continued running. Bullets started to rip into the grass alongside him as he ran. He zigzagged and veered away. The gunfire caused groups of tourists to scream and run like stampeding cattle. The helicopter stopped firing for a moment as the panicked civilians crisscrossed the area.

Zhukov reached the boat slips and saw all kinds of vessels. One small cabin cruiser had its twin outboard engines idling as the people on board were preparing to depart. He ran toward the boat.

CHAPTER 115

Easton arrived at Pier 39, parked the Suburban near the stolen police SUV and reported the situation to McKay. Jake got out and took off sprinting as fast as he could. Greene rushed to catch up with Jake, and Easton ended the call with McKay and followed them.

Moments later, Beth and Terrell arrived. He saw the two SUVs there, empty and parked on the lawn. He looked at his police SUV's shot-up windshield and shook his head. "Well, at least I know the bulletproof windshield works as advertised."

A police radio crackled from a vehicle parked off to the right. Beth ran to the car and made a positive ID of Denton's license plate.

Cody ran off and began following the scent trails of Jake and Zhukov. Sarah ran after him and stayed close as he worked.

Beth looked in the car's open window and saw a police walkie-talkie and a bottle of gin on the passenger seat. There was also a bottle of prescription meds and a folded piece of paper. She checked the meds and the paper and was surprised by what she saw. She hated to do this, but she had no choice. She called the chief, and he answered immediately.

"Chief Pierce here. What do you have, Cushman?"

"I found Denton's vehicle. She's here at Pier 39. There's an open container of alcohol in her car and a bottle of medicine."

"What kind of drug is it?"

"It's a psychiatric drug, but it wasn't prescribed by our police psychiatrist. There's a paper with it, listing all kinds of potentially dangerous side effects. I believe she's suffering from a lot of these. It explains her changes in behavior. The anger, paranoia, and constant pacing."

"I'm giving you an order to find her and detain her. Use a Taser and put handcuffs on her if you have to. It's for her own good."

"Yes, sir. If those are your orders, I'll follow them."

"Denton is probably a good cop, but right now she's having an emotional breakdown. We can't allow that to happen. We need to prevent her from harming herself or anyone else, or causing a media nightmare for the police department."

"Understood." Beth took off running toward another walkway to her right that Denton had probably taken down to the boat slips. Hopefully, if she ran fast enough, she might come up behind Denton and stun her with a Taser. Beth looked at Terrell and saw that he was already moving toward the other entrance to the boat slips. They gave each other hand signals and then ran even faster.

Zhukov sprinted down the wooden dock and climbed onboard the boat that had its engines running. He punched a man who tried to stop him, knocking him into the water. Another man and a woman came charging toward Zhukov, but he fired a shot into the air and yelled at them to abandon ship. The woman was smart and leapt onto the dock, but the man grabbed a speargun and pointed it at the intruder. Zhukov shot him in the arm. The man dropped the speargun and cried out in shock. As he tried to get off the boat, he stumbled and fell into the water.

"Untie those lines," Zhukov said to the woman and pointed his weapon at her.

She hesitated, paralyzed with fear, so he fired a shot into the wooden dock between her feet. She dropped to her knees and began to quickly untie the lines. For a moment, Zhukov was tempted to take the woman as a hostage, but he decided she would just slow him down.

The woman understood the look that passed across Zhukov's face as he thought about kidnapping her, and she vomited into the water in primal fear.

Zhukov thought she reminded him of a nice neighbor he'd had in Brighton Beach, Brooklyn. He'd always liked that woman. "Lie facedown on the dock with your hands on the back of your head. There's going to be gunfire here, but if you stay down and don't move, you'll probably survive."

The astonished woman went prone on the dock and placed her hands as instructed.

Zhukov worked the boat's controls, making the twin engines roar, and took off toward the Bay. He ignored the no-wake zone signs, and made waves that rocked many of the other boats, causing a chorus of shouted complaints from people on neighboring vessels.

Jake ran up to the boat slips and saw Zhukov at the helm of a fast-moving cabin cruiser. He fired off several rounds at the boat.

Zhukov heard the gunfire behind him and ducked as a bullet zinged through his windshield. He turned and saw Jake, then fired his weapon as he yelled, "Since when did photojournalists become vigilantes?"

"Welcome to America," Jake said and returned fire.

Jake took cover behind a large wooden storage box as several rounds splintered the wood behind his head. He scanned the nearby boats for one that could catch up with the escaping vessel. A sport cruiser with an open cockpit was docking at the guest boat area and he ran to the boat and jumped on board before the surprised man had even brought the boat to a complete stop. Jake showed the man his pistol and his U.S. Marshals badge.

"I'm commandeering your vessel. You'll be compensated by the U.S. Marshals Service. Get off the boat right now or go to jail. *Move.*"

The man looked at the pistol and badge and quickly jumped onto the dock. Jake took the helm, maneuvered the boat out of the slip, and turned the vessel toward open water. He was about to increase speed when Sergeant Denton came running down the dock and yelled, "Wolfe!"

Jake reflexively turned his head in response to hearing his name, and Denton shot at him several times. One of the rounds grazed Jake's side, above his hip. His Kevlar vest deflected the bullet, but the impact spun him sideways onto the controls. His shoulder flattened the throttles against the dash, causing the boat to roar ahead at full speed with nobody steering it.

Denton took aim again, resting her right hand on her bleeding left bicep with the self-inflicted cuts as she lined up a head shot. But before she could fire off a round, Agent Greene appeared out of the dark and said, "Federal agent, drop your weapon!"

Denton ignored Greene and shot at Jake, missing him as his borrowed boat rocketed across the water at full throttle. Greene was about to fire her weapon at Denton, but then she saw the SFPD badge on her belt. Greene holstered her pistol and tackled Denton instead, slamming her onto the wooden dock and knocking her pistol out of her hand. Denton began wrestling and punching and kicking at Greene.

Greene fought hard, but Denton was under the influence of meds and alcohol and anger. She elbowed Greene in the ribs, grabbed a fistful of her hair and then punched her as hard as she could on the injured spot on her forehead. Greene saw stars and ducked her head to the side to protect her injury. She threw several brutal jabs to Denton's face, using the tactile feedback of her striking fists to find the vulnerable area around the eyes and nose.

Denton was feeling numb and highly agitated, so she shook it off. She was getting to her knees to attack again when Greene used her faster reactions to stand up quickly and kick Denton so hard in the stomach that it knocked the wind out of her. Denton doubled over and grunted in pain, but she swept her arm behind Greene's ankles, knocking her onto her back.

Greene hit the dock and saw Denton leap at her with a raised fist, but she used her position of being flat on her back as an advantage. She bent both legs at the knee and kicked her feet up hard, sending Denton flying right over her and into the water.

Denton landed in the water with a splash, thrashed around, and came back to the surface. She started to climb back onto the dock, cursing at Greene as she did.

Greene stood up, drew her pistol and pointed it at Denton's face. "U.S. Secret Service. You're under arrest for assault with a deadly weapon and interfering with a federal investigation."

"You're the one who is going to be under arrest after I get done beating the hell out of you," Denton said, and she continued to climb onto the dock.

"Don't test me, I *will* shoot you."

Denton got onto the dock, stood up and balled her hands into fists, tensing her legs for an attack. Greene fired a round into the dock in front of Denton. "The next one goes in your chest, and I won't lose any sleep over it."

"I'm a police officer, you cow."

"Then you should know better. You're under arrest. Lie down and put your hands on the back of your head."

"Shut up, you can't arrest me. I'm an official, I'm important, and I'm well protected."

"Then we'll send you to an official, important, and well-protected prison. Now lie down or I'll put a bullet in you. I'm in the mood to do it, so go ahead and give me a reason to shoot you."

"You're going to be sorry for this."

"Not as sorry as you. Now do it!" Greene fired another round into the dock close to Denton's foot and then pointed the pistol at her face.

Easton arrived at that moment. He didn't say anything. He just aimed the red laser sight of his pistol at Denton's chest and gave her his stone-cold stare that said "I'll kill you" in every language on earth.

Denton spat at Greene and then slowly dropped to her knees and went facedown on the dock. Easton stood where Denton could see him, aiming his pistol at her while Greene handcuffed her. Denton's left bicep was bleeding freely now, after the bandage had been soaked in the water of the Bay.

Denton's partner, Kirby, ran up to the scene. Easton trained the red laser sight on his heart to show him where the bullet would enter his body if he moved an inch.

Kirby slowly raised his hands. His left hand held a badge. "SFPD, I'm on the job." He noted the US Secret Service badge on the front of Easton's belt. "That's my partner you have in cuffs. What's going on here?"

Easton ignored him and pointed his weapon back at Denton. Greene grabbed her by the back of her shirt collar with one hand and pressed her pistol against Denton's back with the other hand, then power-walked her toward the walkway leading to the vehicles. Easton followed.

When the group passed by Kirby, Denton said, "I called your phone, but you had better things to do than answer a call from your partner."

Kirby had an agonized look on his face after finding his partner a few minutes too late. "I called you back repeatedly. You didn't answer."

"Do something," Denton said. "Help me, dammit."

Kirby held his hands out by his sides. "What can I do?"

Beth came running up to them. Easton put the laser sight on Beth's chest. She raised her hands. "SFPD Sergeant Beth Cushman. Hold your fire."

Easton saw the police ball cap and the badge on a lanyard around her neck. He nodded once at Beth and then turned his attention back to Denton and Greene.

Kirby watched helplessly in disbelief as the two federal agents took his partner away and put her into the backseat of the black Suburban. He cursed and made a phone call he didn't want to make. A call to Chief Pierce to report that he had news about Denton and it wasn't good.

CHAPTER 116

Jake wrestled with the boat's steering wheel and raced after Zhukov. The engines roared as he pushed them to their limits.

At the harbor, Terrell ignored the arrest of Denton and ran to the boat slips. He found a powerboat to borrow and Sarah and Cody climbed on board while he started up the single outboard engine. As Terrell was pulling away from the dock, Beth ran up and leapt across a few feet of water and onto the boat. Terrell looked impressed. "Nice jump, Scooter."

"How did you start the engine?"

"The keys were in the ignition. But now I'm going to drive it like I stole it."

Terrell pushed the throttle to make the engine growl and the boat shot out of the harbor like a rocket. It made a huge wake in the no-wake zone, causing another round of angry shouts from resident boat owners.

Beth looked at the ignition and didn't see any keys there; she shook her head but smiled. He obviously had some hidden talents from his past life on the streets of Philadelphia that he'd never told her about.

A uniformed police officer drove up to the boat dock on a four-wheeled ATV. He didn't stop, just kept right on going and drove off the dock into the water. He pushed a button, and the *quadski* vehicle's wheels retracted into the body, turning it into a jet ski. The quadski then took off across the water and raced after the fleeing boats.

Out on the Bay, Zhukov and Jake raced their stolen vessels at full speed across the choppy water. They took shots at each other, but accuracy was difficult with the boats bouncing across the waves in the dark.

The FBI helicopter appeared in the sky above them and shone its spotlight down on Zhukov's stolen boat. The vessel was in an open area of water now and away from other vessels. Reynolds started firing repeated bursts from her weapon at Zhukov.

Zhukov took evasive maneuvers and moved the boat in an unpredictable pattern, but some rounds struck the vessel, and a window on the bridge shattered. Jake's motor yacht was newer and faster. He soon caught up with Zhukov's boat and rammed it from behind. The two men took more shots at close range. Rounds tore into both boats but missed their human targets.

Reynolds spoke on the loudspeaker of the helicopter. "Ivan Zhukov, this is the FBI. Stop your engines and lay down your weapon or we will sink your vessel."

Zhukov ducked out of sight, took a folding-stock assault rifle out of his backpack and sprayed rounds at the helicopter.

Reynolds leaned out the door of the helicopter, wearing the safety harness, and returned fire at Zhukov. She blasted the boat below her with withering fire from her automatic weapon.

Jake began firing round after round into both of Zhukov's boat engines, trying to disable them and leave his enemy's boat dead in the water.

The battle between Zhukov and Reynolds ended quickly when Zhukov scored a lucky hit on the FBI helicopter. Smoke began streaming from the engine, and the helicopter spun in a circle three times until the pilot regained partial control. The pilot attempted to steer the copter toward Fisherman's Wharf and made a wobbly course while losing altitude.

~

When the helicopter spun around, Reynolds was tossed out of the door. Her safety strap coupling had taken a hit, and it let loose now with the slack of her strap, leaving her hanging and twirling in the wind below.

The pilot checked the gauges and fought with the controls as the helicopter went up and down, dunking Reynolds into the icy water several times like a puppet on a string.

At Alioto's waterfront seafood restaurant, the dinner customers stared out the windows with their mouths agape as the helicopter flew toward them. Just when it seemed like the helicopter might crash into the building, it flared and struggled to gain altitude. Then it barely cleared the edge of the roof and landed on top of the building with a heavy thud. Reynolds was still hanging below from the strap and slammed against the thick glass windows that covered the side of the ocean-view restaurant.

Some dinner customers screamed, but a little girl at the table closest to Reynolds just stared in wide-eyed wonder, then waved her hand at the woman outside the window who had the side of her face pressed against the glass. The bruised and sore FBI agent grunted in pain and waved back at the child. Then she started climbing up the strap, hand over hand toward the rooftop, walking up the wall of thick glass like a Ninja warrior.

Out on the water, Zhukov threw a grenade into the bow of Jake's boat and yelled, "I saved one more grenade just for you, Wolfe. Have a nice swim." Zhukov steered his boat to starboard in an attempt to escape the impending blast.

Knowing he only had seconds before the grenade went off, Jake followed closely and rammed the bow of his boat against the other boat's stern, where fuel was leaking out of one of Zhukov's engines. The grenade exploded and blew up the bow of Jake's boat and the stern of Zhukov's boat simultaneously. It ignited the leaking fuel, causing the engine to explode. The burning fuel created a flaming lake of fire on the ocean's surface.

Both men were thrown through the air and into the water by the shock wave of the explosions and the violent tilting of the decks. Their boats burst into flames and began to take on water and sink. Oil and gas spilled onto the surface of the water, adding fuel to the fire. Jagged and burning chunks of wreckage floated in the flaming oil slick.

The police boat *SF Marine 1* shined its spotlight on the water all around the flaming wreckage, searching for the men. A police sniper stood on the bridge looking for Zhukov. His secret orders from Washington were to capture the man dead or … dead.

The SFPD officer driving the quadski was able to go forty-five miles per hour on both land and sea, and he quickly caught up to the boats. He began patrolling around the flaming wreckage with his police lights flashing as he searched for survivors.

Below the surface of the cold water, guided by the glowing light of burning wreckage above, Zhukov spotted Jake and started swimming toward him. Bullets from the police sniper above zipped into the water near Zhukov like small fast fish, leaving short trails of bubbles in their wake.

Jake quickly took off his boots and bulletproof vest, and began swimming away from the burning oil slick so he could come up for air. When the police spotlight swept past, he saw Zhukov swimming toward him. Jake changed direction and the two government-trained killers closed the distance toward each other.

Zhukov had some kind of weapon in one hand that looked like a pistol-grip shotgun. Jake was surprised to see it because he knew that any kind of conventional firearm could not shoot a round more than a few feet underwater. When Zhukov got closer, Jake recognized the weapon as a pneumatic speargun—the kind designed to work underwater and shoot a slender spear shaft attached to a strong fishing line. Zhukov must have found it in the stolen boat.

Zhukov fired the speargun and though Jake tried to dodge the spear, he couldn't move fast enough in the water. The spear flew straight as an arrow and hit Jake on his left side above his belt. It was a smaller spear, a foot and a half long, and it sunk into the fleshy area of Jake's waist. It went through and stopped with about a foot of the stainless steel shaft sticking out of the front and just the small spearhead sticking out the back.

The spearhead had a barb that opened and prevented Jake from pulling the slender shaft out. He couldn't push it through either because it was attached to the extra-strong fishing line.

Zhukov tied his end of the fishing line onto a metal bar protruding from the bottom of a large piece of boat wreckage that was floating past. It began to drag Jake along with it, pulling him out to sea by the strong line. Zhukov dropped the speargun into the deep sea, gave Jake the middle finger, and smiled, then swam toward the surface, leaving Jake to drown.

Jake felt a sharp pain every time the bobbing wreckage yanked on the line and tugged the spear. Panic rose in his throat, and he fought against the urge to cry out. He grabbed the line with his left hand and twisted it to relieve the tugging on his wound. He then reached his right hand behind him, pulled out his KA-BAR knife and slashed through the fishing line.

Once the line was cut, Jake clenched the knife in his teeth like a pirate and started kicking his feet and swimming after Zhukov. As Jake swam, he reached back and unscrewed the spearhead, then pulled the spear out of his side. The shock and pain from that made him dizzy, and he almost gasped and dropped his knife. But he used the pain to spur himself on as he swam with all his strength toward the surface.

Zhukov was swimming as fast as he could, desperate for oxygen. When he reached the surface near the edge of the burning oil slick, he took deep breaths of the foul, smoky air.

Jake was a faster swimmer. He caught up with his enemy, burst above the surface of the water, and attempted to stab Zhukov in the chest with his knife. Zhukov got lucky and saw Jake's glistening knife blade just in time to avoid the point that was aimed at his heart. He grabbed Jake's knife hand by the wrist and then kneed him in the stomach.

Jake threw a punch with his left hand at Zhukov's jaw, hitting him on the side of the head. The blow sent jolts of pain through his skull and he pulled his own knife and tried to stab Jake in the throat. Jake grabbed the wrist of Zhukov's knife hand in a crushing grip and then tried to force the blade of his own knife into Zhukov's eye.

Each man held his knife in his right hand and held his enemy's wrist in his left, knowing that any moment, one of them would deliver the death stroke. They fought hard, wrestling and kicking and thrashing in the water. Zhukov forced his knee into Jake's side, right on the spear wound. Blinding pain shot through Jake's body and he head-butted Zhukov in return, breaking his nose. Blood spewed from Zhukov's nostrils.

Nearby, there was a sudden bright flash of light as the gas tank in Jake's boat exploded. The men were illuminated in the flash of light as they fought in the water among the wreckage.

The police boat spotlight then targeted the area where Jake and Zhukov were locked in hand-to-hand combat, their knife blades glinting as they wrestled in the water.

The bright spotlight shone from behind Zhukov and hit Jake right in the eyes, temporarily blinding him.

Zhukov repeatedly kneed Jake, said "*Do svidaniya,*" and then forced his enemy's head below the surface.

Jake held his breath, wrapped his legs tightly around Zhukov's waist and rolled over in the water with a powerful wrestling move. He brought his own face up for air and put Zhukov's head underwater.

Jake took deep breaths as he held Zhukov's surprised face below the surface. Zhukov fought to get him off, but Jake managed to keep him down. Jake was losing blood and his strength was fading; he knew what he had to do, even if it meant he might die.

In a hoarse voice, Jake said words he hadn't spoken for quite some time and had believed he would never speak again. "The avenger of blood … shall put the murderer to death."

He took one last deep breath, let go with his legs and kicked the water behind him. Swimming forward and downward, he pushed Zhukov backward and deeper in the water. They continued to hold onto each other's wrists in death grips.

Zhukov fought and kicked, but Jake continued swimming deeper. Jake stayed true to his promise as he dedicated his last breaths of life to ending Zhukov's. He was betting that he could hold his breath underwater longer than his enemy could—betting his life. But he would willingly die along with Zhukov if that was what it would take to protect his family and friends.

The look on Zhukov's face indicated he sensed this moral resolve and knew deep down that he had no answer to Jake's selfless willingness to die for his loved ones and for his country. As Zhukov was forced downward, he began to knee Jake in the gut repeatedly, focused on knocking the air out of him and increasing the damage to his spear wound.

Jake took several kicks to the abdomen before he bent his knees, tucked his legs under him and brought his feet up and forward fast as he shoved both feet hard into Zhukov's stomach—like an Olympic swimmer kicking off the wall at the start of a race.

Zhukov took the fierce jab in the gut and was barely able to keep the air in his lungs from bursting out of his mouth. Yet he never let go of Jake's wrist, and he continued to press his own blade ever closer to his enemy's face.

After Jake slammed his feet into Zhukov's gut, he wrapped his legs around his midsection again and squeezed him tight. Then he used the leverage of his grip on his enemy's body to force his elbow into the man's throat. The hard blow hit Zhukov's windpipe at the same time his midsection was being crushed like a vise.

For a moment, Zhukov's face looked … insulted. It was as if he could not believe in the possibility that this fool might actually be able to beat him. Zhukov then focused all his anger into one violent thrust to bring his knife closer and stab Jake through his eye and into his brain.

Jake was expecting it. He let Zhukov's knife hand come toward him but moved his head to the side so the blade missed his eye. The momentum of Zhukov's thrust brought his face closer to Jake's, which was what Jake wanted. Jake wrenched his knife hand sideways, climbed Zhukov's body with his legs, and forced the tip of his knife partway into his enemy's throat.

Zhukov's face revealed he was caught by surprise by Jake's move, shocked to feel the cold knife blade slice into his flesh, and stunned when foaming bubbles of air and blood burst out of the wound in his windpipe and rose up in front of his face. He involuntarily inhaled through the throat wound and sent ice-cold water into his lungs. His strength began to fail, and his hands weakened their grip.

Jake twisted Zhukov's right wrist as hard as he could. His enemy lost his grip and dropped his knife. Jake then brought his left hand up to join his right on his knife's handle, as his legs continued to crush Zhukov in a tight grip.

The two fighters looked into each other's eyes as Jake used both hands to force his knife into Zhukov's chest, all the way to the handle, burying all seven inches of the blade deep into his enemy's heart.

Zhukov's eyes rolled back in his head as his heart bled out and stopped beating. He wheezed involuntarily in the death throes, and his lungs filled with water.

Death was something that Zhukov had always known could come at any time. He felt no fear, only shock and pain from the blade that now pierced his heart. As Zhukov's dying brain accepted his inevitable death, his thoughts turned not to hatred or revenge, but instead to Tatiana, his one true love.

While his eyes grew dark, he saw a vision of his dacha in the Russian countryside. Tatiana was there, alive again and laughing at him as he shoveled snow and sang poorly rendered versions of old Russian folk songs.

In Zhukov's dying heart, he knew that all he'd ever wanted was to live in peace with his beloved wife. To work at a decent job and come home to enjoy her companionship. To share a meal and share their bed. He'd only wanted the same things that most people in the world wanted, but instead, fate had made him into an assassin. Now he was dying in this cold ocean bay so far from home. Killed by an American Marine Corps bastard devil dog.

Jake saw the life go out of Zhukov's eyes and he released his leg lock from around his dead enemy. He kicked off against Zhukov's shoulders and swam toward the water's surface. Jake hadn't focused on survival, only on his mission of killing Zhukov and protecting his loved ones. Now he faced the fact that he might not live through this.

Although he was making a huge effort to use his arms and legs to fight his way upward, his limbs felt increasingly numb and lifeless. His lungs were burning with the need for oxygen and a deadly chill was seeping into his body. Hypothermia was taking hold of him in the cold water. His heartbeat began to slow down, along with his brain activity.

Jake knew that he needed to breathe and he needed to do it soon. There was a distinct change in the light in his eyes. Something from his memory told him that this was a dangerous sign. The one other time he'd seen that fading light was when he'd nearly died in a hostile desert in a foreign land.

The glow from the police boat spotlight swept the surface, showing Jake the way home. Things began to blur as his vision got darker. Jake felt as if he was going blind. He thought that if he didn't make it out of here, a watery grave was a fitting way for a Marine to go. He'd die with honor, serving his country and fighting to protect the people he loved.

Jake continued his efforts to reach the surface, but he also began to accept reality. Even as he fought hard to live, he began to think of everyone he was leaving behind. He knew deep down that he might never see his friends and family again—or the beautiful Sarah Chance, or his new best buddy, Cody. He hoped Sarah would adopt Cody, and they would become close friends. A new family he wouldn't be a part of.

In Jake's memory, he heard the padre giving the eulogy at the recent funeral. "Rest in peace, Marine. Fair winds and following seas, brother. We got it from here. Semper Fidelis. Until we meet again."

It was a struggle for Jake to move his arms and legs at all now. He could barely feel them. He tried to kick his feet, but his legs were numb. Blood trailed from the wound in his side. He could see the surface now, so near yet so far. Bubbles escaped from his mouth and a sound choked in his throat as he tried to stop himself from calling out a name with his last breath.

People had often told Jake his luck would run out someday. Today was obviously that day. But as Jake's eyes began to close for the last time, he thought he glimpsed a golden animal clawing the cold water and moving toward him like a thing possessed. The seemingly mythological creature appeared as if the fur on its back was smoldering with fire, even while underwater. The beast was all paws and teeth and animal fury as it swam toward Jake relentlessly. Jake gazed calmly into the creature's intelligent eyes as it got closer, and he saw its bravery, loyalty, and determination.

As Jake wondered if he only saw Cody in a hallucination due to a lack of oxygen, a chunk of boat wreckage floated past and struck him in the head. His world went completely dark.

CHAPTER 117

When Jake's heart stopped beating, he didn't realize that he was actually dead. He had no previous experience with being dead. What could prepare you for it?

Like many people, Jake had heard the stories about near-death experiences. Thousands of people claimed they floated above their bodies. They could see the doctors trying to revive them. Next, they were flying through a long tunnel and seeing a bright light. They were greeted by people they'd previously known who had passed away before them.

Jake had never really known what to think of it all, but now it seemed to be happening to him.

At first, all Jake knew was the dark and cold. Such a cold as he'd never felt before. Cold right down in his bones and his heart and soul. But after the darkness and cold passed, he was numb for a while and then a strange thing happened. He dreamt that he found himself outside of his body and floating up above it. He was looking down at the scene below and feeling warm all over.

In Jake's dream, he saw Cody swimming to the surface of the water, dragging him along. Cody was biting down on Jake's shirt collar with his teeth while dog-paddling upwards with all of his heart. Terrell was waiting there in the water, wearing a wetsuit and lifejacket. He grabbed Cody while the quadski cop grabbed Jake's body and put it on a rescue stretcher. The cop closed the top of the stretcher. Terrell sat on it and held Cody in his arms as they were lifted up to the deck of the police boat.

Jake saw people trying to revive him. He wasn't breathing. Someone was bent over him, giving him mouth-to-mouth resuscitation.

Cody stood nearby, soaking wet and shivering. Terrell dried him with a towel as best he could and wrapped him in a warm blanket. Cody's eyes never wavered from watching Jake.

For a moment, Jake also dreamt that he was surrounded by a bright light. Next, he saw his deceased grandfather, Patrick Wolfe, along with his dogs, Gracie and Duke. In the dream, Patrick spoke to him. An understanding passed between them that Jake's work was not done. He had to go back … to the ship of fools.

The next thing Jake knew, he was back inside his injured body again. His skin felt cold, but his spear wound felt like it was on fire. He took that as a good sign. The pain meant he was alive. Pain was weakness leaving the body. That was what his boot camp drill instructor always said. Jake looked out through slitted eyelids and saw a group of people peering down at him. Someone's hands kept pressing on his stomach, making him cough up seawater.

"He might be coming to," somebody said.

"I don't know," another voice said. "It could just be the death throes. His heart has been stopped a while. He looks dead to me."

"Shut up," a woman said. It was Sarah. Jake recognized her voice.

"Come on, Jake," Sarah said. "Breathe. Don't you quit on me. Breathe now!"

Jake felt Sarah's warm lips pressing on his. Her sweet breath blowing into his lungs. Her DNA joining with his in what seemed like a merger that fate had ordained.

Sarah's breath and her touch felt like medicine going through his whole body. He felt a strong tug on his heart, like a rope being pulled. Sarah's hands were pressing down right over his heart, doing chest compressions again and again. There seemed to be some kind of electric energy connecting them.

She alternated between administering chest compressions and mouth-to-mouth resuscitation. Jake didn't mind this one bit. Sarah gave him something to live for. *Just keep kissing me and maybe I'll make it,* he thought. Jake felt the tug on his heart again, stronger now.

"Get the defibrillator!" a man said. "What is our ETA to the dock? Is the ambulance there yet?" It sounded to Jake like Terrell's voice.

"ETA five minutes or less. The ambulance is standing by," another voice said. Jake didn't recognize the deep, gravelly voice, but it had a commanding sound to it.

Sarah redoubled her efforts at CPR, with tears on her determined face. She did more chest compressions and mouth-to-mouth. Then she slapped Jake across the face and cried out, "Jake, come back to me ... to us, I mean."

Everyone else got quiet as they understood what seemed to be at stake here between Sarah and Jake and they held their breath. Sarah continued to work tirelessly on Jake, as if she never would've stopped until they dragged her away. A cop ran up with a defibrillator and opened the case. Sarah got it working and said, "Clear!" She pressed the paddles against Jake's chest, giving him a powerful shock.

Jake's body bucked upwards off the deck from the jolt, and then fell back. Sarah gave him another shock, and then another. On the third try he suddenly gasped for air, his chest heaved and he began a ragged breathing. His eyes opened halfway, and he blinked a few times. Cheers went up from the people around him.

Sarah looked as if she might faint from relief. She took a deep breath, put her cheek against Jake's, and whispered in his ear. "Welcome back, Jake. Don't ever drown again, or I'll kill you. Understand?"

He was just lying there, unable to move, exhausted after coming back from the dead. But he managed a smile. Sarah put her hand on Jake's cheek. He tried to talk, but his lips felt like they'd turned blue. Maybe they had. Jake made a strange sound in his throat, and then tried again to speak. Sarah's hands on him felt like life-giving healing magic medicine. With a hoarse voice, he managed to get out two words. "Cody ... okay?"

"Yes, Cody is fine," Sarah said, pushing some stray hair off his forehead with her hand. "He's cold and wet and exhausted, but alive and well."

Jake was greatly relieved to hear that. If he lost another dog, his heart might break once and for all. The last thing he remembered was that Cody had saved him from drowning.

As if reading Jake's thoughts, the soaking wet dog slowly walked up and licked Jake's face and grinned at him with that famous smile retrievers have, and then he wagged his tail. The hair on the top of Cody's back was charred as if it had been exposed to fire, and the stitches on his long flesh wound had pulled loose again and were bleeding a little bit. Jake managed to smile back at Cody.

A gravelly voice accompanied by the aroma of pipe tobacco said, "Cody pulled you out of the Bay. He dove off the boat right into a flaming oil slick to get you. He went underwater for so long we thought he was ..."

"Where am I?" Jake said.

"You're aboard the SFPD patrol boat Marine 1. I'm Captain Leeds."

"Thank you, Captain."

"Give thanks to Cody, he's an amazing dog."

"Yes, he is."

Cody barked once and nodded, then licked Jake's face again and breathed on him with dog breath. It definitely wasn't quite the same as Sarah's sweet breath, but it was all good to Jake. He was glad to be alive.

Captain Leeds looked at Cody. "I'd heard about these dogs, but actually seeing one in action was incredible."

Terrell said, "Some dogs are trained to jump out of helicopters into dangerous waters and rescue people who are drowning. They can even swim while pulling a rope and towing a life raft full of people to safety."

Captain Leeds nodded. "Jake, when Cody came to the surface, our officer on the quadski was there to lift you into the stretcher. Lieutenant Hayes insisted on getting into the water so Cody would recognize a friend and let Terrell grab hold of him. Terrell held Cody in his arms while we lifted you all up to the deck."

"I owe that quadski officer a beer," Jake said. "I owe all of you. Thank you." He looked at Terrell, who just smiled and nodded.

"You're welcome; it's all in a day's work," Leeds said. "Speaking of work. I understand you're the rascal who sent us chasing after your phone on the ferry boat."

Jake grinned. "Sorry about that, Captain."

Sarah bandaged up Jake's puncture wounds on the front and back of his waist, then hooked up an IV from the ship's sick bay to give him some fluids.

Leeds looked toward the shore. "Hang in there, Jake—we're reaching the dock now. Paramedics will be coming on board to take you to the hospital."

"I don't need to go to the hospital. I've seen all I want to see of that place. But I sure could use some aspirin and a hot cup of coffee with a shot of Baileys."

Leeds twisted the cap off a flat silver flask and handed it to Jake. "Here's a drink that might help."

Jake drank some of the amber liquid and coughed hard afterward. It brought the color back to his cheeks.

"Christian Brothers brandy," Jake said, and he coughed again.

"That's a good sign; it means the booze expert is going to be okay," Terrell said and took a small bottle of ibuprofen out of his pocket. He shook out two pills and put them into Jake's hand. Jake took them with another swig of brandy and Terrell helped him to his feet. He stood up with a groan and was a little bit wobbly on his legs, but Sarah came close and put her arm around him and held on tight.

Jake looked at her, took a deep breath and said, "Sarah, are we still on for our date? Let's have dinner tonight on the *Far Niente*. We can go out on the water, and I'll grill some steaks on the barbecue."

Sarah just smiled at him as if thinking the man was irrepressible. Captain Leeds laughed and slapped Jake on the back. Cody barked once and nodded his head. The police boat thumped against the dock and two paramedics boarded the vessel and ran to Jake. One paramedic put a blood pressure cuff on his arm while the other one shined a penlight in his eyes, then he checked the bump on Jake's head and the wound in his side. "Who put these bandages on you?"

Sarah raised her hand.

"Nice work; are you a police doctor?"

"No, I'm a veterinarian."

Jake shrugged as if being treated by a dog doctor was his standard operating procedure. While he stood there being examined, he looked over at Terrell. "Grinds, I think I died, and I saw my grandfather, Patrick."

Terrell raised his eyebrows. "If you say so, then I guess you did. They threw you back, though, huh, like a small fish?"

Jake smiled at his friend. Nobody else spoke for a moment. They just looked at each other with confused expressions. Jake had a bump on his head; he'd been unconscious and had nearly drowned. It wasn't surprising that he might be disoriented and imagining things.

"Did I take out Zhukov? Is he dead?" Jake asked. "The last thing I remember is stabbing him in the chest with my KA-BAR."

"Our other police boat is searching for his body right now," Terrell said. "But your KA-BAR is missing, and I have no doubt it's buried deep in Zhukov's dead heart right now."

CHAPTER 118

Jake finally convinced the paramedics he was well enough to go home and rest in bed. They advised him to get a full medical checkup the next day, and he promised he would. The paramedics then disembarked the police boat and walked up the dock.

Jake, Cody, Sarah, and Terrell followed and when they reached the parking lot, a black Chevy Suburban with darkened windows drove up. Agent Easton sat behind the wheel with his window down. "Get in and have a seat, Wolfe. McKay needs to have a word with you on a conference call."

Jake sighed. "No rest for the wicked. Is that it?"

"You would know. Now get in. McKay has a private message from President Kaufman."

"I'll make a deal with you," Jake said. "You give Sarah and Cody and me a ride to my boat—and I can talk with McKay while we drive."

Easton let out a breath and nodded. Jake helped Cody get into the back cargo area of the Suburban and patted him on the head. Sarah got into the back passenger seat and Jake got into the front.

Terrell waved at Jake and walked down the dock to meet up with Beth Cushman who was bringing back the citizen's boat that Terrell had "borrowed."

Jake gazed at the dashboard screen that displayed an image of Shannon McKay. "Agent McKay, you have a message for me?"

McKay nodded. "Easton, give the noise-canceling headphones to Sarah."

Easton handed the headphones to Sarah. "You're not cleared to listen to this private conversation. I need you to wear these and listen to music."

Sarah nodded and put on the headphones.

McKay said, "Jake, the president wants to talk to you about a possible job offer."

"With all due respect to you and President Kaufman, whatever this is about, it's going to have to wait until tomorrow."

"I'm in charge of this operation, and it's not over until I say it is."

"It might not be over for you, but it's over for me," Jake said. "I did my job and I buried my knife in Zhukov's heart. I almost died doing it too. So I'm taking tonight off for a date with Sarah Chance, whether you like it or not."

"That reminds me—they haven't found Zhukov's body, so there's no proof of his death. Chet Brinkter said he's not going to pay you the reward."

Jake shook his head. "Brinkter the sphincter can sit on it and light it. I didn't do it for the money anyway. When I tried to make him pay me money, it was just to make him pay me respect."

"The president respects you, and he wants to talk. This is top secret. It's an offer he doesn't make lightly."

"He can propose it to me top-secretly and non-lightly tomorrow. Tell the president I'm still disoriented from nearly drowning. Tomorrow I'll be awake and alert, full of coffee, and hopefully relaxed from a night of amazing sex with a very special woman. Then I'll be able to converse somewhat intelligently with the current temporary leader of the free world."

McKay stared at Jake for a moment as if thinking nobody ever said no to the president, let alone gave him a line of smart aleck BS. "You can't be serious."

"After you've died and come back to life, you don't worry so much about meetings and memos and what other people might think you should do," Jake said. "Not that I ever worried much about that stuff in the first place."

"You'd turn down a meeting with the president just to take a boat out on the water with your girlfriend and your dog?"

"Yep. Any day of the week."

Cody barked once, nodded and panted, Ha-Ha-Ha.

"Why do I get the feeling I should make that dog wear headphones too?" McKay said.

"Don't worry; Cody won't tell anyone what you say here. Will you, boy?"

Cody barked twice, and McKay stared in surprise as he shook his head from side to side.

McKay studied a tablet for a moment. "The president is sending me to San Francisco on the red eye. You and I will meet in person tomorrow at noon and have a teleconference with him."

"Okay, we can do lunch at a great place I know. We'll have hot toasted crab sandwiches on sourdough bread, along with cold pints of Flying Cloud San Francisco Stout. You're buying."

CHAPTER 119

Easton gave Jake his phone and he noted there were a lot of missed texts and calls. "Sorry, but I need to check this real quick," Jake said.

McKay nodded and checked her tablet.

Jake's boss, Norman, had sent a text saying that he was fired from his job as a photojournalist. No problem, that was fine. Hopefully, the buffalo head prank would work out as planned. Jake's only regret was that he'd lost his job without kicking his boss in the crotch. That seemed like a missed opportunity. The next time he got fired, he was going to get his money's worth.

There were plenty of angry texts from Gwen. Now she claimed she was pregnant with his baby. Jake had a feeling she was lying. He'd always made sure she took her birth control pill every day. Except for that time she'd traveled alone to the Caribbean for a swimwear photo shoot. His guess was that during her travels, she'd forgotten to take her pills and had cheated on him with one of the ridiculously handsome male models.

He texted Gwen and tested his theory: *I'm sorry Gwen, but the baby can't be mine. I had a vasectomy before we met. We'll do a DNA test to be sure, but I guess you had an affair. We both had our secrets, but congratulations and best wishes to you and the father.*

Jake didn't want to be cold-hearted, but after everything Gwen had done to him, he was simply fighting fire with fire.

Gwen texted back and cursed him for not telling her about his vasectomy. But she didn't deny having an affair. Jake's hunch had proven correct. He'd never actually had a vasectomy, but he'd discovered her unfaithfulness.

A text from Bart said a judge had dismissed Gwen's restraining order and Bart had filed one against her. He'd negotiated a deal that required drug and alcohol rehab for her own good.

Denton had been charged with multiple felonies and was being held without bail until her trial. If convicted of all charges, she could be sentenced to dozens of years in prison. She was currently receiving psychiatric treatment.

A sum of fifty thousand dollars had shown up in Jake's name from a mysterious corporation in Virginia. However, nothing had been paid to Sarah by the FBI.

After his near-death experience, money didn't seem all that important to him. He sent a text and told Bart to give the fifty thousand to Sarah and tell her it was the FBI reward that she'd previously been denied.

Bart texted back and asked Jake about his dream of opening a winery. Jake replied that Sarah had a dream too, about running a veterinary clinic. *She brought me back from the dead. Let's work on one dream at a time—hers first.*

Jake also asked Bart to file an appeal in Sarah's lawsuit. Keep the recently deceased Max Vidallen's law firm busy and prevent them from collecting from Sarah. Look for a way to win the appeal and overturn the verdict.

McKay put her tablet down, gazed at Jake from the dashboard screen and said, "That was Congressman Anderson. He asked me to give you his thanks and tell you he and Katherine now consider you a friend of the family. You're always welcome at their house."

"I'm glad I was able to help them."

"Do you realize what that means? If Daniel wins the presidential election, the house you will always be welcome at will be the White House."

"I don't care about the White House. How are Katherine and her baby?"

"The baby is doing fine, but I'm sorry to say that Katherine has breast cancer and will start treatment soon. If she becomes the next First Lady, she'll begin her term in D.C. with a bald head and a newborn baby."

"She's a strong person. My bet is she and the baby will come through this okay."

"Jake, I also want you to know that you were instrumental in putting a stop to a conspiracy."

"What was Zhukov planning? Why was he trying to stop Congressman Anderson from going to Washington?"

"To prevent him from voting on a bipartisan bill that would authorize appropriations for biomedical research."

"Why would that be important to an assassin?"

"This bill had a little-known rider added to it. An additional provision regarding funding for a university scientist who found a mouse that's immune to cancer. When the white blood cells from that mouse are injected into other mice, they become immune too."

"If that could be duplicated in humans, we'd have a world without cancer."

"That's right, and the vote was to determine whether or not to award government research grants for the project. Zhukov was paid to make sure the bill for funding did not pass. But thanks to the Secret Service and our friends in law enforcement, Daniel was able to vote and sway other voters. The bill passed in spite of Zhukov and his employers."

"A potential cure for cancer could be worth billions. Wouldn't Zhukov's masters want to profit from that somehow?"

"Yes, but the cure is so promising that the scientist is keeping his company private, to avoid the stock market and all the compromises that come with it."

"That might not sit well with the elite, who want their fingers in every pie."

"Once this treatment is proven successful, their lucrative cash flow from the current science would drop overnight," McKay said. "So, their plan was to put a stop to the progress of the new medical science, protect their investments in the competing companies, and continue to earn windfall profits."

"Meanwhile, thousands of people would die because the cure was sabotaged."

"Many of the people affected would've been children. The potential new treatment is very promising for childhood cancers."

Jake frowned. "Were any of the drug manufacturers involved in this?"

"No, the corporations that manufacture the various treatments currently in use were not aware of this new competitor on the horizon."

"I admire Daniel for putting himself in danger so those children will have a chance to live."

"You should be proud of yourself too, Jake. You probably helped to save the lives of an untold number of cancer patients for years to come."

Jake thought about that as they drove. He was reminded of the times he used to take his dog Gracie to visit the child cancer patients at the hospital. He decided that when he had the meeting with the president, he'd give his full attention to whatever it was that the man wanted to talk about.

Easton drove the Suburban into the parking lot at the Juanita Yacht Harbor and stopped near the docks. Jake, Sarah, and Cody got out and walked down Dock A, to Slip A-37.

They boarded the *Far Niente,* and Jake opened two bottles of beer for himself and Sarah. He poured bowls of food and water for Cody. Sarah went to use the head.

When Jake was alone and had a moment of quiet, he thought that perhaps he was finally at peace. But out of nowhere, a strange sensation washed over him. He got goose bumps on his skin and heard an odd little song in his head. It reminded him of something he'd read about—how people with epilepsy sometimes hear music right before the onset of a seizure.

He went out onto the aft deck of the *Far Niente* and looked around the marina. He didn't see any threat, but the hair on the back of his neck stood up. He seemed to smell danger, if that was even possible. He could only guess that he might be experiencing some kind of new phenomenon related to his recent near-death experience.

Cody ran up and stood by Jake's side, then growled and showed his teeth, his hackles bristling.

"What is it, Cody, what's wrong here?"

Cody barked and ran to the lines that held the *Far Niente* tied to the dock. He pulled on one of the lines with his teeth.

Jake decided to trust his gut instincts and trust Cody's attempt to warn him. He untied the cleat hitch knots and freed the lines so the boat could leave the dock. Cody suddenly alerted and looked up above them as if he was looking at a bird. Jake followed his gaze and saw it too. A flying object in the sky that looked like a drone, coming straight at the boat, and coming fast.

CHAPTER 120

Cody barked and ran back and forth. Jake opened a cabinet and took out a pump shotgun with an illegal Salvo 12 suppressor attached. His weapon had a long barrel and a choke set for maximum distance. A drone came into range, one of the new Russian designs that looked like a sawed-off shotgun with a top wing and two propellors attached. It was aiming at Jake and his dog. Jake opened fire and shot it out of the sky. It fell into the Bay and sank under the water.

Jake took his shotgun with him as he ran upstairs to the bridge. He started up the twin engines and cruised out of the harbor and onto the open water of the Bay. Once he'd left the shore behind, he felt like a load had been lifted off his shoulders. He hoped there was only one of those drones, but he continued checking the sky around him and kept the shotgun within arm's reach. He was thinking that Zhukov must have had an accomplice. Or else he'd left behind a surprise with a mind of its own.

The *Far Niente* cruised along smoothly, sunshine sparkled on the blue water and Jake smiled in spite of it all. He was alive, and life was good. Sarah came upstairs and joined him on the bridge, bringing cold beers with her. Jake heard her coming and hid the shotgun in a storage cabinet. He didn't mention the drone to her; he only said that he'd felt like getting away from it all. After a pleasant cruise, he set anchor in a quiet spot and they went downstairs to the galley.

He found some spaghetti sauce from Amborgetti's Restaurant in the freezer, so he threw together an easy dinner of pasta and salad and opened an amazing wine to go along with the humble meal. An aged vintage bottle of Château Margaux red blend from Bordeaux, France. Dylan had given his wine collection to Jake, due to health problems. Jake knew he could probably sell the bottle for over a thousand dollars, but Dylan had said to enjoy his wine collection, and Jake was going to do just that. When Sarah tasted the wine, her eyes opened wide and she looked at the bottle in wonder. She'd never tasted anything quite like it before. It tasted like bottled poetry.

Jake checked the timer for the pasta. "Would you mind keeping an eye on the red sauce and pasta while I take a quick shower and put on dry clothes?"

"Sure, I'd be happy to," she said, picking up the wooden spoon and stirring the sauce.

"Be back in five minutes." Jake took a quick shower, and returned wearing jeans and a t-shirt.

Sarah rebandaged his puncture wound. "This isn't too bad, you were lucky. How's the pain level?"

"It doesn't hurt much," Jake said.

She gave him another shot of novocaine.

They enjoyed dinner, wine and conversation, and afterwards sat on the couch. Jake dimmed the lights and played a slow version of the song "Free Falling" on his acoustic guitar, similar to the way John Mayer had played it live at the Nokia Theatre.

Sarah kicked off her shoes, took off her glasses and removed the band holding her ponytail, letting her hair fall loose about her shoulders.

Cody sniffed the air as if his nose smelled plenty of pheromones in the room. He went out through the open sliding glass door and sat on the aft deck in the cool, salty air.

Jake finished playing the song and set the guitar on the coffee table, then put his hand possessively on Sarah's thigh.

She gave him an innocent look. "Jake, are we ever going to consummate this relationship?"

Jake smiled and leaned in for a kiss, as did Sarah. He kissed her sweet mouth and she kissed him back with raw desire, making the urgency of her feelings for him very clear. The setting sun painted pastel colors on the sky and water, seagulls called to each other, the boat rocked with the movement of the sea, and the two souls who were destined to be lovers wrapped their arms around each other.

Jake kissed Sarah all over her face—her lips, her cheeks, eyelids, nose, and chin—then kissed his way down her neck and shoulders.

Sarah slid onto her back on the couch. She enjoyed how Jake's lips and fingertips traveled all over her body. As he slowly removed one piece of her clothing at a time, he lovingly kissed each area of newly exposed skin. Sarah felt like he was playing her body the way he'd played the guitar, coaxing a sweet melody from the musical instrument, and making the chords sing with true feeling. Soon she was wearing nothing but white cotton bikini briefs with a whimsical Hello Kitty design.

Sarah whispered, "You missed a spot."

"Oops," Jake said, and he kissed her belly button.

"Sorry, I'm not wearing sexy panties," she said.

"That's okay, I'm not either," he said.

She giggled and her tummy bounced up and down against Jake's lips as he kissed her there.

Jake pulled off Sarah's last piece of clothing and then his kisses made her head spin like she'd taken a new drug. The feeling grew more urgent and more intense by the minute and she put her arms up over her head and gripped the couch cushion behind her. Her breathing was ragged, and her body rocked, and then she cried out his name. After the stars collided in Sarah's brain and she came back to earth, she reached down and grabbed the hair on top of Jake's head and pulled him toward her. Her voice was thick with emotion as she spoke only three words.

"Come. Here. Jake."

The romantic style of lovemaking was over now. She kissed him hard on the mouth with hunger as she wrapped her arms and legs tightly around him. Jake pinned her down with his muscular body and they rocked the yacht in a storm of spontaneous combustion that sent waves rippling across the water. Sarah spoke passionate words in French as they made love and time seemed to go on forever. They each felt as if they had become one entity, where two souls connected and joined into something brand-new and magical.

After the moon had smiled down on the lovers for some time, and they were spent and exhausted, they curled up in each other's arms under a throw blanket. In the moonlit waters outside the yacht, small waves splashed against the hull. Fresh, salty sea air came through the open sliding door and caressed their warm skin. They held each other close while the yacht gently rocked with the movement of the water. Their breathing slowed, and they fell asleep and dreamt of a future and a life together … until they were retired and gray-haired and spending their time sailing the *Far Niente* in warm blue waters and visiting tropical islands.

Shooting stars flew overhead and burned glowing trails across the night sky as the astral constellations seemed to align and foretell a highly emotional future for Jake and Sarah. But what kind of future it would be was still an open question that only the two of them could answer, together.

CHAPTER 121

Epilogue:

Early the next morning in San Francisco, the sun sparkled on the water of the Bay. An ocean breeze drifted across the city, carrying with it the familiar aromas of freshly baked sourdough bread from local bakeries and gourmet coffees being brewed at endless neighborhood coffee shops.

At Aquatic Park, the urban beach park across the street from Ghirardelli Square, people were walking and jogging on the promenade, doing yoga on the grass, and tossing flying discs to their dogs on the beach. Tourist couples were taking photos with selfie sticks and several people were sitting and drinking cups of sea salt caramel mocha lattes that they'd purchased at the nearby Ghirardelli Chocolate Company.

A woman was walking her dog on the sand at the water's edge when she noticed something up ahead of her that looked like it might be a beached sea lion. Her dog yanked the leash out of her hand and ran ahead, barking at the strange thing. The woman ran after her dog and called for it to stop, but the dog kept on barking. When she reached the supposed sea creature, she realized it was actually a human body.

A dead man was lying on his back. He'd washed up onto the beach halfway, with his legs still in the water. His shirt was torn open, exposing his chest. He had strange tattoos all over his upper body, depicting foreign words and exotic signs and symbols.

The dead man's throat had been slashed and his mouth was wide open. Flies were buzzing around his swollen tongue and his eyes had been pecked out by birds. The worst thing was that there was a large, wicked-looking knife buried deep in his chest. The leather-wrapped handle protruding like a warning to others.

She screamed and people came running to her aid. A man wearing a San Francisco Fire Department ball cap took one look at the body and immediately called the police. The off-duty firefighter gave a description of the scene to the police dispatcher and his call was routed to the Homicide Department.

Beth was at work early and took the call. She listened as the fireman described the details, then asked him to send a photo to her phone.

The photo showed a dead man's face that looked similar to a photo of Ivan Zhukov taken by a hospital security camera—but now his eyes were missing. Beth told the fireman that she and her partner were on their way and to please tell everyone they were not to touch anything. Beth called Terrell on her phone as she was driving in her police SUV, and they raced to Aquatic Park.

They arrived quickly, and Beth used her phone to take more photos of the body. Terrell put on latex gloves and slowly pulled the large knife partway out of the dead man's chest and heart. It was not the best crime scene protocol, but he already knew what he was going to find. He immediately recognized the knife as a KA-BAR, the infamous Marine Corps fighting knife that had also been adopted by the Army, Navy, and Coast Guard.

This particular KA-BAR had a black blade that featured a gold-colored commemorative etching with the words, "Operation Enduring Freedom." The other side of the blade had an added custom engraving in a smaller script of just one word: "Jukebox."

"This is Jake's KA-BAR, no doubt about it," Terrell said. "We don't usually engrave our knives, but Jake's father had this one etched with the word 'Jukebox' when he gave it to him as a gift. I know he'll be glad to get it back."

"So, the dead body has to be Zhukov. I'm sure Katherine Anderson will be relieved to hear that he is definitely dead."

"Everybody will be relieved. Not that I doubted Jake."

Beth took a close-up photo of Zhukov's face. "Should I send these pics to Agent McKay?"

"Good idea, but send them to Easton and Greene, from our local office. Let them forward the pics to McKay. They'll appreciate the professional courtesy."

Terrell held up his phone so Beth could see the numbers that the agents had given to him at the hospital. Beth forwarded the pics to Easton and Greene. She received a reply from Greene saying they were both en route to Aquatic Park and would be there shortly.

Several uniformed SFPD officers arrived, along with the Crime Scene Investigations Unit, the Forensics Photographic Unit, and the Morgue Unit. Uniformed officers set up the yellow crime scene tape to keep the crowd back. The investigators and morgue technicians took photographs and got the body "tagged and bagged" and loaded into the forensics van.

Someone from CSI found a waterlogged phone in Zhukov's pants pocket. He put it into a plastic evidence bag and handed it to Roxanne, the Computer Forensics technician. Roxanne smiled at the phone and said, "Come to Mama. Your memory chip is going to tell me all your secrets."

Television news reporter Dick Arnold showed up with his cameraman, and they began to broadcast video of the police scene for the media. The camera zoomed in on the KA-BAR knife as a police technician put it into a clear plastic evidence bag. The TV camera feed showed the knife and its custom engraving on live television, and on the news website.

Arnold spoke in a hushed dramatic voice to the news viewers as he speculated that the word "Jukebox" on the knife blade was probably the criminal nickname of the attorney assassin. This dead body that had washed up on the beach was yet another of the killer's lawyer victims—perhaps killed on a luxurious yacht and dumped overboard. On the screen below Arnold's report were the words, "Reporting Live: Benedict "Dick" Arnold."

Moments later, as Arnold watched a replay of his report, he became angry about how his name was incorrectly listed in the credit line. But then he smiled with malice about how he was finally getting the scoop on Jake Wolfe for once. Arnold didn't realize that he'd just helped his rival get paid the fifty thousand dollars he was owed by Chet Brinkter. His news broadcast was providing proof that Zhukov was dead and that Jake had made it happen.

Unknown to Arnold, back at his office, there was a giant buffalo head hanging on the wall above his cubicle. His nameplate had been changed to read "Benedict 'Dick' Arnold." And there was a memo on his desk saying that he was to report to his boss *immediately*.

~

In a faraway computer cloud system, a software program was preparing to help a dead man have the last laugh. It was Ivan Zhukov's worldwide network of malware-infected machines that had previously been set up to seek revenge.

The botnet was programmed to carry out a sequence of automatic murder and mayhem if Zhukov was ever captured or killed. And since the system had not been contacted recently with the stop code, the programs awakened and the zombie botnet came to life with a vengeance. Algorithms went into motion automatically. Predetermined codes began to execute commands without any human intervention, in what was known in the trade as a "dead man's switch."

The hacker software program began running through a list of actions predesigned to trigger events that had been carefully preplanned and arranged to occur by remote control in various parts of the world. A series of maps, file photos, and bios of targets flashed across the computer screens in the network.

Target number one was in France. A wealthy and ruthless dealer in priceless art was walking his dog in a garden and smoking a Gauloises cigarette when a hidden weapon trained a green crosshair target on his back.

A video feed of this target was shown on an unmanned computer's screen in a server room connected to the botnet. Only the video camera could see the circular target with the crosshairs. It was similar to a sniper scope. Preprogrammed directives guided the actions of the hidden camera, weapon, and targeting.

The Frenchman stopped and looked around as if he had a strange feeling that he was being watched. The computer's facial recognition software scanned the side of his face from the video feed and got a match. This triggered a code in the software program, giving an electronic command to the weapon.

TERMINATE.

The man was immediately shot in the head. A thermal scan from the high-tech camera confirmed his death. The computer program then moved on to the next target on the list, ruthlessly, efficiently, and automatically.

Across the world, similar preplanned scenarios began playing out with deadly consequences in every country where a powerful person secretly belonged to the Global Assets Council.

In Russia, the engines on a private jet suddenly exploded in midair, blasting both wings off of the aircraft and causing it to fall from the sky like a missile. Everyone on board screamed all the way down until the final violent impact that left flaming wreckage and dead passengers scattered across a frozen mountainside.

In Switzerland, a woman's coffeemaker excreted a tasteless, odorless poison into her morning brew. One sip caused her to foam at the mouth, fall to the kitchen floor, and go into spasmodic convulsions as she died in agony while kicking and screaming on the cold tile.

In the United States, a man was seated at his office desk when he heard his mobile phone buzzing. He answered the phone and held it up to his ear and said, "Hello." A voice recognition software app signaled the phone to explode, sending sizzling hot magnesium shrapnel into his brain. He collapsed facedown on the desk while smoke came out of the holes in his head, eyes, nose, and mouth, as the magnesium continued to burn white-hot and sizzle like fireworks inside his skull.

In Belgium, a princess walked out of the grand entrance to her castle and got into her limousine, pushing a button to close the thick dark Plexiglas privacy window between herself and the driver. As the car drove along, exhaust smoke started pouring into the back passenger area through the many climate-control vents. The woman frantically pressed buttons to stop it, but all the controls were frozen. Nothing worked, not the privacy screen, the intercom, the windows, the doors, or the climate control.

The princess screamed and beat her fists on the glass screen, but it was bulletproof, soundproof, and darkened. She tried to call the driver on her cell phone, but the display screen said *No Network*. The limousine's passenger area quickly filled up with smoky exhaust, and the princess choked and died from carbon monoxide poisoning. Her employee in the front seat continued driving along, oblivious to it all, as he listened to music.

In Germany, a man who lived in a well-protected country estate went into his private master bathroom and used the toilet. Unknown to him, a high-voltage electric current had been turned on through a hidden wire, electrifying the water in the bowl. When the man peed into the bowl, the enhanced and amplified electric current ran up the urine stream and into his body.

He was violently electrocuted in much the same way as someone being executed in an electric chair. He shook like a leaf in a storm, with smoke rising from his skin. His horrified screams brought the security team rushing in to help him, but it was too late. He was dead. They found him on the floor, his body jerking in spasms from the electrical overdose. Sizzling smoke that smelled like burnt bacon was coming out of the front of his unzipped pants.

These and many more men and women of the Council who had believed they were untouchable were murdered one by one on autopilot. The criminal organization was being wiped out by computer-controlled actions, set up by the ingenious Russian assassin named Ivan Zhukov … a man they had all underestimated.

Chairman Banks' empty limousine was parked at a deserted roadside overlook in the Marin Headlands—the hills just across the Golden Gate Bridge from San Francisco. Banks was a safe distance away, sitting in the backseat of a rented Mercedes SUV, with his trusted driver, Abhay, at the wheel. They were parked a mile up the road, overlooking the scene from the hillside above. As they watched the limousine below them, a bomb went off inside the limo, and the vehicle exploded into a twisted steel inferno of flaming wreckage.

"We can be on our way now, Abhay," Banks said.

"As you wish, sir." Abhay began driving back toward the Golden Gate Bridge, and the city of San Francisco.

Banks turned his head and watched his limousine burn until they went around a curve on the winding mountain road. "Such a waste of a fine automobile, isn't it?"

"Yes, sir," Abhay said. "But better the car alone than us along with it."

"Right you are. Thank you for finding that hidden explosive device left there by our recently deceased Russian friend."

"My pleasure, sir, only doing my duty. I noticed how many times Zhukov checked the car for hidden devices. It made me wonder if he might also have placed one there."

"You were wise not to touch the device when you found it."

"I could see that it was rigged to go off if anyone tried to disarm it. And it was placed right next to the gas tank."

"Now I'll report the vehicle as stolen and let the car insurance company pay me to replace it," Banks said. "Oh, and what about my cheating wife? How is her day going?"

"Not well at all, sir."

Abhay tapped the screen of a tablet that was attached to the dashboard with a holder that stuck to the windshield glass with a suction cup. "According to our intel at the scene, your home in London has burst into flames as well. It is currently burning up, along with your wife and her lover."

Banks leaned forward and looked at the news video on the tablet that showed his London mansion on fire. On another tablet, his bugging devices inside his home provided video and sound of two people screaming.

"Such a tragedy about my home, but I suppose it does save me from giving away half of my fortune to an adulterer. The home insurance policy will pay to have the mansion rebuilt. I never did care for the way my wife had it redecorated anyway."

"All of the Council members have met similar fates in the past hour, just as you predicted."

Banks smiled. "My plan worked out perfectly. I made millions by shorting the investments that the other Council members had bet on to go up, but they went down instead. I also became the sole living survivor of the group. The millions of dollars' worth of gold coins in our numbered Swiss bank account are now all mine. I can begin rebuilding the Council with new members, and this time I'll serve as the permanent chairman and absolute dictator. Anyone who opposes me will be killed by ... oh, I suppose I'll have to find a replacement for Zhukov."

"The only loose end is the surprising survival of that unusual man, Jake Wolfe."

"True, but he is no longer a threat to me. All he knows is that he was successful in killing Zhukov and thwarting the plans of a mysterious conspiracy. The other members of the group are all dead. Nobody has any idea that I am the lone survivor behind the scenes."

"Shall I drive to the airport now, so we can board the private jet and be on our way?"

"Actually, I'm thinking of staying in the United States for a bit. I have my heart set on stealing vast sums of money from these Americans who seem to trust anyone with a fancy accent," Banks said.

"Very well. Where to, then?"

"At the moment, I want to visit a restaurant in San Francisco that serves Dungeness crab pizza on a sourdough crust. They also offer seafood sausages, calamari steak sandwiches, and a lovely clam chowder served in a hollowed-out round loaf of sourdough bread. I simply must try those dishes, along with another half dozen of the California white wines I have on my tasting list."

"As you wish, sir."

"Having people killed and stealing their money always gives me an appetite."

Abhay drove the car onto the Golden Gate Bridge and headed across the Bay.

Banks looked out his window as they approached San Francisco. He couldn't help but think that it seemed like a magical city of sparkling hills beside blue water, where one always feels that anything is possible. He was going to enjoy his extended stay here very much.

~

Unnoticed by Banks, a helicopter was flying high in the sky above and behind his vehicle as it shadowed his car. FBI Special Agent Reynolds sat next to the pilot and watched Banks's rental car through the aircraft's high-powered surveillance system.

"Whoever designs the seats in helicopters should be made to sit in one every day until his butt goes numb," Reynolds said to the pilot.

The pilot shrugged. "Your butt has it easy in this multimillion-dollar spy bird. Try flying in a Black Hawk at a hundred fifty miles an hour through turbulence while terrorists on the ground are shooting at you."

Reynolds nodded at the pilot. He had a point. She contacted Agent Knight and spoke into her headset. "We have a visual. The target is on the Golden Gate Bridge and heading for the city."

"Roger that, continue your air surveillance until he reaches the other side of the bridge," Knight said. "Then I'll follow his vehicle in my car."

"Why don't we put up roadblocks at both ends of the bridge to trap him on it and take him down right now?" Reynolds asked. "Maybe he'll jump off the bridge and save us all some time and trouble."

"Director Walker wants us to gather more evidence, to make such an airtight case against this guy that his lawyers can't possibly beat the charges. Walker wants to make an example out of him with a life sentence."

"Were you able to hack into his car's OnStar system and hear any of his conversations?"

"No, his driver disabled the OnStar and the LoJack," Knight said. "The next time that car is unoccupied, we'll install listening devices and GPS beacons. Meanwhile, we're hacking into the target's encrypted mobile phone. He has some unusually strong private-source encryption on it, but our people will get in. They always do."

"That's right. We're good, and that guy is going down."

~

Knight ended the call and sent a text to FBI Director Walker. The director had a special interest in this case. The tipoff to investigate the man known as Chairman Banks had come from Secret Service Agent Shannon McKay. Her infamous intuition had been accurate once again.

The idea of the FBI and the Secret Service working more closely together was proving to be a very good one. Who had thought of it? Oh, that's right, it had been suggested by Knight's ornery friend Jake Wolfe.

Knight thought to himself that he was going to have to take Jake up on his offer to sail the *Far Niente* out on the San Francisco Bay and do some fishing and drink a few beers.

Jake might be a rebellious guy who was always getting into some kind of trouble, but deep down he was a good man who loved his country and had made great personal sacrifices to help protect it. The man seemed to have nine lives and a lot of luck going for him.

Knight sincerely hoped that Jake's luck wouldn't run out anytime soon.

—The End—

Thank you for reading Dead Lawyers Don't Lie. I had a blast writing it, and I hope you had fun reading it.

Continue reading about the adventures of Jake and Cody in the next book in the series, titled: Vigilante Assassin (Jake Wolfe, Book 2).

If you'd like to receive my reader newsletter, please sign up on my website:

www.marknolan.com

DEAR READER

Dear Reader,

I do a lot of research while writing novels for you, and I try to include interesting and surprising facts for your reading entertainment.

Quite a few readers send emails asking me which things in my books are real. To answer that for everyone, I've put together a quick list pertaining to this book.

Note: The following list contains spoilers, so if anybody skipped to the back, I advise them to please read the book before reading this list.

~

First, what is *not* real:

The Juanita Yacht Harbor in Sausalito is imaginary. There are several nice yacht harbors there, but I made up this one so people wouldn't visit a real marina looking for the *Far Niente's* boat slip. That happened quite often when the late, great John D. McDonald wrote about his character Travis McGee living aboard *The Busted Flush* docked at slip F-18 Bahia Mar in Ft. Lauderdale.

~

Names, characters, places, events, incidents, and dialogue are all products of the author's imagination or are used fictitiously. Any resemblance to actual persons living or dead, businesses, organizations, events, or locales is entirely coincidental.

Second, what *is* real:

The following things really do exist but are used fictitiously in this novel. You probably know many of these, but a few might surprise you. Noted in order of appearance:

Yes, it's true: US scientists found a mouse that is immune to cancer. When doctors inject its cells into another mouse, that one becomes immune too. There are over 800 of these cancer-immune mice now. The mouse was discovered by a biochemist at Wake Forest University in Winston-Salem, North Carolina. If you'd like to know more about it, search Google for: Are you immune to cancer - Discover Magazine.

Kevlar was invented by a woman named Stephanie Kwolek who worked at DuPont. Her invention is now used in over 200 applications, but most importantly in the manufacture of bulletproof vests. Kwolek, who was inducted into the National Inventors Hall of Fame, lived to be ninety and to see over one million bullet-resistant Kevlar vests protecting people. She once said, "I don't think there's anything like saving someone's life to bring you satisfaction and happiness." Rest in peace, ma'am. Much respect to you. Your work lives on, doing good and making the world a safer place, just like the folks who wear those protective vests.

Do dogs laugh? Many readers are delighted when Cody pants Ha-Ha-Ha. However, a small but vocal minority write angry reviews and emails. Oh, the humanity! This leads us to the question: do dogs actually "laugh" or not? Yes, they do!

In her book, *Inside Animal Hearts and Minds,* Belinda Recio notes that many people believe their dogs "laugh" when playing, and now science is proving them right. At the Animal Behavior Center in Spokane, Washington, researchers Patricia Simonet, Donna Versteeg, and Dan Storie discovered that dogs pant in a specific way when they want to initiate play. To the human ear, it sounds pretty much like a regular pant, but when scientists used a spectrograph to analyze various pants, they found this particular pant has a different pattern of frequencies. When dogs hear it—named the "dog laugh" by researchers—they respond favorably, with play bows or play chasing.

As part of their research project, Simonet and her colleagues recorded dog-laugh panting and played the recording to shelter dogs. The dogs responded by wagging their tails, playing, and engaging in other positive social behaviors. The recording also seemed to help decrease stressful behaviors. Researchers are hopeful that dog-laugh recordings will soon be widely used to soothe shelter dogs across the nation, which could potentially result in faster adoption times.

This delightful information is quoted in fair use as part of a review, from Chapter 1 of Ms. Recio's book, in a section titled "Laughter Is a Dog's Best Medicine."

ACKNOWLEDGMENTS

First of all, I would like to thank *you* for reading my book. I'm honored to have you as a reader and I hope you were entertained by the adventures of Jake and Cody. To find out what happens next, check out the second book in the series, titled *Vigilante Assassin* (Jake Wolfe book two).

Thank you to all of my family and friends who had faith in me and offered encouragement, especially my two amazing kids. Thanks to my early readers of the manuscript's first drafts who gave helpful feedback. Thanks to my many beta readers, proofreaders and editors who all worked hard on the story. I couldn't have done it without you.

Thank you to the talented artists at Damonza for designing the book cover. You were a joy to work with.

Thank you to Maureen Feldman of Transaction Publishers for kindly granting permission to reprint the passage regarding the over 50 million citizens randomly murdered by the previous government of the Soviet Union, quoted from the book, *Death by Government*, by R. J. Rummel.

Thank you to Captain David J. Danelo, US Marine Corps infantry officer and war veteran, for writing the book, *The Return: A Field Manual for Life After Combat*. The book helped me to have a better understanding of our returning war veterans. It was also helpful in the readjustment to civilian life for my war veteran son. He served as a US Marine Corps 0311 Infantryman Lance Corporal and "Pointman," leading the way at the front of foot patrols outside the wire in the sandbox. He risked his life alongside the dog handler and war dog as the three of them performed their highly dangerous jobs.

Thank you to Mike Dowling, US Marine Sergeant and dog handler, for writing the book, *Sergeant Rex: The Unbreakable Bond Between a*

Marine and His Military Working Dog. In the book, Sergeant Dowling explains the "alpha roll" and why you should *never* attempt it unless you are a trained military war dog handler.

Thank you to Harris Done, director of the film, *Always Faithful*. This documentary shows the lives of US Marine Corps dog teams deployed on the front lines of war. The close bond between human and canine is a matter of life and death for themselves and countless fellow troops who are counting on them. This movie is available to stream and watch on Amazon.

Thank you to Mike Earp, grandson of the legendary lawman Wyatt Earp, for writing the book, *U.S. Marshals: Inside America's Most Storied Law Enforcement Agency*. In the book, Earp reveals: "The Old West tradition of deputizing citizens to form a posse and chase the bad guys has been updated and enabled the Marshals Service to form task forces. Unique in law enforcement, the Marshals Service has formed regional and local fugitive task forces, under the direction of deputy marshals, that may include contributing officers from any local, state of federal law enforcement agency that chooses to participate. After being trained, the participants also have national arrest authority."

Thank you to Marc Benioff, CEO of Salesforce, for giving the quadskis to the San Francisco Police Department.

Thank you to San Francisco Police Sergeant Adam Plantinga for writing the book, *400 Things Cops Know: Street Smart Lessons from a Veteran Patrolman*. In the book, Sergeant Plantinga shows you what cops face in real life. It is far different than what you see on television.

Special thanks to San Francisco Police Officer John J. Nolan, who gave his life in the line of duty on March 19, 1912, and is listed on the wall of honor at the SFPD headquarters. I don't know for sure if we are related in a close branch of the Nolan family tree, but I wanted to pay my respects. I also wish to thank, honor and pay tribute to all the military members, law enforcement officers, first responders and service dogs who have ever given their lives in the line of duty to protect their fellow citizens. Rest in peace, your sacrifice will always be remembered.

Thank you to all the good people who work at book websites, bookstores, e-book retailers, and libraries. Yours is a proud profession, and you make the world a better place.

ABOUT THE AUTHOR

Mark Nolan is the Amazon bestselling author of the Jake Wolfe thriller series.

You can see a current list of every novel about Jake and Cody on Mark's Amazon author page. And while you're there, click the Follow button below Mark's photo so Amazon will let you know when the next book is available.

Visit here:

Amazon.com/MarkNolan

JAKE WOLFE SERIES

Did you enjoy reading *Dead Lawyers Don't Lie*?

If so, would you consider leaving a short review? Word of mouth is really helpful to an author. Thank you!

Novels about Jake Wolfe:

Book 1. Dead Lawyers Don't Lie

Book 2. Vigilante Assassin

Book 3. Killer Lawyer

Book 4. San Diego Dead

Book 5. Deadly Weapon

Book 6. Key West Dead

Please subscribe to my reader newsletter at marknolan.com and I'll send you an email when I publish another book or give away a Kindle.

Made in the USA
Middletown, DE
12 January 2023